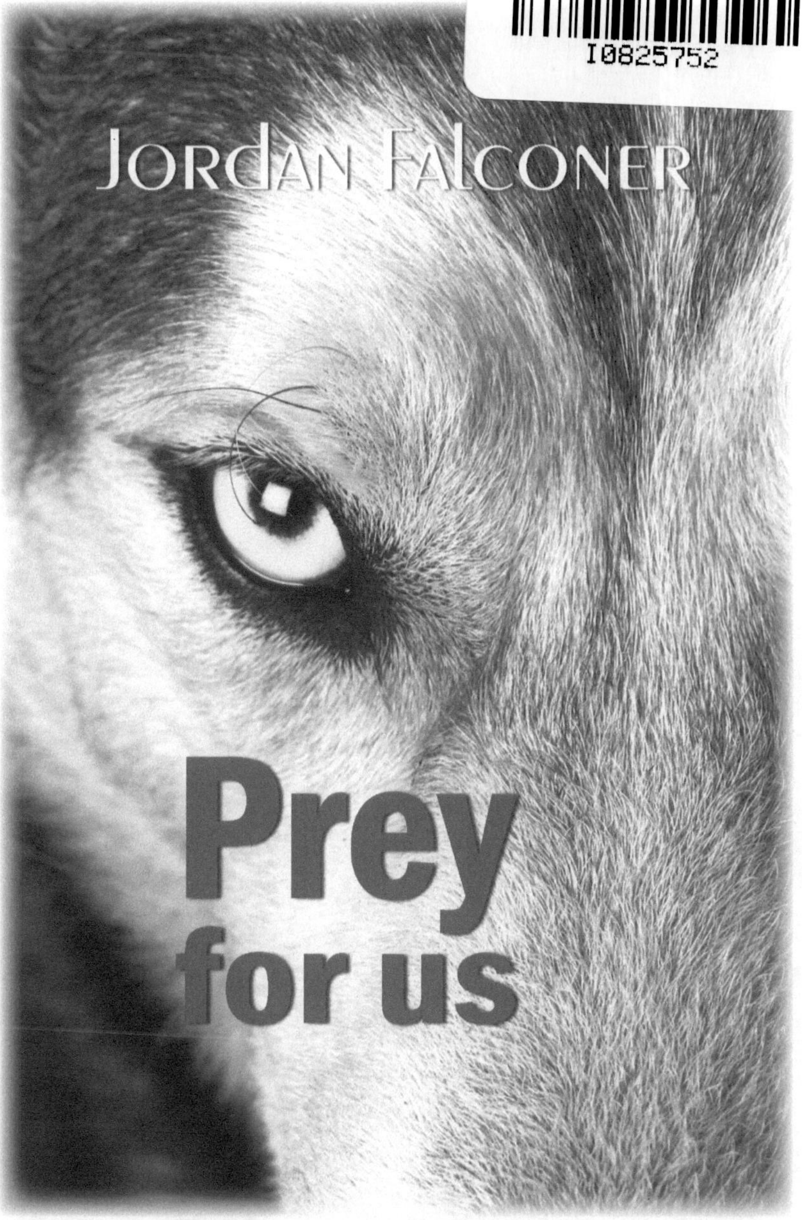

Jordan Falconer

Prey for us

Mindancer Press

Bedazzled Ink Publishing Company * Fairfield, California

978-1-949290-55-4 paperback

Cover
by

Mindancer Press
a division of
Bedazzled Ink Publishing Company
Fairfield, California
http://mindancerpress.bedazzledink.com

To Tammy who never lets me quit

Acknowledgments

Thank you to Casey and Claudia who make me sound much better than I am.

CHAPTER 1

"WELL, WELL, WELL, and who do we have here, hmm?" a stocky, slightly overweight woman said with a shock of thick, almost greasy, black hair. She bent forward, hands on her knees, vicious eyes burning bright yellow, staring at Kilkenny Sharp. The broad smile that graced her thin lips didn't touch her eyes.

Kilkenny Sharp, eighteen-year-old werewolf, wanted to recoil but couldn't.

I feel like I'm super glued in place. She strained to stand up off the benches that lined the courtyard beside the auditorium in the dreamscape version of Sacred Heart College. The only things she was able to move were her eyes. She looked helplessly into Therese "Monk" Monkhouse's bright, blue gaze, as she sat on a bench directly opposite her.

Monk's eyes flickered off to her right and she grunted softly.

"Got nothing to say, *hmm*?" the black haired woman asked.

"Actually I do," Kilkenny ground out, focusing on her and shifting her vision into the shape shifter spectrum. The world became a riot of grey shapes with swiftly moving golden sparks forming the outline of the woman and Monk, nearby.

The woman slapped Kilkenny. "No shifting for you, little lady." She dropped easily onto the seat beside Monk and slung an arm around her broad shoulders. Monk's eyes showed her helpless fury, and her muscles bulged as she tried to move away but couldn't.

The woman whipped her head up, her yellow eyes burning with barely controlled rage. "Now then, little pig, what was your question?"

"Who are you and what do you want?" Kilkenny ground out.

The woman squeezed Monk's shoulder leant over, and kissed her on the cheek.

"She's just adorable, isn't she? I could just eat her. Maybe I will later," she said with a jovial grin. "Ah. Yes. Back onto more pressing matters." Her smile disappeared and her thin lips tightened. "I'm Ingrid Hellstrom and I'm here for Terri Warland. Who, I understand, is one of your friends. Where is she?"

"I barely know Terri Warland," Kilkenny said. "And I certainly don't know where she is."

"Bullshit." The grotesque good humor fell away from the woman and she stilled, golden eyes glittering, pinning Kilkenny with an unforgiving stare. "Oh, but I think you do. I think you know exactly where she is." She turned her attention to Monk. "Perhaps," she studied Monk's chiseled profile, "you need some incentive." She leaned over and snuffled Monk's neck, and then licked her lips. "You're kinda cute, aren't you? I'll bet you're a good fuck. Pity I'm a bit busy now. Maybe later." She ran her tongue up Monk's neck, across the line of her jaw, ending at her cheekbone.

Monk's eyes blazed with impotent fury and her muscles strained. Kilkenny felt sick and tried again to move. It was useless. She was completely paralyzed.

"Is your memory coming back?" Hellstrom asked.

"I don't know where Terri Warland is," Kilkenny said, looking helplessly at Monk.

"Really?" Hellstrom said with polite disinterest. She squeezed Monk's shoulder again. "Let's see how good you could be," she said, kissing Monk full on the lips.

Kilkenny's temper flared. "For the last time, I don't know where Terri Warland is."

"I suggest you find her," Hellstrom said coldly. She lashed out in a blur of speed and sank her teeth into Monk's throat and tore. She spat out a chunk of flesh. Blood dribbled down her chin. Monk's eyes widened as the blood spurted out of her body.

Burning shock and revulsion tore through Kilkenny. "Why, Hellstrom? Why did you do that? She didn't do anything to you."

"I wanted to be sure I had your attention," Hellstrom said, standing.

Monk's body, released from Hellstrom's grip, slid off the bench and into the thick pool of blood on the ground beneath her. She twitched and lay still.

Kilkenny's tears flowed, the pain of Monk's loss overwhelming her and robbing her of the ability to speak. She struggled to remain expressionless as she stared at Hellstrom.

"You have a week," Hellstrom said. She grew translucent. "In the meantime I'm going to gather all your friends and family and start killing them, one for each day Terri remains undelivered to me." Almost completely transparent, she gave her another grotesque smile.

"What are you worried about? She's dreaming. I didn't really hurt her. I will, though."

She faded completely out of the dreamscape, and Kilkenny felt her body relax as the immobility left her.

"Oh my god, Monk," Kilkenny said in a wavering voice, on her knees before Monk. "I'm so sorry. I'm so sorry."

Monk's throat had already closed over with raw, pink skin. She stirred and coughed, moaning in pain. She cleared her throat.

"Kilkenny," Monk said, after a few, dull, excruciatingly painful moments. "Look at me."

Kilkenny tore her eyes away from the wall, her face hot, and forced her eyes to Monk's.

"I don't understand why you're apologizing," Monk said softly. "This is not your fault."

Kilkenny nodded around the lump in her throat. "I'm sorry, Monk."

"For what? I'm supposed to be a master of the dreamscape, and I really didn't see this coming. I also had no idea other shape shifters could do that to me. You can't."

"Master of the dreamscape? Do you even know what that means? I don't," Kilkenny said, wiping the tears from her eyes. "Do you even know how to tell if there are other shape shifters in your dreams with you? And I just don't seem to count."

Monk shook her head. "No, I don't know. All I know is that I have control over the dreamscape. All I really have to do is get Hellstrom in here and collapse it and this whole problem is going to go away."

"And how do you propose to do that?" Kilkenny said.

"The same way I brought us here to begin with," Monk said. "I open a doorway and go through it with her. I should be able to get myself back out again."

"I can't believe we're even having this conversation," Kilkenny said. "A monster just tore out your throat."

"Then don't you think it's the *best* time to be having this conversation?" Monk asked. She held out her hand. "Do you mind? I'm tired."

Kilkenny felt her face heat. She levered Monk to her feet.

"I'm going to open a hole into my place," Monk said, her hands shaping an invisible door in front of them. A door materialized, and Monk put her hand on the knob, stopping for an instant to grin at Kilkenny. "Aren't you glad you told you parents you were staying at our place with us?"

Kilkenny shook her head. "Michelle is going to notice, and that won't be pretty."

"She'll be fine. Trust her," Monk said, opening the door and gesturing for Kilkenny to go through.

Kilkenny did so and found herself standing in the front hallway in Michelle's and Monk's unit.

"Hi, guys," Michelle Coopersmith called from the living room. "Back so soon?"

Monk nudged Kilkenny forward, and she led the way into the living room on shaking legs.

"Michelle," she said softly.

Red headed Michelle Coopersmith, at six feet eye to eye with Kilkenny, stood and stared at them and frowned. An open novel lay on the coffee table in front of the sofa. She frowned and her eyes widened when she saw Monk drenched in blood and shuffling from foot to foot.

"Oh my god. Monk? What happened to you?" She rushed forward and eyed her closely. "Your neck?" She touched Monk's neck with shaking fingers, and Monk flinched.

"I'm okay, Mitch," Monk said softly. She released a breath. "We have something to tell you and it's not good."

"Okay," Michelle said, frowning. She glanced at Kilkenny and Kilkenny flinched. She didn't know what Michelle would say but thought it wouldn't be good, despite Monk's wordless reassurance.

Michelle's eyebrows contracted and her gaze stayed on Kilkenny. "Why don't you go and change your clothes, Monk?" She rubbed Monk's arms. She kissed Monk and Monk smiled, relief shining in her eyes. She smiled at her and gently stroked her cheek. "Go on."

Monk nodded, looking down and grimacing. "Yuck, I'm a mess. Yeah." She made her way down the hallway to their bedroom.

Michelle turned to Kilkenny, who felt a little sick. "Sit down, Kilkenny." Michelle said. She steered her toward the sofa. "You look as white as a sheet."

Kilkenny nodded, numb, and allowed herself to be pushed down, but scooted over so she was as far away from Michelle as possible. Michelle flopped down at the other end of the sofa. Kilkenny studied her, feeling herself tear on the inside. Michelle's face was a study in classic beauty, her gaze gentle and intelligent. Kilkenny fought down tears.

"Do you want something hot to drink?" Michelle asked.

Kilkenny shook her head, not trusting herself to speak.

"Relax, Kilkenny. We'll just deal with whatever it is."

Kilkenny nodded. "We don't have a choice. And this was unexpected."

"You can say that again," Michelle said.

"I'm worried about my family," Kilkenny said.

"Why?" Michelle asked.

"I don't think I can protect them," Kilkenny said.

"Now I *really* want to know what happened on the dreamscape," Michelle said.

Monk came into the living room, flicking back her wet shock of dark brown hair. "Sorry. I had to have a quick shower."

Kilkenny nodded, jaw trembling.

Monk dropped down onto the sofa, and Michelle snuck her arms around her. She kissed Monk and smiled.

"Now, how about you tell me what happened?" Michelle said.

Monk peered into Michelle's eyes. "We have a problem, Mitch. And it looks like a nasty one."

Michelle frowned. "As nasty as your last year of high school?"

Kilkenny nodded, feeling tears run down her face. "Yes, that bad."

"Okay," Michelle said. "What are we looking at?"

Monk and Kilkenny exchanged a glance.

"Well Kilkenny said. It goes like this." Kilkenny told Michelle about Hellstrom and her threat against Terri Warland. By the time she'd finished, Michelle had gone pale.

"Oh, no," she said. "Oh, no."

"Yes," Monk said, nodding. "We're fucked unless you know where Terri is."

"Uh," Michelle said. "Let me think for a sec. I kind of kept in touch with Terri after she left, but I haven't heard from her for a couple of years." She disentangled herself from Monk, stood, and touched Monk's face with shaking fingers. "I'll see if I have her old number. Back in a moment."

She headed toward the bedroom, and as soon as she was out of earshot, Monk smiled at Kilkenny. "See? That wasn't so bad, now was it?"

Kilkenny shook her head. She felt dim relief that Michelle seemed to be taking Hellstrom in stride.

"Don't worry," Monk said. "We'll stand with you."

"I don't want you to get hurt."

"Stronger together than apart, remember?" Monk said. "I learnt that the hard way. I should have trusted you when you were young."

"God, I wish we had a better plan than collapse the dreamscape."

"Well, it's a start. Something is better than nothing."

Kilkenny started to open her mouth when Michelle walked in again, leafing through an address book.

"She's right, you know," Michelle said conversationally. "We *are* better off together. And something *is* better than nothing." She found an entry in the address book and grabbed the telephone. She dialed, listened for a moment and then grimaced. "Disconnected."

"That's not good," Monk said. "We *have* to warn her. Do you know anyone else she might have given her details to?"

Michelle thought for a moment. "Maybe Gab McCann? Gab's friends with everybody and everybody loves her."

Kilkenny smiled, despite herself.

"Sounds to me like we have a few fires to put out," Michelle said slowly. "Terri's best protection at the moment is that you don't know where she is. Your family is also safe for the moment because they're overseas. You're staying with us for another month, so we can all keep watch over each other."

"Yeah," Monk said, nodding. "I don't doubt that Hellstrom is going to be keeping a close eye on you, unless she's not doing it already. If you call Terri on the dreamscape, all Hellstrom has to do is barge into your dream like she did with us and it's over for Terri. I don't want to do that."

Michelle shook her head. "Neither do I." She sighed. "I'm sorry you don't know more about the dreamscape."

"So am I," Monk said. "It hasn't been easy to learn by ourselves either. But I've never been keen on meeting any other werewolves face to face because I just don't trust them not to get nasty."

"There *have* to be some exceptions to the rule," Kilkenny said. "I'm one, for example."

"So am I," Monk said.

"But both of you are very different to most people," Michelle said. "We *all* are."

"True," Monk said.

"So what do you want to do?" Michelle said.

"I want to hear what you have to say," Kilkenny and Monk chorused. They exchanged a glance and wry grins.

Michelle slipped behind Monk on the sofa, put her arms around her and smiled. "Okay, this is what I think. Hellstrom is watching you and probably has been for some time. She's made threats against your family that we have to take seriously. She's threatened us and Terri. We can take care of ourselves but I'm worried about the others. We *have* to find out how she's watching us, Kilkenny. And we also have to find *her* before she finds anyone else."

Monk nodded. "I agree with all of that. On top of that, we have to keep an eye on everyone. We have to tell Jackie. She can keep an eye on your parents for you."

"You can take care of them when they go to sleep, can't you, Monk?" Michelle asked.

Monk nodded slowly. "I think so."

"Here's the big question. Do you know how to keep Hellstrom out of your dreams?"

Monk looked pensive for a moment. "I don't know."

"You can normally keep me out of your dreams," Kilkenny said.

"I know," Monk said. "But you *really* aren't the same as me. We're *very* different as werewolves. I've *never* met anyone like Hellstrom. She's not the same as either one of us. Did you feel how strong she was?"

Kilkenny nodded. "Yup, she's a strong shape shifter all right."

"That's not what I meant," Monk said. "She's *physically* strong. She's *a lot* stronger than I am."

A memory of Monk easily subduing her and throwing her across a gym in the dreamscape tore through Kilkenny's mind and she grimaced. *Oh, I think we're in bad trouble here.*

"I'm going to try and find Hellstrom," Michelle said. "We *have* to find her *first* in the physical world."

"Yeah," Monk said. "We do."

"If she's watching me then I should be able to spot her," Kilkenny said. "Tomorrow's the first day of school. If she wants to breathe down my neck then she has to be either a teacher or a new person in my form. Both of those things make her relatively easy to spot."

Michelle smiled. "Yep. I can agree with that."

"Okay," Monk said. "And I'll do the good, hovering friend thing and stick around you on the dreamscape."

Kilkenny shook her head. "I have to call Terri."

"We'll *all* be together when you do that," Michelle said.

Monk heard the tension in her voice, caressed her hand, and kissed the knuckles. Michelle glanced down at her, expression strained.

"I promised you that I'd *never* walk into a situation like this again without you by my side," Monk said. "I hate it that you're going to be in harm's way with me, but I can't think of anyone I'd rather have by my side." She looked like she wanted to say more, but nothing emerged.

Michelle's arms tightened around her. "I understand. I get it."

"I'm going to have to shadow you at school," Monk said, glancing at Kilkenny. "I don't like you being there all by yourself."

"I'd agree with that," Michelle said. "Times like these it's a real pity I changed schools, huh?"

"Guys," Kilkenny said. "Don't worry about that so much. She can't just kill me at school. Don't forget, I've got friends there, including Riordan Kendrick."

Monk and Michelle exchanged a glance at the mention of Kilkenny's math teacher.

"What is it with math teachers?" Monk asked, smirking.

"We get around," Michelle said, a smile playing about her lips.

Kilkenny felt her face heat. "It's not like that, we're just friends."

"Right," Monk said. "Of course. That's why you blush whenever you see her and you can't look at her in the eye."

Kilkenny's temper sparked and she was about to throw a sharp comment at Monk, but Michelle raised her hand.

"We're just teasing you," she said. "Whatever you feel for her is your business."

Kilkenny nodded once, sharply, an image of Kendrick's beautiful face, ash blonde hair, and arctic grey eyes flashing before her mind's eye. She felt her heart skip a beat and she sighed. She *did* feel more than friendship for Riordan, and thought the feeling was mutual.

"Kidding aside, I can get Rio to give me a lift to school and pick me up. She won't kick up too much of a fuss about that."

"It would be a good idea," Monk said. "I can go with one of you but not both."

"I should probably call her before it gets too late. It's already close to ten," she said, glancing at her watch.

Monk and Michelle nodded.

Kilkenny levered herself up off the sofa as Monk disentangled herself from Michelle and drew her to her feet.

"We're going to turn in," Monk said, gazing into Michelle's eyes. "I'm going to play with warding dreams. I'll call for you when I get to the dreamscape."

"Maybe I'll come, maybe not," Kilkenny said. "I'm not really tired."

"Okay," Monk said. "But come if you do sleep and feel like it."

Kilkenny snagged the phone as Michelle led Monk toward their bedroom.

She dialed a number from memory, and after six rings, a woman's out of breath voice answered. "Hello?"

"Hi, Rio," Kilkenny said.

"Kilkenny? What time is it? Is everything all right?" Riordan Kendrick asked.

"It's close to ten and there's nothing to worry about," Kilkenny said. "I'm cool. But I do have a favor to ask you."

"Ask away," Rio said. "What can I do for you?"

"I kind of need a lift to and from school for a while," Kilkenny said, grimacing.

"Is everything all right?" Rio asked. "Is everything working out? You can stay with me if you want, no problem, you know that."

Kilkenny almost laughed. "Thanks for the concern, but I'm fine. Monk just can't be in two places at once and Michelle lives in the black hole of public transport."

"Okay," Rio said easily. "When do you want me to pick you up?"

"How about quarter to eight?"

"Sure," Rio said, and Kilkenny heard dim rustling in the background. "You want to give me the address?"

Kilkenny gave it to her, and they chatted for another few moments. Kilkenny regretfully said good night and they hung up.

Kilkenny sat on the sofa again, staring out into the darkness, thinking about Riordan Kendrick. Thinking about her felt a lot like thinking about Monk. She seemed eternal, as though they'd known one another their whole lives. Kilkenny couldn't imagine living in a world that didn't have Riordan Kendrick in it.

Maybe they're right. Maybe I am *in love with her.*

She stared out into the darkness beyond the balcony doors. She felt too restless for sleep. She got up, opened the balcony doors, and went out onto into the darkness.

It was a warm summer's night and Kilkenny took a deep breath, savoring the smell of Eucalyptus mixed with unpleasant undertones of car exhaust and ash from distant bush fires.

A flash of memory of she and Jackie glued to the television, watching bushfires approach Autumn Park flashed through her mind, followed by Hellstrom's harsh features. *What a bitch. What the hell is it with some people that they think they can stroll into other people's lives, wreak carnage, and breeze out again?*

A flash of anger tore through her. She wasn't truly worried for herself; her talents as a shape shifter had always run toward healing and spotting other shape shifters. She shifted her vision now, bright, almost incandescent yellow gaze piercing the darkness with contemptuous ease.

The world lightened and became a panorama of grey tones, objects easy to distinguish. Humans walking past were columns of red, green, or blue sparks, sometimes purple or, like the one walking down the road past the block of flats, bright orange. Monk was a column of shining golden sparks, and when Kilkenny looked down at her hand, she saw the same shimmering gold.

She saw the animals in the trees, brown sparks surrounded by a reddish haze, slowly moving through the trees, almost as though they were watching her.

Yeah, we have a good jump start on Hellstrom. Now all we have to do is find Terri before she does.

She hadn't thought about Terri in a few years. After her initial nervousness of interacting with such a tall, beautiful woman, she'd realized that Terri was one of the sweetest and most charming women she'd ever met. She'd been sorry when Terri had gone without explanation.

Why had she left without any kind of good bye? What would they say to one another after so much time apart? Would they be welcome? Would Terri even listen to them?

She gave a wry grin. *It doesn't really matter what Terri says. Monk'll look out for her. God, I'm so not looking forward to this. It's going to get ugly and I* hate *hurting things.*

She sighed. *No matter what happens, I have to be strong. We have to work together to get rid of Hellstrom.*

She turned, went back into the living room, and closed the balcony doors and locked them. She flopped down onto the sofa, abruptly exhausted. Her eyes fluttered closed and she felt a strong thrust upward and a dislocation as she entered the dreamscape.

She stood, bathed in warm sunlight, in a field of waist high wheat, as far as the eye could see. The sky overhead, an immense, bright blue, reminded her of Monk's eyes. She smiled automatically and immediately thought of Jackie, her sister's dark blue eyes and red hair, and wanted her to come.

Come, Jackie. Come to me. She waited, feeling the breeze blowing through the wheat stalks, making them hiss.

After a few moments, she heard footsteps coming close to her.

"Hey, Kilkenny," Jackie Sharp said cheerfully, a wide grin on her beautiful face. "This is an unexpected pleasure."

Kilkenny sank into her embrace, squeezing her and feeling the sting of tears in her eyes. "It's so good to see you, Jackie."

"Same here," Jackie said, pulling back. "How are you doing?" She frowned slightly. "Is there something wrong?"

"Yeah," Kilkenny said. "There is."

"Okay," Jackie said, sinking down onto the stone bench that materialized in the small clearing that now surrounded them. "Tell me. What's wrong?" She patted the bench beside her.

Kilkenny sank down onto the bench and told Jackie everything that had happened to them. When she finished, Jackie was quiet for a little while.

"Oh, my god," she said at last. "What a mess."

Kilkenny nodded. "I know." She steeled herself and met Jackie's eyes. "I'm sorry, Jackie. I promise to watch out for Monk."

Jackie snorted. "Monk is a lion." She glanced at Kilkenny. "She and Michelle will be with you and you'll look out for each other." She bit her lip. "I'm sorry I'm not there with you."

"Well, that's kind of why I called you here," Kilkenny said. "I need your help. I was hoping you could keep Mum and Dad safe. Can you build a construct for them so they'll be safe when they go to sleep?"

Jackie nodded. "Monk showed me how to do it. I've gotten better with warding as well. I think I can keep other shape shifters out of it."

"That's pretty much what I'm hoping," Kilkenny said. "You're my trump card. You're the last thing I have left to keep us all safe with."

Jackie nodded, blue eyes boring into hers. "Take care of Monk and Michelle. I don't know what I'd do if . . . you know, if . . ." She blinked away tears.

"I won't let anything happen to your girls," Kilkenny said, gently squeezing her shoulder. "I know how much you love them."

Jackie nodded, jaw trembling. “Thanks.” She took a deep breath. “I don’t want anything happening to *any* of us. Take care, Kilkenny. Be careful.”

Kilkenny smiled. “I will. Don’t worry about me.”

Jackie closed her eyes and then opened them. “I can feel Monk calling for me. I have to go.”

Kilkenny stood and hugged Jackie. “Have fun.”

Jackie faded out of the dreamscape, and Kilkenny sank back down on the bench, closing her eyes, feeling around the edges of her construct, making sure it was solid. She wanted some peace before facing reality and her first day of school began.

CHAPTER 2

THE FOLLOWING MORNING, Kilkenny sat on the low, brick wall outside Michelle's block of units, enjoying the warm, late summer sunshine.

I'm not sure how I'm going to do this. I have to find out how Hellstrom is watching me but I don't want to shift if I can avoid it. I don't know what I'm looking for and I don't want to draw attention to myself. Maybe I should just stake things out first and then decide who I'm going to Look at.

"Hey, Kilkenny," a woman called.

Riordan waved at her from a BMW convertible idling by the side of the road. The top was down and Riordan leaned back comfortably in the driver's seat, ash blonde hair swept away from her classically beautiful features.

"Hey, Rio," Kilkenny said cheerfully, jogging across the road and dropping her backpack into the back seat of the car. She jumped into the passenger side and landed neatly in the seat.

Riordan Kendrick pushed her sunglasses up and eyed Kilkenny with her arctic grey eyes, glittering with amusement. "Don't you every worry about missing or landing in an untidy heap by the side of the road?"

Kilkenny laughed softly. "Oh, god no. I'm just not that uncoordinated."

"Uh huh," Riordan said, glancing over her shoulder and pulling out onto the road. "Says you until you've bruised your behind." She glanced at Kilkenny. "And I'm so not kissing that better for you."

Kilkenny burst out laughing. "Oh, come on, that's a *terrible* image to plant in my head before school."

"What? Me bending over and puckering up?"

"I'm warning you."

"What are you going to do to me?" She stared at Kilkenny for a second and then nodded firmly. "That's what I thought. Now. Where were we? Ah, yes. Right: then you'd have to drop your—"

"*God,* Rio," Kilkenny said, waving her hands and snorting laughter. "You're *terrible*."

"Yes, but I'm good at it."

"Yes. Yes, you are." Kilkenny grinned at her. "What's gotten into you this morning? You're in an abnormally cheerful mood for a first day of school."

Riordan smiled. "Why not be? Why spend every day of your life not looking forward to something? Besides, I like my job and I get to meet a lot of interesting people."

"Even if they are school girls?"

Riordan shot a glance at her. "School girls aren't school girls forever, you know."

Kilkenny felt her interest spark. "And teachers aren't teachers forever."

Riordan pulled up at a stop sign and looked at her, eyes hidden by her dark glasses. "Nope."

Wonder if I could ask her out on a date? "That's a good thing. A *very* good thing. Although I'd wonder about ethics in such a situation."

"You wouldn't have to," Riordan said, smiling. "Nothing can happen while either one is in school but after that there's no conflict of interest or unfair influence to a developing mind."

Okay, so she'd turn me down flat for a date. I get it. "I'll remember that," Kilkenny said. *The day I finish school I'm going to ask her out.* An image of Hellstrom flashed through her mind. *If things don't go badly.*

"Come on, Kilkenny," Riordan said, glancing at her. "It's just school. It's not that bad. It's also your last year."

"Huh?" Kilkenny said, looking around as she realized Riordan had already parked in front of the school. "Oh. Yeah."

Riordan laughed. "Look, do you want to do something after school today?"

Kilkenny could not refrain and her disobedient gaze took in Riordan's slim body and full breasts. She bit the inside of her cheek. *God, she's beautiful.* "We'll have to see. I'm not sure how I'm going to end up going for homework and I'm gonna have to let Michelle and Monk know."

Riordan smiled. "No problem. Let me know later, okay?"

"No problem," Kilkenny said as they split up. She headed toward the side entrance to the school, Riordan to the front.

Kilkenny made her way through timid first years, clustered in small groups off to one side of the top courtyard; older junior girls playing an odd mix of basketball, handball, and touch football on the lower courtyard; a row of girls outside the science labs with their skirts pulled up, sunning themselves; frightened first year seniors outside the auditorium, eyeing each other suspiciously; and finally the year twelve girls all milling around together and trading stories about their summer vacations, frantically doing homework, curled up in an English novel, or just looking as though they'd opened their eyes that morning and realized they'd landed in hell.

Kilkenny spotted her two closest friends, Kristin Taft and Lauren Sonderby. They were sitting on a bench and idly watching a senior gesturing wildly before a small, entranced group a few benches away from them.

"Hi, guys," Kilkenny said, flopping down on the bench beside them. "What's up?"

"Just watching Clare," Kristin said, nodding toward the pontificating senior. "She's being a moron, as usual."

"Oh? What about this time?" Kilkenny asked, digging into her backpack for her diary. She flipped it open. *English first period, then Modern History with McCann.*

"Oh, she's just making noise about an alleged yowie she saw last night."

Kilkenny's eyebrows shot skyward. "A *yowie*? She's trying to convince people she saw *Sasquatch*?"

"Yup."

"Okay, okay, okay," Kilkenny said. She paused and thought for a moment. "I'll give that one a . . . seven . . . on the Clare scale."

"Oh, come on, Kilkenny," Lauren said. "That one's gotta be a nine at least."

"But it's *stupid,*" Kristin said. "That alone makes it no more than a four."

"Really?" Kilkenny said. "Really?" She nodded toward the crowd of girls. "They look like they're taking it in, hook, line, and sinker. Believers make it a score over five."

Kristin frowned, eyeing the girls closely. "All right. I can see that." She looked at Kilkenny. "But I *still* say it's no more than four."

Kilkenny and Lauren exchanged a glance and laughed.

"I'm going to be so glad when this year is over," Lauren said. "I'm so over this shit."

Kilkenny felt her good humor drain away as an image of Hellstrom flashed through her mind. "I hear you." *And I'm looking forward to the next few weeks being over.*

"What's up, Kilkenny?" Kristin asked, looking closely at her. "Is there something bothering you?"

The first bell rang, sparing Kilkenny an answer. She stood up with a sigh, picking up her backpack and slinging it over her shoulder. "I'll see you guys at recess, okay?"

"No worries," Kristin and Lauren said, shooting her a quick wave and heading in the opposite direction.

KILKENNY TOOK HER seat in English, pulling out her notebook and novel, watching the other girls trickle into the room.

They all look normal to me. But I'd have to shift to be sure. I'll put it at the bottom of the list for now.

A tall woman filled the doorway, catching Kilkenny's attention with an almost audible snap.

She towered over the dregs that filtered into the class. She was dressed entirely in black from head to toe, collar length hair pitch black, with eyes to match. She had a muscular build eerily similar to Monk. Kilkenny stared. The woman radiated magnetic, edgy energy, and an intensity that was almost palatable. Kilkenny sat up straighter in her seat.

"Good morning, girls," the woman said into almost pressurized silence. "I'm going to be taking you for English this year. My name is Mackenzie Moriarty. You can call me Miss Moriarty."

A hand shot into the air.

Moriarty eyed the girl with glittering, black eyes. A smile played about her lips. "If it involves a Sherlock Holmes joke, you realize I'm going to have to get violent, right?"

The hand went down again.

Moriarty smiled. "Wise decision." She stood up and strolled across the platform, red lips curved into a grin. "Although, Sherlock Holmes really isn't that bad."

"Really?" Kilkenny said, smiling slightly. She put on her best English accent. "If you'd read my monograph on bootlaces, you would know this man worked in Manchester as a stenographer, bit his fingernails, had a background in blacksmithing, and suffered from an advanced case of piles."

Moriarty's lips twitched and she slowly strolled across the room so she was standing directly in front of Kilkenny's desk.

"Ah, Holmes," Moriarty said, folding her arms and looking down at Kilkenny. "I knew there was a reason I tossed you over a cliff."

"If I remember correctly, I was bear hugging you at the time, Professor Moriarty."

"I escaped. I got a handhold on the slippery rock and was able to drag myself all the way back up the waterfall. Not a mean feat since I was shaking you off my leg at the time."

"Ah hah. So you finally escaped in your guise of a hunch backed peat salesman with a wooden leg?"

"Of course." Moriarty leaned forward. "The game is afoot."

"Outstanding," Kilkenny said softly, looking into Moriarty's glittering black eyes.

"Who might you be, young one?"

"Kilkenny Sharp."

"I'm pleased to meet you, Kilkenny Sharp."

"Klaatu barada nicto."

Moriarty folded her arms and they looked at each other closely. Kilkenny studied her beautiful face and decided in an instant that she liked Moriarty. Moriarty grinned and Kilkenny saw that the feeling was mutual. She itched to shift her vision.

"Okay," Moriarty said, breaking the spell by moving away back to the front of the room. "Has anyone else ever read any Arthur Conan Doyle?"

The class remained silent and looked at their teacher expectantly.

"We all *do* know how to read, don't we?"

"Kind of," piped up Kelly Featherstone piped up from beside Kilkenny.

"Excellent," Moriarty said. "I suck at drawing pictures."

Kilkenny snorted a laugh.

"Especially when it involves nineteenth century dead people."

"Which dead ones did you have in mind?" a voice asked from the front of the room.

"*Great Expectations*," Moriarty said and the class groaned. "Oh, come on, it's not that bad." Silence. "Really, it's not. You have a complete bitch, a man who's a doormat, and an old lady who can hold a grudge worse than *Jaws*. Oh, and she ends up dead in the end. Plus, we're also going to cover *The Crucible* this year. Anyone know what that one's about?"

"The Salem witch trials," Kilkenny said with a grin.

"Oh, yeah. And it involves love, lust, and a woman—or two—scorned. That'll wake you up toward the end of the term."

The class relaxed and Kilkenny realized she was actually enjoying herself.

"Everybody, open *Great Expectations* to chapter one." She gave an arch grin. "Since I'm sure you're going to need a bit of a kick start to get into this one, we'll read some of it in class and I'll give you some homework. How's that sound?"

The class remained silent.

"I thought you'd enjoy that idea," she said. She zeroed in on Kilkenny. "You're in trouble because I know your name. How about you start us off, Kilkenny?"

"No problem," Kilkenny said, returning her grin. She took a deep breath and read.

"HEY, KILKENNY," GABRIELLE McCann said at the end of Kilkenny's second period Modern History class. "Can I see you for a moment?"

"Sure," Kilkenny said, leaving her backpack by the side of her desk and making her way to the front of the room. "What can I do for you?"

"You going to see Michelle Coopersmith today?"

Kilkenny nodded. "Sure am."

"Can you give her a message for me?"

"No problem."

"Tell her I don't have Terri's number. I tried calling her a couple of times but never heard back from her. The last time I tried her number was disconnected."

Kilkenny felt her blood run cold. "Okay."

"Hey, are you all right?" McCann asked, looking concerned as she scooped up her books. "You look pale."

"I'm fine, just first day blues, you know," Kilkenny said smoothly.

McCann looked at her doubtfully. "You sure?"

"Yeah, I'm cool. I don't think I got enough sleep last night."

McCann nodded. "I know, I get you. I'll see you later. Say hi to Michelle for me," she said as she left the room. "Oh, excuse me." She dodged a tall form coming into the room.

Kilkenny studied the woman who'd just entered the room. She was tall, a couple of inches taller than Kilkenny's six feet. Dark brown hair cascaded down to her mid back, framing perfect features and creamy skin. She was muscular and full breasted. She moved with panther like grace until she stood before Kilkenny. Timeless, unfathomable, dark green eyes captured hers.

"Would you like to take your seat?" she asked, her voice as wonderfully deep, smooth, and enigmatic as the rest of her.

Kilkenny felt her face heat. "Uh. Yes."

She hurried back to her seat and sat down, unwilling and unable to tear her eyes away from the woman. *God, she's hot. Absolutely gorgeous. Wow.*

The woman leant comfortably back against the teacher's desk and folded her arms across her full breasts. Kilkenny saw another flash of creamy skin as her shirt—barely buttoned above her breasts—fell open slightly. *Thank god this is only roll call because I* cannot *concentrate with her anywhere close to me. She's so distracting. And oh my god will you look at that fantastic body?*

"My name is Miss Roth," the woman said, eyes sweeping the room. "I'm going to be your roll call teacher this year."

The girls settled back and relaxed, watching her closely. Kilkenny felt cursed to stare at her. *If I want to stare, that's okay, I can explain it, but absolutely* no *drooling.*

"It seems," Roth continued, "that the speakers in these rooms aren't working. So I'm going to have to read out all the announcements for the next couple of days until the P.A. system is fixed."

Kilkenny felt like an uncoordinated dolt and stared at the way Roth's muscles moved beneath her skin and the way her shirt framed her muscular torso as she shifted around to grab a piece of paper. *Jesus wept. I never thought covered underwear could be* that *exciting.*

The class remained silent as Roth read out the announcements, and for the first time in her school career Kilkenny clung to every word the administration had to say to them.

Lauren Sonderby nudged her. "Close your mouth, Kilkenny," she whispered. "You're being a bit obvious."

"I can't help it," Kilkenny muttered. "And knowing my luck she's probably straight."

Lauren snorted a laugh. "Don't bet on it."

The bell rang, signaling the end of roll call.

"What do you mean?" Kilkenny asked.

"I'll tell you later," Lauren said. "I'll see you downstairs. I have to go and see Mr. Smith."

"Okay," Kilkenny said. The entire room of girls swarmed toward the door, and Kilkenny sat down and waited until the throng had begun to clear.

She glanced at Roth, trying not to obviously stare, when a flash of light caught the corner of her eye. She quickly zeroed in on the doorway and saw the air shimmering inside it.

Oh, no. That's not good.

"Are you all right?" Roth asked.

"Huh?" Kilkenny asked, watching as a girl walked through the doorway and disappeared in an explosion of ghostly sparks. She glanced at Roth, noting with dismay that they were the last ones in the room. "I'm fine."

Roth looked at her curiously. "What's your name?"

"Kilkenny Sharp."

"Well, Kilkenny," Roth said, approaching the doorway. "After you."

There's no rescuing this, Kilkenny thought. *I'm just going to have to toss her out of the dreamscape before she even knows she's in it. Assuming, of course, that there's going to be a hallway on the other side of the door.*

Roth was halfway to the door, and Kilkenny quickly jumped up and smoothly cut in front of her. Roth's eyebrows contracted.

"Age before beauty," Kilkenny said, inwardly flinching as soon as the words came out of her mouth. *Where did* that *come from? Maybe Jackie's right. Maybe I* have *been soaking up too much of Monk.*

She felt a dim heat as she walked through the doorway. She stopped just on the other side, and Roth bumped into the back of her. She felt her heart skip a beat, despite herself. She looked around as Roth murmured an apology.

"S'okay," she said, focusing on a soft sound in the silence of the dark hallway ahead of them.

"Are you going to move any time soon?" a soft voice asked almost directly in her ear.

Kilkenny smiled despite herself. *Not if it makes you put your hands on me to move me out of the way.* "Yeah, sorry." She looked out.

It *was* the school hallway, Kilkenny noted with relief, but it was much darker than it should have been at that time of day, and utterly deserted. There was not just silence but an absence of life that made Kilkenny dimly grateful that Roth was with her.

Roth, she thought with a start. *I have to get her out of here.*

"This isn't right, is it?" Roth said softly, directly into Kilkenny's ear.

Kilkenny shot her a quick glance.

Roth's eyes were sharp and calculating. She looked carefully around the hallway, her gaze finally coming to rest on Kilkenny.

Kilkenny shook her head, distracted by a sound she heard in the distance. It almost sounded like a voice.

"We should get out of here," Roth said.

"No," Kilkenny said softly. "*You* should get out of here."

Footsteps pounded along a concrete floor in the distance. "*Sharp*," a voice screamed from far away, growing in volume as the footsteps came closer.

"What—?" Roth took a step toward Kilkenny.

"What do you mean, what?" Kilkenny whipped around, slamming her shoulder into Roth's chest.

Roth instantly over balanced. She grunted as the air exploded from her lungs and she sailed back into the doorway to the classroom. She disappeared in an explosion of sparks.

Kilkenny shifted her vision, eyes cutting through the darkness with almost contemptuous ease. A column of swiftly moving golden sparks ploughed along the hallway. The shrieking from the shape shifter gaining in volume and strength until Kilkenny was afraid her ear drums would burst.

Suddenly the column was airborne and a heavy figured pounced on her. She crashed to the ground, Hellstrom on top of her. The breath exploded from her lungs, and she felt burning pain as what felt like a yard of skin came off her back. She lay still, temporarily stunned.

"You haven't done what I told you to do, have you?" Hellstrom said, knees digging into Kilkenny's shoulders and keeping her immobilized.

"I'm trying to find her," Kilkenny said.

"You're not trying hard enough," Hellstrom said, tilting her head to one side and eyeing Kilkenny calculatingly. "Maybe you think I'm not serious."

She shifted her weight, and Kilkenny cried aloud as her arm felt mashed into the ground and the bone threatened to break.

Hellstrom leaned down and pulled Kilkenny's uniform blouse out of her skirt. Her fingers were capped with sharp, metallic claws. She pushed a razor sharp tip into the skin below the left side of her rib cage.

Kilkenny moaned in pain as the skin beneath Hellstrom's fingertip dimpled and tore with excruciating slowness. She screamed as she felt flesh and muscle tear with exquisite slowness.

"There," Hellstrom said, smiling and nodding as she twisted the talon and pulled it out, drawing another sharp grunt from Kilkenny. "That should give you some incentive." Hellstrom leaned forward, bile yellow eyes boring into Kilkenny's. "Bring me Terri Warland or I'll strip the skin off your friends and family."

She stood up with stunning speed and tore Kilkenny off the floor. One hot hand held Kilkenny's shirt, the other her bunched up uniform skirt.

Hellstrom swung her arms and hurled Kilkenny toward the door. Kilkenny shot through it and collided with Roth, unceremoniously knocking her over and pinning her to the ground.

Kilkenny instantly rolled off Roth, her side a blaze of agony, radiating out of the cut Hellstrom made to the skin below her ribs.

"What just happened, Kilkenny?" Roth asked, reaching for her.

"Nothing," Kilkenny said, rolling out of her reach and to her feet. She held out her hand and Roth took it, allowing Kilkenny to lever her to her feet.

"Don't lie, Kilkenny," Roth said softly. "That wasn't normal."

"I never said it was normal, Miss Roth," Kilkenny said.

The silence played out between them for a couple of moments.

"You're not going to tell me what this is about, are you?" Roth asked.

Kilkenny shook her head. "There's nothing to tell."

The bell signaling the start of third period rang. Kilkenny internally sighed with relief. She had a double period of maths with Riordan.

"I have to go, Miss Roth," Kilkenny said, breaking the intense silence between the two of them. "I have to get moving or I'm going to be late."

Roth nodded slowly, her dark green eyes intense and measuring.

Kilkenny felt Roth's eyes on her back as she scooped up her backpack and left the room.

Kilkenny could feel the blood covering her side and looked down quickly. The left side of her uniform blouse was soaked with blood. She looked underneath her blazer and saw that her uniform was ruined.

She quickly ducked into the nearest toilet, locked herself in a stall, and pulled up her blouse with a grimace. The cut beneath her ribs was covered in half crusted blood.

She shifted her vision and saw her body as a column of golden sparks. The cut was a brown mess of slowly moving sparks. She covered it with her hand, hissing at the stabbing pain that shot through the cut. Her stomach rolled slowly, threatening to expel its contents. She took a deep breath and pulled the sparks around the cut over the top of it. The pain receded a little.

Her vision flickered back to normal and she looked down at the cut. The skin was whole and pink with a troubling, grayish undertone. It hurt abominably.

Kilkenny felt alarmed. *This isn't normal. I need Michelle's help. I hope it holds out until she gets home.*

She left the bathroom and went to her maths class. She was the last to arrive and Riordan was already at the front of the room. She drew a sharp look from Riordan as she entered. She smiled an apology to Riordan even though she'd never felt less like smiling in her life.

She dropped down into the seat beside Kristin Taft, hissing as her healed cut caught and radiated pain up and down her body.

Kristin looked at her. "Hey, Kilkenny, are you all right?"

Kilkenny shook her head. She felt Riordan's eyes on her and looked up. She smiled and it seemed to satisfy the teacher.

"Morning, everyone," Riordan said cheerfully. "Welcome to Year Twelve Maths."

The class groaned.

"Love the positive energy in the room," Riordan said, grinning. "Let's keep it up." She hefted her textbook. "Let's not open this up for the moment. I think we need a little recap of where we left off at the end of last year."

KILKENNY WAS QUIET throughout the double period. When the bell rang signaling the start of lunch, she found Riordan standing by her desk.

"Are you all right, Kilkenny?" she asked. "You look as white as a sheet."

"I don't feel that crash hot," Kilkenny said. Pain radiated throughout her body in waves and she could barely sit down. She tried to stand but wasn't prepared for the shock of agony to her system. She staggered forward into Riordan's arms.

Riordan held her up and put a hand on her forehead. "God, you're burning up. You should get to bed and lie down."

Kilkenny nodded. Bed and sleep felt like a good idea.

"Can Monk pick you up?"

Kilkenny shook her head. "She's got a full load of classes today."

"You want to crash at my place?"

Hellstrom's face flashed through Kilkenny's mind. "No, that's fine. I'll go back to Michelle's place."

"Okay," Riordan said. Her expression spoke volumes. She didn't like the idea of Kilkenny being by herself.

"I'll be fine after some sleep," Kilkenny said softly. "Really."

"Okay, grab your stuff. I'll take you back to Michelle's place."

Kilkenny nodded and grabbed the straps on her back pack. She moaned in pain as she tried to pick it up.

"Hey, I'll take that for you," Riordan said, neatly grabbing Kilkenny's back pack and shouldering it.

She led the way out of the classroom, Kilkenny close behind her, biting her lip at the tugging sensation in her side at each step.

Riordan stuck her head in the staffroom on the way by.

"Gab, I'm going to be back a couple of minutes late," she said.

"I'll let Rod know," McCann's voice floated out to them.

Kilkenny looked out into the courtyard. It seemed as though there were a million girls down there, either playing some complicated ball game with minimal rules, sunning themselves, or headed from nowhere to nowhere. A teacher slowly made his rounds around the courtyard, surrounded by a cloud of followers, some of them staring at him adoringly.

Kilkenny put on her sunglasses and shifted her vision.

The world became a riot of sparks, in a field of varying shades of gray. She felt unsettled, as though eyes were on her. *Hellstrom's here, all right*. Yet when she looked around at all the girls, they were all columns of varied colors, every shade imaginable under the spectrum except for gold. The magpies sat on overhead wires, a gentle breeze ruffling their brownish sparks, a soft red haze surrounding them.

"Are you ready?" Riordan asked from directly behind her.

Kilkenny instantly shifted her vision back. "Yep. I'm ready."

"Come on, then," Riordan said with a cheerful grin.

She led the way out of the school and toward the car.

Kilkenny felt as though sights were aimed right between her shoulder blades.

"Whoa," Riordan said softly as Kilkenny got into the car. "What happened?"

Kilkenny looked down and saw that the flap of her blazer had fallen back and her bloody shirt was showing.

"I'm okay, it's just a cut," Kilkenny said, awkwardly pulling her blazer closed and glancing at the teacher.

"Show me," Riordan said softly. She reached for Kilkenny.

Bugger. Kilkenny stood still and allowed Riordan to pull aside her blazer and uniform shirt.

Goosebumps followed in the wake of Riordan's fingertips as she gently brushed Kilkenny's skin. Kilkenny looked down. The cut, torn slightly open again, was weeping blood. Kilkenny yelped as Riordan's fingertips brushed over the wound.

"Ah," Kilkenny said sharply. "That hurts." She flinched away from Riordan's soft touch.

"That's infected, isn't it?" Riordan said, looking closely at her. "What happened?"

"I'm fine," Kilkenny said, pulling her shirt closed. "It's fine. I'll get Monk to put some disinfectant on it."

"I can do it. I'm right here with you," Riordan said softly, her gaze searching Kilkenny's face.

Kilkenny looked closely into Riordan's concerned, startling light gray eyes. "It's going to take two people to do it. Someone's going to have to hold me down. You wouldn't believe how painful this is."

"I think I can," Riordan said. She started the car and pulled out into the light traffic. "There's a lot of heat coming off it." She glanced at Kilkenny. "Promise me you'll go to a hospital if it hasn't eased up by tomorrow morning."

"I promise," Kilkenny said. *I'll kick it. I'm glad my blood works for me when I get hurt.*

Riordan remained quiet for the trip to Michelle's flat, and Kilkenny was glad of the silence. She tried to remain relaxed but it took every ounce of self control she had not to gasp in pain at every bump and turn of the road.

Just as they were pulling up to Michelle's flat, Kilkenny saw Monk striding down the road. She spotted them and jogged toward them. Kilkenny could see her concern as she got closer.

"Hi," Riordan said as Monk got within earshot. "You're Monk, right?"

Monk smiled briefly and nodded. "Hey, Riordan. Pleased to finally meet you," she said absently as she leaned over the side of the car. "Kilkenny? What's up? You look horrible."

"Hi, Monk," Kilkenny said. "I'm—"

"No you're not," Riordan said, giving her a sharp glance. "Monk. Kilkenny has an infected cut on her side."

Monk frowned and pulled her sunglasses down, peering closely at Kilkenny. "Show me."

Kilkenny sighed, defeated, and allowed Riordan to pull back her blazer and shirt.

Monk gave a low whistle. "What the fuck, Kilkenny? Jesus. We're going to have to get some disinfectant on that little sore of yours."

She stood back and opened the car door. Kilkenny stumbled out, pain radiating throughout her body, her knees treacherously weak. She fell and Monk caught her neatly, slinging her arm over a broad shoulder. Kilkenny stood, leaning into Monk, thankful for her solidity and strength. Her knees felt rubbery.

"I'm going to park," Riordan said, expertly pulling into the driveway and stopping in a visitor's parking spot.

"Shit," Monk said when she was out of earshot. "You couldn't shake her?"

"No," Kilkenny said. "And that's fine. You're going to need her help."

"We need Michelle's help and she's on her way."

Kilkenny gave her a half grin. "You know perfectly well she can't heal me."

"Maybe not but she can tell us why *you* can't seem to heal yourself."

Riordan strode toward them, carrying her briefcase and Kilkenny's back pack.

"I'm going to call in when we get upstairs," Riordan said shortly.

Kilkenny gave a ghost of a smile as she almost felt Monk trying her hardest not to roll her eyes in frustration.

She tried to take a step forward but her knees gave out. *No.* She headed toward the ground.

Monk neatly caught her. She scooped Kilkenny up and pulled her in close. Kilkenny moaned as pain stabbed through her side.

"I gotcha," Monk said.

She hurried toward the security doors, Riordan close behind her. She balanced Kilkenny's weight and quickly stabbed the buttons on the security pad. Kilkenny felt herself grey out from the pain. Monk jogged, each footstep agony for Kilkenny.

She was only distantly aware of Michelle's front door.

"Keys are in my front right hand side pocket," she thought she heard Monk say.

Monk shifted her weight as Riordan dug in her pocket for the keys.

"Monk," Kilkenny whispered. "I can't anymore."

"Let go, mate," Monk said softly. "It's okay. I'll take care of you."

Kilkenny surrendered to the pain and went off into welcoming darkness.

CHAPTER 3

CHRIST, MONK THOUGHT. *What the fuck happened to her?*

Monk quickly put Kilkenny on the sofa, smoothing back her hair from her forehead. She frowned as she felt the heat coming off her.

She glanced up at Riordan, hoping her discomfort at her presence didn't show on her face.

The teacher was tall, taller than Monk, and had the most arresting eyes Monk had seen on another woman. She was beautiful, but Monk wasn't moved. Riordan's jaw set and she looked down at Monk, almost challengingly.

Shit, I don't know how to get rid of her. Maybe Michelle's got some bright ideas. She could feel Michelle in their shape shifter bond, sending her gentle reassurance and support. Monk could almost feel Michelle's raised eyebrows at the alarm that filtered to her through their bond. She could feel Jackie, too, the question that came to her.

She sent reassurance to both of them and looked up at Riordan. "Do you know how she got hurt?"

Monk pulled aside Kilkenny's blazer and frowned when she saw the blood. *It almost looks like she got into a knife fight.* She pulled up Kilkenny's shirt and saw the jagged edges of the cut. They were almost purple and a thin channel of yellow ran through the center of it.

"Oh my God," Riordan said. "That's a hell of a lot worse than I saw it half an hour ago."

The heat radiating off the cut was tremendous, and Monk caught Riordan's shaking hand just before she could touch it.

"We're going to have to lance it," Monk said.

"Are you fucking kidding me?" Riordan said.

Monk glanced at her. The expression on Riordan's face was indecipherable but it somehow suggested that Monk form a close acquaintance with a pair of handcuffs and straight jacket.

"She's right," Michelle said, leaning over Monk's shoulder.

Monk almost collapsed with relief and barely refrained from throwing herself at her beloved lover.

"Look at what it's doing," Michelle said, indicating the cut. "That's getting exponentially worse. I don't know what it'd look like by the time an ambulance came, let alone the hospital." She caressed Monk's shoulder, a brief touch that instantly made her relax. "Can you get her into the bathroom?"

"No problem," Monk said, easing her arms under Kilkenny's shoulders and knees.

"You're Michelle, aren't you?" Riordan said, eyeing Michelle and giving her a similar look to the one she'd given Monk.

"Michelle Coopersmith," Michelle said, giving her a winning smile, designed to distract her.

"Riordan Kendrick," Riordan said shortly.

"Bathtub, Monk," Michelle said. She turned toward Riordan. "I should really ask you to leave, and I suspect you wouldn't go without a fight. I'd ask you to stay put but I suspect you wouldn't do that either. So are you going to help or keep looking at me like I'm an axe murderer?"

Riordan colored and studied Michelle closely for a moment. "I think you really want to help Kilkenny. I'll help you. What do you need me to do?"

Michelle trailed after Monk into the bathroom.

"Hold down her legs," Michelle said. "Monk? You want to take her shoulders?"

Monk nodded.

"Good," Michelle said. You guys get her clothes off and I'll be back in a sec."

Monk nodded. "I can manage that."

Michelle left the room and Monk sat Kilkenny up, laboriously stripping off her blazer.

Now's not a good time to be playing statue. "Are you going to help me or just look at me?" Monk asked. "I know you think we're both a pair of barbarians, but we're not. Kilkenny is a special needs kind of girl."

Riordan finally bent down and helped Monk strip off her skirt and uniform blouse. Her hands shook and her eyes were wide in her pale face.

Kilkenny, still senseless, lay in the tub in her underwear and Riordan stared at her. Monk wryly noticed Riordan trying hard not to stare at her breasts.

Well, that sort of explains why she won't leave, I suppose.

"You ready?" Michelle said, striding into the bathroom, opening up a kit, and pulling out a razor sharp Exacto knife.

"I'm ready," Riordan said, bending over the tub and grabbing Kilkenny's ankles. Monk gently took her shoulders and glanced at Michelle.

"Ready," she said. *God I hope Kilkenny doesn't wake up for this. It's going to hurt like a motherfucker.*

Michelle tensed, and Monk could feel her unease through their bond. Jackie's attention was focused on them, and Monk sent her gentle reassurance. She tightened her grasp on Kilkenny.

Michelle ran the knife along Kilkenny's open wound with swift precision. The congealing blood and pus instantly spurted out of the wound.

"Christ," Riordan muttered.

Michelle grimaced, touching the cut. "There's something hard in there," she said to Monk. "Brace yourself, I'm going to get it out."

"I don't think you have to worry about Kilkenny," Monk said. "She's out like a light. She's not waking up any time soon."

"I'm still going to make this quick," Michelle said, seating her hands around the sides of the cut. "Here goes."

She brought her hands together and the pinched skin bulged. A spongy mass of pus came up in her hands and blood flowed out of the wound in a steady stream.

Kilkenny moaned and moved but stilled after a few seconds.

"And what do you propose now?" Riordan asked acidly. "You have a sewing needle in your kit?"

"I don't need to have one," Michelle said. "It's already clotting over." She pointed at the wound. "Look."

Monk watched, fascinated, as the wound scabbed over.

"Give it another minute or so," Michelle said. "We can clean her up."

"I'll do it," Monk said. She looked at Michelle. "Please."

Michelle nodded. "All right." She put a friendly hand on Riordan's shoulder. "I'm going to make us all some coffee."

Riordan nodded dumbly and allowed Michelle to lead her out of the bathroom.

Monk sighed and looked down at Kilkenny. The cut had already scabbed over and a thin layer of skin formed over it.

Monk took off Kilkenny's blood soaked underwear, gently bathed her, and brought her into the spare bedroom. Her mind worked furiously, wondering how Kilkenny had gotten the cut and thanking God that Michelle had come as quickly as she had.

She turned her attention back to Michelle, bathed in a river of calm strength. *She's amazing. Does anything* ever *faze her?*

She made her way into the living room. Michelle and Riordan were sitting on the couch, and Michelle's face creased into a broad grin at the sight of her. She patted the couch and Monk comfortably flopped down beside her. Michelle leant back and handed her a full cup of coffee.

"Riordan here is still afraid we're a pair of brutal killers," Michelle said conversationally. "I was just explaining to her that we're not." She tilted her head. "Well, *I'm* not. I'm not sure about you."

"Have you ever found any dead bodies? No. Have you found my barn full of flaying equipment? No. Shallow graves in the garage? No."

"That just means I'm unobservant, not that you're harmless."

"Does that teacher gene of yours *ever* become recessive?" Monk asked plaintively. "Besides, I'm *much* neater than you at body disposal."

"One mistake, Monk. Just one. It was only *half* the police force. Not *all* of it."

"Half was enough. Did you *ever* stop to think about how much work hiding body parts in such a short period of time would be for me? No. Do you ever think of how *I* might feel about all of that? No."

"I don't have to care about any of that stuff," Michelle said imperiously. "That's *your* problem."

"Fine. Next time get rid of your own damn corpses. I have my own stuff to worry about."

"Lovers spat, anyone?" Riordan said, smile playing about her lips.

"No, we're good," Michelle said brightly.

"No problem at all," Monk said, just as brightly.

"Okay, can we drop this for a few minutes, then?" Riordan asked, leaning forward. Her light gray eyes glittered. "Good. All right. What are you both hiding?"

Monk felt Michelle's disquiet through their bond.

"We're not hiding anything," Monk said, tensing her muscles. "*You* were the one who came barging into our home unannounced. *You* were the one who insisted on staying."

Riordan flushed. "I did it because I care one hell of a lot about that woman you have there in your spare room." She eyed them both. "Let's get one thing straight. If you hurt her in any way, shape, or form, I will come after you. Do you understand? *I will come for you.*"

"Are you threatening us?" Monk asked softly. *I don't understand this. This is just weird. We just sliced open a young woman and bled her. That should have sent her out of here screaming. We really* do *look like a pair of serial killers and she's not frightened. She's not threatening to call the cops and she didn't sneak away to call them. Why?*

"No," Riordan said coldly. "I'm stating facts." She put her full coffee cup down and stood. "Thank you for the coffee and afternoon entertainment."

"Who are you to Kilkenny?" Michelle asked.

"I'm crazy about her and it's not one sided," Riordan said, her eyes still hot with anger. "Remember what I told you, ladies."

She stood and strode out of the room. Seconds later the front door shut with a quiet snick.

Monk looked at Michelle, feeling mutual disquiet and Jackie's full attention on them.

"Great," Monk said. "Now we just bought a whole raft of trouble. And an unwanted human hovering over her."

"I know," Michelle said. "On top of everything, we have a dyke drama. I'm sure she's right; I'm sure Kilkenny feels a hell of a lot more for her than she's letting on. And I'm sure that the more mysterious Kilkenny gets, the closer Riordan's going to *try* and get to Kilkenny."

Monk nodded. "And I'm sure Kilkenny is going to tell her to back off, so we're going to have broken hearts in the middle of broken bodies."

"That's one hell of a way to put it," Michelle said. She smiled. "I don't disagree."

"I'm going to call Kilkenny on the dreamscape tonight," Monk said. "She'll probably come. If only to tell us how she got that charming slice on the side of her body. Do you think we should tell her about Riordan?"

"It's going to come out when we tell her how this afternoon went."

Monk was silent for a moment. "Don't you think that was a weird conversation? She wasn't frightened by us."

"Yeah, that *was* weird. If it'd been me I'd have been on the phone to the cops."

"You couldn't *look* at her, could you?"

Michelle bit her lip. "No. I didn't. I couldn't do it without attracting attention. I'm not totally sure she's human."

Monk nodded. "Fair enough. I agree with you, by the way. If she's not human, it would explain how she reacted. If she was a werewolf she'd know what we're doing."

"Great. *Another* one." Michelle sighed. "I'm not sure she's a bad guy, though. She's been around Kilkenny for a year. Way before Hellstrom showed up. And she brought Kilkenny to us. She didn't try to hurt any of us."

"Agreed." Monk shook her head. "We're just going to have to let it go until after we've had a chance to talk to Kilkenny."

Monk nodded. "Agreed."

"I think I should check Kilkenny," Michelle said. "That cut wasn't normal."

"No, it wasn't."

They stood and went into the spare room. Monk pulled back the covers to Kilkenny's waist.

Michelle's eyes faded to bright, bile yellow, and she carefully looked at the raw skin on Kilkenny's side.

"I don't know," she said, shaking her head. "Golden sparks but it looks like there's a brown nodule just under the skin in the middle of the cut."

"Wonder what that means?" Monk said.

"I don't know," Michelle said. "Could be something, could be nothing. But we have to keep a close eye on it."

Monk nodded, pulling up the covers as Michelle's arms slipped around her waist.

She leant back into Michelle with smile. She closed her eyes and breathed deeply, loving Michelle's perfume and Michelle herself.

Michelle's arms tightened around her, and she gently nuzzled Michelle's neck.

"Have I told you how much I love you lately?" Monk asked, kissing Michelle and allowing her disobedient hands to wander. Michelle moaned softly and pulled her toward their bedroom.

Michelle's hands began their own movement. "Show, don't tell," Michelle whispered, moving in on Monk, making her forget everything.

MONK AND MICHELLE sat touching on a Victorian sofa in an ornate drawing room. Large French doors opened out onto a marble patio, lace curtains gently lifted by a late summer breeze. The sun shone into the room, making the antique furniture seem much lighter and elegant than it would otherwise have been. A thick, Persian rug lay underfoot, and a clock ticked on the mantelpiece over a cold fireplace.

"I'm always amazed by this room," Michelle said, looking around. "Where on earth did you get this from?"

"It's not mine," Monk said. "Kilkenny found it when her blood first gained ascendancy. We've been playing in it ever since."

"And you've never seen who owns it?"

"Nope," Monk said. "Are you ready?"

Michelle nodded.

"Okay," Monk said. "Here goes." She shifted her vision and the world became a riot of color and swirling, bleeding auras. An image of Kilkenny swam into her mind and she allowed longing to flow through her. *Come to me. Kilkenny, come.*

She allowed herself another moment of enjoyment and she released her vision. She felt Michelle's hand resting on her thigh, squeezing gently. She could almost feel Michelle's bare body snuggled against hers as they slept.

"I love you," Monk said. "Sometimes I can barely believe you took Kilkenny's blood."

Michelle smiled back at her, looking deep into her eyes. "How could I not? I love you so much it should be illegal. I can live without you, Monk, but I just don't want to. I'd spend every moment of my life haunted by your beautiful, blue eyes, and I'd regret not being by your side."

"I honestly don't know how life is going to work out for us, but I know it's more fun with you by my side." Monk smiled. "I'm going to live up to my promise to you. No matter what happens I'm going to come back to you."

"And I'll make the same one back. I'm going to come back to you, too, Monk. As long as we stay and work together we'll be fine."

Monk nodded. "Yes, we will."

"Hey, guys," Kilkenny said, striding through the French doors.

"Hey, Kilkenny," Monk said. "Take a seat and tell us what the hell happened. How did you get that cut?"

Kilkenny, dressed comfortably in jeans and a tee shirt, flopped down into a chair opposite them. "I went to school today and did see some new faces. My English teacher, Moriarty, is new. So is my roll call teacher, Roth." She colored slightly at the mention of Roth's name. "I didn't get to find out who else I might have had. To answer your question about the cut, I got pulled into the dreamscape—with

Roth—at recess. I managed to toss her back out through the doorway before Hellstrom arrived. Hellstrom swiped me as a gentle reminder that I'm supposed to be finding Terri Warland." Kilkenny's light brown eyes shone with irritation. "Bitch." Pause. "*Bitch.*" She gave Michelle a sad smile. "By the way, McCann gave me a message for you, Michelle. She said she didn't have a good number for Terri."

"Ugh," Michelle said. "That means we're going to have to call her on the dreamscape."

Monk nodded. "No kidding."

Kilkenny leaned back in her chair, the very image of calm relaxation. "Monk, is this dream warded?"

Monk shifted and looked around the room. It seemed perfectly normal and when she extended her senses, it felt as though a glass dome surrounded them. She pushed against it but it didn't give. She nodded. "Do you want me to do the deed?"

"In a minute. What happened with Riordan? The last thing I remember is you carrying me upstairs."

Monk and Michelle exchanged a wry glance.

"She insisted on coming upstairs with us. We ended up lancing your cut, Kilkenny." Monk leaned forward, elbows resting comfortably on her thighs. "She stayed for the whole thing and threatened to hurt us if we hurt you."

Kilkenny frowned. "That's the last thing I'd have expected. I'd have expected her to run miles in the opposite direction."

"Yes. She owes us an explanation. And now *you* owe *her* an explanation," Monk said. "She cares more about you than the bounds of friendship dictate. How do you feel about her?"

Kilkenny blushed. "More than the bounds of friendship dictate." She sighed and rubbed her eyes. "Although I suspect that's going to be a moot point since I'm sure I will have lost on that side of the board after I tell her about me."

"You *have* to level with her about your species," Monk said. *And that'd be one conversation I would* not *want to be there for, although it looks like I'm going to be.*

"Forget my emotions toward her at the moment. I think we should try calling her before we try Terri."

Michelle nodded. "Because you don't know who's watching you and you want us for backup."

"And since we're not here in our physical forms the danger to us is minimized." Monk grinned. "I like it."

"Not only that," Kilkenny said. "If I'm going to level with her about shape shifting, then I want to be able to do the same thing I did with you, Monk. *Raggedy Anne sent me.*"

Monk nodded. "All right, we can go with that."

"I'll do the deed, Monk," Kilkenny said as her light brown eyes faded into a vicious, virulent yellow. Her eyes changed back to normal a moment later.

"Interesting," she said. "You're both columns of gold, like me."

"If you say so," Monk said doubtfully.

"Because you're both shape shifters."

"Okay."

Just at that moment, two tall figures strode into the drawing room.

"Kilkenny," Riordan said happily. "You're alive." She lost no time in pulling Kilkenny into an enormous bear hug. Kilkenny quickly disentangled herself.

"Indeed you are," Roth said, folding her arms and taking them all in.

"How did you get in here?" Kilkenny said, quickly putting herself between Riordan and Roth. Her eyes lightened.

Roth looked at her, as her own eyes lightened.

"She's a fucking werewolf," Monk said. Her heart rate picked up as her muscles tensed.

Roth held up a hand. "Calm yourself. I mean you no harm."

Monk stared at Roth, feeling the alarm from Michelle drift down the bond to her. It caught Jackie's attention and Monk could almost feel her turning toward them.

Monk allowed her vision to shift, watching the gold aura swirling around Roth. Her muscles almost hummed with tension. She heard an explosion, dulled by distance, and frowned.

"What was that?" Michelle said, scenting the air and looking around.

"I don't know," Monk said. "But anything that sounds like that can't be good."

Kilkenny glared at Riordan. "You lied to me."

"You weren't exactly telling me the truth either, Kilkenny," Riordan said, her arctic eyes sparking with anger.

"Are you one too?" Kilkenny asked bitterly. She looked as though she'd been punched in the stomach.

Riordan's arctic eyes faded to bile yellow.

There was another explosion and this time the dreamscape trembled.

"Christ," Monk muttered, feeling Michelle's alarm and her own. "We'd better wrap this up quick."

The explosion returned and the entire world shuddered. Monk stumbled forward, supporting Michelle's weight as she fell into her.

Roth neatly caught Riordan. Kilkenny balanced on the floor on one knee, knuckles resting on the ground.

"Young one," Roth said, glancing at Kilkenny, yellow eyes wild and intense. "What's going on?"

"*Here I come*," Hellstrom screamed.

"We're out of here," Kilkenny said shortly.

Adrenaline flooded Monk's system and she whirled around, slashing a hole into the dreamscape. "Everyone. Out."

Kilkenny gave her a brief nod and shot forward, sailing neatly through the air, crash tackling Roth and Riordan, her forward momentum pushing them through the slit. As soon as they hit the opening, they disappeared in a shower of sparks.

Michelle glanced at Monk. "I'm not leaving you."

"You *have* to," Monk said. "Wells bit me, remember? I have her blood. According to what Lightman once told me about Wells, I should now be a dream walker with total control over the dreamscape. This shouldn't be happening." She nodded. "We have to know more. Like, does she have company?" She gave Michelle a quick kiss. "Go. I'll meet you in few."

Michelle growled. "I don't like this at all." She ran forward and dove through the opening to the dreamscape and Monk promptly sealed it behind her.

The world boomed again and this time the concussion knocked her onto the floor and an end table fell and landed on her in a shower of splintered wood. Footsteps pounded up the marble patio toward her.

She sat up and the doors exploded open.

Hellstrom bounded in, monstrously jovial, bile yellow eyes zeroing in on Monk.

She's working alone. Monk tried to tear a hole in the dreamscape, but found to her horror that she couldn't. *Oh, dear. She* has *to be a dream walker.*

"*There* you are," Hellstrom cried. "The red headed whelp left me a present."

"I'm *not* your present." Monk snarled, easily flipping to her feet. "Hands off."

Hellstrom shot across the room before Monk could blink, and she found herself in Hellstrom's iron grip. "You are whatever I say you are. You're dead if that's what I choose."

"Blah, blah, blah," Monk said. "I've heard that before." She shifted her vision. Hellstrom's golden aura seemed more toward orange, an ugly, unhealthy color.

"You're a shape shifter," Hellstrom said. "Good. You can call Terri for me."

"There's no way in hell I'm doing that," Monk said through gritted teeth, gamely hanging on to her vision. Her muscles bulged as she tried to break out of Hellstrom's grip. She felt Michelle turn to her, her pain and worry.

"Yes. You are."

"No. I'm not. And you can't make me." Monk tilted her head. "What I really want to know is why you don't call Terri yourself. You're a shape shifter. You have the same powers I do. Why don't you do it your bloody self?"

Hellstrom's eyes narrowed in fury, and something flickered in them so quickly Monk couldn't catch it. Sudden realization made her widen her eyes.

She can't. She can't, that's why she's not doing it. What the hell could stop a shape shifter from doing that?

Hellstrom gave her a savage shake. "Call Terri."

"Nope," Monk said, mustering up as much cheer as she could.

Hellstrom snarled, released her, and punched her in the stomach, hard. Agony flared in her midsection and she could taste blood in the back of her throat. The force of the punch threw her backward. She hit the sofa and tumbled over the back of it.

She lay still for a moment, stunned. She hurt so badly she was incapable of rational thought. Something pulled and tore every time she took a ragged breath.

The floor opened up beneath her and she tumbled through a hole in the dreamscape. She felt wrenching dislocation as she sailed through the air to land in a strong pair of arms, which cradled her to a woman's chest.

"Thank you," Monk whispered, surrendering to the pain in her stomach. Her vision darkened.

When she opened her eyes, she heard the soft murmur of water rushing over rocks. A fragrant breeze blew across her damaged body. Her head was resting in a lap.

"Oh, god," she moaned, her eyes fluttering open.

Jackie's dark blue eyes gazed into hers. "Are you all right, Monk?" she said softly, pain in her voice and evident in the shaking hand that gently pushed Monk's hair back off her forehead.

"I'm about as good as I'm going to get," Monk said, yelping as she struggled to sit up.

"Was it Hellstrom?" Jackie said, pulling Monk into her arms and giving her a gentle kiss on the cheek.

"Afraid so." Monk smiled. "Thank you for coming for me. How did you know?"

"I felt you in our bond," Jackie said. "Your dream was a bitch to cut into, Monk."

"Hellstrom managed it like I hadn't done it at all."

"I figured," Jackie said. "You know what that probably means, don't you?"

"A dream walker," Monk said.

"Yeah. On top of everything, Hellstrom is a dream walker," Jackie said. Her arms tightened around Monk. "I'm sorry I'm not there with you and Michelle."

"I don't like you being so far away from us," Monk said.

"I don't like it either," Michelle said, striding down the grassy bank of the river toward them. She slid down next to Jackie and kissed her. Jackie settled back into her arms with a soft sigh of pleasure.

"At least we can meet like this," Jackie said.

"Monk, there's blood coming out of your mouth," Michelle said. "What happened?"

"Hellstrom happened. And she punched me. Jackie cut me out of the dream."

A dull rumbling began.

Michelle looked up, alarmed.

Monk stiffened. Pain stabbed through her and her breath caught. "Not again. We'd better get out of here."

Jackie nodded.

The world wrenched and fell away. Monk felt herself flying backward through the air, plummeting downward. She woke with a start.

Her eyes fluttered open and she coughed. Blood spurted out of her mouth and into her hand, dripping on the covers.

"Let me see," Michelle said gently, pushing Monk back down again and shifting her vision. "Oh, God."

"What?" Monk asked. *God, my stomach fucking hurts.*

Michelle gently put a trembling hand on Monk's aching stomach. She felt a warm, tingling sensation where Michelle's hand was and the pain faded away into memory.

"She hurt me, didn't she?" Monk asked.

"Yeah, she did."

"I didn't think that translated into physical damage."

"Looks like it does."

"It shouldn't."

"But it did." Michelle was pale and trembling. "What happens if she does something to you and I'm not close by?"

"I'd call for you," Monk said, cupping her face with her clean hand. "I'm not letting her get that close to me again. I'll stay out of her reach. Besides, since we bonded I heal faster. The bond seems to give me access to energy from you. The bond alone would help me hang on until you got there."

Michelle rested her forehead against Monk's. "It'd better."

"It will." Monk smiled. "We better go check on Kilkenny." She gave Michelle a gentle kiss.

They got out of bed, pulled on robes, and went to the spare bedroom.

Kilkenny was still laid out on the bed, her chest rising with deep, even breaths.

"She's still asleep," Michelle said, disbelief in her voice. "Do you think she's safe without us?"

"I'm guessing Jackie's given her a safe place on the dreamscape."

"I hope so."

CHAPTER 4

KILKENNY OPENED HER eyes the next morning, surprised and pleased to find that her side didn't hurt as badly as it had the previous day.

She pulled back the covers and looked down at herself. *I healed. Why do I feel like there's still something in there?* She shifted her vision and saw a couple of brown nodules. *Oh, no. I think that might be silver. No, it can't be. If it was, I'd be dead.* She put her hand over it and pushed a thin stream of sparks out of her hand toward the cut. They surrounded the nodule and she tugged. The resulting stab of pain almost made her scream in agony. She bit the inside of her cheek, tasting blood, an instantly withdrew the streamer.

She lay down again, chest heaving, waiting for the pain radiating through her to subside. *I won't be trying that again any time soon.*

When she felt normal again, she slowly sat up, distantly amazed that it didn't seem to hurt at all. She tried to stand, and her vision grayed out for a second. She felt abominably weak.

Great. I hope that *passes soon.*

She was naked and she looked down at the bed, seeing the robe Monk had left for her. It had a note pinned to the lapel.

You looked like you could use the sleep, it said. *I'll be back around lunch time.*

Kilkenny smiled as she slipped it on. *That's one of the reasons I love Monk so much.*

She made her way out of the bedroom and into the kitchen after a quick stop in the bathroom. She made herself a cup of coffee and sat down on the sofa to sip it. She glanced at the clock. It was close to nine o'clock. She wasn't going to school and would miss roll call. A great wave of sadness rolled over her.

I so wish Roth wasn't a shape shifter. She's so hot. *And Riordan. What am I going to do about her?*

How could she have been friends with Riordan for more than a year and not know that she was a shape shifter? Why hadn't Riordan told her? *Dope. What were you expecting her to say? Hey, Kilkenny, by the way, I'm a werewolf?*

The biggest question was what they were going to do now. Riordan now knew *she* was a werewolf. Did that mean Riordan would come after her? Kill her?

Roth's gentle voice floated through her mind. *Calm yourself. I mean you no harm.*

If they meant no harm, why were they there?

"Kilkenny?" Riordan's soft voice came from the patio.

Kilkenny looked up and saw Riordan's outline in the doorway. She blinked sudden tears from her eyes.

"I'm here," she said, her voice cracking slightly.

Riordan silently entered the living room and knelt before her. She gently took Kilkenny's hands. "Hey, are you all right?"

"No," Kilkenny said. "What on earth makes you think I'd be all right?"

"I can guess why, and I'm sorry." Riordan nodded. "When were you planning on telling me you were a shape shifter?"

"Last night, actually. Well, today more like. I was going to talk to you today about shared dreams." She studied Riordan, her pale eyes, still and watchful. "Why are *you* here? What would you have done after I'd told you? Why are you even talking to me now?"

"I'm not here to hurt you," Riordan said softly.

"It's a bit too late for that," Kilkenny said. "Do you realize our entire relationship has been built on a lie?"

"That's a bit harsh, Kilkenny. First, how was either of us supposed to have broached the subject with the other? Second, I'm not *just* a werewolf. I'm also a woman. Everything we've built up so far is true and fair. I'm a werewolf in all my life, not just part of it. Everything you've known of me so far has included the fact that I'm not human. Do I really sound any different to before?" She sighed. "Not every werewolf is a psychopath, or likes hurting things." She studied Kilkenny. "Who did that to you? Who hurt you so bad you'd think we were *all* like that?"

Do I believe that? And she's right. I've done to her what I'm angry at her for doing to me. All the time they'd spent together streamed through her mind, a mix of images and feelings and the utter trust she'd built up in Riordan. *I haven't been honest about my species either. And my species doesn't alter the fact that I loved watching hokey 3D movies with her, prowling through the art gallery giggling at modern art, building sandcastles with her on the beach or, god help me, staring up at the stars in the middle of the night, handing her my heart and soul.*

"I'll tell you what happened to me later." She nodded. "I've done exactly the same thing with you and I'd be a hypocrite if I denied it."

Riordan smiled and caressed her hands. "Do you mind if I sit next to you?"

"Sure," Kilkenny said.

Riordan eased up onto the sofa next to her, so close their bodies touched. "I'm sorry, so sorry to have hurt you."

"And I'm just as sorry to have hurt *you*," Kilkenny said.

Riordan snuck her arm around Kilkenny's shoulder and leaned over and claimed Kilkenny's lips. It started gently, Riordan delicately tasting her, and Kilkenny deepened it, allowing all of her tangled emotions to reveal themselves in it. Riordan responded with gentle passion and when she pulled back, Kilkenny felt as though she'd been knocked off her feet.

"Wow," she said, sinking into Riordan's body as Riordan pulled her in close.

"Yeah," Riordan said softly. "I care about you, Kilkenny, more than I should."

"I care about you exactly as I should," Kilkenny said. "If I'd told you I was a shape shifter, would you still have been interested in me?"

"Yes," Riordan said. "Interest's what made me come. I care about *you*. We can't date until school is over. But don't ever think it's because I'm not interested."

"I can live with that," Kilkenny said. She allowed herself to relax against Riordan, feeling her strong, hard body and beautiful breasts pressed against her arm. *She's so easy to love.*

"Now, then," Riordan said, pressing her lips against Kilkenny's temple. "How about you tell me what's going on? Maybe I can help you."

Kilkenny hesitated. *What would Michelle and Monk advise? Would they tell me to tell her the truth? Yes. Monk can't lie to save her soul.* She studied Riordan's eyes. There was no sign of deception in them, just a gentle concern that warmed Kilkenny's soul. *I feel safe. Besides, Roth was right. If they'd wanted to hurt us in the dreamscape they could have. In fact, if Rio really wanted to kill me she wouldn't have kissed me and we wouldn't have discussed dating at the end of the year.*

"Where to start?" Kilkenny said. "Would you like some coffee? I think you're going to need it."

Riordan nodded. "Actually, that would be really cool. Thanks."

Kilkenny smiled. "No worries." She gently disentangled herself from Riordan and made her a cup of coffee. She settled herself down on the sofa with a soft sigh, relishing the feel of Riordan's arm around her as she pulled her in close again.

Kilkenny began softly and told Riordan about her interaction with Hellstrom, ending with throwing them out of the drawing room.

"Oh, fuck," Riordan muttered when she'd finished. "*Fuck.*"

"Do you know Hellstrom?" Kilkenny asked, looking at her curiously. "One thing I will find odd in all of this is that it's awfully coincidental that you and Roth show up at the same time Hellstrom did."

Riordan frowned. "Are you suggesting that we're somehow working together?"

Kilkenny shook her head. "No. If you were with Hellstrom you'd probably have hurt me by now. You sure as hell wouldn't be sitting on this sofa with me in your arms. I'd have been sailing around the room by now." She looked carefully into Riordan's eyes. "But I suspect you know something about Hellstrom that you need to tell me."

"Oh, sweetheart, that's a really long story. And it's not mine to tell. I don't think we have time for that now. What you need to know right now is that your gut is right. Hellstrom is about the worst news any shape shifter can get." She shook her head. "The cut on your side, how does it look?"

"I'd show you but I'm not wearing anything under this robe," Kilkenny said. "It hurts and it looks like there's a brown thingy in it."

Riordan frowned. "That doesn't sound good."

"Is it possible that it's silver?" Kilkenny asked.

"If it was silver you'd probably be dead. When did you turn into a werewolf?"

"I didn't turn. I've always been this way."

Riordan's eyes widened. "You were *born* a werewolf?"

"Yes. Does that mean anything?"

"It's so rare is almost unheard of," Riordan said.

Kilkenny nodded, looking out the window at the row of crows on the telephone wires. A breeze blew in through the open patio doors, cooling her heated skin.

"If it *is* silver in your cut then the reason you're still alive is that you were born and not made. Silver is not so much poison to us but more like an allergic reaction. It's worse in those of us who were made and not born."

"If I'm having an allergic reaction, is it going to go away or do I have to remove the source of it?"

"I honestly don't know," Riordan said. "It's a question for Roth. But every instinct I have screams at me to get it out of you."

"Yeah, so do mine," Kilkenny said. She glanced at Riordan. "Who is Roth to you, Rio?"

"Roth is my bond mate and my lover," Riordan said.

Kilkenny sighed. *I suspected as much. And that hurts so badly.* "And what am *I* to you?"

Pain flickered in Riordan's eyes. "I don't know the answer to that one. You're so young."

Ouch. Kilkenny shifted her vision, seeing Riordan as a column of golden sparks, almost as bright as the sun. She was surrounded by an aura of silver sparks, which reached out into the distance. They looked the same as they did between Jackie, Michelle, and Monk.

She released her vision. Riordan was studying her.

"I don't want to be your piece on the side," Kilkenny said. "I'm sure Roth knows about me. She can't possibly *not* know. But I don't want to the one you turn to when things aren't going so well for you and Roth. I'm not a consolation prize."

Riordan flinched. "Ouch. That hurt." She was silent a moment. "I'm not a player, Kilkenny. I've been alive for a long time. I've *never* done this before. Roth means the world to me. She's my lover, my teacher, and my friend. She *owns* me. But that doesn't mean there isn't room enough in my heart for you, too."

"I have to get to know Roth before anything happens between us," Kilkenny said. "I want to know for myself that she's not going to go nuts about us."

"*I'm* hoping I'm not *all* you want," Riordan said, biting her lip and studying Kilkenny carefully.

Kilkenny smiled at her. "I'm not unfamiliar with what you're hoping. Monk and Michelle aren't just a couple. Jackie's part of them as well. I'm okay with that."

"Good," Riordan said, nodding. "Then my other concern is if I'm just a passing interest for you."

"Hey, *I* might just be a *passing interest* for *you*," Kilkenny said. "I can't read the future and neither can you. Why don't we just relax, keep getting to know each other, and see what happens?" *This hurts but at least now everything's out in the open. What would have happened if we'd started dating and I suddenly found out she was attached? It'd kill me. Who am I kidding? It'll kill me now if she dumps me.*

Riordan nodded. "I'm glad we actually talked about this," she said after a moment. "I can't stand the thought of not having a chance with you. I felt so bad last night."

Kilkenny nodded. "Yep, so did I." She smiled. "You have no idea how badly I want to kiss you right now."

Riordan smiled, leant forward, and kissed Kilkenny again. This time when they broke, both were breathing hard and Riordan's eyes had darkened.

"God, Rio," Kilkenny whispered. "I don't want to, but you have to. *Stop.* We have to talk about Hellstrom."

Riordan smiled. It lit up her arctic eyes. "Don't blame me if you're as distracting as hell to me. But yes, I understand we have to talk about Hellstrom."

"Hellstrom is watching me. I don't know how close she is. She doesn't know about you or Roth, which is something that's working in my favor."

"Roth and I will stand with you and your friends, Kilkenny. We have to be very careful. Hellstrom is an expert at hiding in plain sight. We all are."

"How come? What does that mean?"

"Shape shifters are all about their blood. Her clan is the same as mine. I'm from the strongest clan. We have super speed and super strength." She studied Kilkenny. "Do you know what blood you have? Can you tell me what you see when you shift?"

"I can already tell you my vision is different to Monk's and obviously yours. I see the world in shades of grey and the living things in it as columns of sparks. Shape shifters are golden. I can see you're different to me because there's a cloud of silver mixed into you, and the silver goes off into the distance, and I'm just plain gold. You look the same as Monk, Michelle, and Jackie so I'm assuming the silver I see is your bond." She was silent a moment. "Oh, and I heal really quickly. I can heal other people as well, including shape shifters. Although, that doesn't seem to work well on Michelle. She's of my clan. I may have figured out how to fix that, though. I'm going to have to get her to hold still so I can try out my theory."

Riordan gaped at her.

"What?" Kilkenny asked. *What's gotten into her?* "Isn't that normal?"

"It's normal but it's not common," Riordan said, her eyes wide. "When Roth and I shift, it's like there's very little darkness in the world. Every sight, scent, and sound is ultra keen. Even if it's pitch black, we can still see. My God, you really don't know, do you?"

"Know what?"

"You're something the shape shifter world hasn't seen in a few hundred years. You're a bond master."

"A what?"

"A bond master. You can see and manipulate shape shifter bonds. You want to try a little experiment?"

"Okay," Kilkenny said.

"Touch my bond," Riordan said. "But please, be very careful. I don't want my bond to Roth damaged. It'd kill both of us."

"I won't hurt you, Rio," Kilkenny said, looking deep into her eyes. "It's the last thing I'd *ever* do to either one of you."

Riordan nodded. "Okay. I trust you."

Kilkenny shifted her vision and carefully studied the silver sparks that came off Riordan. As she watched them move it seemed almost as though they were stuck to her. She stretched out a cautious streamer of gold and caressed Rio's silver sparks, pulling them away from the golden ones. As she pulled one, another followed. Fascinated, she tugged a handful. Suddenly a whole collection of silver sparks exploded out of Riordan, forming a bright cloud around her, which streamed off into the distance. Kilkenny released her vision.

Riordan's breath caught. "Oh my god, what did you do? It almost feels as though Roth is inside me."

"Isn't that what it always felt like?" Kilkenny asked.

"No. Before it was just a general knowledge of her presence. I'd have been able to tell you where she was in a crowded room. Or I'd be able to tell what general direction she's in, but now . . . this . . . it's amazing. I can feel *inside* her. I feel everything she feels for me." A tear made its way out of her eye. "I don't know how to thank you for this."

"Don't thank me until it doesn't go away," Kilkenny said. "But I'm pretty sure it won't. The changes I make seem to be permanent."

She suddenly found herself in a smothering hug courtesy of Riordan.

"God, I wish you could feel this," Riordan said, kissing her. "It's amazing."

One day. "You're welcome, Rio. Say hi to Roth for me."

Riordan nodded. Her arm tightened around Kilkenny.

Kilkenny smiled, watching the crows on the power lines outside the window. They were still brown with a thin red cloud of fuzz around them.

I'm with one of the few people I really care about, we've kissed and I'm in her arms. So why do I feel so uneasy?

MONK WALKED QUICKLY around the outside of the engineering buildings, overtaking a couple of other slow walkers headed toward Redfern train station. She glanced down at her watch.

Ten forty seven. Plenty of time before my train comes at eleven. Thank god today wasn't a long day. I'm too distracted to deal with it.

She walked up the main road, aware of the eyes that followed her from the students walking down the road toward her, headed to classes. She was adept at dodging them, and did so now as a group of five abreast powered toward her as though they were the blade of an oncoming bulldozer. They didn't move, simply stared at her, and she was forced to skirt the edges of them. The end one adjusted her back pack as Monk went past and elbowed Monk.

Monk ignored it.

She kept walking up the road, glancing at one of the houses. A boy of about fourteen stood in the doorway, rubbing his bulging crotch.

Shit, that kid's really fucking freaky. She felt his eyes on her, calculating and measuring. *That little prick really has a fucking porno playing through his head.*

His eyes followed her and she almost felt it as twin laser beams boring into the skin of her back between her shoulder blades. She refused to hurry but still increased her stride so she was power walking toward the station entrance.

A filthy homeless man sat outside the station, holding out his hand, mumbling, "Got some change?" to every student pouring out of the entrance.

Shit. Monk stood directly before him as a young man shot around the side of a slow moving group, forcing Monk out of the way.

A hand tugged on her jeans and she jumped. *I'm more nervous than I thought.*

She looked down at the beggar. His red rimmed, bloodshot brown eyes were intense and the stench of vomit and caked feces drifted off his unwashed body.

"You're going to die," he said, eyes drilling into her.

"What?" she asked. "*What?*"

He looked past her. "You're going to die!"

The group of girls walking past him turned to stare. "Fucking shit for brains," one of them snarled. "Why don't *you* do the world a favor and die?"

"Bitch," he muttered.

One of the girls shot him an obscene gesture.

"*Bitches!*" he screamed at their retreating backs. He looked up at Monk again with an expression she thought was supposed to be ingratiating. "Got some change?"

"No, sorry," Monk said, pulling out of his grasp and glancing down at her watch. Ten fifty five. *Plenty of time to get down to the platform.*

Monk got into motion again and powered through the crowd determinedly. This time people dodged her. She quickly swiped her weekly ticket and went through the turnstiles, past a small convenience store, and down to the end of the station.

The trains headed south were underground. She went through the mouth of the building that housed the escalators and grimaced as she was blasted by the wind from the trains roaring out of the tunnel. Sunlight flashed in her eyes and she blinked.

She breathed deeply, scenting the hydraulic fluid and ozone from the trains below. One roared to a stop in the station, disgorging more passengers.

The ones coming up the escalators all turned to stare at her.

God, what is *it with everyone today? Thank god that crowd's finished with.*

She caught a flicker of movement out of the corner of her eye. She automatically turned to track it but saw nothing in the shadows. She continued her power walk to her normal bench.

This whole thing with Hellstrom is just making me jumpy.

She heard the sound of an oncoming train and almost sighed with relief. It shrieked to a stop before her and the doors slid open. She quickly got into the carriage and headed to the upper level. She took the steps two at a time, almost shaking with relief as she flopped into an empty seat. She kept her backpack on her lap, looking around the deserted carriage.

Five minutes later, she was in Sydenham, which was utterly deserted.

Uh, oh. There should be more people here. Shit.

At the same time, she heard feet pounding through the carriage and up the stairs. Suddenly she found herself face to face with Ingrid Hellstrom.

"Hiya, Monk!" Hellstrom said with grotesque joviality.

"Hiya, Hellstrom!" Monk shot back, adrenaline flooding her system.

Hellstrom's grin fell away. "You won't be cutting yourself out of this dream, Monk. And you're going to call Terri for me."

"*Yes*, I will and *no*, I'm not."

Hellstrom's orange aura swam into focus and the colors in the train carriage bled.

"I won't stop you from shifting," Hellstrom said. "Angela!"

Monk's heart almost stopped when she saw Angela Michaels ascending the stairs, cold smile playing about her lips. Her eyes were bright yellow.

Oh, Christ. I wondered what happened to her after she got expelled. It kind of explains why she got so vicious. When did Wells find time to make her?

Monk felt Michelle's attention turn toward her, her alarm.

"How did you find me?" Monk asked.

Angela smiled and studied her fingernails. "I have you under my skin."

"Fuck," Monk said. *She was made before she clawed my chest. It's always been me. That's how Hellstrom has been tracking Kilkenny.*

Angela's eyes narrowed.

Hellstrom grabbed her shaggy fringe and pulled her head back.

"Now that I have your attention," she said coldly. "Call Terri."

"No," Monk moaned. "I won't do it."

"Fine." Hellstrom turned to Angela. "Make her."

A red aura grew around Angela, sliding toward Monk with deadly accuracy. The second it touched her, she felt as though a million daggers were stabbing into her mind and she screamed in pain. She was distantly aware of a spurt of blood out of her nose.

"Stop," she screamed. "Just stop."

Angela hacked away at her in earnest and the world finally went mercifully dark.

THE TELEPHONE RANG.

Kilkenny, clutching a towel around her wet body, ran to the kitchen and grabbed it on the seventh ring.

"Hello?" she said, trying to catch her breath.

"Kilkenny?" Michelle said.

"Hi, Michelle," she said, an automatic smile coming to her face.

"Is Monk there?"

Kilkenny looked around at the deserted living room. "Nope. Hang on a sec, let me check your room." She put down the receiver, not waiting for an answer. She quickly checked the master bedroom and their office. Monk wasn't there. She frowned, and her heart beat faster. She glanced up at the clock. It was almost one o'clock. *Didn't Monk say she was going to be home around lunch time? Shouldn't she be here?*

She scooped up the receiver. "No, Mitch, she's not. What time is lunch for her? She left a note saying she'd be back by lunch."

"She should have been home half an hour ago," Michelle said. "I already checked with her friend Cally."

"Slow down, Michelle. Why do you think there's something wrong? Maybe she just stopped to pick up a bite to eat on the way home," Kilkenny said uneasily.

"No, she didn't. Not judging by what I just felt in our bond," Michelle said. "Jackie felt it too."

"What did you feel in your bond?" Kilkenny asked.

"She's in terrible pain," Michelle said. "And then it went out."

"It was Hellstrom, wasn't it?"

Silence. "Yeah, I think so." A sigh from Michelle.

Kilkenny flinched at the pain in her voice. "How did Hellstrom know where to look?"

"Good question," Michelle said. "How do we find her?"

"You can track her in your bond, can't you?"

Michelle was silent for a long time.

"Michelle?" Kilkenny asked.

"I'm still here," Michelle said, sounding uneven. "My bond feels the same way it does when you're both on the dreamscape."

"Then we can find her, no problem. We can call her, and if she can't come to us we can go to her."

"I don't think it's going to be that easy," Michelle said.

"Why?" Kilkenny asked.

"Because I—we—think there's another dream walker on the dreamscape. It would explain how easily Hellstrom is getting through Monk's dream warding. I'm guessing Hellstrom is a dream walker."

Kilkenny heard a flutter of wings and turned to look at the crow on the patio. It almost stood in the doorway, tilting its head as though studying her.

"What you're saying makes sense," Kilkenny said. "But the other dream walker isn't Hellstrom. She's the same clan as Riordan and she's *not* a dream walker."

"You've already talked to Riordan?" Michelle asked.

The memory of Riordan's hands on her breasts shot through Kilkenny's mind, and she nodded. "Yeah. I don't think she's got anything to do with what's going on here."

"Is that just your own bias talking?"

"*No*," Kilkenny said. "I'm sorry. I didn't mean to bite. I'm just on edge. No. It's not Riordan. She knows Hellstrom but hasn't yet told me how. She doesn't like Hellstrom either. She and Roth want to help us." She bit her lip. "I think we should let them."

Michelle was silent a long moment. "All right. I'm going to trust you on this one. How are we going to get Monk back?"

"We're going to have to call Terri," Kilkenny said, hanging her head. *I* so *don't want to do that.* "When we do, we're *all* going to be there. You. Me. Roth. Rio."

"I don't want to do it either, but God help me it doesn't look like we have a choice." She sniffed and Kilkenny realized she was crying and flinched.

"It's going to be fine, Mitch," she said softly. "We're going to get her back. Monk is a lion. She's waiting for us to come to her and will hold out until we do."

"Okay," Michelle said, sounding uneven. "Okay."

"We need Jackie," Kilkenny said. "Can you call her?"

"She's already on her way. She won't stay away."

"Monk is in the dreamscape in her physical body. That's how we have to be as well."

"Why? Why not just go in as dreamers?"

"Because," Kilkenny said, eyeing the crow that stared at her with alien, cold yellow eyes, "if we don't, we're going to find ourselves walking through a portal. It's easier for Hellstrom to play with us on the dreamscape that way. Body disposal."

"Ugh. Christ." Michelle's intake of breath hitched. "Hurry, Kilkenny," she said softly. "I don't know what they're doing to her but it hurts."

Kilkenny nodded, feeling the sting of tears in her eyes. *God, Monk, I'm so sorry. Please be all right.*

"I will," she said.

"I'll see you in thirty. I can't stay here. I'm not up to it."

"All right," Kilkenny said. "I'll see if I can get a hold of Rio."

They said their goodbyes and Kilkenny hung up the telephone.

She felt a deep, melancholy sadness as she picked up the telephone and dialed a number from memory.

The phone picked up after a couple of rings.

"Hi," an out of breath voice said.

"Rio? It's Kilkenny."

"Kilkenny?" Riordan said, alarmed. "What is it? What's happened?"

"Monk didn't come home like she was supposed to. Michelle just called me. She said it felt like Monk was on the dreamscape." Kilkenny wiped the tears from her eyes. "Hellstrom has Monk, Rio."

"Oh, no," Riordan said. "No. I'm so sorry, Kilkenny."

"I need your help, Rio. You and Roth. I really didn't want to drag you into this," Kilkenny said. "We have to hurry. We have to get Monk before she gets Terri."

"No problem. Monk is a shape shifter. If she calls Terri it'll be in her dream form and Hellstrom won't be able to take her."

"No, they'll make Monk pull her into the dreamscape," Kilkenny said softly. "She's a dream walker. She'll cut a hole out of the dreamscape and she'll *get* Terri."

"Oh, shit," Riordan said, dismayed. "Shit."

"That's not all," Kilkenny said. "When we called you in the dreamscape last night, someone sliced through Monk's warding like it was nothing. It was *another* dream walker. It has to be the same person that pulled Monk into the dreamscape from reality."

"*Fuck.*" She sighed. "No problem. I'll bring Roth. Roth will know how to deal with this. She'll know how to get Monk back *and* keep Terri safe."

"Why, Rio? Why can't Hellstrom or her friend call Terri? If they're both shape shifters, one of them a dream walker, why can't they call her?"

"We really don't have time now for me to tell you everything, but I promise you, I will. I will." She paused a moment. "To answer your question, it was Roth. Terri's dreams were warded by one of Roth's friends. The warding stops *anyone* from entering Terri's dreams.

Almost no one can. Only a *very* powerful dream walker could do it and yours obviously can't."

"Does that mean Terri can *only* walk in her own dreams or can she willingly enter another person's dreams?"

"Are you asking me if you can call her? Yes. You can. All it really means for Terri is that she can go to sleep and she won't end up in nightmares controlled by other people. And, like anyone, she can choose to ignore a summons issued by people she doesn't want to interact with. It also means that if anyone goes looking for her, they won't find her."

"Okay," Kilkenny said.

"What time do you want us there? As soon as we can?"

"Yes, please."

"We'll be there, love. Don't you worry. We'll be there. For everything."

"Thanks, Rio," Kilkenny said. "It means a lot to me."

"I know," Riordan said. "I know."

"Thanks," Kilkenny whispered, and they both hung up.

Kilkenny listlessly went back into her room to put on some clothes. As she pulled on jeans, a tight tee shirt, and her joggers, she thought about what to do next.

Time passes differently on the dreamscape, isn't that what Monk once told me? When we lost Monk we lost someone who knows me well. So Hellstrom is going to know about Riordan, Michelle, and Jackie. I mentioned the new faces I saw in school yesterday. So she'll know about Roth and Moriarty. God, I hope Moriarty doesn't get dragged into this. The last thing I need is for a human to get tangled up with this.

She went back into the living room and looked at the row of birds on the power lines, and the crow that sat on the railing, staring at her balefully. She shifted her vision and stared at it closely. It looked like brown sparks surrounded by an almost imperceptible aura of red sparks.

Kilkenny frowned and walked toward the crow, and it watched her with its beady yellow eyes. She stood almost next to it and it didn't move.

"You should be afraid of me," she said to it.

It tilted its head. *CAW*.

Kilkenny narrowed her eyes and looked down at the street. A column of iridescent blue sparks walked past with a small mass of brown next to it.

She frowned, focusing on it very closely. “It doesn’t look the same as the other animals.”

A shower of red sparks exploded around the brown mass and slowly sank into it so they became almost imperceptible, like the birds.

“What *is* that?” Kilkenny muttered.

Suddenly the brown mass stopped dead, and the blue column of sparks stopped.

She shifted her vision back.

A woman was down on the street trying to coax her beagle into motion. It was sitting and staring at the block of units, in Kilkenny’s direction.

“Is that how you’re doing it? Are you controlling the animals?” Kilkenny said softly, scalp crawling with shock.

“*Caw. Caw. Caw,*” the crow screamed from beside her.

The dog gave a single, yipping bark.

She looked up and the birds on the wires cried out, flying off the power lines and landing on the patio.

Kilkenny backed into the living room, closing the door with trembling hands.

“Oh, no,” she moaned. “The animals. Hellstrom has the animals. That’s how she’s tracking me.”

She sank down onto the sofa, head in her hands. “God.” *She’s been listening the whole time. She knows what we’re going to do next. We’re in deep trouble.*

That was how Michelle found her ten minutes later.

CHAPTER 5

MONK MOANED, THE swirling fishhooks inside her head pulling her to full wakefulness.

The side of her face felt stiff, and rough cloth dug into her cheek. Her neck hurt. She opened her eyes, hissing as light bored into them like twin lasers.

She squeezed them shut, but tears leaked from her tightly closed lids. Her stomach churned.

She felt the warmth of a body and a hand roughly jabbed her shoulder.

"Unh," she said. "Hurts."

"I know it does," Angela Michaels said soothingly. "Drink some water." A smooth, cool plastic bottle touched the side of her face. "Sit up."

Monk winced and slowly pushed herself off the train seat she was curled up on. Her eyes were hot and stung. She stared at Angela's smug face.

Fuck, I wish I had the energy to cream her. She roughly grabbed the bottle out of Angela's hand.

Angela nodded. "There's more where that came from."

The pain in Monk's head flared and she leant forward, vomiting on the floor beneath her feet.

"That's disgusting, Monkhouse," Angela said coldly. "We're going to have to shift seats."

Monk took a deep swig of water, waiting to see if it would stay in her roiling stomach. After a dreadful, uneasy moment, it stayed. She took another mouthful and swallowed carefully.

"Make me," she said.

Angela's eyes lightened toward bile yellow and her muscles bunched as though she wanted to throw herself at Monk and begin pummeling.

"Your dog told you not to hurt me?" Monk asked wryly.

Angela gave her a cold smile. "No. I'm just not allowed to until we have Warland."

"Sucks to be you," Monk said.

"Pour the bottle over your head, fuck bag. You look disgusting."

Monk ran a finger under her nose. It came away with blood. Her ears were the same. She glared at Michaels and poured the rest of the bottle over her head.

"That didn't help," Angela said, tilting her head and studying Monk. "Now you look worse although I'm not sure how that could be with someone as ugly as you already are."

Monk's temper snapped, and she shot forward in a blur of motion and grabbed Angela by the neck. The muscles in her forearms bulged, and Angela clawed at her wrist.

"You don't get to talk to me like that," Monk said. "I never did anything to you. Watch your fucking potty mouth."

A hand grabbed the back of her neck and tee shirt hard enough for her bones to creak. Angela fell forward, slipping out of Monk's grasp. The hand yanked her backward. Monk's lower back hit the neck rest of a seat and she tumbled over backward. She saw stars as her head and shoulders slammed into the back of the seat behind her. She collapsed into the space between the seats, sobbing in pain as black flowers bloomed in her vision.

Daggers shot through her head and she curled up into a ball.

"How are you going with bonding her?" Monk heard Hellstrom say through the stabbing pain.

"Not very good," Angela said. "She's not as easy to do as animals are. I think I'm pretty close, though. Another session or two and she's going to be a mobile vegetable, I think."

Hellstrom snorted a laugh. "As long as you get her to call Terri I don't care. You can kill her for all I care."

"Why, thank you," Angela said, her tone suggesting a broad grin.

Fuck. Fuck. She can control other things with her mind.

Angela's face appeared over the seat above her. "Hear that, Monkhouse? You're mine." Her eyes flared yellow, and Monk screamed as the fishhooks moved again.

"Watch this," Angela said. "Lift your hand, Monkhouse."

Monk watched in horror as her hand twitched. A fresh bolt of pain tore through her head and she screamed. Her throat felt raw. Suddenly the terrible hacking stopped.

"Very nice, Angela," Hellstrom said. "I like. How long do you think?"

Angela's head disappeared from view. "Like I said, not all that long. She's strong but not as strong as me."

"Good. Let's get going."

"Lead the way."

Footsteps descended the stairs and their voices faded away. The hydraulic doors between carriages hissed open and then closed. Their voices ceased. Monk was alone.

Monk slowly and painfully levered herself back up onto the seat. She saw the flicker of a sign as the train passed through a station.

Autumn Park station. Okay, let's think this thing through. Angela's trying to put some kind of controlling bond over me so she can make me call Terri and it's starting to work. I don't know what that bond is. If I assume the worst, I'm going to feel her sitting inside my mind and I'm going to be a spectator in my own body. I won't be free of her. And whatever she's doing to me to make it happen is damaging me.

She cautiously felt for Michelle and Jackie and her heart twisted at Michelle's pain. She wanted to send reassurance, but didn't have enough strength left.

The others will come for me, but when? How long?

The scenery shot by, suburbs giving way to a terrible, twisted amusement park. Monk looked away, unable to stand the terrible, fog enshrouded darkness and stomach turning angles of the rides.

I can't break out of this dream. If I do and I try and find the others, Hellstrom and Michaels will go straight for them and kill them. I couldn't stand it if anything happened to Michelle, Jackie, or Kilkenny. And Kilkenny would be devastated if anything happened to Riordan.

She glanced out of the window and quickly looked back, not wanting to remember the nightmare figures she'd barely glimpsed in the godforsaken gloom.

If I do *call Terri, they're going to kill her. If I* don't *call Terri, they'll make me do it. She'll come because it's me doing the calling. They'll kill her. Both of those options suck.*

Light crept into the gloom and Monk looked down at her watch, stunned to see half an hour had passed. The scenery gave way to nature again, low coastal trees and sandy soil.

Deep, blue sea appeared in the distance. She could see blue skies and the ramshackle buildings of a coastal town.

God, this world is beautiful. She sighed and levered herself out of the seat. There was no sign of either Hellstrom or Angela.

I'm getting off this train. She moved, slowly and painfully, along the upper aisle, clutching the hand holds on the seat for balance and against the gentle rocking of the fast moving train. She carefully made her way down the stairs, each step an exercise in agony. She stumbled down the last one, falling to her knees. Fresh daggers of pain tore through her body, and she closed her eyes against the tears.

She crawled toward the door.

It's just a construct, right? It doesn't matter who made it, it should behave the same way as all the others, right?

She used the pole to drag herself to her feet. She held on grimly as she extended a shaking finger to draw an outline in the door. A square section of door wobbled and then fell out as the train jostled around a sweeper.

Monk braced herself and then fell out of the train. She screamed as she crashed into the gravel beside the tracks and rolled down a slope into thick undergrowth, momentum bleeding away. She held her breath and slowly sat up, listening for the train. She heard it power down the tracks, uninterrupted, and sagged back into the undergrowth, breathing deeply and relaxing for the first time in what felt like years.

She levered herself to her feet with a groan and looked around. She heard cars in the distance and jogged toward them.

With every step and each moment of passing time and no sign of the train or Hellstrom, she relaxed even more.

The cars sounded closer, and she broke through a line of trees and found herself by the side of a deserted road.

She frowned as she looked around. The traffic sounded heavy and directly in front of her but she couldn't see anything at all. It looked utterly deserted.

The road was in good condition, and the shops lining the other side of the road were neat and well kept. Their doors were open and inviting, as though expecting a teeming mass of customers.

Monk looked around. *Wow. This place is deserted. There aren't any people around to* be *customers.*

She cautiously made her way to the middle of the road, closing her eyes. She braced herself against the cars she could hear. She half expected to be run over.

Yet nothing happened.

The invisible cars swarmed around her.

She grinned, despite herself.

She trotted across the other side of the road and onto the footpath, teeming with life that she could hear but couldn't see.

The store in front of her looked like a small convenience store and she went into it, immediately zeroing in on the refrigerators at the back. She inspected the contents and grabbed a bottle of Gatorade and a sandwich. She ran back out of the store and into the street.

She listened carefully for the sound of the train, but all she heard was the peaceful sounds of summer tourists on vacation.

She breathed deeply, biting into her sandwich and devouring it in three bites. She walked toward the beach, past deserted houses, basking in the warmth of summer sunshine.

She hit the boardwalk and went to the public showers under a stand of trees. Brine air filled her lungs and she felt better. She gingerly turned on the water and put a hand underneath the stream. It was mercifully cold. She stripped off her tee shirt and stepped under it with a sigh.

The cold water ran over her body, and she washed the blood off her face and out of her hair. She looked across the road and saw an open surf shop.

Five minutes later she was in a fresh tee shirt, sitting down on a bench, watching the ocean and eating ice cream.

The train hasn't come back. That has *to mean they don't know I'm gone. They went to a lot of trouble to get me and I don't see them letting go of me without a fight. If Angela could feel me it'd mean that she'd know I'd gone. So the train would have stopped. So chances are that she can't really feel me. I don't know how the marker works. Maybe it's just a general awareness of where I am. If I'm really lucky it only works if I'm* not *in her construct. So if I were to cut my way out of here she'd know and come after me.*

Monk smiled.

I don't really have proof that my reasoning is sound but at least I have a workable theory. After all, when I call someone in the dreamscape I know when they're not *inside my construct. If they are, I don't know* where *they are in it, but I know they're there.*

She bit her lip. *All right, what do I do now? I know Kilkenny got pulled into the dreamscape with Roth, because she got hit with silver. I wasn't there, so Angela wasn't using me to find her. She was using the animals. She said as much to Hellstrom when she was bragging about how she was about to break me. If I was Hellstrom, I'd just begin opening portals to the dreamscape and capturing people close to me to flush me out and make me call Terri.*

The choice I had with Terri hasn't changed. Now all I have to do is minimize damage to the others. Michelle. Jackie. Kilkenny. They'll come for me.

Hellstrom is going to be super pissed when she finds I'm gone. Then I guess it's show time.

Monk levered herself to her feet, eyeing a shadowed alleyway. "That'll do," she whispered.

Once she was under cover of the alleyway, she slumped down against the rough, red brick of the wall marking the alleyway, and drew her knees up to her chin. She rested her aching head against her knees and took a deep breath, allowing longing and melancholy pain flow through her. *Terri. Come to me. Please, Terri, come to me.*

She sank back against the wall with a sigh and waited.

Five minutes later, she heard footsteps coming down the road toward her.

She levered herself to her feet just as Terri appeared in the mouth of the alleyway.

Monk gave her a broad grin, despite herself. Terri was as beautiful as ever. Her blue black hair hung free, framing her perfect features and cascading to her waist. Her mouth creased in a grin as she saw Monk.

She jogged down the alleyway, and Monk found herself in Terri's arms, held close to her perfect chest, breathing deeply of her perfume.

"Monk," she said. "God, it's so good to see you."

"Yeah it is," Monk said, squeezing her eyes closed to hold in tears.

"Come, come, come," Terri said, releasing her and taking her hand. "Let's sit down and talk." She tugged Monk back across the road to the bench she'd sat on before.

Terri frowned as she saw Monk in the full sunlight. "You look terrible."

Monk gazed into her stormy gray eyes. "You, on the other hand, look fantastic. You always do."

Terri grinned. "Thank you. That's very sweet of you to say." She leant back. "How are you? How's Michelle?"

Monk felt in her bond for Michelle and groaned softly as she realized she couldn't feel it and hadn't felt it since she left the train. She was isolated.

"What's the matter? You're so pale."

"Michelle's just as beautiful as she always was and I love her more than ever," Monk said.

"Then what's the problem? I'm sure it's not the desire to see me that made you call me here."

Monk snorted. “Ah, problem.” She sighed and looked directly at Terri. “It’s not true that I wouldn’t call you just to say hi. I like you. But in this case, you’re right.” She studied Terri’s beautiful face. “You’re so beautiful.”

Terri frowned. “Okay.”

Monk felt her face heat. “I’m sorry, I didn’t realize I’d said it aloud. And no, before you ask, I’m not hoping that this turns into some upside down wet dream.”

Terri blushed. “Good.”

“I always wanted to see you again, but you drifted away and I didn’t want to bother you, you know?”

Terri nodded, as though Monk’s rambling conversation was making sense.

“You’re right. I called you here for a reason,” Monk said.

Terri’s eyes instantly became alert and intense. “What is it?”

“Do you remember you once told me that I should level with you because then at least you’d have a choice?”

Terri leaned forward. “With Wells. Yes. I remember.” She paused for a moment. “There’s another shape shifter, isn’t there?”

Monk nodded. “Yes, there is. A charmer by the name of Ingrid Hellstrom.”

Terri’s eyes widened in shock and she went pale. “*Hellstrom? A shape shifter?* Oh, fuck. *Fuck*. She’s *really* bad news.” She drew in a deep breath.

“Oh, yeah, you could say that,” Monk said sourly. “Do you remember Angela Michaels?”

Terri’s eyes narrowed. “She was the shit who decided to hit me with a broom during detention when you were a senior.”

“That’d be her,” Monk said. “It looks like Wells made *her* into a shape shifter as well as me.”

“*Double* fuck.” Terri sighed. “Okay, fill me in on what’s happened.”

Monk sat back against the bench and studied the calm ocean before them. “Okay, this is how it goes,” she said, and told Terri about her and Kilkenny’s first introduction to Hellstrom and Kilkenny’s first day of school. When she’d finished, Terri’s face was set in a horrified mask of dismay.

“There’s more, Terri,” Monk said softly. “I was on my way home from uni and I blundered my way through a doorway constructed by Michaels and into the dreamscape. It’s a long story and I won’t bore you with details, but it looks like Michaels can control animals and probably people in the physical world through some kind of shape shifter bond. She—and Hellstrom—can't call you on the dreamscape for some reason, so they're hammering away at me to do it. I can't hold off Michaels, Terri. She's going to smash her way into my mind to make me call you, and I'm sure they'll pull you in here in your physical form and hurt you or worse. No matter where I go she's going to find me. When she pulled the skin off my chest it created a link from her to me. It's how she keeps zeroing in on me. I wanted to call you here and warn you. I wanted to do it so you'd have a choice. If you hear me call, don't answer. Run from me as far and fast as you can."

Terri blinked away tears. "I'm so sorry, Monk. I never thought my past would spill out all over everyone."

Monk painfully put her arms around Terri, gently stroking her back. "It's all right, Terri. It's okay."

"No, it's not," Terri said, pulling back and looking into her eyes. "It's *not* okay. Hellstrom is a maniac. She won't just destroy you, she'll destroy *everyone* you love."

Monk nodded. "I know."

"I *won't* sit by and watch you do this," Terri said after a moment. "It's not right. She's *my* problem and I *have* to deal with her." She was silent as she studied Monk. "Can you pull me in here in my physical form?"

"If I do that you're going to get badly hurt. I don't know how well I can protect you. You may even end up dead."

"I realize that. If I *don't* do it, she's going to end up finding some way to hurt or kill me anyway. You're proof of that. I'd rather it happened on my own terms."

"Are you sure?" Monk said.

Terri studied her for a moment. She finally nodded. "I don't want to lose you. *Any* of you. Yes, I'm sure."

Monk smiled. "Then I agree. Okay, where are you?"

"I'm in my house in Autumn Park. Can you open the door into the living room?"

Monk nodded. "I can. I remember what it looked like." She stood. "Go. I'll open the door and wait for you."

Terri nodded. "I'll be back in a moment." She slowly faded into transparency and disappeared from the dreamscape.

Monk drew an outline of a door into the air beside the bench. When she blew on it, the center imploded and the outline shimmered.

Monk looked through into the darkness of Terri's living room. *Two minutes. Hurry up, Terri.*

A minute and a half later, Terri Warland herself, pulling a tee shirt down over her bare torso, strode across her living room and through the doorway into the dreamscape. The doorway collapsed in on itself and closed.

There was a tremendous shrieking of brakes and a train whistled shrilly in the distance. Monk grimaced. She grabbed Terri's hands. "Location shift."

Monk and Terri were wrenched sideways and collapsed in a puddle in the middle of George Street in Sydney, tearing away about a yard of skin as they skidded across the asphalt.

Monk stood, brushing off her behind and levering Terri to her feet.

"I don't think Angela can find me if I relocate inside her construct," Monk said.

A tremendous bolt of pain tore through Monk's head, and she fell to the ground, screaming. She was distantly aware of being pulled into Terri's arms. Finally the terrible pain subsided. She swiped her nose and it came away with blood.

"Monk?" Terri asked.

"Angela just said hi," Monk said wryly.

"She's trying to force her way into your mind to see what you're up to, isn't she?" Terri said.

Monk nodded unwillingly.

"Take me to her," Terri said softly. "Take me to Hellstrom."

"No," Monk said, and Terri's face darkened in anger. Monk held up her hand. "Hear me out."

Terri nodded.

"I didn't want to tell you about Hellstrom but I had to, you know?" Monk said. "I knew you'd want to make the choice to be involved."

Terri nodded again.

"Okay, well, I'm going to give you another choice," Monk said. "I told you I wasn't sure if I could protect you. If I'm brutally honest with myself, I have to admit that I don't think I can hold off Michaels or Hellstrom. I don't know when the others are going to be here to help either of us. A lot of bad things could happen to us while we wait for them. I don't want you to get hurt, Terri. You're my friend. You always were. You stood beside me when I was at my worst and I've never forgotten that. I'll take that memory to my grave. Friendship is rare and it shouldn't be thrown away on a whim." Monk smiled. "So as your friend, I'm going to give you a choice. I'm a werewolf, Terri, and I can give that gift to you. It means you'll be strong enough to fight Hellstrom and it gives you a fighting chance at living."

Terri mulled it over.

Monk fell to her knees to wait. Her reserves depleted and she trying desperately to control her queasy stomach. Her head throbbed.

Mitch, I love you. I wish you were here to help.

"Give me the gift, Monk," Terri said quietly. "Give it to me. Hellstrom already stole my future and the love of my life. I won't let her take my friends and *my* life as well."

"Why, Terri? Why is she so fixated on you?"

"I have no problem telling you, but I think time is running short for you. We'd better get this thing on the road."

Monk leaned toward Terri, but suddenly the ground beneath them fell away and they were tumbling through air in a sickening, gut wrenching sensation of weightlessness.

Monk blindly groped for Terri, pulling her in and holding her close. She shifted around, nipping Terri on the palm of her damaged hand. Terri yelped. Suddenly the ground rushed up to meet them and they crashed down onto pristine white carpet.

Terri looked at her, pale and resolute.

"I'm sorry, Terri. So sorry," Monk whispered.

Terri shook her head and smiled. "You done good, Monk." She looked around at the blindingly white house. "Where are we?"

"This is Wells's house if I'm not mistaken. Before it burnt down," Monk said.

"Figures," Terri said sourly.

Monk started as an arm descended around her shoulders.

"Heya, Monk," Hellstrom said, pecking her on the cheek. "You brought my toy. I'm so proud of you." She turned to Terri, her eyes bright, bile yellow. "And you, Terri. We need to have a serious talk."

"Yes, we do," Terri said through gritted teeth.

"Good." She turned toward the stairs. "Angela. Your friend is down here."

Angela Michaels slowly sauntered down the stairs, eyes burning yellow. A smile played about her lips when she saw Monk.

"They're both here," she said. "Told you Monkhouse wouldn't have a choice. Let her go and she'd call Warland. I *told* you breaking the warding on the dreamscape would work." She gave Monk a cruel smile. "You didn't even question why you could suddenly break through into the physical world, did you? Fucking stupid moron."

Monk felt her face heat. *I hate to agree with her but I really* am *a fucking stupid moron. She can track me* anywhere. *Shit.*

Hellstrom laughed. "That *was* good, Angela. Now, come on down here so we can entertain ourselves with our guests."

"GUYS," JACKIE SHARP said, striding down the hallway to the living room. "I'm finally here. Have the others arrived yet?"

Michelle, sitting by Kilkenny on the sofa, turned to Jackie. She shook her head. Jackie took one look at her and was instantly by her side, and Kilkenny found herself quietly pushed off the sofa.

Michelle's tears were flowing down her face, and Jackie, blinking away her own, pulled Michelle in close.

"I can't feel her either," she said. "But it's okay. It won't be forever. We'll find her." She glanced at Kilkenny.

Kilkenny felt as though she'd been shredded. She glanced out of the patio window and saw a line of sparrows sitting on the railing, staring silently at them.

She shifted her vision and saw the red sparks.

"We're still being watched," she said, nodding toward the birds.

"What?" Jackie asked, frowning.

"The birds. That's how we're being tracked. The dream walker with Hellstrom is controlling the animals."

"Shit," Jackie muttered. "And now they've seen me."

"And if you keep talking, they're going to hear you as well," Kilkenny said pointedly.

"Not unless they can read lips," Jackie said. "I'm not sure what the hearing of an average sparrow is, but I'd reckon it would suck."

Kilkenny snorted and Jackie gave her an odd look. It made Kilkenny giggle until finally she was holding her stomach, howling with laughter. Jackie stared at her for a few seconds, and then laughed herself. Finally, after a minute or so, they both quieted. Even Michelle was smiling.

"That's quite an image, Jackie," Kilkenny said, wiping her eyes.

"What? A sparrow with a hearing trumpet?" Michelle asked.

Kilkenny and Jackie exchanged a glance and snorted a laugh.

"What time is it?" Michelle asked. She glanced at the clock. "Okay, four. The others should be here soon."

Just at that moment, the buzzer for the security door rang and Kilkenny got up to go to the intercom.

"Who is it?" she asked.

"Riordan."

"Come up," Kilkenny said. She punched in the security code to open the front doors.

She looked at the other two. "Jackie, they're both shape shifters. It's all right. They're here to help."

Jackie nodded. "All right."

A few moments later there was a knock on the door.

Kilkenny opened the door and found herself tangled in Riordan's arms. She squeezed hard. "I've never been so glad to see you, Rio."

Riordan pulled back and smiled. "We'll get her back, Kilkenny."

Kilkenny nodded and they stood aside to allow Roth, looking cool, elegant, and stunning, to come in after her. Roth gave her the briefest of smiles, but it touched her eyes. Kilkenny relaxed, surprised that she'd been so stiff.

She began to shut the door but it was caught by a strong hand. "One more coming in, Klaatu barada nicto, Kilkenny." Moriarty, eyes burning a brilliant yellow, gave her a disarmingly friendly grin. Kilkenny stared at her in shock.

"You're a . . . a . . ." she began.

"Yes. I'm a toaster," Moriarty said comfortingly, ruffling her hair. Her now black eyes twinkled.

Kilkenny grinned and ducked her hand. "Where would one stick the slices of bread?"

"Well, you could put them in my—"

"You don't have to answer," Kilkenny said.

"You did ask, Kilkenny," Moriarty said.

Kilkenny smiled, despite herself.

"She's a friend, Kilkenny," Roth said softly, exchanging a glance with Moriarty.

Moriarty nodded. "I am. I won't hurt you, young one."

"I trust you," Kilkenny said, finding to her surprise that she meant it. She nodded and gestured down the hallway. "After you. You can take a seat in the living room and we can talk."

Riordan, Roth, and Moriarty went in the way she indicated, and Kilkenny found herself behind Roth. She tried as hard as she could not to stare at Roth's perfect rear and broad back. She wept inside.

"Michelle," Riordan said, flopping down onto the sofa beside Michelle and Jackie.

Kilkenny and Roth sat side by side on the floor next to the sofa.

"Rio," Michelle said. Her impassive mask was in place and her elegant features gave away none of the inner turmoil Kilkenny knew was there.

Moriarty flopped into a recliner opposite them. "What's going on?" she said without preamble. "Rio told me that we have a shape shifter in our midst who's targeting Kilkenny and has Monk?"

"Mostly," Riordan said, exchanging a glance with Roth.

Roth shifted uncomfortably on the floor beside Kilkenny. "Mack. It's worse than that. Ingrid Hellstrom is back and she wants Terri."

Moriarty's black eyes widened and she went pale. "Oh, no, not Terri. Roth, I thought you said she was safe."

"And so she still is while the dream warding is in place."

"How did Hellstrom become a shape shifter?" Jackie asked, taking in each of them. "How do you all know her?"

Moriarty, Roth, and Riordan all exchanged a glance.

"I'll tell," Moriarty said. "This is *my* fault."

CHAPTER 6

"ELEVEN YEARS AGO, I was teaching at Corpus Christ," Moriarty began, settling back into the chair with a sigh. "I was happy. I was finally teaching senior school, I had a permanent job, I was the head of the English department and even had my own office. I had my choice of classes. I decided to coast for a year, and chose mostly senior classes.

"Terri was in her final year of school. I remember the first time I laid eyes on her. She'd already grown to her full height so she was taller than I was. She was also devastatingly beautiful. Perfect body, perfect face. I think my jaw was scraping along the ground, you know how it is with her."

Michelle smiled wryly and Kilkenny saw Riordan flash a glance in her direction. Roth nodded.

"She ended up in my English class, and we just clicked. I put on my best teacher persona, but she already had me, hook, line, and sinker. She stayed and talked to me after class, she kept me company when I was on bus duty after school. She wanted to know *everything*. We became friends very quickly, and I found myself breaking all kinds of rules with her. Nothing that could be construed as a conflict of interest, but really close to the line.

"At the same time as I started talking to Terri, I had a girl in my English class by the name of Ingrid Hellstrom, trying to get my attention. I got on reasonably well with her, but it was obvious she had a crush on me. She loved bending over in front of me, giving me a wonderful view of her goods, but I just wasn't interested. I didn't care how high her skirts got or how open her blouse got.

"I just didn't care. I got on with her, that's it. I always tried to be fair with my classes, and I tried to be nice to her, but all she seemed to do was consider my polite interest as playing hard to get. She began to snag me after class, she started to stake a claim on me around Terri, and she kept staring at me and looking like she wanted to eat me.

"It was taking its toll on Terri. She began to avoid me. She tried not to look at me when we were together. It hurt. I loved her sense of humor, her intelligence, and her gentle, sweet nature. She really liked me, I could tell, but she was pulling back.

"I just couldn't stand it. One afternoon I saw her coming out of the library, and it was obvious to me she'd been crying. It broke my heart to see her so miserable, so I snagged her and pulled her into my office.

"I asked her what was bothering her.

"She wouldn't tell me.

"I tried to touch her.

"She flinched and tears formed in her eyes.

"It nearly killed me to see her like that. I never wanted to see her get hurt. I realized I'd been an idiot.

"I told her I knew what was bothering her. I told her I knew it was Hellstrom. She was jealous, but had no reason to be. I saw a flash of guilt and humiliation in her eyes, and then that gave way to anger.

"Before she could yell at me, I kissed her, and she began kissing me back. I took her home with me.

"God, it was like being possessed. We couldn't stop. I held her afterwards, and she cried again, but this time she wasn't angry or hurt. She was happy.

"That was the first time. We tried to be discrete in school, and every night she came to my place and we went nuts with each other. She was so open to me, so passionate and so giving, and it made it okay to be the same way with her. I'd never before—or since—been that close to a lover.

"Our affair continued for several months, and while it was going on, Hellstrom tried harder and harder to get my attention. I won't go into details but suffice it to say I saw almost everything she had more than once. I didn't pay any attention to her. I was crazy about Terri. But sometimes I had to poke Hellstrom back like I'd done before so no one would think anything of my relationship with Terri.

"Terri kept hinting that Hellstrom was bothering her, and I kept telling her not to worry. One day she finally exploded. She was jealous. She hated the way I kept looking at Hellstrom. I told her it was nothing she had to worry about. She really didn't. But she wasn't being rational right then, and I walked away, figuring we'd be able to talk when she'd calmed down a little."

"She didn't calm down, did she?" Michelle said.

Moriarty shook her head ruefully. "I thought so but I was badly mistaken. When I headed home I found a note on my car. *I'll come by tonight,* it said. I felt as though every fiber of my being relaxed. I could talk to Terri and I could make it right. I went home and when I got there I saw that the front door was open. I went in and got the shock of my life.

"Hellstrom was waiting for me.

"I felt sick.

"Hellstrom's shirt was half unbuttoned and she handed me a drink. She told me it was time to stop hiding how we felt.

"I immediately told her there was no hiding involved. I wasn't interested in her. I had no interest in being her lover. Whatever she was looking for wasn't going to come from me.

"She snapped and began screaming at me. It was Terri, wasn't it, who I was interested in. Terri, who was taller than she was. She was thinner and more beautiful. Her hair was longer. She was the school captain and Hellstrom was only the vice captain. Terri had higher marks than she did. The list seemed endless. It finally seemed to finish when she told me Terri got me despite the fact that she wanted me for herself. And to add insult to injury, Terri wasn't a virgin anymore.

"I got angry and asked her what the fuck she was talking about.

"She told me she'd seen us together and I really blew my stack. Staring at me was one thing, watching us in bed was something else entirely.

"I told her she made me sick. I didn't like her. I was being professional when I spoke to her. What I really wanted her to do was stop coming on to me. Terri was twice the woman she'd ever be.

"You know how arguments sometimes go," Moriarty said with a sigh. "It devolved into us screaming at each other. It finally ground to a halt when I felt my vision shifting. I asked her what she'd done and she proudly announced she'd poisoned me. If she couldn't have me, Terri sure as hell couldn't.

"I began to feel sick and I couldn't control my shifting. Things got all fuzzy after that. Roth can fill you in on the details. Suffice it to say, Hellstrom really didn't poison me with anything that would actually hurt a shape shifter. She gave me the shape shifter equivalent of bad LSD." Moriarty hung her head and glanced at Roth. "You tell the rest. I can't."

"All right." Roth nodded. "I was at school, harmlessly minding my own business, when I got a frantic call from Rio. She'd seen Hellstrom put the note on Mack's car. We lived in the same building so she was going to drop down later and ask Mack what was going on. Her plans changed when Mack got home. Rio heard some of the screaming between Mack and Hellstrom. She headed toward Mack's place to break up the fight, but stopped outside when she heard Mack growling. It sounded very bad. She called me and told me. I asked her to wait for me to get there. It would have taken both of us to restrain her if she'd shifted.

"I left as quickly as I could and met Rio by Mack's front door. She was right, it *was* open. I decided to go in and asked Rio to hang back in case I got into trouble. I went in and you can imagine my surprise when I found Moriarty, yellow eyed and covered in blood, chewing on Hellstrom's neck."

"*You* made Hellstrom?" Michelle said, staring at Moriarty. "She's *yours?*"

Moriarty nodded, convicted. She hung her head. "I'm sorry I dragged you all into this."

"By accident," Roth said. "I won't go into grisly detail, but in the end, Hellstrom left the school and Mack went on leave until the end of the year. I wasn't sure what Hellstrom would do so I had a friend ward Terri's dreams so Hellstrom couldn't get into them." She shook her head. "It was so sad. Suddenly Mack was gone and it broke Terri's heart. You could see it. She just wasn't the same after that. She ploughed through her final year and left without looking back."

"If both of you loved each other so much, why aren't you still together?" Jackie asked. "Your apology is accepted, by the way. It sounds to me like Hellstrom is a bully no matter which way you slice it."

"Thanks, Jackie." Moriarty's eyes shone with a mix of guilt and relief. "I always waited for Terri to come back to me but she never did. I realized it meant she only had a crush on me but I really loved her. I've never loved any woman like I loved her. I don't want anyone else." Her eyes were sad. "But all of that's beside the point. The point is now Terri and Monk are both in danger and I have to end it. I'm going to go in there to face her."

"We're *all* going to face her," Michelle said. "First things first. How are we going to find Monk?"

"Why don't you use your bond?" Moriarty asked.

Michelle's eyes looked haunted.

"She can't," Kilkenny said. "It's muted."

"It feels pretty awful," Michelle said.

"It's really there, it's only muted," Kilkenny said. "I can still see it coming up off you and Jackie but it fades away."

"Yeah," Jackie said. "The dreamscape where I can feel Monk is warded. I can't get into it. The dream walker on the other side is *strong*."

Kilkenny nodded. "You know about the animals?"

Roth and Riordan exchanged a glance. "They're watching us."

Kilkenny nodded. "Do you guys know how it works?"

"Dream walkers are able to form controlling bonds over other species, but I'm sure you already realized that," Roth said. "In that bonding process, something is given and something is taken, and if the practitioner continues to use that talent, they go mad. An insane werewolf is bad but an insane werewolf who can manipulate dreams is much, much worse."

"We know," Kilkenny said. "Believe me, we know." She looked straight at Roth, drinking in her beautiful features. "We have a dream walker who's using that talent. I'm guessing if they're not nuts, they're most of the way there. Hellstrom and her dream walker friend now have Monk. I'm sure they're doing their damndest to get her to call Terri. If the other dream walker hasn't put a controlling bond on Monk yet, I'm sure they're close."

"Monk won't let them do it. She'd rather die," Jackie said.

"I know. Which is why we have to get into the dreamscape. We have to get Monk before they can *make* her call Terri." She glanced around at the other shape shifters. "Are we agreed?"

"Yes," Moriarty said. Her black eyes flashed.

"Jackie," Kilkenny said. "Can you cut us into the dreamscape?"

"Cutting in is easy. Being in the right place isn't."

"Michelle, can you see your own bond?"

Michelle's eyes flared yellow. "Yes," she said after a moment.

"Okay," Kilkenny said. "I'm going to try something." She shifted her vision and zeroed in on Michelle's and Jackie's silver sparks. *Here goes.* She grabbed a handful of the silver sparks and pulled. The cloud between the two of them brightened and the streamer that led off into the distance quivered uneasily and flashed a few times. It finally settled on a steady stream. Kilkenny looked at it closely. "Is it better?"

Jackie nodded and sagged with relief.

"Yeah," Michelle said. She smiled. "She's still alive."

"Can you feel her the way you did before?"

"No," Michelle said after a moment. "I can feel enough to know where she is, like knowing someone's in a room with you. But that's it." She smiled at Kilkenny. "Thank you. It's all about the sparks, right?"

"Yep. You can give them, you can take them and you can move them around." She turned to Jackie. "Okay. Can you feel enough now to know where Monk is in the dreamscape?"

Jackie smiled. "Give me a minute, I'll have a look." She closed her eyes and Michelle pulled her in close. Her body went limp.

It felt as though Jackie was gone for days. Roth adjusted position and leaned back, brushing against Kilkenny. Kilkenny felt her face heat and looked up at Riordan, who grinned at her. Kilkenny felt as though her face was ready to spontaneously combust. Moriarty looked at her, smirked, and opened her mouth.

Kilkenny was mercifully spared Moriarty's teasing when Jackie moved and her eyes fluttered open.

"Yeah, I found the dream," she said. "But it's heavily warded. I tried to break through it a couple of times but it didn't give."

"We need time," Kilkenny said. "Cut us into the dreamscape. To a dream that intersects with Hellstrom's. We'll cut our way in from there."

"Okay," Jackie said. Her eyes flared yellow. "It's done. All we have to do is walk up the hallway."

Kilkenny grinned and levered herself to her feet. "Excellent," she said as she held out a hand for Roth. "Let's get moving." Roth took her hand, pulling herself to her feet, her eyes glued to Kilkenny's.

What a beautiful shade of green. And she's so calm. How does she do *that?*

Roth leaned down and whispered in her ear, "well done, Kilkenny."

Kilkenny smiled and felt like wagging her tail.

Kilkenny and Roth led the way down the hallway, the others behind them. Roth was so close behind her that Kilkenny could feel the heat from her body.

They made their way through the doorway.

THE TERRIBLE FISHHOOKS finally slowed and stopped.

Monk lay on the white carpet, blood trickling from her eyes, nose, and ears. She drew in a sharp, shuddering breath.

She felt the heat from Terri's body and the touch of her hands as Terri clumsily put Monk's head into her lap.

"Why don't you leave her alone?" Terri said coldly. "You have me. You don't have to hurt her anymore."

Angela gave her an unpleasant smile. "I like doing it, that's why."

Monk looked up at Terri through a haze of red. Terri's beautiful face was twisted into a mask of revulsion.

"There's something bad wrong with you," Terri said.

"You told me that once before," Angela said. "I have news for you. There's something *worse* wrong with Ingrid. She told me some of what she wants to do to you and it's not going to be pretty. You're going to wish you'd never been born."

"Could we compromise and say I'm already wishing *you'd* never been born?" Monk shot back. She slowly and painfully sat up.

Suddenly Monk's head was ringing and she was back in Terri's arms. Her face throbbed from the force of Angela's blow.

"Love pat, anyone?" Monk said to Terri.

Terri glared at Angela with impotent fury.

"There's more where that came from, Monkhouse," Angela said.

"She's kind of right," Hellstrom said, silent until now. She leant comfortably back on the sofa, watching them. "Although I will admit it's fun to watch Terri squirm." Her eyes blazed yellow. "This is almost as much fun as throwing a bucket of petrol on you and watching you burn to death, Terri. Your screams would be fun to listen to." She gestured toward Monk. "You really care about her, don't you?"

Terri looked pale and had dark rings around her eyes. She stared at Hellstrom expressionlessly. Monk could tell by the ginger way she held her arm that her hand was aching abominably.

I'm sorry it hurts, Terri. I wish I could take the pain from you. I wish it was different.

"Ingrid. Trouble," Angela said suddenly, her eyes flaring yellow and her gaze turning inwards. "They're trying to get onto the dreamscape. They're going to cut into the dream."

"Okay," Hellstrom said. "It's time to kill them, then. Why don't you *let* them cut into the dreamscape? We'll scatter them throughout the worlds. It'll be fun to watch them die slowly."

Angela nodded. "That'll work." She jabbed her chin toward Monk and Terri. "What do you want to do with them?"

Hellstrom shrugged. "Leave them."

"Don't you want to tie them up or something?"

"Doesn't matter," Hellstrom said. "They can't translocate without *you* knowing and they can't run without *me* knowing. Even if they did they're boxed in. Chasing them as prey is fun anyway."

"They're going to escape."

"I know. It doesn't matter. All that's going to happen is that they're going to get a front row seat as their friends die." Hellstrom laughed, patting Angela's cheek as they became transparent. "You worry too much," she said as they faded out of the living room.

The second they were gone Monk painfully lurched to her feet, swaying back and forth as her head pounded and her stomach grumbled uneasily. She held out her hand for Terri, grunting as Terri pulled herself up.

"You want to run?" Terri asked. "Where?"

Monk grabbed her bad hand and she hissed in pain.

"That hurts," Terri said.

"I know," Monk said, jogging toward the front door. "I know. I'm sorry. C'mon."

She pulled the door open and stumbled out into an overcast world. She blinked and jogged, Terri close behind.

"Where are we going to go?" Terri asked, breathing raggedly.

"We're going to get on the train," Monk said.

"Do you even know where it is?" Terri asked.

"When I went back to Lightman's house last time, I saw that they lived in an expensive part of Autumn Park. It's, I think, about a ten minute walk from the station. Even if the train's not there it has to come in some time, doesn't it? That's provided the geography here is the same as it is in the physical world. There's only one way to find out." Monk dug deep into her reserves. "C'mon, Terri. We *have* to run. Hellstrom outclasses me physically. I'm guessing her sense of smell is way beyond mine. Once she sees we're gone it won't be hard for her to find us."

Terri barely kept pace with Monk as they tore past streets of deserted houses almost identical to the real world. Monk almost sobbed with relief as they ran past the post office, florist, delicatessen, and sandwich shop that marked the side of the road opposite the train station.

"Yes," Terri said, pointing. "It's there. That's your train, right?"

Monk nodded, almost sobbing in relief at the sight of the Tangara parked peacefully in the station.

She grabbed Terri's good hand, and they ran through the turnstiles onto the station. They ran toward the front of the train, stumbling into the first carriage. Terri fell to her knees and threw up. Her chest heaved with exertion. She clutched her hand.

Monk fumbled for the latch on the door to the driver's compartment. Much to her dim amazement, it was unlocked. The door slid open and she fell to her knees with a yelp.

She crawled in and quickly looked at the control panel. There were four buttons. One was labeled *Stop/Go,* the second *Open /Closed*, the third *Emergency* and the fourth *All Stations*. There was a lever that had a *Fast* and *Slow* setting.

Thank god. Her hands were slick with sweat.

She hit the *close* button with a trembling hand and in the distance they heard beeping and a whoosh as the train doors closed. She pushed the speed lever upwards and the train lurched into motion.

Terri sagged back against the wall, her breathing harsh and ragged. "I'm done," she said softly. "I'm done."

"Not quite yet," Monk said, easing down next to her and relaxing.

"How long's it going to take for the werewolf blood to kick in, Monk?" she said, cradling her hand.

Monk looked down at it and saw the inflamed skin and weeping wound. *Not quick enough.* "When I turned it took me about three days."

"Three days? We're not going to last three days doing this," Terri said.

"I know." Monk looked deep into Terri's eyes. "It's not just the turning it's also the amount of time you have to be physically dead before you wake up as a werewolf."

"I think I know what you have in mind," Terri said. "Will it hurt?"

"I don't know," Monk said. "But it's gotta hurt less than this. I know how bad your hand is feeling." She was silent for a moment, allowing sadness to flow over her. "I'll keep running from Hellstrom. I'll leave you on the train, Terri. When you wake up you'll be just like me." She pulled Terri into her arms. "Close your eyes."

"I'm afraid," Terri whispered.

"Don't be," Monk said, tightening her grip. "I'm just your buddy, Monk. I'm gentle."

"I know. That's one of the things I always liked the most about you," Terri said. "I trust you." Her eyes fluttered closed.

Monk could feel her tension and traced circles on Terri's stomach with her fingertips. She kept going until Terri finally relaxed.

Monk felt her vision shift and she took a deep breath, scenting Terri. Something deep inside her snarled as it drank in the smell of hot human. Monk's teeth sharpened to tusks and she whipped her head down. She tore out Terri's throat. It was over before Terri could react.

Terri stiffened in her arms and let out a gurgling breath.

Monk gently held her. Terri's blood coated her clothes and skin, forming a wide puddle beneath them.

Terri opened her eyes and she stared at Monk. Her mouth framed words. *I'll see you again, Monk.*

Monk leant down and gently kissed her bloody forehead. "Relax and let go. I'll see you again soon, my friend." She tightened her arms around Terri, holding her close, soothing her.

Terri stilled and her eyes glazed over.

It hurt to look at her and Monk felt sick. *God, I* never *thought I'd do that to her.*

She studied Terri's beautiful face, peaceful in death.

Okay, now what? If any of the others find her, I'm not sure they're going to realize that she's going to come back. I'm going to have to leave a note on her. That sounds really fucking stupid but I don't want to risk her getting buried alive or something equally horrible. I wonder if my backpack is still on the train.

She levered herself to her feet and jogged out of the driver's compartment. Her skin crawled as she ran back four carriages. She quickly looked down between the seats in the upper deck and to her amazement and relief found it resting on the seat where she'd last left it. She quickly shouldered it and ran full tilt toward the front of the train.

She dropped it on the only clean space of floor she could find. She tugged it open and rifled inside for a pen and her notebook.

She took my blood. Wait for her to wake up, she wrote.

She nibbled her lip. *What else should I add? Will that be enough? I dunno. It's simple and to the point. Gonna have to do. I've gotta get off the train.*

She folded the note paper and very carefully printed *READ ME!!!!* on it.

She grimaced as she leaned Terri back against the wall of the carriage and put the note into the pocket of her blood soaked jeans so the *read me* was obvious.

She made her way back into the driver's compartment. She hit the *All Stations* button on the train board and glanced out of the window. The train was passing through the seaside world, the landscape outside a blur. It sped along an immense bridge, out over the sea water. Monk could see the blue horizon rising in the distance, and the water pulled away from the shore.

A tidal wave. Her heart rate picked up. Would the wave destroy the train?

Suddenly the train was over land again, the coastal trees giving way to a terrible, dank marshland. The roar of the ocean was far behind them. She shuddered. *There's no fucking way in hell I'm getting off there*. She waited until the train entered a vibrant, jungle landscape. The train tracks cut through thick undergrowth.

Monk saw a flash of light in the distance and a train station came into view. The train slowed. She bent down quickly and kissed Terri's cooling forehead.

"Love you, Terri. I'll see you later."

She jogged through the open train doors. She stood on the station, looking back and forth. It was an incongruous structure of asphalt, concrete, and steel in the middle of what looked like mutant Brazilian rainforest.

The train beeped behind her and she turned to see the doors sliding shut. The train whistle sounded and it slowly moved out of the station, quickly picking up speed. It shot away through the jungle almost as though it'd been fired from a gun.

Monk heard a deep rumbling from the mountains in the distance. They belched plumes of smoke.

The ground shook.

Awesome. It's probably a fucking super volcano.

She took a deep breath and scratched the side of her face. She looked down at her fingernails, caked with dried blood. *Yuck.*

Her headache had faded back and was now only a dull thump in her temples. She jumped up and down a couple of times and swung her arms. Her body felt much better than it had, she noted with dim relief.

She glanced up at the mountain. The stream of smoke shook her to her core but she didn't know why.

Fuck it. I'm gonna make Michaels drag her fuzzy little arse all over her stupid fucking playground.

Monk grinned as auras filled her vision.

She drew a hole in the air and jumped through it.

KILKENNY KNEW THE second they'd gone through the doorway that something was horribly wrong. It was almost like stepping off a precipice. She plummeted downward through pitch blackness, a warm body by her side. A strong pair of arms pulled her in close as the ground rushed up toward them. They both hit the ground with grunts and the impact forced the air from Kilkenny's lungs. She lay, stunned, for a moment. She was distantly aware of lying on a soft surface that seemed to be moving up and down.

She shifted her vision quickly but only saw two columns of gold, her and the woman she was lying on. The rest of the world was layered shades of gray.

She looked up and saw Roth's face at startlingly close range. Her eyes widened in shock as she realized her head was resting comfortably on Roth's breasts. She quickly sat up, closing her eyes against dizziness.

Roth's eyes flickered open a few seconds later.

"Oh, my goodness," she said. "That could have gone better."

Kilkenny nodded. "They must have felt Jackie poking at their section of the dreamscape."

"And they opened their own door and we fell right on through." Roth looked around, eyes flaring yellow. "Where is everyone? And where are we?"

Kilkenny looked around. It was dark and a thick, swirling, acrid fog hung around them. She shifted, feeling wood beneath her feet. She looked up and saw a fly eaten mirror behind her, surrounded by fading frescos of circus animals. Ahead of her she saw animals connected to the poles. An elephant, a horse, a sea horse, a dolphin, and others she couldn't clearly make out.

"We're on a carousel," she said, glancing at Roth.

Roth smiled. "So we are." She levered herself to her feet and held out a hand for Kilkenny. "Shall we?"

Kilkenny gingerly took her hand, amazed at her physical strength. She looked deep into Roth's shadowed eyes.

Roth smiled.

In the distance, a train whistle shrieked.

"Hah," Roth said. She turned to Kilkenny. "What do you want to do now?"

"Let's head toward the whistle," Kilkenny said. *A train might mean people. I want to get out of this god forsaken darkness.*

Roth nodded. "That sounds as good a plan as anything else."

They got down off the carousel and began walking. Kilkenny could see shapes moving in the fog and drew close to Roth.

Roth glanced down at her. "Are you frightened?" she asked softly.

Kilkenny looked up at her, wondering if she should tell the truth. *Rio loves her.* She fought down a stab of jealousy. *It's got to be for a good reason.*

"Yeah," she said. "I'm scared."

"Don't be frightened, Kilkenny. You're not alone. And with me around, you'll never *be* alone. We're both shape shifters, and there's *nothing* we can't handle if we work together."

They walked past a warped shooting gallery and a twisted fun house that looked anything but.

"Do you really mean that? I don't know much about being a shape shifter. I don't know that I'm of any use to you."

Roth pulled her to a halt and looked at her. "Are you *kidding*, Kilkenny?"

Kilkenny bit her lip and shook her head.

"In the short time I've known you, I've seen that you're *very* intelligent and you're very brave. I don't know of many people that would have been game enough to throw someone out of the dreamscape because they were afraid that they'd get hurt, knowing the cost to themselves. You care enough about your friends to run into a hornet's nest of trouble, knowing full well what the cost to yourself could be."

"I can't do anything else," Kilkenny said. "Monk is my best friend."

"Do you want to know more about being a shape shifter, Kilkenny? I can teach you and so can Rio." Roth ran a gentle finger down Kilkenny's face. "Rio *wants* to help you. So do I."

"I want. I can't do this by myself anymore. Neither can Monk. Or Michelle. Or Jackie." Her vision shifted and she studied Roth's column of golden sparks, her bond a thick, silver cloud around her.

"Rio's doing fine," Roth said softly. "She's worried about you. I let her know there's nothing to worry about." She smiled. "I meant to thank you for what you did for us. I can feel her like she's inside me. It's like we're one person."

This time Kilkenny could not control the stab of jealousy that tore through her.

"Rio's in love with you," Roth said softly. "She's fairly certain you love her as well."

Kilkenny hung her head. "I do." *Why lie? God knows how this is going to turn out.* "Can I still trust you?"

"*Of course* you can," Roth said. "Of course. Why couldn't you? What on earth do you think I'm going to do to you?"

Kilkenny shrugged.

"What happened to you, Kilkenny? Who hurt you so badly you're afraid of any other shape shifters who come near you? Not all of us are insane maniacs hell bent on revenge."

She pulled Roth into motion. "If I tell you that, will you answer my questions as well?"

"Yes."

"Just like that?"

"Just like that," Roth said. "Now, how about you tell me what happened to you?"

Trust has to start somewhere. Kilkenny glanced at Roth. *I have* so *got to stop staring at her.*

Kilkenny took a deep breath and told Roth about Wells targeting her, Monk stepping to help and being turned into a werewolf. She also found herself telling Roth about Wells's and Lightman's demise. Her throat was sore and she felt husked out when she was finished.

Her face was wet with tears and dull humiliation flowed over her in harsh waves.

"Oh, you poor thing," Roth said, she held out her arms and Kilkenny was in them, a steady stream of tears wetting Roth's chest and shirt.

"God, I felt so helpless," she said, clutching at Roth. Roth gently stroked her back and suddenly all the terrible fear and pain that she'd bottled up for years erupted from her.

"I *never* wanted any of them to get hurt for me. It's *my* fault Monk is a shape shifter. It's *my* fault that Wells came after us at all."

Roth remained silent, stroking her back and holding her close.

"Why, Roth? God, why?"

"Wells was an insane dream walker. I'm sure what she was doing made perfect sense to her and none at all to any one of the rest of us. She never needed a reason, only a place. *None* of that was your fault." She studied Kilkenny. "I must admit I'm quite curious to meet your Monk. She sounds like a unique character. Also someone with exceptional courage and stupidity."

"Michelle said she did it because she had a death wish. I'm pretty sure that was true at the beginning. But Monk realized how stupid that was after Terri left tire marks over her for dragging them into our mess without asking them if they wanted to be dragged."

"Oh, yes," Roth said. "I go where *I* want to go. I'm the mistress of my *own* destiny. No one else is responsible for me and my actions but me."

"I miss Monk. I miss Terri."

"Terri sounds like she grew into a fine woman."

"She was amazing."

"You were all very good friends, weren't you?" Roth said.

"Yeah, we were."

"Okay, then, suppose you tell me what you think Monk has done in this dreamscape."

Kilkenny looked carefully at Roth. There was only peace in her green eyes, and still no sign of deception or duplicity.

"Monk isn't suicidal. Terri knocked it out of her and so did Michelle. She loves Michelle more than anyone else on the planet. She loves Jackie and she wants to see both of them again. I'm guessing Hellstrom is hammering away at her to put a controlling bond on her to call Terri."

Roth nodded.

"I know Monk wouldn't be able to live with herself if she broke down enough for Hellstrom to use her to call Terri into the dreamscape. The most logical thing for Monk to do would be to escape Hellstrom and call Terri onto the dreamscape. Terri isn't a coward, nor is she irresponsible so I'm sure she'd want to stay to fight Hellstrom."

Roth winced.

"Monk is *very* smart. The smartest thing for her to do would be to give Terri the choice to become a werewolf. It evens the playing field. She and Monk could work together to take out Hellstrom. She wouldn't worry about being outclassed because she knows there's no power between heaven and earth that would stop us from going to her. If you're transformed into a werewolf, what happens when you get bitten?"

"You die. You stay dead for a while. The time varies. From an hour to a day. Then you wake up as a werewolf." Roth was silent for a moment. "If I were Monk, I'd put Terri's body somewhere safe until the transformation is complete. I'd make sure I created a fuss so that Hellstrom would have her hands full."

Kilkenny nodded. “And if I were *Hellstrom*, I’d make sure Monk’s friends couldn’t reach her.”

Roth snorted. Her eyes flared yellow and she looked carefully around the amusement park. “Where would you hide a body?”

“You’d hide it where the dream walker and Hellstrom couldn’t zero in on it.”

“Something moving. Like a train, for example?”

Kilkenny nodded. “Exactly like that.”

“The train whistle came from that direction,” Roth said, pointing. “Let’s go.”

“Can you see? When you shift?”

“I can see other people but not objects very well.”

Roth nodded. “Shift. I’ll steer.” She took Kilkenny’s hand and they jogged.

CHAPTER 7

MORIARTY LOST HER footing as she stepped through the doorway and grabbed Jackie for balance. Suddenly they both flew over the edge of a precipice and were sailing down through an overcast sky to a vast, stinking marshland below.

Moriarty clung to Jackie and spun around a second or so before they fell into thick mud. As it spurted up all around her body in a foul smelling blast, she found herself distantly amazed that they hadn't sunk further into the ground, considering how hard they'd hit.

She sat up, groaning, and looked down at her black blazer in disgust. *Ruined.*

"Oh, my aching butt," Jackie said, slowly sitting up and wincing. "That hurt."

"Yeah, it did," Moriarty said. She grinned. "But at least we landed together." She got up out of the mud, grimacing at the sucking sound as she stood. She held out her hand and levered Jackie to her feet.

"Where are we?" Jackie said, peering around.

Moriarty followed the direction of her gaze. The marshland was just as vast, dank and bad smelling on the ground as it had been while they were hurtling downward through the air toward it. The sky overhead was overcast, and an unnerving, steady wind rushed over them in a stream. They were in the middle of a fork in the water, on a small island, now churned to mud. Broken vegetation lay all around them.

"I'd tell you we're in a marshland but I don't think that's the answer you want to hear. Besides that, I'd say you'd already noticed, right?"

Jackie nodded. "You'd have guessed right, Mack." She looked around. "You got some kind of werewolf super sense that tells you which direction we should be going in?"

Moriarty stared at her. "I'm not psychic, Jackie, despite what my students say about me. What does *your* werewolf *super sense* tell you about the direction we should be heading in?"

"It doesn't say anything. And I think my crystal ball is cloudy." She looked sadly at Moriarty. "Michelle's a ways away from us and I can't really feel Monk. She's got to be further away."

"We got split up. Figures. We'll find them." Moriarty snorted. "*My* werewolf *super sense* is just full of mud." She shifted her vision and stared off into the distance. "What the hell is that?"

"What's what?" Jackie asked, eyes flaring yellow.

"That looks like a *Tangara* of all things," Moriarty said, watching a perfectly normal Cityrail train hurtling down a train track.

"Pardon me?"

"You heard me."

"Not right, though." Jackie frowned. "That *can't* be right."

"Oh, you heard me all right," Moriarty said, grinning. "You just don't believe me is all."

"Yeah, well, you wouldn't believe me if I'd said that to you, either."

"We're on the dreamscape. If you tell me you're holding hands with a purple gorilla I'm not likely to argue with you."

Jackie blinked. "You'd better. What the hell do I want with a purple gorilla?"

"I'm sure I don't know. You're just going to have to ask if you ever end up holding hands with one."

"I'll remember that." Jackie smiled and put her hands on her hips. "Maybe we should follow the train tracks."

"All right. Why not? We should probably keep on the lookout for a train station, then, huh?"

Jackie nodded. "Makes perfect no sense." She nodded across the water. "Do you think it's safe just to go into the water?"

Moriarty eyed the dark, murky water. "I don't know but that doesn't really matter. Unless we plan to spend eternity on a hillock playing word games we have to get across it."

Jackie nodded. "Fair enough. Can you see anything in it?" Her eyes flared yellow, and she looked into the water.

Moriarty shifted her vision and stared into the water. It was impenetrable murk. "No. Look, why don't you let me go ahead of you to the other bank? If there's anything in the water, I'll just deal with it."

"No way," Jackie said. "I'll go with you. If there *is* something in the water, you might need my help."

"Okay," Moriarty said. She held out her hand and Jackie took it. She gestured to their joined hands. "Well, we should end up less mud covered, anyway."

Jackie grimaced. "That'd be nice."

Moriarty walked forward, pulling Jackie with her. She waded into the water, Jackie by her side.

They slowly waded in up to their knees. The water was cold, almost unpleasantly so, but seemed blessedly free of life. Moriarty relaxed and strode forward. They were about half way across when something brushed against her leg. It felt hard and sinewy. She glanced at Jackie, who hadn't seemed to have noticed.

The ground beneath them kept sloping down gently until it was up to Moriarty's collar bones. It was up to Jackie's chin.

"Piggy back," Moriarty said. "Get on."

Jackie leapt onto her back and something else brushed past Moriarty's leg.

Fuck. Time to get out of the water.

She plowed toward the far bank, grateful as the riverbed sloped upwards again. She felt the same brushing against the side of her body and quickly looked that way. An immense, rubbery body slid past hers, a finned tail flapping past.

It's an eel. But it's a hell of a lot bigger than it should be.

She pushed forward as fast as she could.

"What's up, Mack?" Jackie asked, sounding alarmed.

"What's up *Doc*," Moriarty said.

"What?"

"What's up *Doc,* not what's up *Mack.*"

"Oh. Sorry. Silly me. What's up *Doc*?"

"Nothing, just getting us up out of the water. This shit is cold," Moriarty said, now knee deep in the water. She jog stumbled toward bank, Jackie clinging to her. As soon as they hit the bank, Jackie slid down her back.

"Thanks," Jackie said. She shook her arms and drops of mud and water flew. "Nice one. You got away from the eels."

Moriarty stared up at her in surprise. "You saw?"

"Oh, I saw all right," Jackie said with a shudder. "The last one was about six feet long and the size of a tree trunk. I'm surprised they're not electric."

Suddenly one of the eels breeched the water and Moriarty put a reflexive arm in front of Jackie. The eel *was* about six feet long and fully one foot in diameter. It had an ugly, gray wedge head full of sharp teeth that clicked together. It went back down into the water with a big splash.

"Fuck," Moriarty muttered. "I'm glad I didn't have to fight one of those."

"I really want to drain this swamp."

"I'd love it if you did but somehow I don't think you're going to be able to do that any time soon." She smiled at Jackie. "So how about we just head up to the train tracks?"

"You're on," Jackie said, and they began walking. "I hope there aren't any other big animals in all this shit."

Moriarty laughed. "So do I." She gave Jackie a friendly grin. "You know you're covered in mud?"

"Really?" Jackie said, smiling. "So are you."

"Well, it's meant to be good for your skin."

"So they say."

"*They* say an awful lot, don't they?"

"Yes, they do," Jackie said. She was silent for a moment as she looked around. She grinned. "I spy with my little eye, something beginning with . . . m."

"Mud," Moriarty said.

"Nope," Jackie said.

"Mire?"

"Nope."

"Marsh?"

Jackie smirked. "Not even close."

Moriarty grinned. "Ooh, I know. *Mack*."

"You're good," Jackie said. "Played this before?"

"Maybe once or twice before."

"Cool. Your turn."

Moriarty looked around, watching carefully for anything else that might have been coming toward them. They seemed to be alone. She pushed aside her deep seated unease and allowed herself to become immersed in Jackie's simple game.

BAKING HEAT ENGULFED Monk as soon as she stepped through the tear.

She gasped, coughing as the superheated air baked her lungs. Ahead of her was a massive lake of lava. The air above it shimmered. She felt the heat from the ground almost melting the soles of her joggers.

"Nice place, huh?" Angela said, stepping through a tear in the dreamscape.

Monk didn't think. She swung her fist as hard as she could and felt rather than heard the crunch as it hit Angela in the face. Angela was lifted off her feet and crashed into a sizzling rock. She slid to the ground, out cold.

Fucking bitch. Shit, she's waking up already. I'm out of here. What a bad fucking bank this was.

Angela sat up, and Monk lost no time tearing a hole in the dreamscape. She dove through it, grateful that only Angela had followed her into this one.

"WHAT THE FUCK?" Riordan said, striding through the doorway and crashing into the back of Michelle. "Sorry."

Michelle turned and looked at her. She shrugged. "I don't know."

They were standing in the middle of what looked like a rainforest. It was hot and humid, and Michelle could hear a variety of bird calls and hidden animals foraging in the undergrowth. Mosquitoes the size of sparrows buzzed all around them.

"Where *is* everyone?" Riordan asked, hands on hips. She looked around.

"I don't know," Michelle said, feeling in her bond for Jackie. She felt Jackie's disgust, far away in the distance. "I don't think they landed with us."

"Ugh," Riordan said, dropping down onto a convenient rock and putting her hands on her knees. "That kind of makes sense. I can feel Roth is further away than I'd like." She eyed the canopy.

Michelle nodded. "Yep. I'm guessing that wasn't just a doorway into the dreamscape. We fell through a rabbit hole and got split up."

"Which means, of course, that Hellstrom now knows we're here."

"She must have known all along. No surprises there. Can we go back through the doorway?"

Riordan's eyes flared yellow and she looked back in the direction of the doorway. "No. It doesn't look like it. I'm guessing that was a one way doorway."

"Great," Michelle said, throwing up her hands. "You have any good ideas on what you think we should do now?"

"Well, we could—*wait*. Listen." Riordan cocked her head, eyes bile yellow.

Michelle shifted her vision and focused on her hearing. She could hear the faint sound of a train in the distance. After a few seconds, she heard its whistle.

"A *train*?" she said. "You're kidding me."

Riordan shook her head. "Makes perfect sense, actually. They caught Monk on her way home from university. One perfectly logical place is the train. What's the bet Monk was running for the train and went barreling through a doorway without even realizing it?"

Michelle nodded. "It'd make sense. Monk always tells me that if she misses a train in the middle of the day she normally has to wait half an hour for another one to come by."

"Well," Riordan said, shrugging. "Do you want to head toward the train tracks? If nothing else at least we'll be a little more out in the open than we are now."

Michelle nodded. "Sounds like as good an idea as any. Which direction?"

Riordan pointed to her right. "That way. Yes, I'm sure, before you ask."

Michelle grinned. "I wasn't going to, but okay." She held out her hand and levered Riordan to her feet.

They walked through the thick undergrowth, Michelle in the lead. The air was hot and humid and she soon found herself dripping with sweat and breathing hard. Riordan sounded like wasn't doing much better.

"Geez," Michelle said, leaning forward with her hands on her knees. "What I wouldn't give for a machete or something."

Riordan nodded. "I know," she said, panting.

Michelle looked at the sleeves of her shirt. She tore one off experimentally. It made a little difference. "What a waste of a good shirt," she muttered as she tore off the other one.

"You should use it to tie your hair back," Riordan said.

"Good idea," Michelle said, pulling her hair back and tying it with the ripped sleeve. "That's a bit better."

Suddenly the ground trembled. The trees swayed.

Riordan grabbed Michelle and looked up, watching the canopy as leaves rained down on them.

"An earthquake?" she said.

"Yeah," Michelle said. "And I'm guessing that this isn't going to be good."

Riordan nodded ahead of them at what looked like a clearing. "Maybe we should get out into the open for a few minutes. See what's around."

"Agreed," Michelle said, standing aside as Riordan took the lead.

A few moments later they'd managed to find their way out of the undergrowth and stood at the edge of a wide clearing. It was about the size of a football field, edged to the front and left by thick trees and covered in lush, long grass. It went off to the right and seemed to stop at the edge of what Michelle guessed was a sheer cliff.

The sun beat unmercifully down on them, and Riordan wiped the sweat off her forehead with her forearm.

Michelle glanced up at the unforgiving sky and saw tall, snow covered mountains in the distance. A thick bank of gigantic, black, cumulonimbus clouds scudded half way across the sky toward them.

"We're in for a whopper storm," Michelle said, nodding toward them.

Riordan nodded. "I don't want to be too far away from the jungle when it breaks. I'm guessing this clearing is like a riverbed when it rains." She pointed at the mountains ahead of them. "Water probably flows down the sides of those."

"Agree," Michelle said. "You game to go to the edge of the cliff?"

Riordan nodded. "Well, no, but I can't not go. It's a bad idea that I have to agree to."

Michelle laughed. "I hear you. Come on. Quick run, then back in the jungle."

Riordan nodded and they continued to walk. It only took them a couple of minutes and they found themselves at the edge of a vast cliff, which formed a natural U shape. It was devoid of vegetation for a large distance to either side and Michelle suppressed a shudder. The center of the U sheltered a small stream, ending in a waterfall down the edge of a four hundred foot cliff. She knew the waterfall wouldn't be small for very long once the storm came.

"Look at that," Riordan said softly, breaking her out of her reverie.

Michelle glanced at her and followed the direction of her pointing finger.

In the distance, more or less in line with the stream, was a vast mountain. It gave off a small streamer of steam.

"It's a volcano, isn't it?" Michelle said.

"Yeah," Riordan said. "And I'm guessing it gives off a huge amount of lava. If we stay we're going to get crisped. Look at the ground we're standing on and the bed of that stream. It's all made of volcanic rock. These turn into lava falls when the volcano blows."

"I don't want to be here for that."

"Neither do I," Riordan said. "Let's just trot along and find that little train, shall we?"

Michelle immediately turned and followed Riordan back into the jungle. A cold wind blew through the trees. They saw a flash of light.

"It's starting," Michelle said. She looked up at the trees. "I don't know what the water runoff is going to be like. Maybe we should consider climbing?"

Riordan shook her head. "I don't think so. Look at the canopy."

Michelle shifted her vision and looked upwards. The green sparks of the trees were covered in knobs of brown sparks. She released her vision, focusing on where she'd last seen a brown knob.

"Oh, shit," she muttered.

An ape thing looked down at them, chewing on what looked like a bloody bone. Little chunks of flesh hung off the bone, and the ape thing's lips were smeared with blood. It yawned, revealing a mouth of razor sharp teeth that rivaled a shark.

"Don't make eye contact," Riordan said softly. "Whatever you do, don't make eye contact."

Michelle nodded, immediately looking away. "Apes take that as a sign of aggression. And I'm guessing that although those aren't apes they're going to do some of the nastier things that apes are prone to when they get aggressive."

Riordan nodded. "And I'm sure it won't think twice about tearing either one of us apart."

There was another flash of light, more brilliant than the last one. Michelle looked around. There wasn't much to hang onto when the rain came. *I'm sure this place is going to be underwater*.

"Don't worry," Riordan said. "I can hold onto a tree. I can hold us both. I'm more than strong enough."

Michelle eyed Riordan's sinewy frame. "All right. I can help a little."

"Good," Riordan said. "And I think we'd better start looking for cover."

Another brilliant flash of light came, followed by booming thunder. It was enough to make Michelle wince. *Shit. And it's not even all that close to us yet.*

Riordan pointed further into the forest as the hair on Michelle's arms stood on end.

"Lightning strike," she said, haring past Riordan, heading in the direction she'd been pointing.

"Shit," Riordan said, running by her side.

A blinding shot of light robbed Michelle of her sight and a concussion knocked both of them over.

Michelle grayed out for a second. Her mind frantically screamed at her to get up and get moving again. She sat up slowly. Her ears rang and stars floated in her vision. Riordan groaned softly from the ground beside her.

Michelle leant over, putting a gentle hand on Riordan's back. "Rio? You still with me?"

"Uh," Riordan said, pushing herself up and shaking her head. "Fuck."

Michelle had recovered enough to tug Riordan to her feet. "Trust me, I get it." She put a steadying hand on Riordan's shoulder. She swayed back and forth, clutching her head.

"I'm sorry, Rio," Michelle said. "We *have* to keep moving."

"I know," Riordan said. "I'm coming."

She bumped into Michelle and Michelle put a hand on her elbow, steering her gently as they ran again.

The first cold drops of water came down from the sky, so large they were like water bombs. Michelle and Riordan were almost instantly soaked and it became difficult to see through the curtain of water tumbling down through the trees around them.

"We'd better start looking for a tree to hang onto," Riordan said, barely audible above the pounding rain.

Lightning flashed and thunder boomed all across the darkened sky.

Michelle looked down. The ground was saturated and rivulets of swift-moving water flowed all around them.

"Okay," she said. "Suggestions?"

"This way," Riordan said, grabbing her wrist and pulling her toward a broken branch hanging off the side of a tree.

Michelle stumbled over the rough ground and Riordan caught her easily.

Riordan pulled her up the broken section of tree and into the branches. She quickly straddled the branch. Michelle sat down in front of her, and Riordan encircled her with her arms, pulling her in close in a firm grip.

Water rushed around the base of the tree. Michelle shivered, snuggling in close to Riordan.

A flash of movement in the dead leaves at the end of the branch caught her eye. A small snake with a head that seemed a little too large for its body slithered toward them, pelted by the huge rain drops. Its tongue flicked out as it nosed along the branch.

I hate snakes. Michelle stiffened.

The snake moved closer to her and was now about two inches from the end of her foot. Her heart pounded. She could see it better now and shuddered. It had a thin body and a large, wedge shaped head with tiny horns over its lidless eyes. Its tongue flicked out, hitting the bottom of Michelle's boot.

"Relax, Michelle," Riordan said softly into her ear. "It'll probably lose interest and go away."

The snake slithered forward and bumped into the sole of Michelle's hiking boot. It backed up a couple of inches and stopped dead, remaining unnervingly still, quivering with tension. Alarm bells rang in Michelle's head. Her heart hammered, and she swallowed convulsively. She reflexively tried to back up. Riordan's arms tightened.

"Stop moving," Riordan said. "Sit still."

The snake's head suddenly whipped up in her direction. It opened its mouth, revealing long, needle sharp fangs. Its mouth kept opening until it was a yawning, two foot maw of venom from two rows of upper and lower fangs.

"Shit," Michelle yelled, swinging her leg out of the way. Just at that second it struck, its fangs heading toward Riordan's unprotected leg.

"Jesus," Riordan screamed, yanking her leg out of the way. They overbalanced and Michelle fell off the branch. She blindly grabbed Riordan's leg and hung on for dear life. Her scalp crawled with shock and her heart hammered in terror. Riordan remained dead still and hung onto the tree, staring at the snake with wide eyes.

The snake reared up, poised to spring. Riordan stiffened, desperately trying to keep her balance.

Michelle looked sideways at the water rushing toward her and saw that the leaves and twigs at the end of the broken branch were crawling with more of the snakes. They watched her with cold, alien eyes, tongues flicking. One of them left its twig and slithered toward the thick part of the branch.

"Let go of the branch," Michelle screamed.

"No way," Riordan yelled. "We'll get washed away."

The snake struck, and Riordan grunted, twisting out of the way. She grabbed the snake, snapped its neck, and threw it as far away from them as she could.

"Let go of the branch," Michelle screamed. "There are about fifty snakes at the end of it and they're headed toward you."

More of the snakes were headed up toward the thick branch, and the first one that moved pushed its head out of the leaves.

Michelle let go of Riordan's leg as Riordan let go of the branch. The flowing water almost knocked Michelle off balance and she braced herself. Riordan landed against her and disrupted her already precarious balance. She fell over sideways, washed away by the rushing water. Riordan was swept away along with her. She groped for Riordan in the water and missed.

They tumbled down a gentle slope, whipped and torn by leaves and rocks, over the edge of an embankment.

Michelle landed heavily, Riordan almost on top of her. She grabbed Riordan and rolled clear of the worst of the water.

They leant against a friendly rock, drenched and gasping for air, pelted by gigantic rain drops.

Michelle turned to Riordan, and suddenly Riordan's eyes widened. She rolled to her feet and grabbed the snake that had tumbled over the waterfall behind them. It thrashed and screamed in her hand.

Riordan's face was a mask of revulsion as she tore its head off its body before it could open its mouth.

Michelle felt the metallic taste of fear in her mouth and the aftermath of terror left her shaking.

"Thanks," she said.

"You're welcome," Riordan said, throwing the twitching body of the snake in the rushing water. She stood and held out her hands so they were washed clean of blood and mud. After a moment, she looked down at Michelle and gave her a half smile.

"I hate snakes," she said.

"So do I," Michelle said.

The rain tapered off.

"Let's get moving," Riordan said, looking up at the sky. Holes of blue were appearing in the overcast sky.

"Yeah," Michelle said. "Do you know which way we're headed?"

"Kind of," Riordan said. "We're going to have to listen for the train whistle again."

Michelle nodded. "I figured."

She got up with a sigh and continued to walk.

MONK'S NEXT TEAR in the dreamscape's skin was no better than the first one. She suddenly found herself sailing through the air toward the ocean. *Shit. That's a fucking tidal wave. This was* another *bad bank.*

The wave was gigantic. It was well over five hundred feet high and moving so quickly it was almost impossible to keep in sight. Monk saw a gigantic octopus that dwarfed the wave a scant second or two before she hit the water.

Jesus, Mary and Joseph. Just look at that fucking thing.

She cut a hole in the dreamscape again, just above the surface of the water, and tumbled through it.

"WHAT'S THAT?" KILKENNY asked, shrinking closer in to Roth.

Roth glanced at her. "What's what?"

"What's *that*?" she said, nodding toward two figures standing at the intersection of the pathway ahead of them.

"I think it's what it looks like," Roth said, pulling her to a halt. Her eyes shone yellow. "It's a mother and a child watching us. Beyond them, straight ahead of them, are more men, women, and children. They look like they're enjoying the carnival."

Kilkenny shifted her vision. She couldn't make out any sparks in the dull, grey landscape. She slipped her hand into Roth's.

Roth glanced at her, smile twitching around her mouth. "Are you frightened?"

Kilkenny bit her lip and nodded. *The woman and child look so . . . wrong.* They had regular features and were well proportioned, but were so pale they were almost incandescent. Their eyes were flat pools of black and the boy had a stain on one side of his mouth. They had a menacing air of watchfulness. There was something unutterably sly about woman, and Kilkenny shuddered.

"There's nothing to be frightened of," Roth said. "Come."

She gently pulled Kilkenny into motion. As soon as they got close to the woman and child, they flickered and reappeared about fifteen feet in front of them.

Kilkenny now saw clearly the people that Roth said she'd seen. They were in what looked like an eating area. There were benches set up in a rough circle, and people sitting on the benches and eating. All around them were stands that sold food. The food itself was the only thing that had color and its garishness drew the eye unmercifully.

"Is that blood?" Kilkenny asked.

Roth nodded. "I think so."

The groups of people slowly stopped eating and turned toward them. Their faces and hands were smeared with blood. A chunk of flesh dropped out of a child's mouth, falling down his clothes and leaving a thin smear of blood behind.

"We've got their attention," Kilkenny said.

"And we didn't want it," Roth said. She looked down at Kilkenny. "Remember, young one, these aren't real people. They're constructs. You can't *hurt* something that isn't alive."

One of the constructs stood, then another one until all of them were on their feet, eyeing Kilkenny and Roth with dead and dreadfully aware eyes.

"We're surrounded," Roth said.

Kilkenny glanced around and saw that the vendors had left their stalls and formed a knot behind them. One of them took a step toward them. Kilkenny turned back and gasped in shock. One of the male constructs stood nose to nose with Roth. Roth stared back at him, seemingly relaxed.

Kilkenny heard a sound behind her and looked around. The stall attendants had taken a step toward them.

"We have to fight," Kilkenny said softly.

"Back to back," Roth said, still watching the male construct closely.

Kilkenny swung around and backed up, grateful for the solid warmth of Roth against her back. She felt Roth press against her and heard the sound of the male construct growling. There was a terrible tearing sound and a crash as a body hit the ground.

The sound galvanized the attendants into action. They rushed toward Kilkenny in eerie silence, clawing and tearing at her.

She pushed a few away from them, feeling the movement of Roth's back against hers as she faced down constructs.

They're not real people, she said to herself, seeing the flat, one dimensional skin of the closest construct grabbing at her with greedy fingers. It touched the smooth skin of her chest and her paralysis broke at the cold, slimy sensation. She felt revulsion and quickly grabbed its shoulder and the top of its head, and pulled them apart as hard as she could. The construct's flesh tore easily, leaving a gaping, bloodless maw in its wake. She dropped the head, its mouth opening and closing soundlessly, and the body collapsed to its knees. It was slowly trampled by other constructs rushing toward her.

Roth's strength and solidity against her allowed her to settle into a comfortable rhythm of catching and tearing constructs apart.

Soon they were both surrounded by chunks of torn, white flesh, which gave off a gassy, swampy odor. Kilkenny looked down at the remains and discovered, to her dim surprise, that she felt nothing. They weren't real people and she hadn't killed anyone. All she'd done was shred parts of the dreamscape.

"Now we keep down the path," Roth said, offering her arm.

"What path? We're in a cul-de-sac." Kilkenny offered a slight smile at Roth's gesture. "My hands are filthy."

"So are mine," Roth said.

Kilkenny slipped her arm around Roth's, instantly aware of Roth's nearness and the feel of smooth, hard muscle under her hand. She automatically moved closer to her.

Roth nodded toward the stand in front of them. "That stand is in the center of the path."

"Lead the way," Kilkenny said, gesturing before them. She ran her fingertips over Roth's smooth skin.

Roth drew her in closer, and they walked again. Kilkenny caught a flash of movement out of the corner of her eye and turned to follow it. It was another attendant, looking as lifeless as the ones that had first tried to block their way. She tugged Roth's arm.

Roth glanced at her with a raised eyebrow, and Kilkenny nodded toward the attendant. More attendants and carnival goers appeared from the dark corners.

"Stand behind me and get on my back," Roth said softly.

"A piggy back?" Kilkenny said, quickly darting behind Roth.

Roth nodded and bent her knees. Kilkenny jumped onto her.

Kilkenny's heart skipped a beat, despite herself. Roth's body was rock hard and sinewy, despite her feminine curves. *She's way stronger than Monk. Wow.*

"Ready?" asked Roth.

Kilkenny studied her elegant profile. She nodded. "Yeah."

Roth ran lightly forward and then launched herself into the air. She flipped over the top of the first mass of attendants and landed softly in the middle of another. They swarmed toward her, and she lowered her shoulder and ran forward, knocking them over like bowling pins.

More carnival goers came toward them and Roth continued running and flipping. Kilkenny found that she was actually *enjoying* herself. Roth's grace and acrobatics amazed her. When they were finally clear of all the people things, Kilkenny slid off her back with a broad grin.

Roth smiled back at her. "Did you enjoy yourself?"

Kilkenny nodded. "I should probably say no, but in the words of my friend Monk, *hell yes*."

Roth laughed. "You could do the same, you know."

"I just don't have your strength," Kilkenny said.

"You're stronger than a grown man," Roth said. "And do you really think a twelve-year-old gymnast relies on brute strength to do what they do? I could teach you. It's quite easy."

Kilkenny looked into her light green eyes. They were amused, patient and very kind. She nodded. "I'd love to."

Roth held out her hand. "Let's go. Take my hand and move as I do. All we're going to do is run and jump as high as we can. No flipping just yet."

Kilkenny took her hand, and Roth pulled her into motion. She felt almost as though she'd sunk into Roth. They moved in perfect tandem, leapt high into the air, and landed softly a long distance from where they'd started.

"That was cool," Kilkenny said with a broad grin. "When can we try flipping?"

"We should probably get clear of this mess first before we continue with the gymnastics," Roth said. She gestured toward a troubling smear on the asphalt to their left. It led into a darkened corner. Kilkenny wasn't sure what it was and didn't want to look. *That's blood all right,* her treacherous mind whispered.

"No worries," she said, moving closer to Roth again.

Roth smiled. "I'd be happy to show you more once we're done with Hellstrom. Are you interested?"

Kilkenny nodded. "I'm interested all right."

She smiled easily at Kilkenny. "Then we'll consider it a standing date."

Kilkenny nodded, grateful for Roth's proximity, and they continued walking.

CHAPTER 8

"THIRD TIME LUCKY," Monk said, tumbling out of the tear in the dreamscape and landing face down in a sodden marsh. The ground felt rubbery and slimy. It moved a little and she stood up slowly and bounced on the ground.

Wind rushed around her in a monotone blast, over a blackish purple ground. A flash of lighter color caught her eye and she turned to track it.

What the fuck?

It looked like a white line, which slowly became a circle.

Holy mother of Christ, is that a fucking sucker*?*

She turned and looked around, grimacing at the foul, fishy smell that washed over her in noxious waves. She was surrounded by what looked like purplish black, slimy canyon walls. She poked a section of wall experimentally. It had no give at all and *was* slimy.

She took a step back and studied the walls. *If I could take a step back I think it'd be a pattern. What do I know that could possibly look like this?*

White skin, purple blotches, and so large she could only guess that was what she was looking at.

Oh, no. Oh my God no. A sick feeling of horror creeping over her.

"Did I really say third time lucky?" she muttered, scalp crawling in shock as she realized she was at the tip of a gigantic tentacle. "I don't want to know what's at the other end of this."

She felt a distant, tugging sensation and a desire to see Jackie. *Jackie must be calling me. I can't go. Shit.*

She caught a flash of light in the periphery of her vision.

Shit, Michaels is tearing another hole in the dreamscape. Wonderful, enjoy the squid. I'm not staying.

She tore a hole in the dreamscape and jumped through.

"ARE WE THERE yet?"

"No."

"Are we there yet?"

"No."

"Are we there yet?"

"No. Are you going to keep doing that?" Jackie asked, glancing at Moriarty.

"Only until you lighten up a little bit." Moriarty pulled her to a halt, balancing carefully on a small hassock. "You look far too tense for your own good."

"Look at where we are." Jackie waved a hand around. "Look at *us.*"

Moriarty looked around at the endless marshland. It was mostly low, rough grass and occasional dirt, with streams and rivers cutting a swathe through it. Cattails grew up in places, the only points of interest in the otherwise flat, featureless terrain. The sky over head was a dull, overcast gray. A steady wind blew, low and threatening, throwing them the occasional scent of rot in the dank air. She and Jackie were both covered from head to toe in drying mud courtesy of their fall through the doorway. They'd both taken the time to wash as much mud off their faces and hands as best they could but Moriarty still felt gritty.

"Okay, so we're a bit dirty. Isn't that what showers and washing machines are for, Jackie?" she asked.

Jackie threw up her hands. "*God.* You're impossible."

"No, actually, I'm not," Moriarty said. "I'm just not as fazed by . . . this as you are. What's bugging you?"

"Why would anything other than this be bugging me?"

"Because you've been stomping around without noticing that we're walking next to a perfectly good set of train tracks on dry ground just over there." Moriarty pointed to her left. "And the muttering."

"I don't mutter," Jackie said.

"You do. Now what's bothering you?"

"What *wouldn't* be bothering me?" Jackie snarled. "*Look* at this." She waved a hand around.

"I know, I can see it," Moriarty said calmly. "You're pissed because you thought your steering should have been better, is that it?"

Jackie's shoulders slumped. "I guess so." She sighed. "I was also Kilkenny's trump card and now I'm nothing."

Moriarty's interest perked up at the way she said *nothing.*

"You don't think you're much of anything, do you?"

"What's *that* supposed to mean?" Jackie's eyes flashed.

One, I hit the mark. Two, now she's really *pissed.* Moriarty studied her. Jackie was beautiful and despite being covered from head to toe in drying mud, was the picture of elegance. Moriarty found her intriguing.

"Come on," Moriarty said, nodding toward the tracks. She turned, hearing Jackie's low growl of frustration. She shifted her vision and quickly leapt from hassock to hassock until she hit the low gravel surrounding the tracks. She sniffed and frowned. *Dead fish and brine again. Where the hell is it coming from? And why the fuck does it keep fading in and out?*

She heard a distant, deep plop, barely audible over the wind.

That wasn't close to us. Thank God for small mercies.

"What is it?" Jackie said from beside her.

"What?" Moriarty asked, releasing her vision and glancing at her. Jackie stood close to her, fear lurking in her dark blue eyes. Moriarty grinned. "Nothing. Just relax, will you?"

She began walking, but a hand grabbed her elbow and pulled her to a halt.

"Don't lie to me, Moriarty. What's up?"

Moriarty opened her mouth, fully intending to throw out another teasing comment. What came out instead surprised her. "I don't know but I don't like it. I don't think we're alone here and I really want out of this fucking marsh." Her mouth closed with a snap and she blinked in confusion.

"What do you think is here?" Jackie said.

"I really don't know but it doesn't smell good."

"Yikes."

"Uh, huh."

"We'd better keep moving then, shouldn't we?"

"Yep."

They walked down the tracks again, the wind streaming around them.

"Can I ask you something?" Jackie said after a while.

Moriarty glanced at her. "Sure."

"Why didn't *you* try to find Terri after all that crap with Hellstrom?"

Moriarty thought about it for a moment. The wind flowed over them, carrying an acrid scent in waves. She remembered Terri, her beautiful, creamy skin, and the flush in her cheeks when they'd finished.

I want to know everything about you, she'd said after the first time. *I feel like I want to crawl under your skin and stay there until it's time for us both to die.*

"I'm not human, Jackie," Moriarty said. "Terri always deserved more than me. She deserved to have a lover who was . . . normal. Someone she could grow old with. Someone who wasn't by nature a predator. I didn't know I'd killed Hellstrom until Roth told me. I thought about it and I realized how stupid and selfish I'd been. I'd seduced a school girl. What the hell was I thinking? How could I look Terri in the eye and tell her I loved her after I'd killed her best friend?" She sighed. "Although I'm sure their friendship had gone south by then."

"Yeah, sometimes it's better to think hard *before* you do something," Jackie said. "If you were to see Terri again, would you tell her how you felt?"

Moriarty glanced sharply at her. *Ouch. She has a way of asking pointed questions.* "Yes. Hell, yes. I made a terrible mistake by not going back in there and telling her everything. I should have thrown myself at her feet, warts and all, and begged her to accept me for who I am. I've been walking around with heartache for years. I *never* healed. At least if I talk to her and she tells me to bugger off, I can let go of her and build my life again." She paused. "Well, at least I can *try*."

Jackie nodded. "Is that why you're here?"

"*Here* as in the dreamscape or *here* as in teaching at Sacred Heart?"

"In Autumn Park."

"Kind of. I came with Roth. She tracked Terri down and we came back so I could talk to her. I think she finally got sick of listening to me pine for lost love."

"Is Roth your lover?" Jackie asked.

"*No.* Oh, God no. She's my absolute best friend. So's Rio." Moriarty smiled. "You're bonded to Michelle, aren't you?"

"Yeah," Jackie said softly. "She's doing better, by the way. She's doing something and she can finally feel Monk. We both can."

"Monk's alive?"

"Yeah, she's alive but there's a lot of disquiet coming across from her. The pain has finally stopped, though."

"I'll bet you're going to be glad when you see her."

"Yeah." Jackie sighed.

"You don't sound it."

Jackie looked at her sharply and slumped her shoulders. "I know what everyone thinks but we're not lovers. Michelle and Monk are a couple."

"Then why on earth are you bonded to them? And how did that come about?"

"Kilkenny turned Michelle. I didn't want to be the weak link so I asked Monk to turn *me*. Once I got there I realized I didn't want to be one by myself. Monk and Michelle bonded me so I could be strong."

"What on earth makes you think you're not strong now?" Moriarty asked curiously.

"This scares the shit out of me. *All* of this does. I feel like I'm living in terror all the time."

"Jackie," Moriarty said, smiling. "Listen to me and absorb. I think you're a very brave woman. You got all bent out of shape when you saw your beloved Monk was in trouble and dived right in after her. You did the same with your little sister. Facing down a homicidal maniac takes some guts." She tilted her head. "I can teach you to use your blood, you know." *Time to poke a little.* "But that's not all you're afraid of, is it? You're in love with Monk, aren't you? And Michelle?"

Jackie's expression darkened and she pulled Moriarty to a halt. She put her hands on her hips and growled and then stopped. She took a deep breath and opened her mouth.

"Yes? You wanted to say something?" Moriarty said. "Wanna take a chunk out of me?"

Jackie's shoulders slumped. "What does it matter how I feel? I can't have either one of them." Her mouth shut with a snap, and she blushed.

"Awful, isn't it?" Moriarty said. "I know. Being around *you* makes *me* tell the truth."

"Fuck," Jackie muttered.

"Uh, huh," Moriarty said. She pulled Jackie into motion again. "You know I can't call anyone in the dreamscape, right?"

"What?" Jackie said. "I didn't even think of that. That's pathetic."

"No, not really," Moriarty said. "Most shape shifters can't go into the dreamscape in their physical forms. You're an exception to that rule because you're a dream walker. Part of what makes you a master of the dreamscape is that you can do all of the things that a more common shape shifter can do, but *only* if they're dreaming. Me? I can't call anyone other than a dream walker without great difficulty. In effect, I can only call you or Monk. Even if I *were* able call someone they'd have to use conventional means to reach me. Like walking, for example. It'd take so long that it's essentially useless to even try it."

Jackie mulled it over for a while. "So one of the others would have to call me for us to be able to go to them? By cutting a hole?"

Moriarty nodded. "You could call Monk, you know."

"Interesting," Jackie said. "But I don't know if she'd answer."

"Why not?"

"Her part of the bond feels kind of desperate."

"That doesn't surprise me. How's Michelle doing?"

"She's relaxed. There's a lot of peace coming from her."

"Try calling Monk and Michelle. Let's see what happens."

Jackie's eyes closed for a moment and Moriarty took her elbow and held her steady. She tripped on a sleeper but Moriarty was there to catch her.

"Thanks," Jackie said as she opened her eyes again. "Michelle heard me. I'm getting frustration and disappointment. Monk? She heard me but I'm not getting any kind of positive vibe from her. She's resisting me."

"I suggest that you keep calling Michelle and eventually she might get annoyed enough to call *you* and we can go to them." Moriarty looked up at the sky, feeling a deep seated unease. The clouds above were fluffy and dark, almost as though a thunderstorm was building. They roiled in the wind, which had picked up a notch.

"I don't like this at all," Moriarty muttered.

"You and me both," Jackie said.

"You know what's going to happen when I meet up with Terri," Moriarty said. "What's going to happen when you meet up with either Monk or Michelle?"

"Nothing," Jackie said. "Given that we're bonded I don't know how either one of them could *not* know how I feel. That's pretty embarrassing in and of itself. If either one of them felt the same about me then something would have happened by now."

"Maybe they both do and they're waiting for you to catch up."

"Oh, no. No way," Jackie said. "You're not going to con me into humiliating myself but telling them anything."

Moriarty laughed. "Well, it was worth a try." She heard water gurgling in the distance and she scanned the marshland.

It looked as though a small mound had appeared in the marsh kilometers away. Moriarty shifted her vision and tried to make it out but was unable to. It was too far away. The odd fishy smell came and went in distant waves.

"What's that?" Jackie asked, following the direction of Moriarty's gaze.

"I really don't know," Moriarty said. "I can't see what it is."

The hillock expanded and contracted.

"I really don't like that at all," Jackie said.

"Neither do I," Moriarty said. "What happens if you open a doorway in this dreamscape?"

Jackie's eyes flared yellow. "It's like we're in a closed fish tank. I can feel the edges of the dreamscape but I can't break through them on this side any more than I could on the other side."

"So we'd land somewhere inside Hellstrom's nightmare?"

Jackie nodded. "Yeah. Making doorways isn't that simple anyway. If you want it to come out in the right place you have to know what the endpoint looks like. Otherwise you're just firing at random."

"So you had to know what Michelle's hallway looked like to come out of the dreamscape there?"

Jackie nodded.

Moriarty grinned. "So what happens if you don't know the end point?"

"I can still cut the hole but god knows where we'd end up."

"Maybe we should do that if things get too tough."

"We could end up in the middle of a mountain or something," Jackie said.

"Or even a hundred kilometers down these tracks away from the danger."

Jackie stared at her, jaw clenched.

Moriarty sighed. "Okay, just keep it up your sleeve, then."

Jackie remained silent.

Moriarty looked out over the marsh. There was no sign of the odd hillock. The sky was darkening and the wind was getting colder. *There's no cover here at all. Shit.*

"Hey," Jackie said, touching her sleeve and breaking her reverie. "What's that ahead of us?" She pointed.

Moriarty looked out over the marshland, shifting her vision. "Hah. It's a shelter of some sort. Quite frankly it looks like a train station."

"It's a dream so it doesn't have to make sense," Jackie said.

Moriarty snorted a laugh. "Exactly. I say we go to the station. If we're lucky a train might actually come in. If we're not then at least we might get some shelter from the storm."

"I'm not sure I'd want to get on a train here," Jackie said. "The next place we end up might be more sucky than this one."

"It also might be less sucky. We won't know that until we get there. And we might even find some of the others if we get on it."

Jackie nodded.

They kept walking.

Moriarty glanced up at the sky. *Wonder how long we have until the weather breaks?*

MONK'S TEAR IN reality took her back to the city. *Thank God,* she thought with no small measure of relief. *At least this place looks* normal.

It *did* look normal. It looked like she'd landed in the middle of George Street.

She began jogging along, singing softly to herself.

"Where are you, Hellstrom?" she called out after a moment or so. *Shouldn't be too long now.*

The city street was deserted and the buildings and shops lining the street also looked deserted.

I don't think Michaels has walked down George Street in a long time, Monk thought with a wry grin. Two adjacent office buildings looked exactly the same and the revolving doors looked more like transparent cylinders.

She saw movement out of the corner of her eye and turned to follow it.

Nothing. It really does look deserted. So why the hell do I feel like it's thirteen o'clock?

She heard the sound of roaring water in the distance and turned to look down the street. From where she was standing she could see Circular Quay, devoid of life and ferries. The water sloshed up and landed on the boardwalk.

What the hell caused that*? Oh. Holy fuck a duck.*

Just beyond the ferry jetties was a gigantic ship. It was the largest sailing ship Monk had ever seen in her life. It looked to be close to a kilometer long and riddled with cannons. It was so large it was physically and logically impossible for it to be in the harbor. It hurt Monk's eyes and head to look at it. She shuddered and studied individual elements of the ship. She could clearly see the carved figure under the bowsprit. It was a tied up depiction of herself, painted in garish colors that suggested she was being disemboweled.

The cannons pointed toward her.

"There you are, love," Monk screamed. "I was wondering when you were coming." She ran down George Street, glancing back at the ship.

The cannons glowed red and she could see the heat vapor from the muzzles making the air shimmer.

"Aw, shit. I don't think that's grapeshot," she muttered.

"No," Hellstrom said, leaning comfortably against the façade of a haberdashery. Her eyes burned yellow and a grin played about her lips. "It's not grapeshot at all."

Monk heard the roar of flames and ran as fast as she could. She could feel heat crisping the back of her head and it became so intense she could feel her hair and clothes smoldering. She heard shattering glass and explosions as the buildings burst into flame around her.

Oh, fuck me, that's hot. She tore a hole into the dreamscape and ran through it into blessedly cooler air. The tear closed behind her, cutting off the heat and flames.

She found herself running down the section of highway from the city to Autumn Park that made its way through the national park.

She heard a scream of rage behind her and glanced back over her shoulder.

Hellstrom dove through a closing tear, rolled and landed on her feet.

She bolted after Monk, impossibly quick.

Oh, God, I'm in trouble here. Monk increased her speed. *How the fuck am I going to be able to get a doorway to close before she gets through it? She's really fucking fast.*

Suddenly Monk crashed to the ground, temporarily stunned. Hellstrom's hot breath bathed her neck.

Hellstrom licked her and smacked her lips. "You're a tasty little thing, aren't you?"

Monk shuddered.

Hellstrom's crushing weight left her and a strong hand bunched up the back of her torn tee shirt, yanking her to her feet.

"Angela," Hellstrom screamed. "Come. Come to me."

The air above them shimmered and a black slit formed, rapidly widening.

Angela Michaels easily dropped through the hole. She landed and bounced with grotesque good humor.

"Monky, Monky, Monky," she said, pinching Monk's cheek. "Betcha thought you deep fried me."

Monk slapped her hands away. Hellstrom gave her a vicious shake and Monk could almost feel her teeth rattling.

"Be nice, Monk," Hellstrom said in her ear.

She shoved Monk away as hard as she could and Monk sailed forward, tripped and skidded heavily on her knees, tearing her jeans and skin.

She stood up.

Hellstrom and Angela stood staring at her.

"Run, Monk," Hellstrom said softly.

Monk stared at her, shifting her vision. The auras around Hellstrom and Angela were a sick, vibrant orange.

The low ground cover in the bush to one side of them rustled loudly. Monk turned to look at it.

Oh, fuck, here we go again. Christ, when's Terri going to wake up?

A dog thing with the general outline of a greyhound came out of the bushes, its furnace red eyes glowing.

Look at the size of that thing.

In the distance, the train whistle blew, a shriek of despair in mutant world.

The dog's ear flicked and its head swiveled in the direction of the train whistle. It licked its lips, displaying razor sharp teeth. As its gaze passed Monk, its ears went flat against its wedge head. It pulled its lips back and emitted a low, savage growling.

"RUN," Hellstrom screamed. *"RUN, RUN, RUN, RUN, RUN."*

I'm not gonna run, Monk thought. *I got a much better idea than that.*

The dog took a step toward her, still growling. It was enough to rattle Monk's teeth. She ran backward a few steps and the dog barked, ear splitting howls of pure rage.

Undergrowth rustled as more dog things rushed out to answer the call of the pack leader. They bounded straight toward Monk and Monk relaxed, letting them bowl her over backward.

She gagged at the fetid smell of their breath. She grimly held the contents of her stomach, holding the first dog back by the shoulders. Her muscles bulged and her arms shook.

A second dog came around the side of her and bit her in her unprotected side. She screamed in pain as it twisted its head, pulling away a chunk of flesh. Her side instantly felt cold and soaking wet. After a second or so it felt as though it was on fire.

The other dogs zeroed in on her, frenzied by the smell of her blood.

One of the dogs shot around to the side of her and grabbed her bicep. She howled. She felt as though she'd been burned with acid.

The sound of Hellstrom's roaring laughter and cries of encouragement from Angela were almost inaudible above the sounds of the dogs tearing away chunks of her.

I hope they can't see me. She opened a slit in the dreamscape and fell through it.

Ground rushed up to meet her. Her head cracked against it and she blacked out.

"I CAN'T BELIEVE we're lost," Michelle said, slumping down onto a convenient rock in a rare clearing in the thick jungle.

"I know," Riordan said, slumping down next to her.

They were both breathing hard and sweating freely in the sweltering heat.

Michelle's wet shirt clung uncomfortably to her body. *I wonder if the others are wandering around somewhere in this shit?* She glanced at Riordan. She seemed as cheerful and unruffled as ever.

It felt like hours since they'd heard the train whistle again and moved toward it. They'd spent all that time slogging through thick jungle, complete with low growls, bird calls, and the occasional monkey gibbering at them. The memory of the last one made Michelle shudder and she scanned the tree tops.

"They're still following us," Riordan said, pointing upwards. "Look."

Michelle looked up. The monkey things were above them and one climbed down a thick, vine encrusted tree toward them. As it got closer, she felt uneasy. It was no larger than a standard macaque but its paws had thick, razor sharp claws that almost belonged on a lion. Its teeth, also wickedly sharp, were half again the size of its head. They stopped it from closing its mouth completely. Its breath was a low, uneasy wheezing. It stopped half way down the trunk and stared at them, pitch black eyes dreadfully aware, alien, unknowable, and vicious.

"Nasty piece of work, isn't it?" Riordan said, yellow eyes watching it carefully. "Smells as bad as it looks."

Michelle sniffed. It smelt like rancid, acidic urine. "As long as it doesn't come any closer, I'll be good."

"Yup," Riordan said. She grimaced.

"What's up?" Michelle asked.

"Roth. She's on alert. I really *don't* like the way that feels."

"Yeah. Jackie's still calling me and Monk is . . . *ow*." Michelle clutched her head, trying to fight off the sick bolt of horror and pain from Monk. Suddenly Monk went quiet and Michelle grimaced, frantically feeling for Monk in the bond. The waves of pain crashed over her, and then faded and Monk fell to another low level that meant she was probably unconscious, but alive. Jackie's alarm and dismay at the disturbance from Monk came through to her, strong and clear.

She was distantly aware of Riordan's arm around her, holding her up. She opened her eyes.

"What just happened, Michelle? You look horrible," Riordan said.

"Something awful just happened to Monk. Jackie felt it and she's still calling for me," Michelle said. She eyed Riordan, who was shifting from foot to foot and avoided her eyes. "You don't need to ask. She's still very much alive. They both are."

Riordan nodded. "Can you track either one of them by your bond?"

"Can you?"

Riordan shook her head. "No. Not like I used to. Now Roth's *feelings* are clearer to me. She's fine. I think Kilkenny is with her." She blushed.

"Roth is your lover isn't she?" Michelle said. She felt Monk and Jackie hurt and tried to push it back a little. *I want to go to both of them. We need each other.*

"Yep," Riordan said.

"And you've made moves on Kilkenny?"

Riordan blushed harder and bit her lip.

"Uh huh," Michelle said, smiling and feeling a spark of anger.

"It's not like that," Riordan said.

"So you're putting Roth and Kilkenny together to see if they have the same sparks the two of you do?"

Riordan winced. "We hardly planned it that way but Roth did want to know who Kilkenny is. She wanted to know who she was sharing me with."

"Hurt Kilkenny and I'll kill you."

"I hadn't planned on that either, but the warning is well received." Riordan's blush faded a little. "Can I ask you something?"

Michelle levered herself of the rock, pulling Riordan with her. They slogged their way through the jungle again.

"I know what you want to ask. No, Jackie, Monk, and I aren't a threesome," Michelle said.

"I thought you . . . the three of you are bonded?"

Michelle nodded. "We are but Jackie doesn't seem to want to make a bigger *us*. I think she's getting the flow of what's between Monk and me." An image of Jackie kissing Monk popped into Michelle's head. She wondered if that was Jackie's emotion or theirs.

"Why on earth did you agree to have a bond mate who wasn't intimate with you join in?"

"She didn't want to be by herself. She wasn't comfortable. For some reason she thinks she's not as strong as us mentally, and she felt vulnerable. We told her we would bond her so she wouldn't be alone. We intend to break it when she finds someone she wants to be intimate with." Michelle sighed. "I don't think she really thought it through when she asked for Monk's blood. We weren't cruel enough to leave her alone. We both like her a lot."

Riordan nodded and was silent for a moment.

The ground shook and Michelle grabbed Riordan for balance. "Sorry," she said.

Riordan waved away her apology. "Is Jackie still angry?"

"No, that seems to have passed. Now she's just embarrassed."

Riordan shook her head. "She *has* to be with Mack. Mack has a way of bringing things out of people that they'd rather keep hidden."

Michelle smiled, despite herself. "Poor Jackie."

"Not really. Mack is one of the bravest and gentlest people I've ever met. Jackie's safer with her than anyone else besides Roth."

"Jackie's not a coward but her strength doesn't really run in any ways that would help her in this world."

"I don't know. I think you'd be surprised," Riordan said with a grin. "She came with us, no questions asked. I think if she was backed into a corner she'd probably surprise you."

Michelle smiled. "I know. It's one of the reasons Monk and I both love her so much."

"Are you saying that you wouldn't mind if you guys and she—?"

"She's calling me again. Why? She has to know I can't just materialize by her side," Michelle said. *It all sounds so damn bizarre when you actually say it.*

"You know," Riordan said after a moment. "Just because *we* can't go to her, doesn't mean *she* can't come to *us*. She's a dream walker, after all. Her talents work whether or not she's in the dreamscape in her physical body."

Michelle called for her and half way through, staggered and clutched her head. Jackie was screaming in terror and denial. Michelle fell to her knees, clutching her head.

Riordan was by her side in an instant, an arm around her back, helping her to stand.

"What happened?" asked Riordan.

"Jackie," Michelle said. "Something bad just happened to her."

"Call her again," Riordan said.

Michelle did.

CHAPTER 9

"I REALLY DON'T like the look of this," Jackie said, glancing up at the sky.

"Neither do I," Moriarty said.

The clouds had darkened and the marshland was covered in by eerie yellowish light. The wind picked up in a terrible stentorian howling that set her teeth on edge. Lightning flashed and thunder roared.

The station's a hell of a lot further away than I thought. But at least we're on flat ground we can run on.

Jackie tripped over a sleeper and Moriarty absently caught her.

"Thanks," Jackie said. "Can you make out what that . . . thing . . . over there is? I can't see it." Her eyes shone yellow and she squinted into the distance.

Moriarty shifted her own vision.

"It's definitely bigger," she said. "Weird. It seems to be going up and down. Well, kind of."

Jackie's clothes whipped around her body. "What does that mean?"

"Are you sure you want to know?" Moriarty asked.

"*Yes*, I want to know."

"It's something that lives under the water and it's going up and down. Oh *shit*!"

A dark rope looking thing flew away from the mound, heading straight toward them.

"RUN," screamed Moriarty screamed, grabbing Jackie by the sleeve.

A funnel cloud formed beneath the roiling clouds, a small distance away from them. Thunder crashed so loudly Moriarty's ears rang.

An immense tentacle shot toward them at high speed and the mound grew in size.

Christ. Look at the suckers on that fucking thing.

She outpaced Jackie.

"Mack," Jackie yelled, and Moriarty glanced over her shoulder. Jackie was behind her and leaning into the howling wind. Moriarty cursed and headed back toward her.

The tip of the tentacle flew toward them and crashed into the marsh beside the tracks. The concussion knocked Moriarty off balance and threw Jackie to the ground.

The funnel cloud headed toward the ground.

Moriarty caught her footing, tore toward Jackie, and pulled her up by her tee shirt. There was a purring sound as the seams ripped.

The tentacle withdrew a short distance, and two others joined it, waving above the marsh.

"Piggy back time. Climb aboard," Moriarty said, bending at the knees.

Jackie leapt onto Moriarty's back and Moriarty ran as fast as she could toward the train station.

"Light weight," she tossed over her shoulder with a grin.

"Gee, thanks," ground out Jackie through gritted teeth.

The funnel cloud touched down and instantly the world became a place of flying mud, grass, and sediment from the marsh.

Moriarty looked down at the ground, carefully following the tracks.

"Where's the fucking octopus?" Jackie yelled in her ear.

Moriarty glanced sideways and saw a gigantic body appear above the surface of the water. Its tentacles flailed and gigantic blots of slime joined the debris already kicked up by the tornado.

Moriarty ran as fast as she could but she could feel herself losing forward momentum. She leaned far into the wind so she was almost parallel to the ground.

A tentacle smashed into the earth before them, knocking Moriarty's feet straight out from under her. She fell to the ground and a shower of gravel rained all over them.

The tentacle withdrew and Moriarty stared at it, wide eyed. *Christ, the suckers on that thing are bigger than I am.* She glanced around, looking for Jackie and saw her in the ditch left by the tentacle.

She cursed and ran toward her, finding it harder and harder to move into the wind. She skittered down the crater. Jackie groaned. There was a wash of blood on the side of her face from a gash to her temple.

She groaned and sat up, dazed.

The howling wind seemed worse in the crater.

We have to get out of here, Moriarty thought. *I don't like being down here where I can't see anything.*

She grabbed Jackie and threw her across her shoulders in a fireman's carry. She bolted up the slope one handed, grimly hanging onto Jackie, showers of loose dirt falling around her.

Jackie had rallied enough to clutch feebly at Moriarty, and Moriarty pulled them both over the lip of the crater. Jackie fell off her back and lay panting on the tracks.

Moriarty felt a distant vibration and quickly bent down to touch the twisted wreckage that marked the end of the train tracks.

"The train's coming," she yelled, but Jackie didn't seem to hear her. She slowly sat up, looking dazed.

The octopus thing roared in the distance and the sound overpowered the shrieking of the tornado hurtling toward them fast as lightning. Underneath that was the sound of the train whistle.

"We'd better run, then," Jackie said, barely audible over the rushing wind.

Jackie climbed onto her back and Moriarty pushed forward with all of her strength.

Suddenly concrete appeared and Moriarty realized they were running along the edge of the platform.

Now she could actually hear the train above the cacophonous sound of the tornado and the squid. She jumped up onto the platform and collapsed, chest heaving. Jackie lay next to her, also breathing hard.

"I'm glad the train station is still here," she said to Moriarty.

Moriarty nodded. "It shouldn't be."

"This is a dream," Jackie said. "It's not supposed to make sense."

Now the base of the tornado was almost on them and they shrank back into the station, wind howling around them. The concrete and glass covering creaked around them and the glass rattled in its frame.

"This should be getting torn apart," Moriarty said.

Jackie remained silent. She still looked a little unfocussed.

The train pulled into the station and the doors opened and beeped.

Moriarty grabbed Jackie and dove for the open doors. Jackie was lifted into the air as they reached the small gap between the train and the station's covering. Moriarty gritted her teeth and climbed aboard the train, but could not pull Jackie with her.

She leaned backward, holding onto Jackie's wrists.

"Let go," Jackie screamed. "You're tearing out my arms."

"We can still do this," Moriarty said. "Bend your arms toward me."

"Michelle's calling me. Let go," Jackie yelled.

The train doors began to close.

"Come on," Moriarty yelled. "Come on."

Jackie let go of her. Moriarty felt her slipping out of her grasp.

Let me go. I'll be all right, she mouthed.

Moriarty felt the sting of tears. The train doors were almost on her hands. She let go, and Jackie was torn up into the air. The doors slid shut with a pneumatic wheeze. Moriarty crawled to the door as the train moved, hands on the dull Perspex, looking up frantically for Jackie.

Jackie was a spec far above the ground and a tentacle whipped through the air nicking her. Jackie was knocked sideways and disappeared in a flash of light.

"Oh, god, Jackie," Moriarty whispered. "I'm so sorry."

She watched the world outside, the flying debris. As the train pulled away from the tornado, she was able to see the deep groove in the marshland that it left behind it. The squid thing, so massive it almost reached the clouds, whipped its tentacles through the roiling air, almost as though playing with the tornado.

Moriarty unwillingly tore her eyes away from the spectacle.

She sighed. *I guess it's time to find out who's driving the train.*

She levered herself to her feet. Every muscle in her body protested. The train gently rocked back and forth as it rounded sweepers, and she held onto the poles, working her way toward the connecting doors that led to the next carriage.

She quickly mounted the stairs, only enough so she could see feet. There were none. She went downstairs, jogged along the lower level, and mounted the stairs to get to the small section that had the carriage doors.

She continued on through the deserted train. The only carriage that had any signs of occupation was one with a troubling blood stain on the seats and traces of vomit on the floor.

Monk. This was her train.

She finally reached the front carriage and quickly jogged toward the driver's compartment. Her heart almost stopped at the sight that awaited her.

Terri sat slumped against the driver's door, a wide, drying pool of blood around her. Her shirt was stained dark with dried blood and Moriarty thought most of it must have come from her.

Moriarty knelt in the mess before her. Terri blurred, and Moriarty distantly realized she was crying. She reached out a shaking hand and touched Terri's face. It was cold. Moriarty saw a piece of paper sticking out of her front pocket. She grabbed it.

READ ME, the note said.

Moriarty unfolded the paper.

She took my blood. Wait for her to wake up.

Moriarty took a deep, shaky breath. *You're a smart girl, Monk. Very smart. I'm going to kiss you when we finally meet.*

"Come back to me, Terri," Moriarty whispered, sliding in behind her so Terri's body reclined comfortably in her arms.

"HEY, WHAT'S THAT?" Riordan asked, looking up at the sky.

"Huh?" Michelle asked, bumping into her back. "Sorry."

"I saw a flash of light," Riordan said. "There's something coming toward us."

Michelle looked up. A small figure tumbled out of the sky. "That's a person."

Riordan drew in a sharp breath. "Oh no. That's Jackie."

Michelle's heart beat hard. Riordan took a step forward and Michelle held out a restraining hand. Riordan gave her a questioning look.

"We have to know where she lands. We can't do anything for her. I'm hoping the trees break her fall."

Riordan winced. "I hope there's no wildlife in them."

Michelle glared at her.

Riordan held up her hands. "Peace, Michelle."

Michelle nodded.

Jackie crashed into the tree tops. They heard leaves rustle and shrieks and whistles from the birds and animals as she continued toward the ground.

Riordan's eyes flared yellow.

"Follow me," she said and ran, Michelle on her heels.

The ground shook, the hardest tremor yet. Michelle fell into Riordan and they were both knocked off their feet. Leaves rained around them and a branch fell, drawing a squawk from something in the undergrowth.

"Crap," Riordan said, standing and helping Michelle to her feet. "I want out of here. I don't like those mountains." She nodded behind them.

Michelle turned and looked. The mountains behind them had once been covered in snow but now it looked as though some of it had shaken off. They were now lumpy in places. The clouds above them roiled and looked as though they were getting larger. The sound of rushing water, which Michelle had gradually tuned out, became louder and choppier. She gritted her teeth against the troubling noise.

"I don't like that either but I don't think we have much chance of outrunning whatever's coming next."

"I think we both know that's a volcano."

"Yeah, no kidding. We've gotta find Jackie and get *out* of here."

Riordan nodded. "Let's go."

She pulled Michelle into motion again and they ran in the direction of the trees Jackie had fallen into.

"There," Riordan said, pointing at a broken branch.

Michelle wrinkled her nose. The tree it'd been attached to looked like a mutant fruit tree. The fruit was large, pinkish, and shiny. Maggot things oozed out of the stump and fell to the ground in wet splatters.

They jumped over the trees, barely managing to dodge the worms that shot toward them like flung rubber bands.

Michelle felt in the bond for Jackie. She seemed flat, and Michelle thought it meant she was unconscious. Jackie felt off to their right, so she headed in that direction, Riordan changing direction to run after her.

Michelle suddenly stopped, and Riordan crashed into the back of her.

"Fuck," Riordan breathed in Michelle's ear.

Michelle nodded.

Jackie lay spread eagle in the middle of a clearing, surrounded by birds that looked like vultures. *I don't think vultures are supposed to have beaks the size of toucans. And look at those claws.*

The birds lumbered around the clearing, sharp claws leaving divots in the dirt.

"You're a healer, right?" Riordan asked, eyeing them.

Michelle nodded.

"Good, because I think I'm going to need your services."

Riordan jumped forward before Michelle could stop her and kicked one of the birds out of the way. It stumbled sideways into another and they gave twin squawks of rage. They eyed each other for a second or so and then pecked each other, flapping wings and slashing with their claws. Blood flew.

Riordan barely dodged them but got to Jackie. The other birds watched her closely and moved forward. Riordan lashed out and grabbed the closest one by the neck and hurled it into a trio coming toward her.

The two combatants moved dangerously close to Riordan as the other three shook their heads and squawked in outrage at her.

She grabbed Jackie under the armpits and tugged her toward Michelle, crying out as one of the birds darted toward her with blinding speed and pulled a chunk of flesh out of her neck. She faltered for a moment and another of the birds moved in.

The ground shook with a vicious tremor. Riordan fell forward, covering Jackie. Jackie moaned softly and moved.

The birds flew off, squawking, flapping their wings. The rancid animal odor faded away.

Michelle knelt beside them.

Riordan's shirt was torn and covered in blood. She clutched her neck and winced. "That fucking hurt."

"It looked like it did," Michelle said, shifting her vision. Riordan became a column of sparks, some of which were bleeding away. Michelle touched her sparks, moving them back into position.

Her vision returned to normal.

Riordan was smiling at her. "Thank you."

Michelle smiled back. "No worries." She looked down at Jackie.

Jackie was a mess. Her clothes were torn and her face was covered in blood from a nasty cut to her head. She was covered in scratches from her fall down through the trees.

Michelle shifted her vision and moved her sparks so they were whole again.

She sat back, hands on her thighs, waiting to see what would happen.

Jackie's eyes opened up after a few seconds. "Michelle. You're incredibly beautiful." She gave her an adoring smile.

"Thank you," Michelle said, grinning and standing.

"And I think you're hot."

"Okay."

"And I'm crazy in love with you."

Michelle raised an eyebrow, but she knew Jackie was telling the truth. She could feel it in their bond.

"Love you too, Jackie," Michelle said, grinning and reaching down to help her up.

Jackie took the opportunity to grab onto Michelle in a bear hug and kiss her.

Oh, boy, Michelle thought fuzzily, and gave in to the kiss.

Riordan laughed.

When they finally finished Michelle kept her arms around Jackie, holding her close.

"Why now, Jackie?" she asked softly.

Jackie gave her a sappy smile, eyes unfocussed. "Mack said to. I like Mack."

Riordan laughed harder. "You got clocked pretty badly, didn't you, Jackie?"

Jackie ignored her.

Oh, boy, Michelle thought. *Jackie's . . . Monk's gonna . . . Mack* told *her to do it . . . Aww, shit.*

"Come on," Michelle said with a smile, sliding an arm around Jackie's shoulder.

Jackie leaned into her and hung on.

Michelle turned to look at Riordan, who was trying to suppress her giggles.

"Not one word, Rio," Michelle said. "Not one."

"Nope," Riordan said. "None."

An ominous rumbling began. It was gigantic, all encompassing, and terrifying.

Riordan and Michelle exchanged a glance.

"That's the volcano, isn't it?" Riordan asked.

"You betcha," Michelle said. "It's gonna blow."

The ground heaved from a series of immense explosions, and they were thrown into the air. Michelle landed on her back, Jackie in her arms. Riordan tumbled backward over a rock. The trees around them swayed and leaves rained down. The ground movement ceased after few seconds that felt like an eternity.

Michelle sat up. "Rio. Rio, where are you?" she called.

"I'm here," Riordan said and stood up.

The ground shook again, like a cosmic grandmother shaking a tablecloth, and Riordan was thrown up into the air.

This time the trees cracked and Michelle found herself dodging splinters. She cried out in pain as a splinter tore through her side and she felt the warm wash of blood. Jackie grabbed her by the shirt collar as a tree tore in two and crashed down over the last place they'd seen Riordan.

Oh, shit. "Rio," Michelle yelled, stumbling over to the tree, Jackie close behind her.

"There," Jackie said, pointing. "Oh my God."

Michelle followed the direction of her finger and saw one of Riordan's hiking boots. The torn laces flapped and Michelle's heart hammered. She quickly dived to the boot and looked frantically for Riordan.

She saw a torn jeans clad leg and felt cold.

"Oh, fuck." She glanced at Jackie, who still looked a little dazed but much more focused than she had.

Jackie nodded and they both clambered to the jeans.

Michelle felt her stomach roil.

A terrible, white knob of bone poked out of torn flesh and ragged jeans. Jackie was quickly and tidily sick.

Michelle looked around for Riordan's body. She shook when she saw a sliver of Riordan's torso under a branch.

She dived over to Riordan and saw her unblemished face and neck. She felt for a pulse. It was thready and almost gone.

"She's dead," Michelle said.

"She's a werewolf."

"Can you cut a hole and get us out of here?" Michelle said.

"Sure."

"Nope," a new voice said.

"Fuck," Michelle said, looking up. She found herself looking into Angela Michaels's cold yellow eyes.

"You bitch," Jackie snarled. Her eyes flared yellow. "You're right. I can't a cut a hole anywhere near to me, but I can cut one under you. You forgot the ground, you fucking idiot." A blaze of light appeared under Angela Michaels and before she could react she'd fallen in, screaming in rage.

The tear closed up behind her.

"Nice," Michelle said. "Can you do the same for us?"

Jackie's eyes blazed and the world was suddenly filled with red mist. It boiled around them for a moment and then exploded outward, flattening torn bushes and tree debris.

Michelle felt for Riordan's pulse again. It was almost gone.

"Now I can," Jackie said shortly. "But we could end up anywhere. I don't know this dream so I can't steer."

"Take us to Monk. No more hiding," Michelle said.

The air heated and there was a massive explosion. The ground heaved and the tree bounced off Riordan's body.

Michelle barely held onto her stomach contents. Most of Riordan's body had been crushed and terrible knobs of bone peeked through torn clothing and flesh.

"Shit," Jackie said.

Michelle felt in her bond for Monk, knowing Jackie could feel her too. Monk felt weak and flat.

They heard a hissing roar coming toward them, gaining in strength by the second.

"Now," Michelle said.

Suddenly she was flying through empty space into a terrible twilight, fog enshrouded world.

"RIO," ROTH MOANED, grabbing her head and falling to her knees. "Something terrible's happened to Rio."

Kilkenny quickly knelt beside Roth. She put her hand on Roth's back and Roth leant into her touch. She shifted her vision. Roth's sparks were a bright golden yellow but the silver sparks surrounding her were fading and winking out.

Oh, no. Kilkenny blinked away tears.

She focused on the silver sparks and poured her own streamer of golden sparks into the silver surrounding Roth. The silver sparks stabilized and gained in strength as they poured off of Roth. Kilkenny felt treacherously weak and shook.

She stopped her streamers and released her vision, only fuzzily aware that she was in Roth's arms, wet with Roth's tears.

"Thank you," Roth said, brushing a kiss across her forehead.

"You're welcome," Kilkenny said, digging into her reserves of energy. Her side ached. She sat up. "Do you know where Rio is?"

Roth closed her eyes for a moment. She nodded. "God help us, she's here. She's somewhere in the amusement park."

"Can you find her?"

"I can feel her and *we will* find her."

Kilkenny nodded. Roth's beautiful face was set into a mask of determination.

"Are those creatures gone?" Roth asked.

Kilkenny knelt, shaking, and peeked over the counter. They were inside a booth, a shooting gallery. Outside, searching through the other booths lining the sides of the path, were a strange, motley collection of creatures.

They were torsos melded together at the waists, which ended in ragged skin-covered stumps that should have been necks holding up heads. Both ends of the bodies had a pair of legs and arms, so when they moved they looked like insane humanoid slinkies. The dirty, bloody hands had restlessly moving fingers that grasped and squeezed everything they touched.

One of them approached their booth and was grabbing at the counter, feeling across the top.

Kilkenny ducked down beside Roth, pushing her back against the wall.

The guns clattered and screeched as the hand grabbed them, feeling them. It seized a gun and tore it from its stand. It bent the gun in half with two fingers and then hurled it across the way toward the other booth. It crashed through the rotten wood and fell to the ground with a clatter.

Roth and Kilkenny exchanged a glance.

They're very *strong*, Kilkenny mouthed.

Roth nodded.

Roth abruptly stood up, grabbed the hand, and pulled with all her might. It tore out of the socket with a wet, purring sound. Black blood spurted out of the wound, splashing her. She jumped over the counter.

The slinky thing contracted and reared up, seemingly in agony.

Roth grabbed a leg and pulled it toward the thing's spine and there was a sick crack as the bone broke and its hip was dislocated.

Bone peeked through the skin and the creature collapsed, thrashing.

Roth's foot came down square in the center of it, snapping its spine. It lay still.

The other creatures quivered and flipped with insane speed toward Roth. She was soon engulfed in a wall of blackened, stinking flesh.

Kilkenny dived over the counter, heart hammering. She tore at them, desperate to get to Roth. She grabbed and ripped every piece of suppurating flesh she could reach. Soon they both knelt in a pile of twisted remains, breathing hard.

Roth's head hung and she was pale.

"What's the matter?" Kilkenny asked. "Was that too much for you?"

Roth shook her head. "Normally, no. But my strength is being drained."

Kilkenny shifted her vision. Some of Roth's golden sparks were draining away into the distance through her bond.

"We have to get to Rio," Kilkenny said.

Roth nodded. "I know. I can feel it. She's in a lot of pain."

"Where is she?" Kilkenny said, helping Roth to her feet.

"Down that way," Roth said, nodding at the dark path before them.

"Why did it have to be there?" Kilkenny muttered, eyeing the gigantic roller coaster that seemed to mark the center of the amusement park.

"Because it's *always* the way it works. Haven't you noticed that?"

Kilkenny felt her face heat. She hadn't intended for Roth to hear her.

They walked and Roth nudged her. "Look at the bright side of things. At least we haven't been pulled into the ghost train."

It felt like the darkness was closing in on them and Kilkenny shrank into Roth. Roth glanced at her. "Is the darkness bothering you?"

Kilkenny unwillingly nodded.

Roth settled her arm around Kilkenny's shoulders. "Don't be frightened, Kilkenny."

"Easy for you to say," Kilkenny said.

Roth snorted a laugh. "You think I have an intimate acquaintance with amusement parks like this? You'd be wrong. I'm *much* nicer to my dates, thank you."

"And what *is* your ideal date, Miss Roth?"

Roth's yellow eyes shone with amusement. "A beautiful woman and an amusement park, nestled in the darkness."

Kilkenny laughed. It felt good. The shadows seemed to shrink away from them.

"How close are we to Rio?" Kilkenny asked after a few comfortably silent moments.

"We're getting close now," Roth said. "I'm surprised. I thought this park was much larger than that."

Kilkenny glanced off to one side and saw a ruined carousel. There was an elephant, a horse, a sea horse, and a dolphin amongst others. "It doesn't really matter how big it is. We're going in circles. The carousel? That's where we landed."

Roth stopped and stared at it. She frowned. "I hate to agree with you but I have to."

Kilkenny nodded. "Do you think you can still find Rio?"

Roth glanced at her. "Yes. I can. My bond is working even if the world has become a spinning compass."

"Okay, let's go and find them."

Roth pulled her into motion and they walked again. Kilkenny snuck a glance at her. Roth was terribly pale and looked on the point of collapse.

"Do you need a boost?" Kilkenny asked. Her side ached. It almost felt like she had a stitch but the pain was more relentless.

"Not the best of ideas, young one. You're looking a little pale."

"Well, so are you."

"Not yet, then. You should probably be saving your strength."

Kilkenny bit her lip. She thought about Riordan and nagging worry resurfaced. "Look. What good is strength if it can't be given freely to other people? I know how much you love Rio. It's my gift to both of you." She shifted her vision before Roth could answer and poured sparks into her.

The ache in her side flared, and she released her vision. Her knees felt rubbery and she clung to Roth for balance.

Roth straightened and practically carried Kilkenny.

"Roth, I think I'm . . ." Suddenly black flowers bloomed in her vision and her knees gave way.

MICHELLE KNELT OVER Riordan's body, moving her sparks so they were whole again. The sparks in her leg and ragged stump at her hip were the worst. They were almost completely dark.

"She looks good," Jackie said. "She's breathing and her pulse is a lot stronger than it was."

Michelle nodded, relieved. "Now it's her leg I'm worried about. It's not doing too well."

"Can you take anything from me?" Jackie asked. "Can I help?"

Michelle glanced up at her. They were in the middle of a fairground, and it felt like it was the middle of the night. The sky above was inky black, yet they could see. It was as though the light came from things within the fairground. She could see a suggestion of movement in the background.

"I think you're about to have your hands full," Michelle said. "I don't know what's coming toward us."

Jackie followed the direction of her gaze, her eyes flaring yellow. "What the hell is that? That looks like a bunch of robot things coming toward us."

"Keep an eye on them," Michelle said, shifting her vision. She saw the silver sparks gaining in strength all around Riordan, and her golden sparks brightened. "I've just got to finish this."

She eyed the silver sparks speculatively and extended a golden streamer toward them. They gravitated to her, so she grabbed them and pulled as hard as she could, pouring all of it into Riordan.

The golden sparks seemed to explode to life and moved and gained in brilliance. Her own sparks joined the flow before she could stop them and she grunted, forcing herself to pull them back.

She released her vision, falling backward onto the ground, clutching her aching head.

"Holy shit," Jackie said.

Michelle heard the alarm in her voice and looked up.

Five large, cylindrical robots were coming toward them, clattering noisily across the cracked asphalt. They had stumpy arms ending in sharp, dark looking claws. The claws came together with brisk, snapping sounds. Each of the robots had a cheerfully painted face, chipped and peeling in some places. They rolled purposefully toward them.

"We've gotta get out of here," Michelle said. "Can you feel Monk?"

Jackie hesitated a moment and shook her head.

Michelle felt inside and there was only Jackie. Monk was so flat it was almost as though she was background noise. She felt a bolt of worry about Monk and pushed it down. It would have to wait for later.

"I don't think she's dead, Mitch," Jackie said hesitantly.

"I want to find her," Michelle said. "I *have* to find her."

Suddenly the robots shrieked and moved toward them with blinding speed.

"Fuck," Michelle said.

"Yep," Jackie said, bracing herself.

CHAPTER 10

WHEN MONK OPENED her eyes, she saw a canopy of solid black over her head. She thought she was finally dead.

I shouldn't be in this much pain if I was dead, should I? She grimaced as she tried to move her arm.

"Yuck," she muttered, pulling her hand out from under one of the decapitated dog things that had attacked her on the highway.

She slowly sat up, her head pounding. She felt abominably weak and sick. She looked down at herself. She could see that her once clean white tee shirt was soaked in blood, her jeans were ruined, and her joggers were coming apart at the seams.

I feel like ten tons of shit. She fought a rise of nausea. Her entire side felt as though it was on fire and she pulled up her shirt. A chunk of flesh was gone and she was bleeding heavily. She was covered in scratches and deep gouges on her stomach. Her neck pulled when she turned it experimentally. She put her hand to her neck, hissing in pain at the stinging sensation.

She stumbled to her feet, swaying unsteadily and forcing back the black flowers blooming in her vision.

She pulled off her tee shirt and pulled the ragged remains in to a long strip and wound it around her damaged body. The pain increased and she gritted her teeth.

I've gotta find Michelle or Kilkenny. I need help to heal from this.

She forced herself to take an experimental step forward. Her legs felt rubbery but willing to support her. She pushed a little harder and broke into a shambling run. Her knees gave way and she fell. The pain in her side exploded as her skin tore. She screamed.

She lay on the ground, tears of pain streaming from her eyes. *Oh fuck. I have to get up. I have to keep going.*

She pulled herself to her feet, gritting her teeth and hissing in pain as she did. She walked as fast as she could. *Wonder when Michaels is going to come back?*

She walked past booths and wrecked carnival rides. Horrible things crawled in the dark, dragging across the asphalt. *I don't give a fuck at this point in time.*

She ran with a sick, drunken gait that tore at her side and made her want to vomit with the pain of it. She forced her gorge down and pushed as hard as she could. As she rounded a decaying game of Test Your Strength, sound came to her on the cold night air.

She stopped and tried to control her breathing so she could hear.

It sounded like something being dragged across the asphalt, interspersed with clattering and high, electronic shrieks of rage.

What the fuck? She forced her abused body into motion and shambling toward the sound.

It became louder, and as she rounded a final sweeper, she stared in shock.

Oh, Christ. Is that Jackie? And hell, that's Mitch.

They bracketed a prone figure, and looked to be taking on five robot things. The robot's arms lashed out and slapped at them, causing both to stumble. She saw blue sparks coming from the claws. The acrid stench of ozone filled the air as one of them lashed out at Michelle and hit the next robot instead. There was a bolt of lightning and the second robot was thrown back several meters.

Jackie yelped as a robot touched her, and the sound spurred Monk forward.

She ran toward them as fast as her damaged body allowed and breathed a war cry, simply too tired to try for more.

She hit the first robot with her shoulder. She screamed and collapsed, clutching her side as she felt something deep inside tear. She grayed out.

"Down, Jackie," Michelle called in the distant twilight. "They're overloading."

Monk lay down, tired and relaxed. She felt like sleeping.

There was a tremendous explosion and heat baked Monk for a few seconds. *Michelle. Jackie.*

Suddenly she felt a warm body skid to the ground beside her, and she yelped as her head was pulled onto a soft surface.

She opened her eyes and looked up into Michelle's beautiful face. Michelle knelt beside her, brushing her hair off her face.

"Hi, Mitch," she said softly.

"Monk?" Michelle asked. Her green eyes blazed with pain.

"How'd you get so dirty?" Monk asked, clumsily reaching up for her.

Michelle pulled her hand against her cheek.

"Long story," Michelle said. "What happened to you?"

"Long story," Monk whispered. "I'm tired. I love you."

"Love you too, Monk," Michelle said, brushing a kiss onto Monk's forehead.

"Where is everyone?" Monk asked.

"We don't know where Roth or Kilkenny are. Don't know about Mack either. Riordan's here with us."

The surface Monk's head was resting on shifted, and she found herself looking into Jackie's inverted face.

"How badly are you hurt, Monk?"

"Bad enough to be lying flat on my back when I should be running like hell." She glanced at Michelle's stricken features. "Angela Michaels is here and she's chasing me in the dreamscape. I need you to heal me, Michelle."

"I can do that," Michelle said.

"Take it from me," Jackie said. "Take it all. I don't care."

"It won't come to that," Michelle said, and her eyes flared yellow. She put her hands on Monk's body and Monk felt warmth and a deep seated itch in her wounds. The terrible agony in her side shut down and receded.

Michelle's eyes faded back to their normal green. She had gone pale. Monk sat up, feeling mercifully whole and exhausted, and pulled the equally exhausted Michelle into her arms.

"God, it's so good to see you," Monk said, kissing her hair. She glanced at Jackie. Jackie had an odd expression on her face that Monk hadn't seen before.

Michelle's arms tightened around her. "I thought I'd lost you. I couldn't feel you."

Monk reached for Jackie and Jackie was there in her other arm, squeezing her for all she was worth.

"I don't know why. I've spent most of my time here running from Angela Michaels and haven't had much time for anything else," Monk said. "Michaels is still a psycho bitch, by the way."

"We noticed," Jackie said. "She dismembered Rio. We just finished putting her back together again."

"Fuck." Monk winced. "I don't want to run anymore. I want to stay with you. If you've already run into Michaels she's going to be tracking you as well. It's safer if we stick together. But we have to keep moving and keep her busy."

"Okay," Michelle said. "I don't want to leave you either. Where do you want to go?"

Monk thought about the flamethrowers in the city and grimaced. “We may as well walk around here for a while. This looks dark and creepy but not quite as bad as some of the other worlds I’ve seen.” She sighed. “I found a lovely coastal town that had the biggest tidal wave I’ve ever seen crashing over it. Sydney has an armed sailing ship sitting in the harbor.”

“The marsh and the jungle both sucked,” Jackie said.

Michelle pulled them both to their feet. “I’m going to get Rio.” She quickly jogged to the prone figure of Rio.

Monk made a move to follow her, but Jackie pulled her to a halt, the odd look on her face again.

“What is it, Jackie?” Monk asked gently.

“I love you. I’m *in* love with you. Michelle, too,” Jackie said.

“I know that, silly,” Monk said, gently cupping her dirty face with an equally filthy hand. “Both of us have known that for a while.”

She leaned forward, pulled Jackie into her arms, and kissed her. Jackie kissed her back and Monk moaned softly.

“Are you guys coming?” Michelle asked, breaking their reverie. Monk glanced at her and saw the amusement and relief in her eyes. Rio was slung across her shoulders in a fireman’s carry.

“Yep, we’re coming,” Monk said, taking Jackie’s hand and pulling her into motion.

They jogged off down a darkened path lined by broken lights.

MORIARTY SAT ON the train, watching the worlds go by. They’d been through them more than once and it was fading into a blur for her. The train stopped at every station and every time she half expected to hear the sound of running footsteps toward the front of the train.

The worlds themselves were horrible.

First, there was the normal train trip from Autumn Park into the center of the Central Station. Its course deviated from what she remembered from the physical world. It went senselessly through the middle of the city and over the Harbour Bridge. She’d made the mistake of looking into Sydney Harbor and had seen a sailing ship that was about a kilometer long, its cannons the size of tunnels. They shot flames that leveled half the city.

A carnival world appeared. It was a dreadful blend of fog and darkness.

The next world after that was a coastal town. It was absolutely gorgeous, except for the massive tidal wave that reached from the depths of ocean to the clouds overhead. The wave had crashed over the town, destroying everything in its wake. Yet when they passed the town again, it was whole and untouched.

After that was the marshland she and Jackie had been caught in. Sometimes it was peaceful, sometimes a gargantuan octopus played with the clouds and with a terrifyingly large tornado.

After that was a jungle rainforest surrounding immense volcanoes that periodically erupted, turning the streams into causeways of molten rock and fodder for a massive blaze that baked the inside of the train with heat. It eventually petered out, Autumn Park appeared, and the train headed back into the city.

Will Terri really wake up? She combed Terri's inky hair off her forehead. *Will she be glad to see me?*

The train rolled into the marshland station, slowed, and stopped. The train doors beeped and closed and the train gathered speed. She heard a soft moan from her lap.

Oh my god, it's true. She her heart rate picked up.

"Oh, wow," Terri mumbled. "I feel a hell of a lot better now. Monk?"

Terri pulled forward out of her grasp and swiveled around. Her eyes widened when she saw Moriarty.

"Holy shit, I'm dead. It didn't work," Terri said, reaching out a trembling hand to touch Moriarty.

Moriarty grinned, despite herself. "No, lover, you're very much alive. It's me, Mack Moriarty."

Terri knelt before her, seemingly unaware of all the blood on the floor around them.

"Is it really you, Mack?" Terri said in a small voice, her eyes brimming with tears.

"Hell, yes," Moriarty said, meeting her halfway and they fell into each other's embrace, squeezing hard. Moriarty's neck became wet with Terri's tears. She held Terri as the sobs of repressed pain and grief tore through her. She felt the sting of her own tears.

"I should be really pissed at you," Terri said, pulling back, sniffing and pawing away her tears. "You dumped me."

Moriarty shook her head. "No, I never dumped you. Don't *ever* think that. I *had* to go away." She cupped Terri's beautiful face and Terri leaned into her. "I loved you. I still do. I'm crazy *for* and *about* you."

Terri sighed, lips curving into a smile. "I love you too, Mack. So much. I never found anyone else I wanted to be with as much as you."

"Neither did I," Moriarty said. "I came back to throw myself at your mercy."

Terri gave a shaky laugh. "If you loved me that much why didn't you come back to me before now? Why?"

"That last fight we had . . . all it did was prove to me that you needed some time to explore the world with other humans, and without a lover by your side. You had to be single. It was the right decision and I've regretted it every second since I made it. I thought you had a crush on me. I thought that's why you let me go so easily. I came back because I was going crazy. I *had* to tell you something."

Terri was silent a moment. "Are you back for keeps?"

"Yes."

"God, Mack, I love you so much," Terri said, crawling into her lap. She leaned forward and claimed her lips.

The kiss felt like it lasted forever. When they finally broke, Moriarty's body throbbed. It was like a millstone had been lifted from her.

"I love you too. Do you want to know what I wanted to tell you?"

Terri nodded.

"I'm sorry for hurting you. It was foolish and stupid of me. I love you, Terri, more than you'll ever know. Hellstrom means nothing to me, she never did. I'm not interested in her. I'm *only* interested in you."

"I want there to be an *us* after all of this is over," Terri said.

"There's one now and every day of your life if that's what you want," Moriarty said.

Terri's arms crept around her again and this time her tears were tears of joy.

"I have to ask you, Mack, how did you come to be *here* in this nightmare?"

"I came in with Roth. I came to find Monk and to help get rid of Hellstrom. She's not their problem. She's *my* problem." Moriarty bit her lip. "*I* was the one who made her."

Terri's face became a mask of dismay. "How did *that* happen, Mack?"

Moriarty told her what Roth had told the others. She'd lost her senses and killed Hellstrom.

"Oh, fuck," Terri muttered.

"Okay, now your turn. How did you come to be here?"

"Monk called me. Angela Michaels was trying to put a controlling bond on her. She had a choice. Call me for herself or call me for Michaels. She called me for herself. And she made me a werewolf because she knew I'd never survive as a human."

"Smart move. I really want to meet Monk."

"You will, lover. You will." She toyed with Moriarty's dirty tee shirt. "What the hell happened to you?"

"The marsh world. Long story. I'll tell you all about it later." She smiled, feeling almost drunk with happiness. It warred with her worry and tension. "We'd better get off the train."

Terri kissed her and slowly pulled back, and climbed off Moriarty. "Yep. I'm done with Hellstrom and Michaels both."

"Who?" Moriarty asked.

"Angela Michaels. Wells made her and Monk both. We didn't know Michaels was a werewolf until she showed up with Hellstrom." Terri held out her hand and Moriarty took it with a grin. Terri levered her to her feet and kept a hold on her hand.

She looked out the window.

"Great. Right back at the beginning," Terri said with a sigh as Autumn Park slid back into view. The train slowed.

Moriarty pulled Terri toward the doors and they got off. They left the station and walked down the road, past deserted shops.

"Do you have a plan?" Moriarty asked.

Terri shook her head. "I could call Hellstrom."

"We're all here in our physical forms," Moriarty said. "If she's here the same way, then she's going to have to get to us by some arcane means. If she's with Michaels, she can just pop in with her. If she's in her dreaming form she can whip around like a ghost."

"How do you know which form she's in?" Terri asked, glancing at her.

"You're a dream walker. You might be able to tell, since this is your domain." Moriarty smiled. "Why don't you try shifting and tell me what you see?"

Terri's stormy gray eyes faded to brilliant, bile yellow. She eyed Moriarty carefully, looked down at her hands, and then turned to look at all the deserted buildings surrounding them.

"Well," she said, her eyes returning to gray. "We're both covered in golden auras, with a little silver mixed in. The buildings and everything else is what you see, but it all looks like it has red auras over it."

"We're both shape shifters. I'm assuming that's why you'd see us as gold. Red probably means constructs. Wonder if that applies to people? Would you see red auras if the person was in here as a dreamer?"

"I don't have any answers. I don't know," Terri said. "Okay, so we have a couple of choices. We can take our chances and call her or we can try to find the others and see how they look, then call Hellstrom."

"They've been through enough," Moriarty said. "Hellstrom is *my* fault and *my* problem."

Terri nodded. "I'll call her." Her eyes flared yellow and she closed them.

Moriarty watched the streets carefully.

She saw a flash of light in the distance and turned to follow it. A tear opened and a figure ran through it.

"*TERRI,*" Hellstrom screamed, running toward them. "AND YOU BROUGHT ME A *PRESENT*."

"Bitch," Terri muttered.

Moriarty nodded and rolled her eyes.

Hellstrom was almost on them, and Moriarty shifted her weight to the balls of her feet, ready to spring into action. The world swam into sharp focus as she shifted her vision.

Hellstrom skidded to a halt before them, eyes burning yellow.

"You fucking killed me," Hellstrom said.

"Because you fed me fucking LSD," Moriarty said.

"I loved you," Hellstrom said. "I was crazy in love with you."

"I *never* felt that way about you," Moriarty said, feeling revolted. "You were obsessed with me, you freak. You *spied* on us when we were together. I *hated* you at that moment and it hasn't changed for me."

"You mean *together,* together?" Terri asked. Moriarty snuck a glance at her and her face was set in a mask of humiliation and revulsion.

"Yeah, that way," Moriarty said. She turned back to Hellstrom. "You *violated* us."

"I couldn't help it," Hellstrom whispered. "I loved you. I *wanted* you."

"I was never yours, Ingrid," Moriarty said quietly. "I belong to Terri. I always did."

"Why did you steal her from me, Terri?" Hellstrom asked plaintively.

"I *didn't* steal her from you," Terri said. "I was *never* aiming for her. I *liked* her for God's sake. She was my *friend.*"

"Nobody stole me from anyone," Moriarty said. "I chose Terri. And if you hadn't butted in we'd have been married by now."

She felt Terri's wide eyes on her.

"Let her go," Moriarty said. "You lost."

"If it wasn't for you, Terri, she'd have been mine. You flashed your tits, didn't you? Let her see your legs and your cunt? You betrayed me when you started fucking her under my nose. You were busy laughing at me, weren't you?"

"No," Terri said. "I couldn't tell you either. You really *were* obsessed with her. You drooled over here *every* time I was around. I didn't want to hurt you and I didn't know what to do."

"So you made a fool of me instead?" Hellstrom snarled.

"No," Moriarty said coldly. "You made a fool of yourself. Anyone with half a brain would have realized that they weren't going to get anywhere with me, long before they confronted me."

She stared at Hellstrom. Hellstrom looked as though she'd been kicked. Hellstrom's eyes flickered between Terri and Moriarty. Tears made slow tracks down her face. Her hands flapped helplessly by her sides.

Moriarty watched her carefully. Hellstrom kept twitching as though she wanted to leap on Terri. She suddenly grabbed for the waistband of her jeans and pulled out a serrated hunting knife, surging forward with it and sinking it into Terri's unprotected stomach.

Terri cried out and clutched at the handle sticking out of her.

Hellstrom threw herself backward and disappeared out of the dreamscape in a blaze of light.

"Oh, Christ," Moriarty said, diving for Terri.

Terri fell to her knees and grabbed the hilt with a shaking hand. She yelped as she fell back and into Moriarty's embrace.

"It wasn't silver," Terri said, holding it out for Moriarty to look. "It's just a regular knife." Blood flew from her lips.

Moriarty tightened her arms around her, and she shook with relief. She managed a crooked grin. "You'll heal. If you bond me you can use my strength to heal." She shook as the adrenaline raced through her system. There was a lot of blood staining Terri's already filthy clothes. *I think Hellstrom nicked an artery.*

Terri reached a clumsy hand to her face. "I love you, Mack. I don't want to leave you."

"Shift," Moriarty said. "Bond with me."

"Yeah," Terri breathed, her eyes lightening toward yellow as they fluttered closed. She went limp in Moriarty's arms.

Moriarty looked down at her, saw every line of her beautiful face, memorizing it. She saw a silver string coming off Terri's head and pushed her own toward it. She felt a rushing sensation as she poured into Terri. Terri rose to meet her, overcome her, and she felt Terri rushing into her.

"Take it, Terri, take it all from me," Moriarty said, her vision shifting back and blurring with tears. She forced them back. *No time for that now.*

She pushed herself into Terri as hard as she could, pouring as much energy as their bond could stand into Terri. She lifted Terri's tee shirt and watched the skin slowly knit together until it was unblemished. She pushed still more through.

"Come on, love, wake up," she whispered.

As if on cue, Terri's eyes opened. She focused on Moriarty and smiled. "I can feel you."

Moriarty nodded. "I know where you are. I'll never lose you again."

"Never," Terri said, slowly disentangling herself from Moriarty and standing. She held out her hand and helped Moriarty to her feet.

"We have to find the others," Moriarty said. "Hellstrom's loose in the physical world. She came in here as a dreamer. Michaels may be in here the same way." She eyed Terri. "It would be quicker if we split up. I'll take care of Hellstrom and you take care of Michaels."

"Oh no, no way," Terri said, shaking her head. "No way in hell am I *ever* going to let you go and take on Hellstrom by yourself."

"Terri," Moriarty said gently.

"*No*," Terri said. "I know what it feels like to make a life without you and I'm *not* doing it again. If we go, we go *together*."

"All right," Moriarty said. She kissed Terri. "We learn to fight together."

Terri pulled her in close and kissed her again, a long, slow, gentle exploration with a promise of more to come. When they broke, Moriarty sank back into her embrace, pressing her face against Terri's neck, enjoying the feel of Terri's long, strong body pressed against the length of hers.

Terri gently stroked her back.

When they finally separated, they kept their hands loosely linked.

"Where do you want to start?" Terri asked.

"Unless one of them calls to you, we're stuck with searching for them by normal means," Moriarty said.

"Walk around and shout their names?"

"Pretty much."

"Shit."

"Pretty much."

"Is that all you have to say?" Terri asked.

"Pretty much," Moriarty said with a grin.

"Ugh," Terri said, lips twitching with a grin. She tilted her head to one side and studied Moriarty. "There's another way we can do this. We could just get on the train and get off at every station."

Moriarty grinned back. "That might work."

"Come on, then," Terri said. "We have a train to catch."

She pulled Moriarty into motion and they ran toward the train station.

"OH, FOR THE love of Christ," Monk said. "We're back at this stupid, fucking carousel."

Riordan leant forward with her hands on her knees. "Roth is here somewhere. I can feel it."

Monk watched the auras bleed all around them. She frowned.

"What is it?" Michelle asked softly from beside her.

Monk glanced at her. "The geometry of this place is wrong. It's a lot like a like a Venus Fly Trap. Once you come to a certain point, you end up in like a gigantic glass. You think you're walking straight ahead but you're really walking in a circle around the perimeter. If you want to leave it, you have to go out like it's a labyrinth. To go straight ahead you have to keep turning right."

"You can lead us out of here, though, right?" Michelle asked.

"I think so," Monk said.

She turned to look at Jackie bending over beside Rio, a concerned hand on her back. She shook her head and glanced at Michelle.

"Spill," she said. "What happened with you and Jackie?"

Michelle flushed. "I think I might have pushed her over the edge." She told Monk about Jackie's arrival in the jungle and Monk laughed.

"You're not angry?" Michelle asked hesitantly.

"No," Monk said. "No. I've had a long time to think about it, Michelle. I bonded Jackie because she was afraid. Once you joined, I found out how she *really* feels and thinks on the inside. She's so easy to love. I love you and I want you to be happy. I know you love Jackie. I can feel it in our bond. Not once since I realized that have I *ever* felt that you love me less. I can share your love, Michelle."

Michelle kissed her. "Thank you, Monk."

Monk smiled. "I love you, Michelle. I always will."

"I love you too, Monk."

"Guys," Jackie said.

Monk turned. Riordan and Jackie were both looking at them.

"Shift your vision," Jackie said. "Mitch, can you follow Rio's bond?"

Michelle's eyes faded to yellow. She studied Riordan for a moment. She nodded. "I think so."

Monk studied the aura over Riordan's head. "What does it look like to you?"

"Like a silver streamer. It fades as it goes into the distance."

"I'm looking at a silver aura," Monk said slowly, studying the bleeding colors. "Everything else is surrounded by red auras. They're the constructs. We're the only things here that don't have auras."

"What's a dreamer look like?" Michelle asked, looking up and walking past the carousel and down toward the carnival rides.

"A person with a red aura. Well, maybe more crimson than red."

"Did you ever get to look at Hellstrom or Michaels?" Michelle asked, turning left past a rotting Caterpillar. To their right was the entrance to the rotor.

"Kind of. They were a sickly orange color. I wasn't really paying attention. I was too busy trying to stop Michaels from bonding me." She looked at Michelle uneasily. "I don't know why she hasn't tried to find me here."

"Yeah, I don't like that either," Michelle said. "There." She pointed toward the Teacups. "I think it ends there."

Riordan broke into a run and jumped onto the platform. She searched the teacups. "Roth," she called, sounding ragged.

Jackie, Monk, and Michelle searched the other teacups.

Monk peered over the edge of a cracked teacup and saw Roth and Kilkenny, both unconscious, curled together on the bottom.

"Here," she said. Michelle, Jackie, and Riordan were by her side in an instant.

Riordan jumped over the lip and landed lightly beside them both.

"Just unconscious," she said, breathing ragged. She slumped on the floor next to them. "Just unconscious."

"Okay, let's get them out of here," Monk said, climbing over the rim and landing softly next to Riordan.

Suddenly the bottom of the teacup collapsed and Monk found herself falling through space at a gut wrenching pace.

"Shit," Riordan screamed as they landed heavily on a concrete walkway.

Monk lay flat on her back, stunned. Her body screamed at her. "Oh," she moaned, looking up at the ceiling of the Teacups, far above them. She shifted her vision and saw Michelle and Jackie peering over the edge.

"Monk! Rio!" Jackie yelled. "Are you all right?"

Monk looked around. Roth and Kilkenny lay on the ground, beside them. Kilkenny looked as though she was stirring. Roth was starting to sit up, slumping against Riordan, who was breathing hard and wincing.

"I think we're all right," Monk called. "*Mitch. Look out.*"

Monk saw another aura behind Jackie and Michelle. Angela Michaels gave her a cheeky grin.

Michelle twisted and grabbed Jackie. Suddenly they were gone.

Monk's heart hammered and she closed her eyes, frantically feeling for Jackie and Michelle. Monk felt Jackie's shock—she almost felt winded—and Michelle's consternation. They were both very much alive.

"Holy mother of God," she muttered, breathing a sigh of relief.

Kilkenny was sitting up and looked pale, studiously avoiding looking at Riordan and Roth. Monk glanced at them and quickly looked away, unwilling to intrude on their gentle reunion.

Monk crawled over to her.

Kilkenny blinked at her and opened her mouth several times. Suddenly she was in Monk's arms, squeezing her for all she was worth. "It's so good to see you again, Monk," she whispered.

"Good to see you too, mate," Monk said softly. "I was worried about you."

"I'm good. How badly did they hurt you, Monk?" Kilkenny asked, pulling back.

"They tried hard but you know me, mate," Monk said and Kilkenny grinned. Monk's return grin fell away. "We're dealing with Hellstrom and Angela Michaels. Remember her?"

"Oh, no." Kilkenny looked sick. "I'm afraid so."

"She spent her time trying to put a controlling bond on me," Monk said.

"Is it a red thing?"

"Yup," Monk said. "It hurt like crazy." She smiled without mirth. "That's not the worst of it. She also has a marker on me. I don't know how it works but she's using it to track me on the dreamscape. That's how she kept finding us—me—so quickly."

"I'm sure she's watching now," Kilkenny said.

"It doesn't matter," Monk said. "She has an orange aura. Gold for a shape shifter mixed with red. That probably means she's not in the dreamscape in her physical body. We can do what we like to her here and it's not going to matter."

"That's not fair," Kilkenny said.

"I know," Monk said. "How are you doing? What happened to you? You were out like a light when we found you."

"We? Who's *we*?"

"I was with Jackie, Michelle, and Riordan."

"What about Moriarty? And what'd you do with Terri? You pulled her in here, didn't you?"

Monk bit her lip. "I haven't met Moriarty. She's your English teacher, right? And a shape shifter?"

Kilkenny nodded.

"Cool. *Another* one." She sighed. "No, I haven't run into her in any of my travels."

"Pity. By the way, Moriarty's not like that. I like her," Kilkenny said.

Monk nodded. "Okay. As far as Terri goes, I pulled her in and told her what was going on. She asked to be brought in with her physical body. I did it. I turned her. I was trying to keep Hellstrom busy until she woke up."

Kilkenny grinned, and it did nothing for her pallor. "I thought so. Nice one, Monk."

"Well, at least she's got a fighting chance against Hellstrom."

Kilkenny nodded.

"You're Monk, aren't you?" Roth said, bending over them. She held out her hand.

"Yeah. You're—?" Monk asked, taking her hand.

"Roth," Roth said, pulling her to her feet. Monk was astonished by her sheer strength.

"I got it," Kilkenny said, reddening and rolling away from Riordan's outstretched hand. Riordan looked slightly hurt as Kilkenny moved past her to stand behind Monk.

"Let's get out of here," she said to Monk.

"Uh, okay," Monk said, surreptitiously eyeing all three. Roth and Riordan stared at Kilkenny who steadfastly refused to look at either one. "Toss a coin, ladies. Which way do you want to go?"

Kilkenny's eyes flared yellow. "This way is as good as any other," she said, and began walking, Monk close behind.

CHAPTER 11

"THIS PLACE SUCKS," Terri said, watching the train pull out of the station that called itself *Carnival World.*

Moriarty looked around, wrinkling her nose. "No kidding."

"Why did *this* one have to be first?"

"Because all of the others were being destroyed by natural disasters."

Fog curled around them, damp and unappealing.

"Wonder when the hounds are going to start baying?" Terri muttered.

Moriarty snorted a laugh. "Let's go."

The station opened straight out on the entrance of the park. A row of dilapidated booths, leaning drunkenly against each other, marked the boundary. Moriarty approached one and looked inside.

It was almost empty. There was a skeleton that slumped on the seat before a cash register so old Moriarty was sure it'd come from some time in the previous century. The skeleton was covered in places with mummified skin and the jaw was half unhinged.

"See anything green?" Terri asked from behind her.

"Not green," Moriarty said, steering her away. "Just funky."

Terri frowned at her. "Are you hiding something from me?"

"Just a skeleton. Nothing interesting. Seen one, you seen them all."

"Okay," Terri said. Her eyes flared yellow. "We have to be careful when we go in here. It's easy to get lost in there. The middle of the park looks like it's under a cake dome."

Moriarty nodded, shifting her vision. The darkness bled out of the world and she saw endless rows of booths and carnival rides, most in poor condition. A column of light shot up from the center of the park. She breathed deeply. It smelt of decay and rot, with an undertone of fresh meat.

"First, there's a column of light in the middle of the park. Second, I can smell hot meat. Living flesh if you prefer."

"Sounds like a promising start," Terri said, taking Moriarty's hand.

They walked down the pathway toward the center of the park.

Moriarty caught movement out of the corner of her eye. She turned to track it and saw things that looked like torsos that had been glued together at the waist. They stopped and quivered for a second, and then turned toward them.

"Terri," Moriarty said. "I think we should run."

The slinkies picked up speed and were starting to move quickly toward them with odd, wet, slapping sounds as their dirty hands hit the pavement.

"That sounds bad," Terri said.

"I know. Run," Moriarty said, pulling her into motion.

They bolted for the center of the amusement park and Moriarty felt a tingle as they passed the Rotor.

"We just ran under the dome," Terri said. "Stay close if you want to get out of here."

"You really don't need me to promise that," Moriarty said, haring toward the center of the park, Terri close behind her. She skidded to a halt and looked behind them.

"I think we're supposed to be here," she said.

Terri turned to follow her gaze.

Rows of slinkies stood quivering just beyond the Rotor.

Terri grimaced. "Good god, this place *really* sucks."

"All we can do is keep walking. I'm not sure what we're going to find in here, but I think the others really are here somewhere." She scented the air. "I can smell Roth. And Jackie."

Terri nodded.

Moriarty's nostrils flared as she tried to sort the scents from one another. She smelt drying blood over to the left, toward a teacup ride so old it looked ready to fall apart.

They went to the teacups, Moriarty's nose leading them to one particular one.

"Whoa," she said, raising her eyebrows.

"That's a long bloody drop," Terri said, looking down beside her.

"Surprise," Angela Michaels screamed straight into Terri's ear.

Terri jumped and bumped into Moriarty. The side of the teacup Moriarty was leaning on broke and she frantically scrabbled backward to keep her balance. Terri's hand was instantly under her elbow, pulling her back.

Angela Michaels swung from the ceiling, expression a frozen rictus of good cheer that made Moriarty shudder.

"It's a jack in the box," Terri said.

"What does it look like?"

Terri bent in close. "God, it looks life like." She turned to Moriarty. "It's covered in an orange aura. It looks almost completely real. Pimples, acne, grease, and all." She turned toward Moriarty. "Do you think we should—?"

"*SURPRISE,*" the Angela screamed in the box screamed. "*I* AM *REAL.*"

"Fuck," Moriarty said. She was suddenly given a vicious shove, and she took a step back into space. Terri dove for her, grabbing her wrist. Terri was torn backward, clinging grimly to Moriarty's wrist.

Moriarty twisted, grabbing Terri's wrist and clutching her arm with the other hand. They were torn backward, backs scraping on the cracked, ancient asphalt.

"*Shit,*" Terri screamed. They bounced up a set of stairs, through a doorway filled with raucous, soulless mechanical laughter. They did not stop in the entrance. They slid down a corridor and Terri's back shattered a mirror. Moriarty landed on top of her.

"That could have gone a little better," Moriarty said with a sigh, taking the opportunity to kiss the end of Terri's nose.

Terri grimaced. "I'd kiss you too, but I'm too uncomfortable. I think I have most of that mirror stuck in my back."

"Yikes," Moriarty said, instantly easing herself off Terri. She held out a hand. "Sit up. I'll pull it out."

Terri winced in pain as Moriarty pulled her up.

Moriarty knelt beside her and pulled up her torn and blood-stained tee shirt. She shifted her vision. "There's not much in there, thank god. You just look like you got shredded on the way here." She grinned at Terri. "You'll heal quickly." She bent to work on Terri and pulled out pieces of glass. Terri sat still, the only indication she felt anything in the stiffening of her body as Moriarty pulled out the deeper slivers.

Moriarty saw one piece of glass that was deeply embedded in her back.

"This is going to hurt," she said. "Take my hand. Squeeze as hard as you like."

Terri took her hand and intertwined their fingers. "I'm ready."

Moriarty nodded, grabbed the glass, and tugged it out of her back. Terri's fingers tightened and she moaned in pain.

"Done," Moriarty said. She held up a splinter that was easily six inches long. "That was stuck in your back."

"I felt it," Terri said.

Moriarty pulled her to her feet. "Can you call Jackie? Or Monk?"

"That's what I've been doing since I we got off the train," Terri said, frustration in her tone. "Either they can't hear me or they can't answer."

"Wonder if it's got something to do with the cake dome," Moriarty said. "Try again. They might be able to move inside here."

"Okay," Terri said. "It's worth a try." Her eyes flared yellow and she stayed still for a moment.

"Now we wait and see."

"TAKE *THAT* YOU *fucking, stupid clown*," Jackie snarled, tearing the head off a four foot clown that seemed intent on chewing on Michelle's neck. Jackie's face was set in a rictus of disgust as she tossed the gaily painted head down the darkened corridor behind them.

"Jackie," Michelle said, sitting up. "It's fine. Really."

"That stupid clown could have hurt you," Jackie said. "Badly." She held out a hand and levered Michelle easily to her feet.

"But it didn't," Michelle said easily. She smiled at Jackie. "You ripped it to pieces."

"I *hate* clowns," Jackie said. "Really *loathe* them."

Michelle looked up and down the corridor they were in, seeing herself and Jackie reflected back at them a thousand times. There was something about it that set her teeth on edge. It was as though the reflections watched them as soon as they turned away. The torn, stuffed clown lay beside them. It had followed them and finally attacked when they'd hit the hall of mirrors.

Jackie viciously kicked the remains of the clown and it tumbled down the hallway, shedding cotton stuffing.

"Hey," Michelle said, gently steering Jackie around so they could see each other. She cupped Jackie's face. "What's the matter?"

Jackie bit her lip. "I'm just scared, is all."

Michelle pulled Jackie into her arms, holding her close. "Relax," she said softly. "I'm right here with you."

"I know," Jackie said. "I just wish I wasn't such a chicken."

"You're not a chicken," Michelle said, smiling at her. "Courage isn't about *not* being afraid, it's about being able to move forward *despite* being afraid."

"Monk doesn't look like she ever gets to that point."

"Monk is a lion," Michelle said. "She's truly in a class of her own on that one. Don't compare yourself to Monk. You're very different people."

"You're more like Monk than I am," Jackie said.

"What is this *really* about, Jackie?" Michelle asked.

Jackie's eyes swam with unshed tears. "I'm so sorry, Michelle. I'm an emotional mess. I'm worried about Monk. I'm worried about *you.*"

Michelle studied her. Jackie was pale and could barely look at her.

"Hey, look at me," Michelle said. She gently lifted Jackie's chin and forced her to meet her eyes. "Relax, will you? I'm perfectly all right. So's Monk. We'll find her." She let her love for Jackie through to her in the bond. She leant forward and delicately captured Jackie's lips, tasting her. Jackie moaned softly and when they separated, looked a little dazed.

"Wow," she said.

"Exactly," Michelle said, smiling. "I love you too. We can talk about this later. We have other things to worry about right now."

Jackie nodded.

Michelle pulled Jackie into motion. "We have to keep moving. I want to find the exit to this shitty little anything but fun house."

Jackie nodded. "I hear you."

They continued to walk.

"Mitch?" Jackie said, shrinking into the back of Michelle.

Michelle stumbled slightly as Jackie bumped into her and clung to her.

"What's the matter?" Michelle asked and gasped as one of the reflections in front of her turned to stare at her. She struggled not to look away. There was no expression on its face and its eyes were soulless and dead. Yet something horrible, something terribly *aware* and alive lurked in their blank depths.

Michelle glanced over her shoulder at and beyond Jackie.

Shit. They're coming out of the mirrors. SHIT.

The figures varied in size from their true height, all the way down to centimeters tall. They shambled out and reached for them. Jackie's arms shot around Michelle's waist and tightened.

"Michelle," she said, raw panic in her tone. "They're *grabbing* me."

Michelle felt one set of cold hands grasping at her torn shirt. She slapped them away, but more came in their place.

She heard Jackie's yelp and the purr of tearing clothing.

Jackie's hands left her waist, fingers digging into her but losing purchase. She looked over her shoulder in time to see what looked like hundreds of copies of her and Jackie pulling the real Jackie toward the mirrors.

Fuck. It's an exponential curve of them.

She lunged for Jackie but missed by millimeters as hands closed around her shoulders and arms and pulled her back. She flexed her muscles and flung some of them off, but only long enough for more to take hold. A pair of hands grabbed her ankles, tugged hard, and pulled her off balance. She crashed down onto her back, and they swarmed her. She struggled and thrashed but it was useless. Hundreds of hands held her immobile and dragged her backward toward the mirrors.

She felt a tingle as she went through.

"Jackie," she yelled, calling for her through their bond as hard as she could.

She thought she felt a distant echo from Jackie, but she was alone in a cold and dark place.

KILKENNY WALKED ALONGSIDE Monk along the endless corridor they'd landed in. It was lit by flyspecked bulbs that barely cast any light. She tried not to look at Riordan and Roth, close together behind her. Their linked hands almost drove her insane. A slow, sick wave of jealousy broke over her at the thought of them touching each other. *Focus. Let it go. Can't do anything about it now.*

"This is a long bloody corridor, isn't it?" Monk asked, shaking her out of her reverie.

She glanced at Monk and saw how carefully her tattered friend was watching her.

"S'okay, Monk. But thanks." She studied Monk's bloody face. "What happened to you, Monk?"

Monk told her everything, up until they'd fallen through the teacup ride.

Kilkenny grinned at her. "That's good, Monk. It was a brilliant move."

"I meant to ask you," Monk said. "Who's Moriarty besides being your English teacher?"

"She's Roth's best friend," Kilkenny said. "And she's part of the reason we got into this mess." She took a deep breath and told Monk what Moriarty had told them, although it hurt her to do it.

"What a mess," Monk said, shaking her head. "Wonder where Moriarty is now?"

The pain in Kilkenny's side flared and she was quiet a moment, trying not to limp. "I have no idea. If she's very lucky she's with Terri."

"What the hell is that?" Monk said, eyes flaring yellow. She frowned and focused on something in the distance.

Kilkenny followed the direction of her gaze. "You've *got* to be *kidding* me."

"An *exit* sign?" they chorused.

Kilkenny glanced back at Roth and Riordan.

Riordan shrugged. "An exit sign. It doesn't have to make sense."

"Well?" Monk asked. "What do we think?"

Roth's eyes flared yellow. Kilkenny watched Riordan watching her, remembered the feel of Riordan's hands on her body. She stood close to Roth, studying Kilkenny. She looked like she wanted to say something. Kilkenny looked away. *How did I get myself into this mess? Why did I let it go as far as I did with Rio?*

"—go up," Roth was saying.

"Kilkenny?" Monk asked.

"I don't want to stay in a tunnel," Kilkenny said. "What I really want to do is get out of the dreamscape. Monk, can't you just cut a hole and get us off the dreamscape?"

Monk shook her head. "It's not that easy."

"Why? Why isn't it that easy?" Kilkenny asked, uncomfortably aware of a thick drop of blood oozing from of her cut.

"Ugh," Monk said. "How do I explain this? Okay. When you build a construct on the dreamscape, you just imagine it into being and it's there, right?"

Kilkenny nodded.

"But from my perspective, it's not just a simple matter of it suddenly appearing. It's like a cipher, built of colors and particles, encased in auras. It's the patterns and combinations of those things—colors and auras—that determine what the naked eye can see, right?"

"Maybe like the dots on a television screen?"

"Well, kind of but not really. On a television screen, the thing that makes the pictures is electrons exciting a charged surface and if you excite the surface in the right kinds of patterns, you can see pictures."

"Okay."

"In this case, I put together the dots and auras into patterns and you see something. You see what I want you to see. You do the same thing when you build on the dreamscape, but you can't see it to the same level I can."

"So far so good."

"Right, so if I wanted you to see something different to what was really there, how do you think I'd do it?"

"You could change the colors and dot combinations that people could see."

"Or you could make people *think* they'd changed. It's easy. All you do is push the auras around the dots off in different directions. The auras change so what you *see* changes but the basic structure of the original object remains intact."

"So you'd have to know where the auras are supposed to go if you wanted to make the object look like it's supposed to again?"

"Yep."

"Okay, so what happens when you cut a hole in the dreamscape?"

"You pick up two adjacent lines of dots and put them on top of each other so the spaces between the next pair of adjacent rows becomes a little larger. Then you pull the columns of dots apart."

"Which is why you see light when you cut a hole in the dreamscape," Kilkenny said. "The auras are all mixing together."

Monk nodded. "And when you *ward* the dreamscape, you're actually putting another series of rows and columns of dots on top of the first set so when you pull columns apart the second set fills the gap. You can feel when someone is trying to get in or out. There are flashes of light when they start to pull at the dots."

"So you can't just put two columns of dots on top of each other and tear through the spaces," Kilkenny said. "Because there *are* no spaces."

"Right," Monk said.

"But if you know how it works, why can't you slice through it?" Roth asked.

Monk glanced at her. "The concept of *locking*. You can set up the dots so that if another shape shifter grabs the dots and starts tugging on them, other dots all move together so you can't tear a hole. The auras give off a flash of light in that case as well but only I or another dream walker would be able to see that."

"Which functions as a beacon," Roth said, nodding. "You'd tell dream walkers where you were."

"Right," Monk said, nodding.

"So how does locking itself work?" Kilkenny asked. Her side ached from standing in one position so she shifted her stance a little. She balled her fists, trying not to clutch at her aching cut.

"You blend the auras together. So if I, for example, see a green aura on a wall, it's made up of two layers of dots that have blue and yellow auras. So I decouple the auras in combinations until one layer simply slides away from the other layer."

"Doesn't that take a long time?" Kilkenny asked.

"No, not really. To me this is perfectly natural. So I can kind of *feel* a lock. I usually don't have to think about the simple ones."

"And this one?"

Monk shook her head, eyes flaring yellow as she looked around. "Oh, this one's a total bitch. When I look around, I only see auras around constructs, not the dreamscape itself. It's locked up tight. Michaels did it so that the auras cancel each other out and there's no color at all. So when I dip into the layers of dots—and it looks like there are several real layers and a dummy layer or two—so I can't even make out *one* layer of dots. Every time the layers shift the auras compensate and cancel each other out. It doesn't look any different to me. I can't *see* the lock so I can't pick it. I can't find the key."

"So you can't crack the walls," Kilkenny said.

"Yep," Monk said.

"So if anything happens to Angela Michaels we're going to be stuck here."

"Maybe not."

Kilkenny's arm snuck into her side and it took all of her willpower not to flinch as pain lanced through her. She felt perspiration trickling down her back. "How so?" she asked, amazed at how even she sounded.

"Believe it or not, I just have to watch her when she leaves. If she's here in her body, she's going to have to physically open the lock. I can reproduce it and *we* can leave. Or, I can just remove the lock and warding so everyone can get in and out. If she's here as a dreamer and leaves, I can see the first color of the lock and I'll be able to work out the rest."

"So I suppose our plan is to find Angela Michaels, then?" Riordan said. "Otherwise we're going to be stuck here until she collapses the dreamscape."

"Yup," Monk said. "That's probably the smartest thing to do."

"One thing that's not making sense to me," Kilkenny said. "If you know all of this, why haven't you just pushed her *out* of the dreamscape? You'd have seen it and you could have unlocked it for the rest of us."

"Every time she's come to me it's been with Hellstrom. I've been too busy getting tossed around, or having my brain scraped out, to pay attention to anything other than staying alive," Monk said. "Michaels has been trying to put a controlling bond on me. You have no idea how much that hurts. I haven't exactly been in a position to be able to fight her on a level playing field." She shook her head. "She's *strong*. I don't know where it's coming from." She gestured toward the door. "None of this stuff matters just yet. We have to get out of here before we can do anything. We should also find the others. I'm worried about Michelle, Jackie, Terri, and Moriarty."

Roth nodded. "Let's go."

Monk nodded. "Me first. Kilkenny, you next. Then Rio and you, Roth."

She didn't wait for a response. She turned the door handle, opened the door, and stepped through it.

Kilkenny followed her in, almost glad of how dark it was. She leaned slightly to one side, despite herself. She felt blood dribbling out of the cut.

She felt the warmth from Riordan's body right behind hers and flinched. She was glad no one could see her face.

"Well, this wasn't really helpful, was it?" Monk asked.

"It's no problem," Roth said, her eyes flaring yellow.

The door closed behind them with a solid thud and they were lunged into pitch black.

Monk cursed. "I can barely see a fucking thing. I'm navigating by auras."

"It looks like we're in a large room," Riordan said slowly.

Kilkenny shifted her vision. Rio was right. They were in what looked like the auditorium at Sacred Heart College. She could easily see the columns of sparks that made up the others, but the rest was a field of dark gray, with suggestions of furniture lining the edges of the room.

"School auditorium," Roth said.

"Yeah," Riordan said. "My suggestion is that we just get the hell out of this room."

"You're going to have to lead us," Monk said. She held out a hand and a solid ball of light formed above it. She grinned. "That should help I hope. What the hell. Why not?"

"No problem, Monk," Riordan said.

Kilkenny could almost hear Riordan's grin.

Before she knew what was happening, someone took her hand and tucked it under their arm. "Roth," she whispered.

Roth gently squeezed her hand and remained silent.

Kilkenny pressed in close to her to avoid tripping as they moved forward. She felt cold in the warmth coming off Roth's body.

Monk's light helped a little but they could barely see where they were going so they had to move slowly.

It felt like they shuffled forward forever until finally there was a wash of dim light as Riordan pushed open the rear doors of the auditorium. They all moved out into a shadowed hallway.

"Thank God that's over with," Kilkenny muttered, shifting her vision. The world was still a mass of gray with barely visible red sparks in random places.

"We're still alone," she said. She turned to face Monk. "What now?"

"Let's get outside," Roth said quietly. "Find out if we're in another world or if we're in the amusement park."

Monk nodded. "Agreed." Her eyes flared yellow and she looked carefully around. "Still can't see any auras. What a pain in the arse."

Roth nodded. She turned to go up the hallway. Kilkenny watched Monk. Monk was standing and staring intently into the darkened auditorium.

"What?" Kilkenny asked, trying to follow the direction of Monk's gaze. When Monk looked like that there was always trouble.

"Nothing, I guess," Monk said slowly after a moment.

"Are you coming?" Riordan asked. Kilkenny glanced at her. She and Roth were further up the hallway and Roth's hand was poised on the next set of doors.

Roth studied Monk. "What is it?"

"I don't know," Monk said, shaking her head and taking a step up the corridor. "I thought I heard—*YIKES*—"

A pair of shadowed hands appeared on the floor of the open doorway. They grabbed Monk's ankles and pulled. Monk crashed over and slid into the darkened auditorium.

Kilkenny instantly rushed over to her, dropped heavily to her knees, and yelped as a bolt of pain shot up her body. She struggled not to fall over sideways. She grabbed Monk's hands and tried to brace herself and pull Monk backward.

Monk's face was a grim mask of determination as her hands slid out of Kilkenny's slick grasp. She slid into the shadows and grabbed both sides of the doorway. Her muscles bulged.

"*Monk*," Kilkenny screamed.

"They're too strong. I can't hold on," Monk screamed.

Kilkenny could only helplessly watch as Monk's grasp on the doorway faltered and finally gave out. She disappeared into the shadows.

A body leapt over Kilkenny and ran into the auditorium.

Kilkenny remained almost doubled over with pain, chest heaving with exertion. She felt like crying. A warm body knelt beside her and she felt a comforting hand on her back.

Roth reappeared in the doorway a moment later. "She's gone."

Kilkenny did cry then, and she felt herself pulled into a pair of strong arms. It was Riordan.

"We'll get her back, Kilkenny, I promise," she said.

Kilkenny sank into her embrace, despite her pain. She felt exhausted. She wondered what she was going to tell Michelle.

Roth knelt beside her. "We need to find another dream walker."

Kilkenny nodded. She called for Jackie.

CHAPTER 12

"JACKIE," MICHELLE SAID softly. "Are you there?" She listened carefully, blinking in the darkness. It was so black that her normal vision was completely useless.

She shifted her vision and scanned the area. She could see an unmoving column of golden sparks close to her. She slowly crawled over to it, half expecting to go tumbling through a trap door.

Her hand finally touched a shoulder.

"Jackie?" she asked softly.

"Oh, hell," Jackie moaned, rolling over. "What happened this time? Where the hell are we?"

"I don't know. I can't see a thing," Michelle said.

She felt Jackie sit up, and saw her yellow eyes. "I don't see anything," Jackie said after a moment of silence.

"Neither can I," Michelle said. "That's probably good. It means there are no living creatures near to us."

She felt in their bond for Monk. She felt calm and Michelle sent gentle reassurance to her.

"I'm getting called by someone," Jackie said, breaking her out of her reverie.

"Do you know who it is?"

"No clue," Jackie said.

"Do you want to go on blind faith?" Michelle asked. "Anything's gotta be better than stuck in this insane limbo."

Jackie snorted a laugh. "Okay, I'll cut a hole in the dreamscape for us. Hold on to me."

Michelle helped her to her feet and slipped her arms around Jackie's waist.

A flash of light appeared before them and they stepped through.

MORIARTY LEANED BACK against the wall, Terri in her arms.

"Are you sure you just want to sit here and wait to see if the others turn up?" she asked nibbling Terri's ear.

"Might as well," Terri said. "This is as good a place to wait as any. It's a better idea for us to stay put so they can find us more easily, provided Jackie or Monk are even listening." She settled herself with a sigh. "Besides, don't you want a break?"

Moriarty couldn't help herself. She smoothed Terri's hair away from her neck and planted gentle kisses on the line of her jaw. "Yeah, I'm not going to complain if we get one."

Terri shifted in her arms and kissed her.

"I love you," murmured Terri when they broke.

"I love you, too," Moriarty said, studying her perfect features. "God, you're so beautiful."

"So are you," Terri said. She smiled. "I'm amazed. I was devastated when you left. I felt guilty for so long. I thought I'd pushed you away because I was so jealous. I thought you'd gotten sick of me."

Moriarty shook her head. "Nope. Never. But if we'd stayed together I'm not sure what would've happened."

"You think we would have split up?" Terri flinched.

"It would have been tough. You're beautiful and I'm sure you get women hitting on you all the time. That would have tweaked my jealous tendon. I probably would have let you go so you could go nuts with as many women as you wanted."

Terri sighed. "I *have* gone nuts with a whole bunch of women. But there's only ever been one woman who *really* got to me. I was so sure that I was going to marry you."

Moriarty's breath caught. "Is that what you want now?"

"I've wanted it for so long I can hardly remember a time when I didn't want to."

Moriarty pulled her in close, overcome. She closed her eyes and gently kissed the crown of Terri's head. "I want to."

"Then we're going to have to work out a time and a date." Terri smiled. "And I honestly think we should stay dating for a little while. Who knows? We both might have changed so much that *we* don't make sense anymore."

Moriarty gave her a sad smile. "That's very true, and I'm okay with that."

"Don't look so sad. I'm not going anywhere. Now I'm an adult, and we're the same species. Mostly what I see is a chance to grow with you. Can't you see how good this is for both of us?"

Actually, that's true, Moriarty thought. *We really* are *on an even footing.*

"Yes, I can," Moriarty said. "And I'm sold on the idea."

"Good," Terri said.

Just at that moment a sliver of light flashed before them.

They quickly separated and in unison rolled to their feet, ending in a crouch.

Two women climbed through the tear in the dreamscape.

Jackie and Michelle stood before them. Michelle's eyes widened at the sight of Terri.

"Terri," Michelle said and threw herself at Terri, giving her a hard hug. "It's so damn good to see you again, despite the mess we're in."

"Good to see you too, Michelle." Terri grinned.

"Mack," Jackie cried, smothering Moriarty in a hug. "Did you do the deed?" she whispered into Moriarty's ear.

"Hell, yes," Moriarty said. "You were right. You?"

"Hell, yes," Jackie said. "You were right."

They separated and high fived each other.

Moriarty turned to see Terri and Michelle staring at them. Michelle raised an eyebrow.

"Oh, don't look at me like that, honey," Jackie said, grin playing about her lips. "Tornado promise."

"And squid promise," Moriarty chimed in.

"Of course," Jackie said. "Glued together by mud."

"And train tracks."

They gave their respective lovers large, fake grins.

Michelle and Terri exchanged a glance.

"Spit it out," Michelle said. "*Honey*, you never told us what happened to you before you ended up crashing in the jungle."

"It's a long and sad story," Jackie said.

"And to put it in a nutshell, we ended up in a marshland, watching a squid thing, thousands of meters high, playing with a tornado," Moriarty said. "We were walking on train tracks and made it to the station. The train came in. I managed to get on the train."

"I got sucked into the tornado," Jackie said. "I cut a random hole and ended up in the jungle."

Michelle and Terri exchanged a wince.

"Sounds horrible," Michelle said.

Moriarty and Jackie exchanged a glance. "It was," they chorused.

"Terri," Michelle said. "I'm assuming Monk brought you into the dreamscape?"

Terri nodded. "And made me into a shape shifter."

Michelle nodded, eyes flaring yellow.

Terri stared at her. "You're a shape shifter as well?"

"Yeah," Michelle said. "Kilkenny asked me if I wanted to be one. I said yes."

Moriarty felt a distant tugging sensation and suddenly it felt as though Terri had exploded inside of her.

"Oh, wow," Moriarty breathed, sneaking a glance at Terri. Terri was watching her and had a predatory, proprietary gleam in her eye that made her grin. "What did you do?"

"I strengthened your bond," Michelle said.

Moriarty gave her a gentle hug. "Thank you."

"You're welcome."

"How long have you been here for?" Jackie asked, glancing at Moriarty.

"Not all that long. We've been looking for all of you," Moriarty said. "We got off at Carnival World and got chased into the fish bowl. Then we got sucked into the fun house. Terri called you, and we waited for you to come."

"Can you call Monk?" Michelle asked. "I've tried and no luck." She looked worried and Moriarty gave her shoulder a comforting squeeze.

"We'll find her," Moriarty said.

"We'd better," Michelle said. "She was okay when she was with us, but we got separated. Again."

"What happened?" Terri asked.

"She ran up to us while we were here," Michelle said. "We were with Riordan. We found Roth and Kilkenny in the teacup ride. Monk got in to take a closer look and the bottom dropped out of the ride. We got sucked away into the fun house."

"Okay," Terri said, exchanging a glance with Moriarty. "I think the bottom line here is that we're going to have to find the others and get the hell out of the dreamscape. Monk is almost certainly with Angela Michaels. Hellstrom isn't here in her physical body at all."

"What?" Michelle asked, looking shocked. She gaped for a moment. "How?"

"We ran into Hellstrom on the way here," Moriarty said. "She cut a hole and disappeared from in front of us. A regular shape shifter can't move around the dreamscape that way if they're here in their physical body. They need a dream walker to be able to do that."

"But we're all stuck here," Jackie said. "How can she move around at all?"

"A regular shape shifter can't see the weaves that make up the dreamscape the way a dream walker can. That's why we can't just move around at will. You can only cut rudimentary holes. But, if a dream walker has given you the key and you know where to look, you have more latitude to get around. That only works if you're in as a dreamer because the world *looks* different if you are."

"Monk told me how to ward and lock the dreamscape," Jackie said, eyes flaring yellow. "It's to do with the auras. The problem with this dreamscape is that there *are* no real auras the way there normally are in a dream."

"By auras you mean color, don't you?" Michelle asked.

"Yeah," Jackie said. "Let me see if I can show you the way we see." She studied the wall ahead of her. Moriarty watched in fascination as it glowed a little. The glow disappeared.

"It's about layers of dots and auras."

"Where does it come from?" Michelle asked. "The dots?"

"The raw material for a dream is just there," Jackie said. "It's a bunch of dots in space. Kind of like a forest of trees that you can make tables and chairs from." She glanced at Michelle. "In the case of *this* dream, I can't make tables and chairs because I can't see the forest."

Terri's eyes flared yellow. "What happens if you poke the wall?"

A light flashed before them.

Jackie nodded. "Excellent idea." Another flash of light.

"Can you keep your finger on it?" Terri asked.

Jackie nodded, and there was a sustained burst of light.

"Wow," Terri said after a moment. "Will you look at that?"

The area in front of them exploded into auras and shimmered before their eyes.

"That's how the world looks to me when I shift," Jackie said. "If I want something to appear, I move the dots around. The dots look like this."

Large spheres grew in the auras before them. Jackie frowned for a moment and the dots moved position. She shrank them down again and a rose hung in the middle of the auras.

"I think you do that naturally but can't see it. That's what Monk says."

"Wow," Moriarty murmured. She felt Terri's hand slide into hers. "Since you've just figured out the auras, can't you cut us out of the dreamscape?"

Jackie shook her head. "*I* can't. Maybe Monk can. I don't know." She glanced at Michelle, who raised an eyebrow at her. "It's not that easy. It's because there's a whole bunch of layers. We just broke up the first one that'll allow us to get out of the fun house and the cake tin we're in. But actually breaking out of the dreamscape itself? We need the person who created it to show us how to bring out the auras."

"You saw it, didn't you, Terri? When Hellstrom left?" Moriarty said.

Terri's eyes widened. "Yeah, I did."

Jackie's face lit up. "Can you show me?"

"I'll try."

The auras before them shifted and changed color.

"Yes," Jackie said triumphantly as flash of light followed by a tear appeared in the dreamscape.

"Yep, that's my living room, all right," Michelle said with a grin.

Moriarty hugged Terri. "Beautiful," she whispered into Terri's ear.

Terri grinned. "Let's go get the others."

OH, FUCK, MY aching head. Monk slowly came to her senses. She took a deep breath and felt a tugging stab. *Okay, my ribs are stuffed.* She turned her head from side to side. *Neck's okay.* She tried to move her hands but they were tied behind her back. Her ankles were tied to the legs of a chair. *Well, my knee hurts anyway.*

She looked around carefully. She was sitting in a deserted, fanatically neat living room. There was a balcony with sliding glass doors, and a gentle breeze caressed her, carrying the scent of salt air and feel of warm sun.

She recognized the lip of the bay and the headlands.

She was in the sea world.

"Come out," she said. "I know you have to be close by."

She heard footsteps coming up behind her.

"Hi, Monkhouse," Angela Michaels said softly, kissing her ear.

Monk grimaced. *Yuck.*

"I'm not going to waste time talking to you," Angela said coldly, circling her and kneeling to face her.

"I'm not going to waste time listening to you," Monk said, equally coldly, and tried to stand up.

Her muscles bulged and the burning sensation of the ropes against her skin made her hiss in pain.

Angela laughed. "You're *my* bitch now, *Monk*." She leaned forward and her eyes flared yellow. A second later, fish hooks sank into Monk's brain and she screamed.

"OH, FOR GOD'S sake," Roth muttered. "I never thought I would hate a simple building so much."

"No kidding," Riordan said.

Kilkenny, breathing hard, sank down onto the green painted concrete. Her side was aching and every step was an experience in pure agony. *Where's Monk? I'm worried. I wish I could shake the nagging feeling that I should be with her. Wait, is she calling me?*

"Hey," Riordan said, kneeling beside her. "Sweetie, you look terrible. Are you feeling all right?" Her hand was on Kilkenny's forehead before she could react. "You're burning up."

Roth dropped to one knee beside them, and Kilkenny abruptly felt smothered. She pushed their hands away. "I'm fine. Really."

Roth and Riordan exchanged a glance.

"We're sorry," Roth said. "We're worried about you."

Kilkenny watched them both carefully. She felt like an outsider.

I want Monk.

"Worry about each other," she snapped. "You have each other."

"What about you?" Riordan asked.

"What *about* me?" Kilkenny said. "We were friends and we made out once. Big deal."

Riordan looked like she'd been slapped. Roth flinched.

"Kilkenny," Riordan said. "You can't mean that."

"Yeah, I mean it," she snarled. "What the hell were you thinking? You let me think you were single for almost the entire couple of years we've known each other. I let myself feel something for you, but it's *nothing* to the way you and Roth feel about each other. You're an arch bitch for doing that to *both* of us." She turned to Roth, levering herself to her feet, grunting in pain. "You *like* it when your lover cheats on you? Says a lot about *you*, Roth." She wondered where the words were coming from, horrified that she couldn't stop them.

"Calm down, Kilkenny," Roth said quietly. "We only want to help you. You look sick. You don't know what you're saying."

"I know *exactly* what I'm saying, Roth. I'm telling you to *fuck off!* Fucking *leave me alone. Go away!*" she screamed. She shook with the force of her anger. *Please don't leave me.* Please. *Please don't leave me.*

Riordan tried to touch her but Kilkenny shoved her away as hard as she could. She felt possessed. Riordan stumbled back and Roth caught her and pulled her to her feet.

"We're sorry for hurting you," Roth said quietly. "We won't be bothering you anymore." She gently took Riordan's arm and they walked away.

Kilkenny sagged against the wall. She felt devastated. She'd hurt Riordan and Roth. Her shoulders shook with the force of her sobs and tears streamed from her eyes. She watched them leave her, not looking back.

I'm in love with Riordan. I'm falling in love with Roth. What have I done? What's happening to me?

The wall shimmered beside her, and a figure stepped through it, clapping her hands. A cruel smile played about her lips and her brilliant, bile yellow eyes shone with vicious amusement.

"*Very* nice, lover girl," Angela Michaels said. "Stand up."

Kilkenny felt disconnected from her body and stood, giving a hard, sharp bark of pain as her side tore.

"I wanted to get you alone," Angela continued, almost conversationally.

"What do you—?"Kilkenny began.

"Shut the fuck up, shit for brains," Angela snarled. "And don't call for any of the others."

Kilkenny felt horrified as her mouth closed without input from her. It felt as though she *wanted* to obey each and every one of Angela's instructions. She *had* to obey them. *A controlling bond?*

"Keep standing," Angela said. She stepped forward and punched Kilkenny in the side.

The agony was intense and overwhelming. Kilkenny hurt too much to scream. She grayed out for a few seconds as the pain came and went in sick waves. She vomited blood and bile and then finally was able to scream, but neither of those things helped ease her pain.

Angela laughed. "Suck it up. You're coming with me."

She reached out, grabbed Kilkenny by the collar of her tee shirt, and threw her through the wall.

MICHELLE WALKED DOWN Harcourt Parade, Jackie by her side. Moriarty and Terri were close behind them.

"Are we there yet?" Moriarty asked.

"No," Jackie said.

"Are we there yet?"

"No."

"Are we there yet?"

"No." Jackie turned to Moriarty with a half grin. "Are you going to start that shit up again?"

Moriarty laughed. "At least you're not mad at me this time."

"Keep doing that, *Bart,* and I will be."

"Ow, quit it," Moriarty said in an eerie imitation of Bart Simpson and they all laughed.

"Seriously, where *are* we going?" Moriarty asked.

"I don't know," Michelle said. "I just want to walk down this way."

"Even in the dreamscape you want to go to school?" Jackie asked. "You're dedicated."

Michelle gave her an uneasy grin. "I think I'm being called and I'm not sure who by."

"That's another story," Jackie said, all traces of humor vanished.

Michelle nodded. It felt as though she had a compass in her head, a solid knot that made her shift direction so it always stayed in the center of her forehead. "Just brace yourself. I don't know who it is."

"Right beside you, Michelle," Terri said. "No matter what."

"Yep," Moriarty said.

She felt Jackie give her hand a gentle squeeze.

"Thanks, guys," she said, stopping in front of Sacred Heart College. "In there."

"Figures," Moriarty said.

Michelle glanced at her as she shook her head. She raised an eyebrow in question.

"Even when I'm dreaming I go to fucking school," Moriarty said, grinning.

"I know," Michelle said, rolling her eyes. She jogged up the stairs and into the school. She felt close to the knot's source.

She made a beeline for the stairs by the office, taking them two at a time until they reached the top verandah. She ran down the corridor, the others close behind her. She saw two kneeling figures and her heart sank. She skidded to a halt by Roth and Riordan.

"Guys," she said.

"We were lucky that worked," Roth said to Riordan, standing and helping her to her feet.

"It's good to see you all," Roth said. Her eyes widened at the sight of Terri. "Terri?"

"Roth," Terri said, pulling her into a hug.

"I'm so glad you're not with Hellstrom," Riordan said, taking her turn and hugging Terri.

"No. Monk called me and made me."

"You're a dream walker?" Roth asked, pulling back and looking up into her eyes.

"Yeah," Terri said, shifting from foot to foot as though she'd been caught stealing.

"You'll do fine," Roth said, patting her cheek.

"Roth, I hate to break this up," Moriarty said. "Something's wrong. You look terrible."

"Thank you, Mack," Roth said. "Your assessment of my physical appearance is always deeply appreciated."

"You look like someone ripped your heart out, my friend." Moriarty pulled her and Riordan into a hard hug. They stayed like that for a moment.

"What on earth is the matter?" Michelle asked, frowning. Moriarty was right. They both looked like they'd been punched, and Riordan was still visibly upset. "And where's Monk? Wasn't she with you?"

"No," Riordan said. "We lost her. We've been calling for you."

Michelle felt sick. "No. Not again." She glanced sharply at them. "Why not just call Jackie? We could have gotten here much sooner if you had."

"The type of calling I did," Riordan said. "It relies on the *knowing* of the person. You healed me, Michelle—and it created a type of transient link between the two of us because you gave me some of you. You look drained."

"I am but that's not what Monk needs right now." Michelle forced down her anger.

"She's probably all right," Jackie said, looking as sick as Michelle felt. "She's a lion. She can take care of herself."

"I know but that doesn't mean I don't want to be wrapped up all around her," Michelle said. "I don't want the carnival to be the last place I—"

"No, don't go there," Terri said. "Do *not* go there. We're going to get her, I promise."

Moriarty nodded, black eyes flashing. "To the last, Michelle. I've never met Monk but I owe her. I *owe* her."

Michelle nodded, seeing the truth of what Moriarty said in everyone else's faces. "Okay."

"Kilkenny," Jackie said. "She was with you, too. Where is she?"

"Kilkenny," Roth said. "Look."

"Oh, shit," Moriarty muttered as they looked down at spray of drying blood and vomit on the green paint.

"What happened?" Jackie asked, slipping in close to Michelle. Michelle put her arm around Jackie.

"No matter what, I'm right here," she whispered into Jackie's ear.

"First Monk and then Kilkenny," Jackie said. "Roth, *what happened?*"

"Kilkenny looked sick and when we asked her about it she said some terrible things and told us to leave her alone. She was too upset to be reasoned with so we were going to give her a few moments to compose herself before we tried again," Roth said. "We heard her scream and came back but she was gone. We saw what you see now."

"I called you," Riordan said. Her voice broke and her eyes shone with unshed tears. Roth put an arm around her shoulders, pulled her in close, and gently kissed her head.

"We'll find her," Roth whispered. "I promise."

Riordan nodded.

"Well, at least we're all together now," Moriarty said. "No more hoping that one of us calls a dream walker. Can either of you guys feel Monk?"

Jackie shook her head.

"No," Michelle said. "She keeps fading in and out. At the moment, she's out." She exchanged a look with Jackie. *Jackie's hurting. So am I. I want Monk.*

"She's got a marker on her," Riordan said. "That's why."

"What the hell is this marker thing?" Michelle asked.

"Angela Michaels must have tasted Monk's blood," Riordan said. "So she's kind of linked to Monk. She can *sense* Monk. It's kind of like a controlling bond but not a consciously made one. It's enough for her to isolate Monk, to shield her connection to you."

"You mean that vicious little bitch has been *toying* with us the whole time?" Michelle asked, getting angry.

"They *both* have," Roth said.

"Monk, Kilkenny, and Angela all have some history together. I'm betting Michaels took them," Terri said. "Remember the first day of Monk's senior year and detention?"

Michelle nodded. "I agree. But where are they?"

"Good question," Terri said. She looked at the others. "We'll all go together to find them. We don't know if Michaels is with Hellstrom. And it's going to take *all* of us to take those two down."

"Agreed," Moriarty said.

"Where do we start?" Terri asked.

"Good question," Moriarty said.

CHAPTER 13

KILKENNY FELL TO her knees, retching. She clutched at her side.

"Kilkenny," Monk said. "Kilkenny, look up. Look at me."

"Monk," she moaned, eyes blurring with tears. She looked up and saw Monk tied to a chair. They were in an upper floor room, the scent of salty air filling her lungs.

She tried to call for Roth and Riordan, but it felt like she was pushing against a wall. Next was Jackie, but that didn't work either. She felt like she was stuck in a small box.

Angela Michaels knelt beside her. "You can't call for your friends. We're alone." She smiled. "Just the three of us." She sank back onto her haunches.

"What do you want from us?" Kilkenny asked, grinding out words through the pain.

"I want you to kill each other, of course," Angela said, sounding friendly. "I met the two of you and my life went to shit. You destroyed *it* and *me*."

"I never did anything to you," Monk said. "Neither did she. You did it all to yourself. *You* got you expelled."

"And *you* got me turned into a fucking werewolf," Angela snarled, eyes burning with rage. "And then you fucking *killed* the only person who could actually help me."

"You mean Wells?" Monk asked. "*She* turned you in a werewolf, I had nothing to do with that."

"If you hadn't insisted on pushing her, she'd still be alive and I'd be with the one person who understood me. Who understood *this*."

"She was a fucking homicidal nutcase," Monk snarled. "She destroyed everything she touched. And she *liked* doing it."

"You never understood her. The world she opened up for me."

"You're fucking nuts," Monk said after a moment, shaking her head.

"Yeah," Kilkenny gasped. "She *is* nuts."

Monk's eyes widened. "No, mate. No. Are you telling me she's gone mad?"

Kilkenny nodded. "And I think she put a controlling bond on me."

"Fuck," Monk said. "Are you all right, Kilkenny?"

"*Stop ignoring me*," Angela screamed.

They both stilled. Kilkenny shook. Monk looked dismayed.

"Now that I have both of your attentions," she said. "Good. Don't either one of you forget who's in charge here."

"You're not in charge of your faculties, let alone us," Monk said coldly.

Kilkenny glanced sharply at her. *Stop needling her, Monk. What on earth are you doing?*

"You think so?" Angela said with an equally cold smile. She looked at Kilkenny. "Stand up."

Kilkenny felt as though her body and her legs belonged to someone else. She stood. Blood gouted out of the wound to her side and she felt it dribbling down her body in a warm, sticky wash.

"Kilkenny," Monk said, but before she had a chance to say anything else, Angela was across the room by her side.

"Fucking *shut up,*" she snarled, pulled her fist back, and hit Monk as hard as she could on the side of her head. Kilkenny heard a grisly crunch, and Monk's head fell forward.

Kilkenny felt a shot of panic and her vision blurred.

"Good," Angela said, pulling back Monk's head. Monk's cheek was a field of mottled bruising. Angela shrugged. "She'll do until I'm finished with her."

She stood, crossed to a side table, opened a drawer, and pulled out a knife.

"Come here," Angela said.

Kilkenny fought as hard as she could and tried screaming for Roth and Riordan again. She stood. Her movements were jerky, her forward momentum relentless.

I can't stop her. She sobbed on the inside. *I'm not strong enough.*

She stopped in front of Angela.

"Hold out your hand."

Kilkenny held out her hand, palm up, of its own volition. Her palm burned. The knife was silver. "No. Don't. Don't make me do this." She cried in earnest.

Angela laughed. "I don't care what you do and don't want."

"I can get you help," Kilkenny said as she turned around. "Anything you want." She walked toward Monk, her movements jerky. *I can't stop myself.* She stopped.

"Go on," Angela said with terrible gentleness. "Hold it in both hands and lift up your arms."

Kilkenny did so. *I'm sorry, Monk. I'm sorry. You're my best friend.*

"Stab her in the heart."

Monk's eyes fluttered open, and she lifted her head. Blood streamed out of her nose and she looked dazed for a second. Her eyes widened and flared yellow.

"*No, God no,*" Kilkenny screamed. "*Monk, I can't help it. I can't stop. I'm sorry.*" She fought the savage, downward motion of her arms but it was no use.

Angela's howling laughter echoed in her ears.

"CAN EITHER OF you guys call Monk?" Moriarty asked, glancing between Michelle and Jackie.

Jackie's eyes widened and she gasped. "I don't think we need to. Monk's calling me. She's *screaming* for me." She growled, viciously slashed a hole in the dreamscape, and tumbled through it.

Michelle felt Monk through the bond. She felt almost resigned and with no small measure of regret. It felt so *final* and Michelle dived through the hole after Jackie, the others close behind her.

She was temporarily stunned by the sight before her eyes.

Monk was tied to a chair and Kilkenny, shaking and covered in blood, stood before her holding a knife. She was crying and screaming denials. Angela Michaels leant against a side table, relaxed and laughing. Her eyes danced with mirth.

"No, Kilkenny," Michelle yelled, diving for her, but it was too late. Kilkenny's muscles bulged as she fought her downward killing stroke.

Jackie dove toward Kilkenny, knocking her off balance.

The knife plunged into Monk's chest, just to one side of her heart. Only half of the blade was visible.

Monk's reaction was instantaneous. She screamed, great, throat tearing gusts of agony as her chest smoldered.

The sea roared in the distance.

Roth was the first to move. She pulled the knife out of Monk's chest and dove toward Angela.

Angela, smirking, tensed herself as Roth sprang.

Michelle felt a terrible weakness and the world became a riot of sparks. She fell to her knees, crawling to Monk. Monk was bleeding golden sparks that were darkening toward black.

Michelle pushed her sparks through their dissolving bond, firming it, but it was not enough to stop the spread of black inside Monk. She was dimly aware of Jackie sobbing beside Kilkenny. She grabbed more sparks from Jackie, and both streams poured into Monk. The black stopped spreading. Slowly and agonizingly it retreated, and Monk's sparks became whole again, but were dimming. She drew deep inside but had nothing left, or so she thought. She gave one, final shove and the world faded out as she fainted.

MORIARTY WATCHED WITH a sinking heart. Roth's face was a snarling rictus of rage as she held the laughing Angela up by the neck.

Riordan was kneeling beside Kilkenny, who was lying in a troubling spray of blood. Jackie and Michelle were both unconscious and Monk was turning blue.

"Tidal wave," Terri said, jerking her head toward the sea.

A solid wall of water had built up and was roaring toward them, sound increasing in volume as it approached the shore.

"Bubble," Moriarty said, racing toward Monk.

"Can't," Terri said. "Michaels."

"Roth," Moriarty said. "End it."

"Look at those two fuckwits," Angela said, laughing. "They fucking deserved it."

Roth snarled.

Moriarty dropped to her knees beside Monk, frantically feeling for a pulse. There was none. She glanced at Michelle and Jackie, both out cold.

Just gonna have to do this the old fashioned way.

She snapped the ropes holding Monk and reduced the chair to kindling.

"Stop laughing," Roth snarled, giving Angela a savage shake.

"Do what you like," Angela said. "I got what I wanted." Peals of laughter echoed and ricocheted all around them.

"Shut up," Roth ground out.

Moriarty was dimly aware of the terrible crack as Roth broke Angela's spine over her knee.

"*That* was for Monk," Roth said coldly.

Moriarty tilted Monk's head back and began breathing for her. Terri knelt beside her, eyes brilliant, bile yellow.

"*This* is for Kilkenny," Roth said, plunging the silver knife into Angela's cold heart.

The world went black as the wave crashed over the seaside world, destroying everything in its wake. The water roared over the bubble created by Terri. The apartment creaked.

Roth dropped to her knees beside Monk.

"I got this," Moriarty said, tearing open Monk's shirt and pushing on her sternum. "Kilkenny."

She leant in and listened for Monk's breathing. *Nothing.*

She breathed for Monk again, and the world became lighter again, every sound a cacophony as she shifted her vision. A breath, pump the heart. Ignore the swirling blue that went so high above Terri's bubble that it must have touched the clouds.

The world was slowly sunny again and she felt Terri shift beside them.

Then it was Terri breathing for Monk and Moriarty palpitating her heart.

Moriarty leant down and put her ear close to Monk's chest. *Was that—? I think. Yeah, I do. I hear her heart beat.*

She grinned and felt Terri giving her a questioning look.

"She's doing it on her own. She's alive," Moriarty said.

Terri's eyes teared. She nodded, shifted, and pulled Monk's head into her lap. They watched the rise and fall of Monk's chest, and they kissed.

"We did it," Moriarty said. "We did it. Monk's alive."

"Yeah," Terri said. "But look at Kilkenny. I don't know." She nodded toward Roth. "Go on."

Moriarty nodded. She approached Roth and Riordan.

Kilkenny's head was resting in Riordan's lap. Roth had torn open her tee shirt, and Moriarty grimaced at the look of her side. Her flesh was a mottled black and tendrils of black crept outwards away from it. The cut was a mass of swollen, black flesh with yellow, foul smelling pus leaking out of it.

"That's the result of silver, isn't it?" Moriarty said.

Roth sighed. "I think so." She looked up at Moriarty. Her expression was calm but Moriarty could see, from the ease of long experience, the terrible pain and regret in her eyes.

"She should be dead already," Moriarty said. She pointed to Kilkenny's festering cut. "This isn't new, is it?"

"No," Riordan said. "She got swiped by Hellstrom."

"She's a bond master," Moriarty said. "This is something our world hasn't seen for hundreds of years. She's a rare and wonderful thing in and of herself."

"And a wonderful *woman* in and of herself," Riordan said, her eyes showing a glimmer of anger.

"Peace, Rio," Moriarty said, holding up her hand. "I wasn't thinking self gain, and that wasn't what I meant. I *was* actually thinking about her." She smiled. "She's sweet, smart, and beautiful."

"Where are you going with this, Mack?" Roth asked with a hint of impatience.

"We don't know much about her clan or her powers. All we really know is that as a bond master, she has unusually strong powers of healing of both herself and other people." She nodded toward Michelle. "So does she. You saw Michelle use it on Monk. All three of them should be dead too, but they're not. Maybe all she needs to heal isn't another bond master, it's her own innate powers."

"What are you suggesting, Mack?" Roth asked.

"Bond her and give her the strength to heal."

Roth and Riordan exchanged a glance and Riordan flinched. She shook her head. "She doesn't want us. She made that quite clear."

"How on earth do you know what she does and doesn't want?" Moriarty asked, exasperated. *For smart women, you can both be incredibly dense.*

"She told us outright that she wanted us to leave her alone. That she doesn't feel anything for either of us."

"Oh, yeah? When was that?"

"In the school corridor before she went missing," Roth said, biting her lip as realization dawned in her eyes. "Oh, good heavens, you're probably right."

"Yes. Thank you, Roth," Moriarty said, smiling and nodding.

"What the fuck are you talking about?" Riordan asked.

"You saw how Kilkenny was when we came in here," Moriarty said. "She had a knife ready to plunge into her best friend's chest. She was crying. She was devastated. It was pretty fucking obvious that she didn't want to be doing what she was doing."

"A controlling bond?" Riordan said.

"Oh, yeah," Moriarty said.

"Angela wanted to destroy Kilkenny," Roth said. "Taking Monk was easy. She wanted Kilkenny to see it. She was already weakened because of the silver poisoning, and Angela compounded it with fear and worry. It worked. It weakened Kilkenny and Angela simply took over. She forced Kilkenny to push away the two people she loved the most."

"And we fell for it. I thought she was just delirious," Riordan said, a spark of hope in her eyes.

Roth nodded. "But mind, my love, the words may have been Angela's but the *content* was Kilkenny's. Don't be so sure of her heart, when she herself doesn't seem to really know where it lies. We must leave her be so she can decide for herself what she wants to do. *You've* gone to *her*. Now *she* must come to *you*."

Riordan nodded. "I know you're right." She smiled. "But I want to help her." She smoothed back Kilkenny's hair from her forehead. Riordan's relief was almost palatable. She turned to Moriarty. "Okay, how do you propose we do this?"

"I don't know," Moriarty said. "I don't really have a plan. I never really thought about a scenario where two bond masters were half dead and we had to fix one of them."

"You're such an ass," Roth said, smiling fondly, if a little sadly, at her.

"Maybe *I* can help," Terri said.

Moriarty smiled at her. "Go ahead, love."

"I can't see shape shifter bonds, but since I'm a dream walker, I can make controlling bonds, right?"

"Oh, sweetie," Moriarty said. "That's very dangerous." *I won't ask you not to do it but I don't want to lose you. God, I love you so much.*

"Where does the danger lie? In the mind you link to?" Terri asked. "You can never really know another person's heart because you aren't that person. I understand that. And an animal? Raw instinct and passion, I understand that as well."

"It's not only that," Roth said. "It's more. Every time you form the bond something is given and something is taken until finally there isn't any of the original *you* left."

"I don't plan on risking madness," Terri said, looking deep into Moriarty's eyes. "I have too much to live for. Besides, I can go my whole life without linking with things, right?"

"I've never had the urge," Moriarty said.

"And from what I understand of Monk and Jackie," broke in Riordan, "neither of them has ever done it either. There's no need for it."

Terri's eyes flared yellow. Kilkenny's hand twitched and the others looked at it in surprise.

"That was me," Terri said. "I'm nudging her aura. I want to try something. Rio? Roth?"

"Yes?" Roth asked warily. She yelped in pain. "Stop that," she said sharply.

"Do you mind?" Riordan asked.

"What did you just do to them?" Moriarty asked.

"She tweaked our bond," Roth said.

"Not exactly," Terri said. "If I look hard at either one of you, I can see an almost invisible silver flame in your aura. I touched it."

"With what?"

"Another silver flame. Kind of like the ones both Mack and I have."

Roth's eyebrows shot up. "You tried to form a shape shifter bond with us?"

"No," Terri said. "But I may have just found a way to push Kilkenny's toward you *without* putting a controlling bond on her. Like repels like, remember? If I push it toward you it might meld into yours."

"And it should work even though you're both bonded. We can all only form a single bond with another shape shifter, but bond masters seem to be able to form multiples."

"So it relies on her innate abilities," Roth said. She looked down at Kilkenny and then gave Riordan a sad smile. Riordan nodded. "Do it. Do it."

Terri gave her a nod and stared intently at the three of them.

"How's that?" she asked after a moment.

"I can feel her," Riordan said after a moment. "It actually feels like a regular shape shifter bond, minus the tweaking that Kilkenny did to our bond."

"And Michelle did to ours," Moriarty said, feeling her love for Terri and knowing Terri felt it as well.

"She's pulling strength from us," Roth said. "Can you feel it?"

"I can feel it," Riordan said.

"Look at the wound," Roth said.

Moriarty leaned toward Kilkenny and studied her terrible cut closely. It almost looked as though the black tendrils travelling throughout her body had retreated. It was so slow as to almost be invisible, but inch by agonizing inch it was disappearing.

"Oh," Roth said. "I think I'm going to . . . to . . ." Her eyes rolled up in her head and she fainted.

Riordan looked as close to collapse as Roth. "I was badly hurt," Riordan whispered. Her eyes fluttered closed and then opened again briefly. "Michelle used my and Roth's strength to heal me. I don't have much left and Roth has none . . ." She sighed and passed out.

"Oh, boy," Moriarty said, surveying the unconscious figures. Of the eight of them, all but two were unconscious and hovering close to death. That only left two of them to fight Hellstrom, and they didn't dare go together because it left the others unprotected.

"I know what you're thinking," Terri said. "You think we have to split up to fight Hellstrom, don't you?"

Moriarty unwillingly nodded. "I don't see any other choice. Hellstrom is still running around somewhere and she still wants to use us for sushi practice. I think Angela's madness and Hellstrom's viciousness have kind of combined and ricocheted all through Hellstrom. She's nuts and she has a grudge against us. Roth just killed someone who could have been her bond mate, her lover, or simply her partner in crime. I'm sure that's made her angry on top of being lethally loopy."

"I agree," Terri said with a sigh. "I don't want to but I don't know what choice we have."

"Well, there's a compromise I can suggest," Moriarty said. "I don't want to be away from you any more than you away from me. Let me go and look for her. When I find her I'll call you."

"You promise?" Terri asked.

"Promise," Moriarty said. "Cross my heart and hope I don't die."

"That's not funny under the circumstances," Terri said, anger flashing in her eyes. "Don't joke about it."

"I'm sorry, love," Moriarty said. "I don't mean to upset you."

"I can't help it," Terri said. "I don't think you understand exactly how much it hurt when you went. I can't lose you again."

"Hey," Moriarty said, kneeling before her and gently cupping her face. "No one's going anywhere. We're bonded. Can't you feel what I feel?"

Terri was silent a moment. "You're confident. Like you normally are. And you *want* me with you."

"*Never* think that what's going on inside you is one sided. It's not. I *hate* the idea of you being around Hellstrom, but you have the right to come with me if you so choose. I won't stop you. I would rather you were with me so whatever happened we were together. I can't and won't tell you what to do. Your pleasure, madam?"

Terri leant forward and slowly and thoroughly kissed her. Moriarty was glad that she was kneeling. Her legs were shaking.

Moriarty buried her face in Terri's neck when they broke. She felt Terri nod and tighten her arms around her.

"Be safe, Mack," she whispered. "Please."

"I will."

They separated. Moriarty gazed at her beloved Terri, trying to memorize every line of her beautiful face.

"I think we should get off the dreamscape," Terri said. "This place shows no sign of collapsing and it's crawling with lethal natural disasters. That suggests to me it's not Angela's dreamscape."

"You think it's Hellstrom's?" Moriarty asked. "That *would* make sense. What if Angela carved her a door or two so she could come and go as she pleased?"

"We have to get out of here, quickly," Terri said.

"Yeah," Moriarty said. "Michelle's place. Yours isn't safe, neither is mine."

Terri nodded. "Agreed. I think I've been to Michelle's place once or twice."

"Let's get moving. The ocean's risen a few feet in the distance."

Terri gritted her teeth. "Ugh." She carefully placed Monk's head on the floor and glanced out of the open patio doors. "Shit."

The horizon rapidly lifted another foot or two.

"It's building," Moriarty said, grabbing a hold of Michelle and stuffing Angela's silver knife into her pocket as Terri cut a hole in the dreamscape.

She unceremoniously dived through it and put Michelle and Jackie on the living room floor. Terri followed closely behind with Monk and Kilkenny. Seconds later, Moriarty was putting Roth on the floor next to Riordan as Terri sealed the dreamscape. The sound of roaring from the oncoming tidal wave diminished and died as the tear closed.

Moriarty sank onto free space on the floor and put her head in her hands. "That was close."

"Yeah," Terri said, looking all around that the unconscious bodies and snorting a laugh. She shook her head.

"Yeah, I know," Moriarty said, grin tugging at her lips.

Terri's arm crept around her shoulders. "Where are you going to start looking?"

"Well," Moriarty said. "Hellstrom is a psychopath who's fixated on me and hates you. I told her that she never had a chance with me. Where do *you* think she's going to be hiding?"

"Somewhere she can drool over you and wait for me."

Moriarty nodded. "I'm going to head home to my old place. I don't live there anymore. I moved after all that shit."

"I understand," Terri said. "When are you headed out?"

"The sooner the better," Moriarty said. She knew Terri could feel her unwillingness in their bond.

"Kiss for luck," Terri said, kissing her thoroughly.

Moriarty felt dazed when Terri released her. "You have *got* to stop doing that when I'm on my way out the door."

"I'm doing it that way to remind you what's waiting for you when you come back *in* the door."

"As if I would ever forget that," Moriarty said, gently patting her face and hauling herself to her feet. "I'll call for you."

Terri nodded. "Love you, Mack."

"Love you too, Terri," Moriarty said.

She stood, digging in her pocket for her car keys. *Miracle. They're sill on me.*

Moriarty quickly left, feeling Terri inside her and sending her gentle reassurance.

Five minutes later she was jogging out of the doors toward her Holden Calais. It beeped almost cheerfully and unlocked. She quickly started the engine with an expert twist of her wrist. The car started with its usual deep growl and began purring. She glanced at the dashboard clock. *It's only been an hour*.

She drove out of the parking lot, just above the legal limit. She didn't want any unnecessary delay caused by a friendly chat with the police.

As she absently drove toward her old flat, she wondered what she'd find there. *I think the entire complex ended up being vacant. Roth did tell me everyone was frightened of the demonic presence in the building.* She smiled. *Humans. They're such suckers for ghost stories.*

She turned the corner into her own street, feeling a slow wave of familiarity wash over her. *I don't think Hellstrom's going to have any traps waiting for me. She looked too hurt—devastated—to find out I didn't love her. God I hope Terri's safe until I find Hellstrom.*

She pulled up in front of her old block of units. It was hidden behind a chain link fence and carefully labeled as *Private Property.*

Show time. Moriarty got out of her car.

CHAPTER 14

SHE JOGGED UP the path to the front door and pushed it. It opened with a dull squeal. *I remember the first time I brought Terri here. We barely made it into my unit. It took quite a while until we could last long enough to get to my bedroom.*

Every step along the darkened corridor was a trip down memory lane. *It felt like the entire world was my oyster. And then Hellstrom took it away from me. From* us.

She pushed open the front door and winced as it squeaked and moaned.

It was completely bare, all the furnishings and bookshelves gone. The fireplace was cold and empty, just as she'd left it.

We made love so many times in front of that fire. And that horrible feeling when Hellstrom told me she'd been watching us sleep together.

She made her way into where her bedroom used to be and stopped.

Hellstrom sat cross legged in the middle of the floor. She was looking down and her hair hung in her face. Her forearms rested on her thighs and her hands dangled toward the floor.

"I wondered when you'd come," Hellstrom said, looking up at her. Her eyes shone yellow and Moriarty shifted her vision. She felt Terri's attention turn toward her.

"I've come to end this. Roth already ended it with Angela," Moriarty said.

Hellstrom smiled. "I know she did."

Moriarty wasn't sure what she was expecting, but this wasn't it. *I was so sure they'd been bonded. I wasn't even really expecting to find her here alive.*

"Oh, I suppose you're wondering why I haven't curled up into a little ball and died, aren't you?"

"The thought had crossed my mind," Moriarty said.

Hellstrom closed her eyes, and Moriarty looked around as the room brightened and was restored to its heyday. The floors were deeply polished and thick rugs lay on the floor. Moriarty's enormous four poster bed stood, soft and inviting. A rose lay on the pillow.

Fuck I'm on the dreamscape again. Moriarty resisted the urge to call Terri. She felt Terri respond to her tension. It felt as though Terri turned toward her, paying close attention to her.

"All this time I've been pissed at Terri, and it was *you* I really should have come after," Hellstrom said, tilting her head and studying her. "You toyed with both of us. *You* were the one flirting with *me. You* made me think I had a chance with you. How cruel are you?"

"I *never* flirted with you," Moriarty said. "I was always nice to you but it was always professional."

Hellstrom snorted a laugh. "Staring down my shirt at my tits was professional, was it?"

"No, and having half of your buttons undone so you almost spilled out of your shirt was a really stupid thing to do. Not only was it obvious but it was really crass. It was shit attempt at seducing me. You really think you're the first girl to have done that to me? You really think you were *that* tempting that I wouldn't be able to resist? You really think I'm that starved for physical attention that I'd turn to you?"

Hellstrom colored and looked furious. "You can say what you like but I *know* I frustrated you. I *know* you wanted to do more than look. I *saw* what you were like with Terri. You were a wild animal. You *fucked* her and that was because of what *I* did to you."

Moriarty fought down her revulsion. "This conversation is never going to go anywhere. No matter what I say, you're always going to think I turned to Terri because she was convenient, or some kind of replacement for you. Well, she wasn't." *In fact, she was a little bit* frightened *of sex with me but she wanted me so badly it was shredding her.*

"It's time to end it, isn't it?" Hellstrom said. "Good. I'm tired. I don't want you anymore." She gave Moriarty a bitter smile. "On the other hand, just because I don't want you anymore doesn't mean I'll let anyone else have you. What person in their right mind would you let you loose on a bunch of young girls?"

She leapt up off the floor and launched herself into a dive toward Moriarty. Moriarty was almost unprepared as Hellstrom landed on top of her. She felt sick at the sensation of Hellstrom's flabby body grinding against hers. Hellstrom, despite her bulk, was strong. Moriarty's muscles trembled and stood out in sharp relief as she tried to hold Hellstrom's snapping tusks away from her neck.

Moriarty felt the ground dissolve beneath her.

Fuck. Here we go again. She sailed through empty air, Hellstrom grasping and tearing at her. She felt Terri's alarm and tried to send her reassurance.

The unnerving sensation of falling continued for almost longer than Moriarty could bear it. Hellstrom's eyes shone with fury and madness.

Moriarty yelped in pain as something dug into her back, knocking her off course. *Christ, that was a fucking tree,* she thought, dazed, as they bounced off another branch. It held and groaned mightily beneath their combined weight. Moriarty heard chattering off to one side and glanced toward the place the sound came from. Weird ape-like things with overly sharp claws and teeth sat close to them, chewing on what looked like raw meat. One of the animals saw them and chattered. The other monkeys heard and looked in their direction. As one, they swarmed the branch, howling and shrieking with rage.

The added weight was too much for the branch and it snapped. A monkey was on the broken end, leapt toward her, and sank sharp claws and teeth into her shin. It grimly hung on. She howled in pain and Hellstrom tore a chunk of meat from her neck.

"*Ow. Goddammit,*" Moriarty screamed, blood pattering from her wounds. She was bleeding heavily. They crashed through branches on a headlong descent to the jungle floor, leaves whipping and tearing at them.

The air exploded from Moriarty's lungs as she landed on the ground, instantly crushing the simian's head. Her nose burned from the smell of sulphur and the hot air. She sweated profusely.

"*Terri,*" she yelled.

A hole tore in the dreamscape and water gushed through it, knocking her flat. Hellstrom was pushed over sideways, still grabbing for her as the volume of water washed them away.

Why the fuck is water coming through a hole over our heads? What the fuck is Terri doing*?*

Thunder cracked above their heads, almost deafening Moriarty. A split second later there was a flash of light so bright Moriarty barely had time to close her eyes before being temporarily blinded. She heard Hellstrom hiss in pain.

She sat up but Hellstrom was close again. She held a large, silver knife.

The first drops of rain fell, the size signaling a deluge of catastrophic proportions.

Hellstrom lunged toward her and Moriarty jumped sideways, slipping in the mud. She fell to her knees and looked up and behind her, watching with almost clinical detachment as the knife arced toward her back. She tried to roll out of the way but knew it would be too little, too late.

The blow never landed. Terri, drenched by heavy rain and snarling in rage, grabbed Hellstrom's wrist and used her own momentum to arc the blade up so it slammed into her chest, through her heart.

"Leave her alone," Terri screamed. "Leave *us* alone." She twisted the knife. "Mack is mine. She always was. I'm fucking sick and tired of pretending you ever had a chance."

Hellstrom howled and thrashed but Terri held her down.

"Leave me, my lover, and my friends alone, you fucking bitch. You *suck*."

Hellstrom screamed as the skin around the knife blackened and smoked. She howled as the silver took firm hold of her. She clawed at her chest, pulling out sizzling chunks of charred meat. Her screams faded away as her throat went black and dissolved. She finally tumbled over and shattered as black rubble.

"Mack? Are you all right?" Terri asked in a small voice as Moriarty collapsed on her back, chest heaving.

"Yeah, I'm all right," Moriarty said. "Bleeding like a stuck pig and bit by a pair of fucking apes, but I'm fine."

The rain became heavier. It was almost like being under a warm waterfall. The mud ran around the sides of her, stained with her blood.

Terri took a step toward her, and her feet went out from under her. "Shit," she yelled as she slid away on a river of mud.

Moriarty rolled to her feet. "I'm com-*shit,*" she said as she tried to take a step and slipped in the mud. She slid down the gentle slope toward Terri, coming within inches of her. She lunged forward, fingers grasping empty air, and then they suddenly intertwined with Terri's.

"Hang onto me," Moriarty yelled as the gentle slope became a sharp drop off.

They sailed over the edge of a cliff. There were waterfalls in front and to the left of them. Terri twisted, holding onto her for dear life as Moriarty straightened in a high dive position.

Endless seconds passed before they plunged into swiftly moving water, hurling them toward their next destination.

"Mack," Terri said, clinging to her.

Moriarty spat out water. "Just hold on. I'll keep you safe."

They were carried along a savage river and thrown over the side of another waterfall, this one larger than the last. Water cascaded and roared all around them with bruising intensity. Terri's grip on her tightened and the stomach wrenching sensation of falling continued until Moriarty couldn't stand it anymore. They hit the surface of clean water, going almost to the bottom before Moriarty was able to reorient them and push them to back up into the air. They broke the water, coughing and spluttering.

"Quick, get onto my back," Moriarty said. "*Now*."

Terri instantly curved around her lover and Moriarty swam as fast as she could for the closest bank. She could feel things brushing at her legs.

They got to shallow water and Moriarty found her feet and ran as fast as she could up onto the bank of the river, well clear of the water.

Terri slid off her.

She collapsed onto her back, drenched and bleeding, chest heaving from exertion. Terri flopped down beside her.

"What's in the water, Mack?" Terri asked.

"Anti Flipper," Moriarty said. As if on cue, a piranha the size of a dolphin jumped out of the water, razor sharp teeth clicking together.

"Fuck," Terri said, watching it with wide eyes. She looked around. "This is jungle world, right?"

"Yeah, I think so," Moriarty said as the ground shook and a mushroom cloud of ash poured out of the volcanoes in the distance.

"I hate this place," Terri said. "Let's get out of here."

Moriarty, exhausted, sank back into Terri's arms as she cut a hole in the dreamscape.

They tumbled through and landed on Michelle's carpet. They were both soaked through and the wound on Moriarty's leg bled heavily.

Moriarty felt dazed. "I think I'm going to pass out," she said, and did just that.

WHERE AM I? Michelle's eyes fluttered open. She blinked. *I'm exhausted and I've got a splitting headache.*

The ceiling above her looked familiar and she stared at it for a few moments, trying to decide if it really was her bedroom. She felt warmth to one side of her and rolled over to find Monk, still terribly pale, lying beside her, out like a light. Her chest rose and fell at regular intervals. Jackie was on the other side of Monk, her arm thrown across her body.

"Monk," she whispered. "Jackie."

She pushed herself up, head throbbing, and studied her lover.

Monk was naked, as naked as she herself was, lying under a blanket. They were all clean; someone had taken the time to bathe them. She put a shaking hand on the valley between Monk's full breasts, feeling her heartbeat.

She's alive, Michelle thought, tears in her eyes. *She's alive.* She leaned over and gently kissed Monk's forehead.

She sat up, slowly and painfully, and gray flowers bloomed before her vision. She waited until it'd passed and swung her legs over the side of the bed.

She padded, naked, to her bedroom door and pulled the robe off the back of the door and slipped into it with a grunt of exertion. *I feel like I've gone ten rounds with a rhino.*

She pulled the door open and painfully made her way down the hallway toward the kitchen.

Terri was out like a light, Moriarty nestled protectively in her arms. Both were clean and in cut off shorts and tee shirts. Moriarty had a thick bandage on her calf. There was also a thick pad of gauze on the junction between her neck and shoulder.

She glanced at the counter and saw six power bars lined up, each with a PostIt note with their name printed in neat handwriting. She grinned. *That was probably Moriarty.*

She grabbed hers, tore open the wrapping, and bit into it. *Chocolate. Oh, nice.* She wolfed it down. She saw another PostIt note stuck to the refrigerator. It said *Fridge.* She pulled open the door and snorted a laugh as she saw a bottle with a note on it. It said, *Michelle.* Underneath that, *that was just for you, Mitch.*

Thank you for the chuckle and thank you adding extra food to my fridge. I must've been out for at least a couple of hours.

She pulled out the bottle and opened it with a firm twist. She took a sip. Nothing had ever tasted as good to her and she chugged half the bottle despite the temperature.

She went back into the living room and sank down into a recliner with a sigh. She looked at Terri and Moriarty, and her eyes flared yellow.

We'll try this the normal way. Moriarty's sparks looked dented and Michelle moved them so her outline appeared smooth and unbroken again. Her vision returned to normal.

Moriarty and Terri were both awake and watching her.

"Thank you, Michelle," Moriarty said softly. They disentangled from each other and sat up. "I appreciate it."

Michelle smiled. "You're welcome. What happened after—?"

"Roth took care of Angela. Then we took care of Hellstrom," Terri said.

"Thank you," Michelle said. She pulled at the lapel of her robe. "This was you guys as well?"

Moriarty's black eyes flashed and she nodded, quick grin showing her straight, white teeth. "Yup."

She's really beautiful, Michelle thought. "Thank you for that as well."

"No worries," Terri said. "We stocked your fridge as well."

"So I saw," Michelle said.

"Spit it out, what's bugging you?" Moriarty asked, studying her closely.

"Is Kilkenny still alive? Is Monk going to wake up again?"

"Kilkenny's alive but we'd better check on her," Moriarty said. "As for Monk, she's very much alive and she *will* wake up again. You look exhausted and I think at least half the reason for that is because Monk is drawing on you for energy. Just keep eating good, healthy food, get some rest and you'll both be feeling normal in a couple of days." She got up and went into the kitchen. She came back seconds later with a neatly de-seeded avocado and a spoon. "Here."

Michelle tasted a spoonful of avocado. *Oh, that's good.* She wolfed down the rest, Moriarty and Terri grinning as they watched.

"What happened to Kilkenny?" Michelle asked, going into the kitchen and tossing out the remains of her avocado.

"Angela put a controlling bond on her and tried to get her to kill Monk," Terri said. "The cut under her ribs . . . I don't know . . . that looked like it was spreading . . ." She exchanged a glance with Moriarty.

Moriarty took her hand and kissed her knuckles. "It *will* be all right. Roth is strong enough for all three of them and she's been around for a while. She knows what she has to do to keep them all safe."

"Did someone mention my name?" Roth asked. She looked cool and elegant as ever, despite the robe she wore and her terrible pallor.

"I did, old friend," Moriarty said, standing and giving her a hug. "It's good to see you up."

"It's good to *be* up," Roth said. "And it's good to see you too, Michelle."

Michelle nodded. "I know," she said as Roth grabbed her power bar. "Thank you. *All* of you. I love you guys."

Moriarty and Terri flashed her grins.

"You're welcome. We love you too," Moriarty said as she and Terri squeezed her.

"And I have to say, Michelle," Terri said. "I'm sorry. So sorry. I never meant to drag you into this. I never meant for anyone to get hurt."

"Neither of us did," Moriarty said. "I'm sorry."

"It's all right, guys," Michelle said, pulling them both in close. "If you guys hadn't turned up, I think we'd all be dead." She looked at Roth. "Kilkenny?"

"Rio and I are holding her here," Roth said. "She's close."

Michelle frowned. "Show me."

Roth nodded and led her to her spare room. "Don't be shocked."

Michelle nodded, wondering what Roth was going to show her. *How bad can this really be?*

Roth quietly opened the door and they all went in.

Kilkenny lay on her back in the middle of the bed, Riordan curled up beside her. Kilkenny looked so pale she was almost translucent. Riordan was as pale and her breaths were shallow with long intervals between.

Roth leaned down and pulled back the sheet covering them, careful to keep Riordan covered.

"Oh my god," Michelle said.

Kilkenny's entire torso had a troubling, grayish tint and the cut under her ribs looked swollen and infected. Tendrils of black crept outwards away from it. Michelle held her hand over the cut and felt the heat radiating out from it.

She shifted her vision. Kilkenny's sparks were a dull gold and moved slowly. The mass of infection was black with a knot of dark brown at the center, radiating outwards to grayish white sparks, lightening into golden.

"What do you see?" Roth asked softly.

Michelle looked at her, saw a thin streamer of silver that led into Kilkenny. A similar streamer led from Riordan also into her.

"You bonded her," Michelle said. "Good."

Roth shifted from foot to foot, looking anywhere but at her.

Michelle gently squeezed her shoulder. She turned to Terri and Moriarty. "We're going to lance the cut. It's got a better chance of healing if the infection is reduced."

Moriarty nodded. "Okay, what do you want us to do?"

"Bathtub," Michelle said with a sigh. "Terri, do you think you could—?"

"Sure," Terri said. She scooped up Kilkenny and carried her into the bathroom, Roth and Moriarty trailing behind.

Michelle's exacto knife was still in the bathroom, and she scooped it up from the counter and cleaned it. "Roth. Kilkenny might wake up for this so I need you to be here for her."

Roth nodded. "I will."

Michelle knelt by the tub and looked down at Kilkenny's bare body in the unforgiving bathroom light. Kilkenny looked worse than she thought. She sniffed and struggled to remain expressionless. The smell of death came off her in waves.

She looked up at Roth. "I don't know chapter and verse of what she said to you and it's okay not to tell me. I won't chase you about it. But I *will* tell you that if the content bothers you that much, you should be asking yourself why. Was there even a tiny little inkling of truth in it? Or are you just projecting your own fears?"

"I don't know what I think," Roth said. "I just want to talk to her again."

Michelle nodded. "Somehow we'll fix this. I promise, Roth."

"You think she'll live?" Roth asked hesitantly.

"I honestly don't know. That's not for me to decide. But I can promise you I'll do my level best to make her *want* to live. So will Monk."

Roth nodded. "Thank you. For everything."

"You're welcome," Michelle said. She leant over Kilkenny. "You may have to hold her down."

Moriarty took her legs and Roth took her shoulders.

Michelle braced herself and cut long and deep through the center of the terrible wound. Foul smelling pus and black blood welled out of it. She glanced at Kilkenny. Nothing. She was still dead to the world.

She took both sides of the cut and felt a nodule inside it. She squeezed as hard as she could and a solid knot of bloody, foul smelling matter shot out of the wound. Michelle shifted her vision and looked at the cut. It still looked terrible but one of the knots inside her was gone. The other was still there but was much smaller than the first had been. She tried to move Kilkenny's sparks but they wouldn't budge. When she tried to move some of hers toward Kilkenny, a terrible dagger of pain lanced through her head and she shifted her vision back. She held the heel of her hand against her throbbing temple.

"Michelle," Terri said. "Are you all right?"

"I'm okay," Michelle said. "I just tried to heal her cut. Works as well as it ever did, as you can see."

The cut was still swollen but didn't look as bad as it did. The terrible hint of gray in her skin had also faded a little so it looked healthier, and the tendrils of black had also retreated. The cut on her skin started to scab over and close.

Michelle glanced at Roth. Roth was on her knees before the tub, hanging her head.

"Roth," Michelle said urgently. "Let go."

Roth nodded. "I just wanted to give her enough to stop bleeding."

"You did it," Michelle said. She grabbed a wash cloth and cleaned the worst of the blood off Kilkenny. "All of you, back to bed. Rest."

Moriarty gave a bone cracking yawn. "I certainly wouldn't mind a little more shut eye." She leant over the tub to grab Kilkenny, but Roth gently shouldered her aside.

"I want to do it," she said, scooping Kilkenny up with trembling hands.

Michelle watched her go and rinsed out the tub.

"You think those three are ever going to talk? Properly?" she asked.

"I don't know," Terri said. "I hope so. Roth's hurting pretty bad."

"I've *never* seen Roth that hurt or off balance," Moriarty said. "So I really hope Kilkenny is gentle with her. I do *not* want to pick up pieces of my beloved best bud Roth."

"Same from Kilkenny's side," Michelle said. "We're just going to have to keep pushing them together." She smiled at Terri and Mack. "Now go and get some sleep. Really."

Moriarty nodded and took Terri by the hand and led her out of the bathroom.

Michelle made her way back into the bedroom and slipped into bed beside Monk. She was exhausted and was just beginning to drift off when she felt Monk stir.

She really is *going to be okay.*

She rolled over and snuggled into Monk, resting her head on Monk's broad shoulder and falling asleep, gentle smile tugging at her lips.

GOD, I FEEL like shit. Monk's body ached and she was tired.

She felt two bodies close to her, and turned to see Michelle's beautiful face relaxed in sleep at close range. Jackie was on the other side of her with a possessive arm thrown across her chest. She grinned.

Jackie's eyes fluttered open. She looked dazed for a moment, and then came into focus as she saw Monk looking at her. She leaned up and stared at Monk in wonder for a moment, studying her as if for the first time. Her eyes filled with tears and she reached out a trembling hand to trace her features, travelling down her neck to her chest. Her hand came to a halt on Monk's stomach.

"Hey, Jackie," Monk said softly.

Jackie's tears spilled over and cut tracks down her face. "Hey, Monk."

"You're still here," Monk said. She felt a million emotions slamming into her from all sides, leaving her shaking.

"I'm still here," Jackie said, nodding slowly.

"I'm glad. I was afraid you'd go again."

"I'm not going *anywhere*. I can't stand it anymore."

"Kiss me, Jackie, please," Monk whispered.

Jackie slowly leaned over and kissed Monk, but for Monk it was more than a simple kiss. It was gentle, desperate, loving and lasted long enough for Monk's toes to curl.

"I love you. I'm *in* love with you," Jackie said, looking as raw and vulnerable as Monk felt.

"I love you too, Jackie. So very much," Monk said, and they kissed again.

"I thought I'd—*we'd*—lost you for good this time," Jackie said.

"No way," Monk said. "I *knew* you'd be there for me."

"I nearly wasn't."

"But you *were*."

"Don't ever do that to me again," Jackie said. "I couldn't stand it if anything happened to you."

"I agree," Michelle said.

Monk turned and looked at Michelle. Michelle's beautiful eyes were a deep green, and Monk keenly felt her love for Michelle. She leaned up and kissed Michelle with all the passion she'd ever had for her lover. Michelle, who looked as desperate and raw as she was, returned it, moaning softly.

"I love you, so much," Monk said, trembling. She felt naked, stripped bare.

"I love you," Michelle said. Her heart shone in her eyes. "Forever, Monk. We promised each other forever."

"I *still* promise you forever. I never intended for what happened to happen. I thought Kilkenny would be able to hold off Michaels like I could," Monk said. "She couldn't. I don't know if it was because she's not a dream walker or something else."

"She's sick, Monk," Michelle said, relief and love shining in her eyes warring with concern for Kilkenny. "I don't think she could hold anything off now. The silver cut under her ribs flared up again. It's really bad. We lanced the cut."

"Who's we?" Monk asked.

"Roth, Riordan, and Kilkenny are in our spare room. Mack and Terri are on the couch."

"I had the impression things had gone south between those three," Monk said.

"Not quite. Rio and Roth bonded her and they're feeding her strength so her body can heal. They need to talk when Kilkenny wakes up. She said some awful things to them, from what I can understand."

"Okay," Monk said. "So she's a mess."

Michelle nodded. "I think so."

"Thank god she's still alive," Jackie said. "Do you know what happened?"

"I have no idea," Michelle said. "I was out like a light after I healed Monk."

"I'd better see how she's doing," Jackie said. She looked under the covers at herself. "Oh lord." She blushed.

Michelle and Monk exchanged a glance and laughed.

"We're both quite naked as well," Monk said.

"I'm glad you find this amusing," Jackie said, blushing harder.

"We're all adults here," Michelle said, smiling at her. "Besides, being seen naked by your lovers is part of the deal."

"This *had* to have been Mack's doing," Jackie said. She bit her lip. "My lovers." She seemed to taste the word. She looked at them. "I've never . . . never . . . you know . . ."

"We know it's your first time with a woman," Monk said gently. "And there's no rush. It'll happen when you're ready."

Jackie smiled and caressed her face. "Thanks." She looked relieved.

"No problem," Michelle said. "Can I ask you something off topic?"

Jackie nodded. "Sure."

"Aren't your parents going to be wondering where you are?" Michelle asked. "Aren't you supposed to be on holiday with them?"

Jackie blushed again. "I told them work needed me back so they dropped me off at the airport and I came straight here."

"I'm glad," Michelle said. "I'm glad you were here. I'm *not* glad you got dragged into this mess with us. I couldn't stand it if anything happened to you either."

Jackie smiled. "We're all really in this together, aren't we?"

"Yep," Monk said, grinning as Jackie rubbed her stomach and gently touched the swell of her breasts without seeming to be aware that she was doing it. "I hate to be pedestrian. But I have to get up and eat something. I'm starved and I don't have much energy left."

"Yeah," Michelle said. "I'm in that."

"I'll join you once I've stuck my head in on Kilkenny," Jackie said.

Monk and Michelle got out of bed. Monk could feel Jackie's eyes on them. She turned and tossed Jackie Michelle's robe, slipping her own on. Michelle pulled on shorts and an old sweatshirt.

Monk headed toward the kitchen, Michelle close behind her.

"God she's adorable," Monk said.

Michelle grinned. "Yeah."

"Well, well, well," Monk said, glancing at Terri and Moriarty curled up on their sofa. She grabbed her labeled power bar off the kitchen counter and grinned. "Who's responsible for the label?"

"Me," Moriarty said, sitting up. "Can't have one of you eating *all* of them, can we?"

Michelle pointed to the label on the refrigerator and Monk burst out laughing, trying not to choke on her power bar.

"That's good," she said, turning to Moriarty. "I'm Monk." She held out a hand and Moriarty ignored it. She engulfed Monk in a bear hug.

"Mackenzie Moriarty. You can call me Mack or Moriarty."

"Should I start in on the Sherlock Holmes jokes?"

"Never heard *that* one before."

Monk laughed.

Terri sat up. "Monk."

"Terri," Monk said, heading to the sofa as Terri stood.

They gave each other bear hugs.

"Thanks, Monk," Terri said softly.

"You're welcome," Monk said. She pulled back. "Is it over?"

"Yeah," Terri said. "Hellstrom and Michaels are both gone."

Monk looked between Moriarty, Terri, and Michelle.

"Now that we have the introductions out of the way, I want to ask a question. Why's my chest sore?" she asked.

Moriarty looked as though she was going to give Monk a teasing response but it died at the mild frown on Michelle's face.

"I don't know," Michelle said. "Is your chest sore?" Her eyes flared yellow and Monk felt tingling warmth on her sternum. The pain drained away.

"What happened?" Michelle asked, looking at Terri and Moriarty.

"Um," Terri said. "Monk wasn't breathing after you finished healing her."

"So we gave you mouth to mouth," Moriarty said.

"I died," Monk said.

Moriarty and Terri exchanged a glance.

"Um," Terri said, shifting from foot to foot. "I . . . guess . . . so?"

"You *guess* so. That means yes?"

Moriarty firmed her chin. She nodded. "That means yes."

"Then I'm alive because of you?"

"Only a little."

"Good enough." Monk launched herself forward and wrapped her arms around Moriarty, squeezing hard. "Thankyouthankyouthankyou."

Moriarty returned her hug, and said, "You're welcome."

Monk released Moriarty and looked at Michelle. Michelle was so pale she was almost translucent.

"Hey, Mitch," Monk said. "Hey." She approached Michelle and held out her arms.

Michelle was in them and sobbed against Monk.

"Hey, I'm fine, Mitch," Monk said. "Really."

Michelle squeezed her.

Monk held her and gently stroked her back. *Oh, Christ*. "I'm sorry, Michelle. I *never* meant to hurt you like that."

"I know, Monk," Michelle said, pulling back and looking at her. "You've *always* kept your promises to me. That one was no different to you."

"I will *always* be there," Monk said.

"You can't promise that," Michelle said.

"Maybe not, but I *can* promise to always *try* to be there. To not let myself get sucked into anything I know is too big for me."

"The problem is, Monk, that nothing *ever* looks too big for you," Jackie said quietly. "You're a lion. You always have been."

Michelle pulled back from Monk a little to allow Jackie to join them.

"Just *try* to keep the odds in your favor, all right?" Jackie said, slipping her arms around them both.

"For you two? Always," Monk said. "I promise."

"Same promise to you, Monk," Michelle said. "I'll *always* try to keep the odds in my favor."

"Same," Jackie said.

Michelle's intense eyes showed the truth of her promise, and Jackie's gentle eyes showed her calm confidence.

Monk nodded. She glanced over into the living room. Moriarty and Terri had left.

"I think I want to go and check on Kilkenny."

CHAPTER 15

MONK LED THE way into their crowded spare room.

Roth watched them as they came in.

"How's she doing?" Monk asked.

"She's a little better. The tendrils have retreated and she doesn't have that awful gray color," Roth said.

Monk nodded toward Riordan. "Rio? How's she doing?"

"She's getting a little stronger but she's still weak and she needs to eat."

"And *you*, Roth? How are you?"

"I'm on my reserves," Roth said. "When Michelle healed Rio it took all of Rio's strength and most of mine. I think the silver took hold of Kilkenny when *she* gave *me* most of her strength so I wouldn't . . . wouldn't . . ." Roth looked miserable.

Monk knelt beside Roth. "Let it go, Roth. It's all done now. We go from here. Let me talk to her when she wakes up. I'll try and make her *feel* better so you can all talk. Until then, it's out of your hands. Out of *all* of our hands."

Roth nodded and gave her a sad smile. "I know you're right. But the *knowing* doesn't make it any easier."

Monk nodded. "I agree." She felt a pair of hands on her shoulders, giving them a gentle squeeze. She looked up and saw Michelle's beautiful face. She looked like she wanted to crawl inside Monk.

Monk smiled and stood. "We'll leave you to your rest."

Roth nodded.

Monk left the room, Moriarty, Terri, Michelle, and Jackie in tow.

"Does anyone want a *real* meal?" Michelle asked. "I don't know about you guys but I'm *starving*."

Moriarty and Terri exchanged a look and nodded.

"Now you mention it," Moriarty said. "I'm famished."

"Yes, I am," Terri said. She grinned. "I stocked the fridge and I have an idea. How about some basic pasta and a salad?"

"Sure," Michelle said, heading toward the kitchen. "Monk, Jackie, you guys want a salad and some garlic bread to wash it down with?"

"Love to," Monk said.

"Sounds fantastic, thanks," Jackie said.

"If you don't mind I'm going to go and pull on some shorts. I feel underdressed," Monk said, plucking at her robe.

"No worries," Michelle said.

"Monk, I think I'm going to join you," Jackie said, biting her lip and blushing a little.

"Sure," Monk said easily. *Lord, you really* are *adorable. I can't believe you're so damn shy.* "C'mon."

She led Jackie into the bedroom and slipped off her robe. "You need to borrow anything?" She glanced at Jackie who gaze seemed to be glued on her. "Hey, sweetie. Do you need to borrow any clothes?"

"Yeah," Jackie said. "I do." She advanced on Monk and pushed her back down onto the bed, straddled her, and looked down at her with a predatory gaze.

This is way too fast for you I'm sure. Monk slowly sat up so Jackie was in her lap, facing her. She kissed Jackie, long and deep, feeling her body respond. She pulled back, gazing at her and gently teasing her breasts.

Jackie's breathing quickened. "This isn't really time for a good make out session, is it, Monk?"

"No, not at all," Monk said, nibbling her collar bones.

"That feels good," Jackie breathed, tilting her head back and allowing Monk better access. "We have to stop for now."

"I know," Monk said with an easy grin, despite her body's insistent throbbing. "It's okay." She pulled Jackie in close for a gentle hug. Jackie's arms tightened around her.

"I've gotta be frustrating the shit out of you," Jackie said. Her eyes stuttered to Monk's breasts and she colored slightly.

"I can live with this," Monk said. "We told you we can go at your pace. We both meant it. Give yourself time."

Jackie pulled back and looked into her eyes. "Really?"

"Hell yes," Monk said.

"I want there to *be* time for it to happen," Jackie said, running her fingers gently between Monk's breasts.

Monk caught her hands and pressed them over her heart. "There *is* time. I'm *not* going anywhere."

"All right," Jackie said. "I believe you."

"Just like that?" Monk asked, gazing into her dark blue eyes.

"I *have* to have faith in you, Monk," Jackie said. "I know I *can*. You've changed a lot since school. You see that there's so much in this world to live for. You're more open. It's part of why I let myself fall in love with you. Michelle's always been like that but you . . . you had me worried in school."

"I *have* changed a lot since school. It wasn't until I really let myself believe in Mitch and her love for me that I began to relax. My life up until then was pretty awful, but Michelle showed me *how* to open up. She's always been my lover, my teacher and my friend." She smiled. "Then there was you. You've *always* been there for me. *Always.* So has Kilkenny. I've been so lucky to have you guys. I don't think I'd have made it without you. I'm always going to love you for that."

Jackie smiled, tracing Monk's cheekbone. "I've never met anyone like you, Monk. You never looked at Kilkenny like she was a dangerous freak. You always took it in stride. And then when you got made, you two became playmates. You showed her how to be *normal*. You made it *fun* for her. You saved her, Monk, and I'm always going to love *you* for *that*."

She leaned forward and kissed Monk, gently and lovingly.

"Let's get dressed," she said softly when they broke. Her blue eyes shone and Monk gently pushed her red hair away from her forehead.

"Let's. Mitch is probably wondering where we are."

They disentangled and stood.

Monk loaned her old shorts and a tee shirt, and they headed back to the kitchen.

"Wait, Monk," Jackie said as they went down the hallway.

"What?" Monk asked, turning around and looking at her. *Why are her eyes yellow?*

Jackie was staring at the doorway to the office. "The doorway I created so I could get here. It's still here."

"It's not going to do any harm," Monk said.

"It did when we tried to go through it to get on the dreamscape to look for you. The second we did we fell through trapdoors to weird places in Hellstrom's construct."

"If Hellstrom is gone, and so is Michaels, the doorway shouldn't be there anymore. The dreamscape should have collapsed," Monk said.

"Agreed. We need to talk to Mack. She and Terri were the last ones there."

"In the meantime, why don't we make it so people bounce off it when they try to go into the room?"

"Why bother? Why not just collapse it?" Jackie asked.

"Because we don't know if we can get in there again," Monk said. "We *have* to re-enter the dream. There's a reason it hasn't collapsed and I don't know if this is good or bad."

"True," Jackie said. "We better talk to the others."

Monk nodded and they went into the living room.

Terri was helping Michelle in the kitchen and Moriarty was sitting on one of the stools at the counter.

"Hey," Monk said, sliding into the seat next to Moriarty.

"What *took* you so long?" Moriarty asked, grinning at her.

Monk stared at her. *Wow, what amazing eyes.* "We were *only* getting dressed, Mack. Or is that a strange psychosexual ritual for you?"

Michelle laughed, and Jackie clapped a hand over her mouth to smother her laughter.

Moriarty looked like she was thinking about it. "No, but it could be. Terri?"

Terri snorted a laugh. "You have to do that naked, Mack. *Naked.* Or are you losing your touch?"

Moriarty waggled her fingers. "You decide, lover girl."

Terri leant over the counter and stole a kiss. "You're such a brat, Mack."

Moriarty polished her fingers on her tee shirt. "And I'm good at it."

Michelle stirred the pasta sauce. "I think this is about ready."

"Thank you, Mitch," Monk said, as Michelle handed her plates and bowls.

"You mind handing a plate to Roth?" Michelle asked.

"Sure," Monk said.

"No need to," Roth said from the doorway. "I'm here."

"Excellent," Michelle said. "Let's eat. Do we save plates for Rio and Kilkenny?"

"I'll make sure they eat when they wake up."

"No problem. You can stay here for as long as you like, by the way. I don't think I said that," Michelle said.

"You didn't have to," Terri said, smiling at her.

They filled their plates and soon found themselves sitting at Michelle's dining room table.

Monk took a spoonful of pasta and her hunger sprang to life. She tore into her food and was onto a second helping about ten minutes later, the others close behind.

"God, this is about the best thing I've ever eaten," Monk said. "Thanks, guys."

"You're welcome," Terri said and Michelle together.

When they'd finished their second plates, they all sat back, satisfied.

"I have something to ask you, Mack," Monk said.

"Sure," Moriarty said. "Shoot."

"What happened with Hellstrom?" Monk asked.

"There was a doorway into the dreamscape," Mack said. "I went through it. Hellstrom was sitting in my old bedroom waiting for me. We fought and Terri took her out with a silver knife."

"Terri, did you go in with Mack?" Monk asked.

"No," Terri said. "I stayed after we put you all back here. We wanted to be sure you'd be okay. I went in when Mack called me."

"I called and you came," Moriarty said.

Terri nodded.

"Was the dreamscape still there after you got rid of Hellstrom?" Roth asked.

"Oh, yeah," Moriarty said. "I know we've gotta go in there and find out who's controlling it."

"Geez," Monk said. "I'm starting to get sick of this."

"I hear you," Moriarty said. "I was going to deal with it when I felt stronger. I might as well go to sleep and head in again."

"No you won't. You need some rest as well," Roth said. "I'll go in and do it."

"Oh, c'mon, Roth," Moriarty said. "You don't *look* like you're strong enough to deal with it."

"I *need* to go in," Roth said. "I have to call Kilkenny and see if she's all right. I *have* to."

Moriarty nodded. "All right. I get it."

Roth stood. "Michelle, Terri—thank you for a wonderful meal. Monk was right. That was absolutely fantastic."

Michelle and Terri both grinned.

"You're welcome," Michelle said.

They watched Roth head back to the spare room.

"Wow," Monk said softly.

They all nodded.

KILKENNY STOOD ON the lawn outside the mansion that held the drawing room. *I'm not looking forward to this. I don't want to go in. I want to run but Monk would slap me upside the head if I did. Wonder if I could call Monk? What if it's Monk calling* me? Her shoulders slumped. *I don't think I'm that lucky. I know it's either Roth or Rio calling me. They're close. I'm just going to have to grow up and face it. I said some terrible things and I at least have to say sorry even if Roth and Rio don't want to look at me again. When this is all over, no matter what, I'll* still *have Michelle, Monk, and Jackie. God. Monk. I stabbed her with a silver knife. How am I ever going to face Jackie and Michelle again? What have I done? I can't fix that.*

She squared her shoulders, took the marble steps up to the patio two at a time, and strode across it to the French doors. She kept her trembling hands in her jeans pockets. She made her way through the doors and looked around. She saw the same familiar things she'd always seen—the Victorian sofa and chairs, the ornate coffee table, thick Persian rugs, and high, ornate walls and ceiling.

Monk's face flashed in her mind, and she felt herself twist inside.

Roth leaned idly against the mantelpiece, before the ticking clock, watching her closely, her face carefully guarded.

Kilkenny automatically took in her lean beauty, unable to stop staring at her muscular body, gentle flare of her hips, her full breasts, and her beautiful face. She felt herself melt inside. *God, she's so* hot. As her gaze travelled up Roth's body, she felt herself slam into Roth's wary eyes.

"Roth," she said softly.

"Kilkenny," Roth said, unmoving.

Kilkenny awkwardly crossed to the sofa and sat down. Her knees were trembling. "What happened to Monk?"

"She's very much alive, young one. Michelle healed her."

Kilkenny felt her insides unclench. Monk was alive. "Where's Rio?" she asked.

"She's not here. She's very weak."

Kilkenny felt like crying.

"Is she going to be all right?" Kilkenny asked, peering at Roth.

"I think so. It will take some time." Silence reigned for a moment. "What of *you,* Kilkenny? How are *you* doing?"

"I feel weak," Kilkenny said. "I don't want to know what it feels like when I wake up. It's going to be ugly." She watched Roth's expressionless face closely. "And you? What about *you*?"

"Oh, I'm fine. Just a little tired, but it will pass."

Kilkenny felt her shaking worsen. She took a deep breath. *God hates a coward and I'm not one of those.* "I'm sorry, Roth. For what I said to you and to Rio in the corridor. I didn't mean it."

There was silence for a long time.

Kilkenny felt any hope of reconciliation disappear. The pain returned and she felt her eyes tear. *I won't cry,* she chanted to herself. She stood up.

"Apology accepted." Roth crossed to the sofa and sat down beside her. Roth's beautiful face blurred as Kilkenny's tears finally spilt over. Roth wiped away her tears with trembling hands and Kilkenny felt herself split open and cried in earnest. Roth's arms slipped around her, pulling her in close, and she let go.

Roth gently soothed her, letting her give vent to her misery.

"Neither of us is really upset by your shouting. Angela Michaels put a controlling bond on you, so that was out of your control," Roth said once Kilkenny had quieted a little. "We're both more concerned about *what* you said. Is that what you *really* think? That Rio is an animal who has nothing better to do than cheat on her lover? And that I think so little of myself that I'd turn a blind eye to it?"

Monk always says that truth is best. "The honest truth is that I don't know *what* to think about any of this," Kilkenny said. "I wish to God Rio had told me she had a lover. I would have had a choice. I would have been able to decide to fall in love with her rather than feel it slip away from me. I *do* feel like she took advantage of me. I *don't* know how I fit in with both of you." She studied Roth's face, seeing no signs of building anger in her gentle, green eyes. "And *you,* Roth. I don't know what you think about all of this. I'd like to know because you honestly don't strike me as desperate. You don't seem to me to be the type to let a lover cheat on you. I want to know what lies inside your heart, Roth."

There was silence for a moment.

"*You* lie in my heart," Roth said with a trace of a smile. "You fascinate me. I happened to come across you and your friends playing in my house its grounds. I wanted to know more about you."

"This construct is *yours*? You're *kidding* me."

Roth shook her head. "Yes, it's mine. I was flattered you all liked it so much." She smiled. "I showed Rio and we talked. We came here to meet you. She came ahead of me to Autumn Park to find you."

"How long have you been here for?"

"I was teaching in Queensland until the end of last year. Then I came down to Sydney again. Rio had gotten a job at Sacred Heart the year before." Roth smiled. "This is my house in Queensland."

"How did you handle the time apart?"

"We were never really apart. We were together all the time in the dreamscape. She told me she'd met you and she told me all about you. She told me *everything*, Kilkenny. I could see she was falling in love with you, and I knew I had a choice. I could split up with her—and I've *never* stopped loving her—or I could share her love. *Not once* have I *ever* felt her love for me diminish, despite hers for you. In fact, she loves me more than she ever did because I supported her as she followed her heart."

"Do I really mean that much to either of you?"

"She loves you. You mean a lot to her and to me as well." Roth smiled. "You mean a great deal to me, now, simply because of who you are."

"What do you feel for me?" Kilkenny asked, almost afraid of the answer.

"I'm falling in love with you," Roth said simply.

"*I'm* falling in love with *you*," Kilkenny said.

Roth smiled, leaned over, and kissed her. Kilkenny's desire exploded and took over, and she moved in close to Roth. She pushed her down onto the sofa, covering Roth's body with her own. She moaned at the feel of Roth's strong body pressed against hers, their breasts pressed against each other. Kilkenny kissed her way down Roth's neck, tearing the buttons off her shirt in her haste to feel Roth's soft skin.

Roth moaned and tore at her clothing and Kilkenny felt her mind dissolving at the soft touch of Roth's fingers and lips.

They lay together afterward, Kilkenny draped across Roth's body, arm across her torso, gently kissing the salty skin of her chest.

"Do you feel a little bit better now?" Roth asked. Her green eyes were calm and peaceful.

"Yes, I do," Kilkenny said softly. "I'm glad I haven't ruined things with you and Rio." She settled herself on top of Roth's bare body so she could see her eyes.

"No. We never had the chance to talk, and it hurt but it wasn't unrecoverable. Plus, you had a controlling bond on you." Roth smiled. "Do you think you could be a part of us?"

"I *want* to be. So badly. But you realize I'm in my last year of school? I have to study undistracted." She felt Roth's arms encircle her and her body responded. "And you're both *very* distracting," she added, breathless.

"We will wait for you. No dating until the end of the year," Roth said. "But you have to realize you can't look at me like that in roll call, don't you? You're going to kill me doing that."

"And you can't be staring at me either," Kilkenny said. "Although I admit that I enjoy it."

Roth laughed. "I don't think either one of us is going to win prizes for subtlety."

"We *have* to," Kilkenny said. "I don't want to hurt you or do anything that's going to get you into trouble."

"Don't worry about it," Roth said. "No one said we couldn't be friends, even though my behavior is unethical and unprofessional." She eyed Kilkenny. "I've learnt over the long course of my life that sometimes it's better not to wait despite questions of ethics and morality. I also think that you're old enough for what's happening between us. We wouldn't have just done what we did if I didn't think that." She smiled. "If we want to go crazy with each other, we do it here where there are no prying eyes. If that's something you'd be willing to do?"

"Of course I'm willing. Sounds like a nice compromise." Kilkenny smiled. "I'm sure I could ask Monk to cut a doorway for us . . ." The past days in the dreamscape slammed down on her again. "Monk."

"Easy," Roth said softly, stroking her back. "Easy. Monk isn't mad at you. You just have to talk to her."

"I stabbed her with a silver knife."

"She knows that. She *understands*, love."

Kilkenny's breath caught at the endearment. She gazed into Roth's eyes, seeking the truth. "Really?"

"Yes. Really," Roth said. "Since when have you been afraid of your Monk?"

"I'm not afraid of her, I just feel *horrible* about it," Kilkenny said. "I hurt her badly. I hurt her *wife* and my *sister*."

"Do you want us to be there?"

"No, I think I'm good. I want to talk to Monk alone first." She bit her lip and looked at Roth. "Monk means a lot to me."

"I know she does," Roth said. "We *both* know that."

Kilkenny nodded. "Where's Rio, anyway? I thought she'd be with you—with *us*."

Roth flinched. "She can't be with us just now."

"Why?"

"She's in a coma. Her body has to recover."

"She's *what*?" Kilkenny said. "God, no. No." She looked at Roth. "I'll give you everything I have to bring her back."

"*No,* Kilkenny," Roth said. Her eyes sparked. "You've done enough of that."

"Oh, no," Kilkenny said. "Is it *my* fault she's in a coma? Did I do that to her?"

"I didn't mean it that way," Roth said. "That *isn't* your fault. When you strengthened our bond, you gave too much of yourself to us. The silver poison in your body took over again. That was how Angela Michaels was able to control you so easily. We *all* have to get our energy reserves again, or things will go badly for us, worse than they are now."

"So this *is* all my fault."

"*No.* It isn't."

Kilkenny felt sick and unable to look Roth in the eyes. She studied Roth's soft skin.

"Look at me, love," Roth said gently.

Kilkenny heard the pain in her voice and dragged her gaze away from Roth's chest to her beautiful, green eyes, her inner strength shining in them.

"Shift," Roth said.

Kilkenny shifted her vision and Roth's body dissolved into sparks. She saw a silver cloud of sparks around Roth. They looked healthy.

"Your bond looks fine," Kilkenny said. "That means Riordan is still very much alive."

"That's right," Roth said.

A silver streamer caught Kilkenny's attention. She couldn't see where it ended, but it seemed to be connected to her somehow.

"Why do I see another shape shifter bond? Is that coming off me?" she said, shifting her vision back.

Roth looked a little abashed.

"You *bonded* me?" Kilkenny said. "Why, Roth? Why did you do that?"

"We did it so you would heal from the silver poison," Roth said. "We were able to push it down a little and Michelle cut out half of it. You're still sick but your body is fighting back."

"Thank you," Kilkenny said, at a loss for words. If she went, they would go. The simple action touched her so much she felt like crying. If she'd needed proof that Roth and Rio both loved her, she'd gotten it. She felt vulnerable and exposed. Roth kissed her and tightened her hold on Kilkenny, giving her wordless reassurance.

"You're welcome," Roth said. She tilted her head, studying Kilkenny. "We still need to collapse the dreamscape that Michaels built."

"Shouldn't it have done that by itself?"

"Yes. Something is holding it in place. My original intention was to call you and we could go in together to see why."

"That idea tanked, didn't it?" Kilkenny said. "I know we have to do it. But I want to get back to the physical world and see Rio. I have to *know* that she's all right before we do."

Roth nodded. "I understand. Let's go."

KILKENNY OPENED HER eyes. *Oh God, I'm so sore. The cut's bothering me really badly.*

She felt Roth lean up beside her and felt for her lover. Roth looked down and stole a kiss.

"It's good to see your beautiful brown eyes in the physical world," Roth said. "How do you feel?"

"Like I decided to go and bungee jump without the elastic cord."

"You still look pale but better than you did."

Kilkenny painfully rolled over so she could see Riordan.

Riordan looked dreadfully pale. Her arctic grey eyes were closed. Her chest rose and fell with her even breathing. It looked like she would wake at any second, but Kilkenny knew it wasn't true.

"I'm going to strengthen our bond," Kilkenny said.

Roth frowned slightly. "Don't over exert yourself."

"I won't," Kilkenny said. "It's not like that anyway."

The world dissolved into sparks and she looked at the bonds she had with Riordan and Roth. She pushed her silver sparks forward and they surged toward Roth and Riordan. The bond suddenly roared to life between them. It almost felt like an explosion and Kilkenny was glad she was lying down.

Roth's essence rushed into her, filling every corner of her soul, mixing with the outpouring from Riordan. She could feel the truth of Roth's and Riordan's love, and the passion that lay between all of them.

She also felt Roth's worry, more than she'd let on.

"You're too worried about Rio for my taste," Kilkenny said. "Can you wake her up?"

"It would require giving her energy and I don't dare do that since you're so sick. I *know* how badly that cut pains you now."

I can't keep any secrets from either one of them, Kilkenny thought.

"No," Roth said. "No more secrets."

Kilkenny opened her mouth and felt amusement coming to her from Roth.

"No, I'm not telepathic," Roth said. "I just know what you feel."

Kilkenny smiled, despite herself.

"Take the energy to wake Rio up," Kilkenny said. She held up her hand. "Before you tell me about the energy again, remember that *she* needs it as well. We're all going to eat once she's woken up. If we need energy, that's the best way to do it."

Roth nodded. "I agree. But it means we won't be going back to the dreamscape to collapse it. We don't have enough between the three of us for that. I'm going to ask Mack for help."

"Okay," Kilkenny said.

Roth's eyes flared yellow and she gently touched Riordan's forehead. Riordan moaned softly.

"I'm going to Mack," Roth said. She nodded toward Riordan. "Her eyes will be open in less than a minute."

Roth slid out of bed, and Kilkenny eyed her lean beauty and the flash of her full breasts from the opening in her robe. Her desire ratcheted up a notch despite the terrible pain of her wound. Roth glanced at her with a half smile, her own desire flowing into Kilkenny through their bond.

"You're going to kill me, you know that?" she said.

"I'm killing *myself* by doing that," Kilkenny said. "I can't help it. I just can't help myself."

"Neither can I," Roth said, shaking her head. "I give up." She crossed back to Kilkenny and kissed her hard. Kilkenny felt herself loosen and attacked Roth's lips, wanting to tear her robe off. They broke, and Roth backed up a little.

"That didn't help," she said.

"No," Kilkenny said. "That just made things worse."

"I hope you get better *soon*."

"I will," Kilkenny said. "I'm not about to let you do *that* to me and just walk off."

Roth snorted a laugh and shook her head. "I'm not going to tease you about it. I can't." She looked deep into Kilkenny's eyes for a moment. She looked as though she wanted to say something but shook her head, breaking the moment. "I'm going to go and get all of us a bite to eat."

Kilkenny nodded and watched Roth's behind as she left the room.

"Kilkenny," a weak voice beside her said.

She looked down, transfixed, at Riordan's beautiful, bloodshot, arctic gray eyes.

"Rio?" she asked softly. "I love you. I'm sorry for hurting you."

Riordan's eyes filled with tears, and she reached for Kilkenny. Kilkenny suppressed a yelp as Riordan snuggled into her and brushed against her cut. "I'm sorry for hurting you, Kilkenny. I know I should have told you about Roth early on. I should have but I couldn't. I didn't want to lose either one of you."

"I talked to Roth. I told her I *wish* you'd told me about her because I would have had the choice of falling in love with you. That's wrong. I *never* had a choice about falling in love with you. You stole my heart, Rio, and it hurt really badly when you finally told me about Roth. I felt *betrayed.* You *should* have told me much earlier on in the piece."

"I know. I'm sorry."

"You're forgiven, you know why?"

"No. It's too easy. Why?"

"Because I realized that after I found out about Roth, I never thought about *you* alone. My love for you hasn't changed. It won't. I'm falling in love with Roth. When I think about you and me, it isn't just you and me. It's all three of us. We're *together.* We're equal partners."

Riordan's eyes filled with tears that spilt over. "Thank you, sweetie. Thank you for accepting *both* of us into your heart."

Kilkenny closed her eyes and drank in their bond. She felt as though she had Roth and Riordan cupped gently in her hands. Riordan's heart felt gentle and sweet and a little afraid. Roth was a primal ocean of passion, strength and absolute confidence. In that second, Kilkenny realized she *really* had no choice. She *needed* Riordan's gentleness and Roth's passion. They were the qualities that drew her to Monk and to Michelle and that she valued the most in Jackie. She felt herself slipping over the edge into an abyss with them both.

"I love you, Rio," she said, kissing Riordan's head. "I'm in this for keeps."

Kilkenny felt her relief.

Riordan's arms tightened around her and this time Kilkenny could not stop her yelp as the pain flared and crashed over the top of her. She was distantly aware of Riordan's consternation before she blacked out.

CHAPTER 16

MORIARTY WAS JUST drifting off to sleep in Terri's arms when she heard Roth enter the kitchen. She felt Terri's arms tighten around her, and she kissed the soft underside of Terri's jaw.

"Love you," she whispered. "I want to talk to Roth quickly."

"Okay," Terri said.

Moriarty gazed into her stormy gray eyes. "God, I want you so bad."

"It's going to be all the sweeter when we're alone at last, won't it?" Terri kissed her. "And it'll be a long night. I want *you* every bit as much as you want me."

Moriarty smiled at her and gently disentangled herself. "I know."

"Roth," Moriarty said, watching Roth as she prepared a tray of food for them. Suddenly Roth groaned and clutched the counter top.

Moriarty rushed over and hung onto her. "*Roth.* What happened?"

"Mack," Roth ground out. She looked whey faced. She also looked like she was fighting tears, Moriarty saw with alarm.

"What on earth is the matter, Roth?" Moriarty asked, quickly putting her arms around Roth and pulling her in for a close hug.

"I met Kilkenny but we didn't get around to collapsing the dreamscape," Roth said, arms tightening around Moriarty.

"Okay but that's hardly the end of the world, Roth. I'll just go in with Terri and we'll take care of it." She pulled back and looked at Roth, almost frightened. *Nothing bothers her. She's the most self assured person I've ever known.*

Roth looked like she was fighting herself. Her shoulders finally slumped. "It's Kilkenny. I'm not sure she's going to make it."

"*What?*" Moriarty asked sharply. "Why on earth not?"

"The silver in her system is gaining ascendancy again. I just felt it. Riordan and I just aren't strong enough between us to draw the poison out of her system. Riordan's strength won't return unless she stops giving it to Kilkenny. She's only going to get weaker. *I* don't have enough for them *both* to heal. We have to choose who lives and who dies."

"Oh, Roth," Moriarty said. She could feel that Terri had sat up and was watching them closely. She glanced at her lover. Terri looked horrified.

"That's not a choice I'll stand by and let you make," Moriarty said. She glanced at Terri and nodded toward Michelle's bedroom. Terri nodded and silently left the living room. "We're going to work something out."

Roth's tears came, then. They hurt Moriarty nearly as much as Roth. Every one made Moriarty bleed on the inside. Roth was someone who cried so rarely it was terrifying to see when it happened. Moriarty knew she was torn apart deep inside.

Michelle and Monk, both looking flushed, appeared a few moments later. Terri followed behind them, blushing, and Moriarty caught a flash of her embarrassment. She sent Terri calm reassurance. They'd made love and it didn't surprise her. They'd understand why Terri had gotten them.

"What's up?" Michelle asked, staring intently at Roth and Moriarty.

Roth glanced at Michelle and gently disentangled herself from Moriarty.

"We're sorry to bug you, Mitch," Moriarty said. "We have a bit of a problem. The silver's taking over Kilkenny again."

"Aw, shit," Monk muttered. "Why? How?"

"Rio and I aren't strong enough to give her the energy to push it back."

"Are you saying the silver poison is going to kill her?" Monk asked.

Roth nodded. "We can't help her."

"What about one of us?" Michelle said, exchanging a glance with Monk. "Jackie can't really help. She's passed out. She got wiped out helping Monk."

"No. Michelle, you're not strong enough and you know it."

"How about one of us?" Moriarty asked. Terri nodded. "I've got enough to hold up everyone in the room including you, Roth."

"I can't ask that of you, Mack," Roth said. "And we need you to be whole and healthy to collapse the dreamscape."

"Why don't *I* collapse the dreamscape?" Terri asked. "It shouldn't be as hard on me as it is on you, right?"

"I don't want you to go in by yourself, love," Moriarty said. "It's not safe."

"I don't understand what the big rush is, anyway," Terri said. "Why don't we just help Kilkenny first and deal with the dreamscape later?"

"I think I might know why," Monk said slowly. "When we create something in the dreamscape, the energy comes from inside to move the unformed matter around into constructs and dreams. I know that because I can feel it inside when it happens. Michaels was *too* strong in the dreamscape and it didn't collapse when she died. That means *someone else* is keeping the dreamscape intact and was feeding her energy. She was using a kind of human—or shape shifter—battery to keep everything running while we were inside. It wasn't Hellstrom because she's gone as well and the dreamscape is *still* there. We have to go and help the poor soul who's being drained to death."

Moriarty nodded, her respect for Monk going up a notch. "Very good, Monk. You're right."

Terri growled in frustration. "They were a sick pair of arseholes, weren't they?"

"Yeah, that's putting it mildly," Moriarty said. "Which is why we *really* need to go in there and collapse the bloody thing."

"Monk," Michelle said softly, shaking her head. "Please."

Monk smiled at her and gently cupped her face. "Do you mind going and getting Jackie?"

Michelle nodded. She disappeared down the hallway and returned a minute later, a yawning Jackie in tow.

Monk turned to the others. "I have an idea, if everyone's interested?"

Moriarty nodded, glancing at Roth. Roth looked at the point of collapse. Her color had faded to an ugly white and the burning intensity in her eyes told Moriarty that willpower alone kept her conscious.

"Shoot, Monk," she said.

"Terri, you don't know quite enough yet about being a dream walker to collapse the dreamscape and Jackie's not up to it. So you, Mack and you, Terri, go into the dreamscape and call me. I'll go with you and tell you how to do it. Michelle and Jackie will stay here and do what they can for Roth, Rio, and Kilkenny."

"Oh, Monk," Jackie said.

"Monk," Michelle said. "No. You're still too weak."

"Hey," Moriarty said. She felt the heat from Terri's body as her lover slid into place behind her, giving her a gentle squeeze. She stroked Terri's arms. "You have nothing to worry about. We'll take care of her. I won't let *anything* hurt her."

"Guys," Monk said. "I have an idea."

"What?" Michelle asked.

Monk pulled them into a huddle and they whispered quietly together for a few moments. They separated.

"You think that'd work?" Michelle asked.

"Yes. It'll work," Jackie said. "But listen, Monk. *Be careful*, you understand?"

"I will," Monk said. She looked over Michelle's shoulder, alarmed. "Roth?"

Roth's head hung and the arm holding the counter top was trembling. She swayed and Michelle caught her as her legs gave out and she collapsed.

"I got her," Moriarty said as Michelle carefully lowered Roth to the floor. "I'll take her in with the others."

She went to Michelle's side and carefully picked her up. Roth's body was limp and her breathing was shallow.

Aw, shit, please don't give up on us, Roth. I can't imagine a world without you in it.

She took Roth into the spare room and carefully laid her on the bed beside Kilkenny. Kilkenny's skin looked waxy and her breathing was shallow. Moriarty pulled back the flap of her robe and hissed as she saw Kilkenny's wound. It was black and had tendrils. The center was a pool of yellow pus and she was bleeding.

"That looks terrible," Terri said from over her shoulder.

Moriarty nodded. "Yeah, it does."

"We better get moving," Terri said. "The sooner we take care of the dreamscape the better." She studied Moriarty. "But I still think I've missed something. *Why* are we doing this? *Why?* Isn't Kilkenny at least as important as the person in the dreamscape?"

Moriarty looked at her, studying her beautiful face. Terri looked terrible. Her anguish was clear in her face and through their bond.

"I think I know what Monk has planned," Moriarty said. "Creating a dreamscape has to do with energy. When you create, you give energy. When you collapse, you take it back. That dreamscape that Michaels created was one hell of a whopper. There's a lot to give back. But to do that, you have to *take over* maintaining the dreamscape first. That's going to be a terrible drain to whoever does it. But once it's done and the collapse begins, there's going to be enough energy to fuel a small country. I think Monk is banking on taking it and feeding it to Michelle and Jackie so they can help Roth, Kilkenny, and Riordan."

"That's a really good idea," Terri said. "But I thought Michelle couldn't heal Kilkenny?"

"I agree," Moriarty said. "So I'm going to suggest an alternate arrangement."

"What?" Terri asked. "My only suggestion would be that Jackie and Monk go into the dreamscape and we stay behind here. We can get Michelle to link us to them so we can keep them alive." She studied Moriarty. "We're the only ones who aren't too weak."

"*You* could help Monk, you know," Moriarty said. "*You* could help her in the dreamscape. You're a dream walker."

"I know," Terri said. "And I *want* to."

Moriarty nodded. "Let's go talk to the others."

They went back into the living room. Jackie, Monk, and Michelle were sitting close together on the sofa.

"So, ladies," Moriarty said, flopping down into the recliner opposite them. "I know what you have planned, Monk."

"You do?" Monk asked. "And what would that be?"

"You plan on using the energy that's already on the dreamscape to fuel the others, aren't you?"

Monk nodded. "Good."

"That's all well and good, but how do you plan to get the energy to Roth, Riordan, and Kilkenny?"

Jackie looked miserable. "We can't do it the way we are now. We're going to have to break our bond to Monk and Roth's bond to Kilkenny. Monk is going to bond Kilkenny and give the energy to her directly."

"How do the shape shifter bonds work?" Terri asked. "When I tried to touch Kilkenny's bond—and Roth's—it hurt. Kilkenny's bond shied away from me. How are you three able to be bonded at all?"

"It's hard to describe," Michelle said. She looked pale and miserable. "*I* have the ability to form multiple shape shifter bonds, not these two. I'm guessing you fall into the same category as them. I also *can't* form a shape shifter bond with Kilkenny. We seem to repel each other. I can break and repair shape shifter bonds. Kilkenny showed me how to do it. The only problem is that it takes energy for me to do it."

"If Kilkenny can form multiple bonds, why not just put Monk and Kilkenny together and leave your bond alone?"

"*I'm* part of our bond. It's the *me* part that Kilkenny has trouble with. I can't be there at all in the bond with Kilkenny," Michelle said. She looked at Monk. "We have to break our bond to link her to Kilkenny."

Moriarty could not stop her flinch. She felt Terri and couldn't imagine how it would be not to have her there. She felt gentle reassurance and looked up to see Terri gazing at her, her stormy gray eyes gentle.

"Okay," Moriarty said. "Can you link me to Roth? I'll send them both to sleep."

"Would you consider linking with me?" Michelle asked. "I'm going to need a boost to stop broken bonds from killing everyone."

Moriarty glanced at Terri, who nodded. "Of course. What do you want me—us—to do?"

"Shift and hold still," Michelle said. She turned to Monk and kissed her, tears in her eyes. "When the bond is broken, look at Kilkenny. Take her the way you took me."

Jackie draped her arms over Monk's shoulders and kissed the top of her head. "I don't want this. Thank you for doing it."

"You probably aren't going to want me to rejoin after we get back," Monk said with a grin that didn't touch her intense, blue eyes.

Michelle said nothing, simply studied her with sad eyes.

Moriarty looked at Terri. She could feel Terri's pain for them and sent her gentle reassurance. She shifted her vision and Terri sprang into sharp focus. She could clearly see every curve of her creamy skin, the specks in her stormy gray eyes, her full, red lips, and her long, blue black hair. Now the scent of perfume and her essence came to Moriarty and she took a deep breath, drinking her in, stunned by her sheer beauty.

"Focus, Mack," Terri said softly.

Moriarty felt her face heat and turned her attention to Michelle. She saw the telltale silver glow and studied it. It was like a part of her reached out and touched Michelle, a gentle, feather light touch. She was suddenly seized and pulled forward with incredible force, as though she'd been yanked straight across the room. She slammed into Michelle, buffeted by the emotions that tore through her.

Michelle was upset and worried. She also felt terrible uncertainty. Jackie was simply sad and felt regret. Monk was a calm river of peace and strength.

"Now, you, Monk," Michelle said. She touched Monk's face with shaking fingers. "Come back to me," she whispered.

"I will," Monk said. "I promise."

"When I break the bond to us, grab whatever you can see on Kilkenny," Michelle said.

Moriarty felt Monk flinch, and felt reassurance. She glanced at Terri. It was Terri, and she added her own reassurance to hers. She felt Michelle grab her hand and she squeezed it in return.

Suddenly Monk was gone and Moriarty almost staggered. Michelle's eyes shone yellow and Moriarty felt her knees become rubbery. She sat down.

"What the hell?" she asked.

"Sorry, that was me. I had to trim off Monk's bond so the leaving wasn't fatal," Michelle said. "I needed some of your strength."

"Take what you need," Moriarty said, gently soothing both hers and Jackie's pain.

"Okay," Michelle said. Her voice shook. "Monk, shift. Grab Kilkenny's bond when you see it."

Suddenly Roth and Riordan both moaned, and then stilled. Monk moaned and flinched.

"Fuck," she muttered. Michelle put a gentle hand on her back and rubbed her.

Monk looked at her, anguish in her eyes. Michelle looked back with the same anguish. Tears slowly made their way down Jackie's face. Monk immediately pulled them both in close.

Moriarty called for Terri. They then left the room and headed to the spare room and Roth. Moriarty immediately pulled Terri into her arms, overcome by the anguish from their new bond mates. Jackie felt the worst of Michelle and Terri. She hurt and that was all that seemed to come from her.

Michelle joined them a few moments later, composed. Underneath the calm, Moriarty could feel her emotional wound. It was almost as if she was bleeding. There was an aura of desperation that did not show in her face.

"I'm going to break the bond to me and put you together with Roth," Michelle said. "Ready?"

Moriarty nodded. "Fire away."

Michelle's eyes flared yellow and Moriarty flinched as she felt a strange sensation, almost like a band aid being torn off. She suddenly felt Roth flowing into them, over them, through them. It was like an unstoppable tide, ridden by Riordan.

It was an ocean of primal, elemental passion, covered by a thin veneer of gentleness. It finally stabilized as Moriarty held onto Terri for dear life. It felt as though they were in a small boat on a wide ocean.

"Whoa," Moriarty said and Terri nodded. "Roth."

Terri nodded. "And Riordan."

Michelle dropped onto the edge of the bed.

Moriarty immediately knelt beside her. "Are you all right?"

"I'm exhausted. I think I have to go and lie down for a while."

Moriarty nodded. "Go and lie down. I'll tell Jackie."

Michelle nodded. "Thanks."

As soon as she left the room, Moriarty turned to Terri. "Whatever you do, do it quick."

"Are you all right?" Terri asked, looking at her, concerned.

"No," Moriarty said. "I think I'm going to pass out."

Gray flowers bloomed in her vision and she felt the sensation of falling. She braced herself for an impact that never came. She felt Terri's arms scooping her up before the darkness took her completely.

MONK LOOKED AT her two lovers. It felt so *empty* without them. *Is this really what it felt like before we bonded? I* hate *this. I like feeling as though Michelle and Jackie are always with me.* She looked at them both. *I'm jealous. They have something I want to be a part of.* It felt the same as when she'd first seen Michelle give Terri a hug and kiss goodbye.

"There's no need to be jealous, love," Michelle said, as though reading her mind. "You hold my heart. That's something you've *never* had to worry about."

She felt Jackie's hand on her back and turned. Jackie immediately slipped her arms around Monk, pulled her in close, and kissed her.

Monk tasted her, and when they broke, she pulled back, breathing hard. Jackie looked like she wanted to eat her.

"Don't look at me like that," Monk said softly.

"I want," Jackie said. "Remember that."

Monk smiled, some of her unease receding.

"How's Kilkenny doing? How are *you* doing?" Michelle asked.

Monk felt in her bond for Kilkenny. Kilkenny seemed almost flat. Monk searched the bond for her, almost calling for her friend. She found a tiny spark in the darkness and she rushed toward it, taking in both hands and cradling it gently.

"I can feel her," Monk said. "She's very weak. I've got her."

She pulled the spark in close, feeding it so it became a small flame.

"Hey, guys," Terri said, coming into the living room with Moriarty cradled in her arms. Monk peered at Moriarty as Terri carefully laid her out on the sofa.

Moriarty was pale but still looked in good health. She looked as though she was deeply asleep.

"Is she all right?" Monk asked.

Michelle's eyes flared yellow and she looked at Moriarty. "She's all right. Her sparks are a little dim but they're stable." She shifted back. "How's Kilkenny look?"

"Bad," Terri said. "We'd better get moving."

Monk nodded. "We're going. We're going to use Jackie's doorway."

"We could end up anywhere," Terri said.

"What difference does it make?" Monk said. "We don't really know where Michaels's source of power is. Anywhere we look is as good as anywhere else."

Terri nodded. "True, I suppose."

"How are you feeling?" Jackie asked.

"I'm fine," Terri said. "I'm a bit tired. I feel like I'm walking with weights on."

"Monk?" Jackie asked.

"I feel like I've just run a marathon and need to sit down," Monk said.

Michelle instantly looked concerned. "Are you going to make it?"

"Yep," Monk said. "We only have to go one way. I'll be fine once we collapse the dreamscape."

"I'll come with you," a weak voice said from the sofa.

"No you won't. You aren't up to it." Monk leant over and looked into Moriarty's tired black eyes. "I won't let anything happen to Terri, all right?"

Moriarty nodded. "I trust you." She sighed. "You know to look for the antibodies, don't you?"

Antibodies. I like that. Monk nodded. "I do." She turned to Terri. "We'd better get moving."

"Yeah," Terri said. "Let's get this over with."

They took their leave of their lovers and went down the hallway to the office.

"I'm going to open the door again," Monk said.

Terri's eyes faded to yellow. "Go ahead."

Monk shifted her vision and auras sprang up around the doorway. "Grab a hold of me."

Terri's arms encircled Monk and she suddenly found herself nose to chest Terri. *I'm almost glad Mitch and Jackie can't feel me right now,* Monk thought, distracted by the sight and feel of Terri's perfect, creamy skin.

She smiled at Jackie and Michelle as they watched her take a step backward through the door.

They almost instantly plummeted and Monk held onto Terri for dear life as they were torn sideways, shot upward for a few seconds, and then finished with a stomach turning plunge downward.

"*Shit,*" Monk screamed as they tumbled down into a marsh.

Monk landed heavily, Terri on top of her. The breath exploded from her lungs and she lay, stunned for a moment. Terri lay on top of her, breathing heavily.

"That was pretty fucking awful, wasn't it?" Terri said after a moment, levering herself up so her weight rested on her forearms. She stared at Monk. She looked as dazed as Monk felt.

"You reckon?" Monk asked.

Terri smiled and rolled off her. They sat down in the mud, side by side, resting for a moment. "What do you suggest we do now?"

"We have to find Angela's source of power," Monk said. "We've got Marsh World, Carnival World, Seaside World, Jungle World, and Autumn Park to look in. Where do you want to start?"

"What did Mack mean about the antibodies?" Terri asked.

"Michaels and Hellstrom would have protected their power source. They did everything to stop us from reaching it. They created constructs to function like anti bodies," Monk said.

"Okay. I'm not sure this would be the right world, then," Terri said. She looked around at the almost featureless marsh and the unforgiving, overcast sky. "I can't *believe* how shitty this all is. And a good dose of it is *my* fault."

"Look," Monk said. "Pick up your teeth and keep going. You were bonded to me for a very short while. Do you *really* think I'm actually *angry* at you?"

Terri studied her carefully for a few moments. "No, you're not, are you? Why?"

"What I did to you in high school was much, much, much worse than what's just happened to us. I just stood back and made decisions for *all* of us without *once* thinking of the effect they'd have on you. You have no idea how sorry I am for that." She took a deep breath. "You once told me it was about choice and to consider all the people around you. It is, really. Even this. You told me to *never* write off my friends. I could rely on you. Well, that works both ways. We could have just folded and called you and let Hellstrom do what she wanted, but we didn't. We couldn't. *You* are *my* friend. *Our* friend. We had a choice and we *chose* to help you. *You* can rely on *us*. No matter what, I will be there. I won't leave you unless you tell me to go and mean it."

She watched Terri for a moment. She could see Terri was thinking about it. *She's the most beautiful woman I've* ever *seen.* She felt inside for Kilkenny, and it felt like Kilkenny sleepily nuzzled her, radiating gentle warmth to her friend. Kilkenny felt *safe.* Monk smiled.

"I often wondered why you were single," Monk said. "You've always had your choice of women, but you always seemed so restless."

"I always wanted Mack. I never found anyone even close to her. I fell in love with her the first moment I ever saw her and the emotion just never let me go. I thought she died and a big chunk of me died as well."

"I missed you when you went away," Monk said. "So did Kilkenny, Jackie, and Mitch. You've always been a *real* friend, Terri. Are you going to leave again?"

"I don't think so. Home is where Mack is. *I'm* home for Mack. We both want to stay here. So, I think, do Roth and Riordan."

"I'm glad," Monk said, putting a friendly arm around Terri. "It's good to have you back."

Terri's arms slipped around her and tightened. "You really *are* a good friend, Monk."

Monk smiled. She levered herself to her feet and held out a muddy hand for Terri. Terri took it and Monk pulled her up.

"Train tracks?" Monk said.

"Hell, yes," Terri said, looking down at her feet. She'd sunk into the mud. "I could do without the aerobic walking, thanks."

"I hear ya," Monk said. She looked around. "You know, we could save a hell of a lot of trouble and just cut our way into the next world."

"We could," Terri said. "We could also save even more time if we went straight to the world that we thought had our mystery person in it."

"Where would the most logical place to start be?"

"I don't think this is it. There's nowhere to hide."

Monk saw something move out of the corner of her eye. She turned to follow it and saw a bulge appear in the distance. "Uh, oh. Wonder if that's the squid Mack was talking about?"

Terri turned to look in the direction of her gaze. "Oh, my god. That looks bad."

"Real bad," Monk agreed easily. She shifted her vision and the dreamscape filled with auras. "This is better. Now I can actually *see* something."

The bulge in the marsh land became more pronounced and the flat, steadily rushing wind picked up.

"Tornado time," she said. "We're not staying."

She tore a hole in the dreamscape and looked in it. It was seaside world. Monk shuddered. "Okay, this is where we go next."

"Agreed," Terri said.

A gigantic tentacle tore out of the marsh and Monk felt almost sick at the sheer size of it. Terri saw it and didn't need to be asked twice. She went through the hole Monk held open, followed by Monk.

As soon as they found themselves standing in the main street of seaside town, they heard a gigantic concussion reverberating through marsh world. The ground shook and the wind picked up. Monk hurriedly closed the hole.

"I don't want to know," she said. "I'm not really up to any major fights anyway."

Terri instantly peered at her, concerned. "Are you doing all right, Monk? Is Kilkenny okay?"

"I'm doing fine. I'm tired, that's all," Monk said. That wasn't strictly true. She had a mild headache that she could feel wanted to turn into a major, stomach emptying pain. She felt in the bond for Kilkenny. The small flame still burned, brighter than it had before. Kilkenny still floated, feeling safe. "Kilkenny's hanging in there. She feels like she's sleepy."

Terri nodded. "We need to hurry, though, don't we?"

"Yeah," Monk said. "We do."

"We could search the buildings," Terri said.

"Well, actually," Monk said. "There *is* another thing we could try. If all of these worlds are subject to natural disasters, then we could easily just create a bubble for ourselves so we're not subject to whatever's happening in the outside world. If the person is in any of the worlds, they would have to be insulated. So we'd be looking for a bubble or something that was unaffected by calamity."

"That's a great idea," Terri said with a grin. "I like that."

"So do I," Monk said. "The only thing is that you'd have to be the one looking after us. I have to ration my energy for Kilkenny."

"We have to be smart about this," Terri said. "Mack's drawing on me for strength for Roth. So which world do we think is the most likely candidate for having a sleeper in it? Me, personally? If I were Michaels, I would have gotten something with a building in it."

Monk nodded. "I agree. How many of these worlds have you seen?"

"I saw Autumn Park with you and a bit of Carnival World. That's where we got off the train. Mack saw them all."

"From talking to the others, we know that the jungle, the marsh, and the seaside world all get decimated at regular intervals. The only ones that don't seem to suffer from that are Autumn Park and Sydney."

"Maybe that's where we should start." Terri was silent for a moment. "You know, come to think of it, Hellstrom and Michaels spent a lot of time in Autumn Park. That's where they brought us when they caught us."

"Yeah," Monk said. "And Sydney *does* have that sailing ship with the flame throwers. So it's leveled on a regular basis. I'd forgotten about that. Autumn Park it is, then."

"I'm glad in a way," Terri said. "The other worlds are truly *awful*." She held up her muddy arms.

Monk looked at her. She was a mess. She was covered from head to toe in drying mud. Her clothes were ruined. *She looks like shit and I'll bet I don't look any better.*

"I know," Monk said. "This one little trip into psychopathy has cost me my favorite tee shirt."

Terri snorted a laugh. Then she giggled and finally ended up laughing outright. Monk joined in and they were clutching each other for support.

"I know," Terri said, wiping the tears from her eyes. "I liked the shirt I was wearing as well."

"Moriarty's going to have to dry clean her blazer," Monk said.

"Probably not. I think she's got an entire wardrobe of them. The entire time I knew her I never once saw her in any other color than black."

"Wonder what would happen if you bought her a pink shirt?" Monk said, tearing open a hole in the dreamscape.

"I don't know. Mack's unpredictable, and she has one hell of a sense of humor," Terri said, stepping through the hole. "Given that I've never seen any other color than black I'm sure it wouldn't be pretty."

Monk laughed and followed her through the hole.

CHAPTER 17

MONK AND TERRI stood on the street next to the train station in Autumn Park.

"Does anything seem out of place to you?" Terri asked. "Something immediately obvious that'd tell us there was something wrong?"

"Not really to me," Monk said. "And that would probably be the point. But, we have to start looking somewhere, so I'd suggest two places. First, Wells's house. Angela seemed to like Wells. Then I'd suggest looking at Autumn Park Hospital. That'd be another perfectly logical place to hide a person." She gestured toward the train station. "One moment, please. I need my backpack."

"Your *backpack*?" Terri asked.

"Yeah, I got pulled in here in my body by Michaels on my way home from uni," Monk said, jogging to the station. "I had a couple of text books in there and they aren't cheap. Michelle'd probably kill me if I lost them."

"Fair enough," Terri said. "You want to send it back through into the physical world?"

"Probably not a bad idea," Monk said. "I *already* feel like I've been running for a long time. I'm exhausted."

They reached the turnstiles, slipped through them, and flopped down onto the platform to wait for the train.

They were quiet for a moment. Monk was struck by the *silence* in the world. They couldn't hear anything. She also couldn't *see* anything, just empty buildings and streets.

It's going to take us forever *to find the dreamer. I remember when I was just made by Wells. When I was in the dreamscape, it felt like the entire world was connected to me. Like it was building blocks all around me. Wonder if I could do that now?*

She shifted and closed her eyes, extending her senses. The bench beneath her felt like an odd mixture of hard and porous. She felt herself running throughout the inside of it, felt it as an extension of her body. She tugged on the spheres that made it up, and pulled them toward her.

She was dimly aware of Terri shifting beside her.

She kept tugging, pulling the spheres together and then toward her. The sphere suddenly shot up inside her, exploding, and she felt a wash of energy that she carefully funneled toward the flame of her bond.

The bench dissolved, dumping her unceremoniously onto the platform and disrupting her careful control of the energy. It shot into the flame, making it flare. She felt groggy surprise from Kilkenny.

Wow, Monk thought. *That worked. Why did it work? It shouldn't have.*

She opened her eyes and found herself sitting on the platform. Terri was looking down at her with a strange look of half consternation and half amusement. She held out her hand. Monk took it and allowed herself to be levered up.

"What did you just do?" Terri asked. "I thought you couldn't do that."

"I just collapsed the bench," Monk said.

"You think?" Terri asked, folding her arms.

"Yeah, that didn't come out right," Monk said. "I collapsed the bench and pulled the energy into me."

"Nice one," Terri said. "How did you do that?"

"Here, I'll show you," Monk said. "Just give me a moment to check on Kilkenny."

Terri nodded.

Monk closed her eyes and felt for the flame. It was definitely bigger now, and burned brighter. She felt an affectionate nuzzle from Kilkenny, who seemed to fall back to sleep again.

"Kilkenny's a bit stronger now," Monk said. "Here." She went over to the other bench. "I'd suggest not sitting on it. The back of my front still hasn't quite forgiven me for that. Put your hands on the bench."

Terri put her hands on the back of the bench.

"Shift," Monk said. She watched Terri's eyes change to bright, bile yellow. "Look at the bench. You can see how it's made up. *Feel* it. *Feel* how it's made up. You can feel every atom in the bench. You can touch them all and feel the spaces between them."

Terri smiled. "Yes," she murmured. "I can. I really can."

"Good," Monk said. "Pull them all toward you and into you."

Terri frowned and after a second the bench seemed to liquefy and then flow up into Terri's hands.

"Wow," she said, her eyes returning to their normal gray. She looked down at her hands. "That was fantastic. Mack appreciates it as well." She looked at Monk. "If you can do that why don't we just collapse this entire world?"

"Pushing yourself into the bench takes energy. This was just a small object. If you try and do an entire world you'll probably hurt the others doing it."

"Fair enough," Terri said.

The tracks sang. The train was approaching.

"I'd suggest we both collapse a few more objects in this world. We'd be able to stock up on some energy. After that we can collapse the *worlds* we don't think our sleeper is in. We'll leave that final world alone and let the sleeper take the energy."

"Sounds like a plan," Terri said as the train came into view.

The train pulled into the station and Monk bolted for the driver's car. She jumped onto the train and saw her back pack sitting just outside a pool of drying blood, forgotten. She quickly opened the driver's door and hit the *Stop/Go* button. She hesitated a moment, then pressed the *Open/Closed* button.

"Did you get your backpack?" Terri asked as Monk strode toward her.

"No, I didn't," Monk said. "Thank you." *I'm an idiot.*

She scooped up her backpack and slung it over her shoulder. They got out of the train and she quickly cut a hole in the dreamscape and tossed her backpack into the living room of Michelle's flat.

She snuck a look at Moriarty, passed out on the sofa. She was dreadfully pale. Her eyes fluttered open for a second. *Hurry*, she mouthed.

Shit, Monk thought. *We gotta speed things up.*

"Done," Monk said. "Let's try and collapse a building on our way to Wells's place."

They left the station and walked up the road. Monk snuck a glance at Terri. She looked pale and tired. Monk glanced at the house they were walking past. It was an older style fibro home, surrounded by perfectly groomed lawn and a neat, red brick fence.

"Here," Monk said, pulling her to a halt. "Tank up. Collapse the fence first, then the house."

Terri nodded and her eyes flared yellow. She put her knee against the fence and it shimmered for a few seconds, liquefied and absorbed into her knee. There was no trace that there'd ever been a fence around the house when she'd finished.

"Wow," she said. "That was tough. I thought I was going to pass out."

"How do you feel now?" Monk asked.

"Better. I'll try the house."

She walked across the lawn and put her hands on the house and the process began again. When she finished, she was on her knees, breathing heavily. Monk rushed over to her side and put a hand on her back.

"Terri?" she said. "Are you all right?"

A moment or so later, Terri responded. "Yeah, I'm all right. That one was harder than the fence but I feel better. Now I'm just tired and not exhausted."

"Can you feel how Mack's doing?"

Terri was silent for a moment, her gaze turned inward. "She's better. She's saying thanks. I think Rio and Roth are also doing better."

"My turn," Monk said, going to the next house, Terri behind her. She absorbed the house and promptly threw up. She was dizzy, her head was ringing and her stomach murmured uneasily. She felt as though she'd been hit by a truck. She felt inside for Kilkenny, and saw that the flame hadn't gotten any bigger; but it hadn't gotten smaller either.

"Monk?" Terri asked anxiously.

"I'm okay," Monk said. "I feel like shit." She took a deep breath, trying to get air into her lungs.

Terri gave her a searching gaze. "All right," she finally said. "You'll tell me if you're not all right?"

"I will," Monk said. "You want to try another couple of houses?"

Terri nodded. "Sure. We can *eat* on the way to Wells's place." She grinned.

Monk burst out laughing. "I like that one."

They made their way down the main street.

Terri absorbed two more houses as they walked down Wells's street. She looked better.

Monk felt terrible. She had a headache and felt queasy. She warily eyed the house next to Wells's. *I* have *to do this. I hope I'm still of use to Terri once I'm done.*

"Monk," Terri said softly, looking concerned.

"I really don't know what's wrong. I'm wondering if I'm feeling the effects of silver poison."

"I don't think anyone knows the answer to *that* question, Monk. Kilkenny really seems to be a first for everyone."

Monk nodded. She looked at the house. It was two storeys but didn't look as large as the other houses on the street.

"Here goes nothing," she said. She put her hands onto the house and sank into its raw matter, tugging it back into her. Intense pain tore through her body the moment she started and she moaned in pain as it continued. The house was gone just as she reached the limit of what her body could take.

She sank to her knees, heaving and clutching her aching head. She felt the warmth from Terri's body as Terri knelt beside her. Terri put her arm around her and helped her to stand. Monk nodded her thanks.

She felt inside her bond for Kilkenny. The flame was at the same intensity as before; it hadn't gotten any larger or smaller. Monk inwardly cursed. *So a couple of houses really isn't going to make a dent in her. I'm going to have to absorb a world and see if that makes a difference. Fuck. I don't know how bad this is going to be.*

"Terri," Monk said when she was finally able to speak again. "I think I need Michelle." She sank to her knees. Her head throbbed painfully and she felt weak as a kitten.

Terri instantly knelt beside Monk. "Are you going to be okay for a few moments?"

"Yes," Monk said. "I don't plan on going anywhere and I don't see any antibodies."

"Okay. I'll be back in a couple."

Terri stood and tore a hole in the dreamscape. Moments later she was back with Michelle and Jackie in tow.

Monk felt rather than saw Michelle and Jackie kneel beside her. She felt arms slip around her, pull her in close. It was Michelle.

"Monk, you look awful," Michelle said. She sounded worried.

Monk opened her eyes and looked at Michelle. Michelle hissed. "Monk, you've got a blood spot in one eye." Her eyes faded to yellow.

"That's the least of my worries," Monk said. "Is Kilkenny any better?"

"The rot has stopped but she's looking pretty awful," Jackie said. She caressed Monk's shoulder. "I'm worried about *both* of you."

"I feel pretty bad," Monk said. "Why don't you absorb a house and get your and Michelle's strength back up?"

"Sounds like a good idea," Jackie said. She and Terri approached the large house across the street from Wells's.

"Monk, what's the matter?" Michelle said as soon as they were out of earshot.

"I'm absorbing stuff, that's fine, but it's hurting me. I can feel Kilkenny but to give her a booster shot I'm going to have to absorb a world. Well, that's my next try anyway." She looked deep into Michelle's eyes. "I don't know how it's going to go for me but it'd make me feel *much* better if you and Jackie were with me."

"It's a good idea," Michelle said, nodding. "Where you go, I go."

"When you shift and look at me, what do you see?"

Michelle studied her. "Your sparks are golden, but not as bright as they should be. Your bond, though . . . it looks like there are tendrils of black in it. They've nearly reached your sparks."

"It's coming from Kilkenny, isn't it?" Monk asked.

"That would be a safe assumption," Michelle said. "I'm guessing the silver poison will begin to hit you soon." Michelle's eyes widened and she turned to Jackie. The house was gone. Jackie grinned and gave her a thumbs up.

"Does it feel good?" Monk asked. "Does it help you?"

"It does," Michelle said. "I feel like I've had a night's sleep. So I still feel like I should be resting, but like it's the day after the energy drain."

"Good," Monk said. "It means I can help Kilkenny and maybe push back the rot in my bond." She held out a hand. "Help me up?"

Michelle helped her to stand. She looked concerned but grimly determined.

Terri and Jackie rejoined them.

"Better?" Terri asked.

"A little," Monk said, lying through her teeth. "Okay, let's check Wells's house and then if this isn't it, head over to the hospital."

"Okay," Terri said.

They went over to Wells's house and Terri put her hand on the knob. "Ready?" she asked them.

"Let's get this over with," Michelle said.

Terri nodded and opened the door. They went in.

"Terri and I will go up, you guys do downstairs," Michelle said.

"Works for me," Jackie said. "C'mon, Monk."

Jackie took the lead. They went into the garage. It was dark, painted brilliant white, with a clean, unblemished floor.

"Have you seen any real change in Kilkenny at all?" Monk asked. "Michelle said that the rot didn't look as bad but is it going back a little? And the others? How are they?"

They backed out of the garage and explored the three bedrooms. Each of the rooms was completely devoid of furniture and any other signs of habitation.

"Kilkenny is still as pale as hell. She looks . . . like . . . well . . . what am I going to tell Mum and Dad?"

"Hey," Monk said, pulling her to a halt and looking deep into her eyes. "Kilkenny *will* make it if I have anything to say about it."

Jackie gave her a searching look. "I believe you," she finally said. "I really think that you're sure."

"I am," Monk said. "Nothing worse is going to happen to any of us. I don't want it to. It's already bad enough."

Jackie leaned forward and kissed her. "Thanks, Monk, for helping. You've always been my friend."

Monk nodded. "*You've* always been *my* friend. I don't know what I'd do without either one of you."

Jackie smiled, and they kept looking. "You asked about the others. Mack's perked up a little bit and it looks like Roth and Rio aren't as badly off as they were before. They're not as pale."

"Thank God the houses seem to be working for Terri."

"They work for me as well. Both of us are feeling a little better."

They made their way back into the living room. Further conversation was halted as they saw Terri and Michelle making their way down the stairs.

"Empty," Michelle said when she saw them. "It doesn't look like anyone's been anywhere in the house besides the living room."

"That's pretty much what I thought," Monk said. "We haven't seen any antibodies in this world."

"Absolutely none," Terri said, looking around at the house. "And I've never seen anyone so obsessed with white."

Michelle nodded. "It's flat, all right. There aren't even any pictures on the walls. Personally? I think we'd better get the hell out of here before we end up suffering from snow blindness."

"I'm with you there," Monk said.

She opened the front door and left.

They stopped in the middle of the street.

"So," Jackie said. "What's the plan now?"

"We're going to go to Autumn Park Hospital and see if she's in there," Monk said.

"That's a hell of a hike and a hell of a job to search it," Michelle said. "Monk, are you sure you're up to this?"

"I'm okay," Monk said. "We'd figured it was going to be like this."

"Okay," Michelle said. "Let's get moving."

Monk felt Jackie's hand slip into hers. She caressed it and gently kissed Jackie's knuckles. "Thanks for coming."

"I'm glad you asked for us," Jackie said. "I was going nuts watching Kilkenny and I'm worried about you."

"I'm not sure if you need to actually *worry* about me yet," Monk said. "And to make you feel little bit better, Kilkenny *feels* safe. It's like she's sleeping and every now and again wakes up and gives me a squeeze. It feels warm and loving."

Jackie nodded. "I don't know what's wrong with me. I just keep having this . . . thirteen o'clock . . . feeling, you know?"

"So do I," Michelle said. "The last time we were in a dreamscape like this with Wells, it had more activity in it. There were more creatures floating around. This particular world is so . . . bare."

"I know," Monk said. "But there's a big part of me that thinks this would be a good place to hide someone *because* of that."

"So let's revisit the subject of antibodies and our plan," Terri said. "Monk, the seaside world? Did it have anyone in it?"

"Nope, none that I could see," Monk said. "This world—which is Autumn Park and also Sydney—had rabid dog things in it and that's about all. I'm not counting the sailing ship."

"Marsh world had a squid in it, nothing else," Jackie said.

"Jungle world had monkeys in it," Michelle said.

"And piranhas," Terri said. "*Big* ones."

"Carnival world had lots of stuff in it," Monk said. "The robot things for starters."

"And it was the only world with a bubble inside it," Jackie said.

"I really don't think I'm up to traipsing all over the other worlds looking for a dreamer," Monk said. "I say we go to carnival world and ride the rollercoaster."

Michelle smiled, despite herself. "I'd have thought you'd have enough of that by now but okay, why not?"

Jackie and Terri both nodded.

"Let's do it," Monk said. "Terri, you want to do the honors?"

"Sure." Terri turned and slashed a hole in the dreamscape. They could only see darkness beyond the tear.

"Ugh," Michelle said. "I hate that place."

"I hear you," Monk said, slipping through the hole. "Welcome to Silent Hill."

Jackie followed her, Michelle and Terri behind them. Terri sealed up the hole in the dreamscape and they were plunged into eerie twilight.

They looked around. They were in a riot of carnival rides and games booths.

"Jackie," Monk said. "You want to send out some feelers and tell us what you see?"

"Okay." Jackie's eyes faded to yellow and she closed them. She frowned after a moment. "Well," she said slowly. "This place is crawling with creatures. I can feel them. There's also a bubble in the middle, the cake dome we all got stuck in." She opened her eyes. "I can't feel inside it. That has to be it."

"It's a place to start looking," Terri said.

Michelle, beside Monk, took a step forward and they resumed walking.

Monk looked around. Dilapidated rides, crumbled asphalt, shadows and unseen things made their home in the darkness. She unconsciously moved closer to Michelle.

Michelle glanced at her. "Scared?"

"Not exactly," Monk said, feeling her face heat. "I'm just really glad you're here."

Michelle slipped an arm around her shoulders and Jackie moved in close. Monk caught a blur in the distance. She frowned, trying to focus on it.

"Do you see that?" Terri asked from beside them.

"Can you see what it is?" Jackie asked, frowning and staring into the distance.

"No, not really," Terri said slowly. "Looks like a blur."

"It's a clown, of all things," Michelle said.

"Yuck," Terri said. "I *hate* clowns."

Monk and Jackie both nodded. Michelle smiled and shook her head.

"It looks like it's in our way," Michelle said. She glanced at Monk and Jackie. "Can either of you see another route?"

Jackie shook her head. "We could take any route you like. They all seem to lead to the middle of the fair ground. This way is the shortest, though."

"Shortest works for me," Michelle said. "If it gets nasty we'll just deal with it."

They kept walking toward the clown.

"Maybe you should try absorbing a carnival ride," Monk said to Terri and Jackie. "Things are only going to get nastier from here, I expect."

Monk stood shoulder to shoulder with Michelle as the others jogged toward adjacent booths. As soon as they laid hands on the booths, the clown in the distance sprang into motion. It flipped toward them at a speed Monk found troubling and almost terrifying.

She felt Michelle brace herself and noticed with dull surprise that she felt better.

I'm glad she's here, Monk thought. *It really* does *make me feel better.*

The clown stopped in front of them with shocking abruptness. It was as tall as Michelle was. It had a white grease-painted face, complete with a huge red painted smile and tufts of green hair. It looked like a stereotypical clown, complete with huge, bulbous shoes and pink striped clown suit with exaggerated curves. This visual spectacle was topped off with bright red pompom buttons down the front of its suit.

It bowed from the waist and presented a bouquet of dead flowers to Michelle with a flourish. Michelle recoiled and it slowly stood and growled deep in its throat. Monk tensed. She felt the hair on the back of her neck rise.

The clown stared at Michelle. Its eyes were flat and inhuman.

Oh my Christ, that's its real *skin.* She looked closely at its face. Its eyes were the worst. They were human eyes with nothing human in them. They were the cold, flat eyes of what was almost an organic machine.

Michelle stood nose to nose with it, unmoving. She seemed completely unafraid, and they seemed to be sizing each other up.

They moved at the same time. Michelle took a step back as the clown reached forward and snagged her upper arms. The world moved in slow motion for Monk. She saw its ragged fingernails, razor sharp and the bulge of its muscles as its hands clamped down on Michelle's arms.

Michelle yelped in pain and the adrenaline tore through Monk's system. She leapt onto the clown's back, holding tight, trying not to gag at the smell of old bandages and decay. She reached inside it and it melted in her arms as she pulled its energy into her body. Michelle stumbled back and Monk fell to her knees, retching.

The energy tore through her system like acid, burning her veins and arteries. In too much pain to scream, she funneled the energy toward her bond. The flame flared briefly and Monk collapsed, curling up into a ball as the backwash flowed over her.

She was distantly aware of Michelle and the others leaning over her, of Jackie's comforting hands on her.

"Monk? Monk? Are you all right?" Michelle asked, leaning over her.

Michelle's long hair brushed over her hot arm. "I am now," she said when she was able to speak. She felt as though she'd been burnt inside and the feeling didn't fade away. *God, I feel like shit. This time I'm not coming out of it the way I should. I'm not trying that again until it's time to absorb a world for Kilkenny.*

"You don't look all right," Michelle said, looking closely at her. Her eyes flared yellow and she went pale. "Your sparks are fading, Monk. You're going down with Kilkenny."

"Then we'd better hurry," Monk said, cupping her face.

"Can you bond me to her?" Jackie asked.

"Bad idea," Monk said instantly. "Maybe when I can't go any further but *not* before then."

Monk looked deep into Michelle's eyes and saw how troubled she was.

"Monk, I'm *really* worried about this," Michelle said.

Terri gave Michelle's a shoulder a gentle squeeze. "I saw part of that. You couldn't break out of the clown's grip, could you?"

"No." Michelle unwillingly shook her head. She looked deep into Monk's eyes. "I appreciate what you did, Monk, but please don't do it again."

"I won't, love," Monk said gently. "I'm going to wait until we find the dreamer." She held out her hand. "Help me up?"

Michelle took her wrist and hauled her to her feet. Her abused stomach almost rebelled and she leaned forward with her hands on her knees. She felt Jackie's hand gently rubbing her back.

"Oh fuck," Terri muttered. "There are *more* of those little bastards coming toward us."

Monk stood, trying to ignore her swimming head. A platoon of jugglers and acrobats were coming toward them, flipping and twirling in a way that seemed so *normal* to Monk that she wanted to cry.

"Stay close together and keep walking," she said, glancing at the others. "We have to get to the middle of the cake dome."

They stood shoulder to shoulder, Michelle on one side of her, Jackie on the other, and walked forward. The acrobats leaped toward them with increasing speed.

"Brace yourselves," Terri said.

They closed ranks even further.

The acrobats leapt toward them. One of them flipped onto another's shoulders and then onto the ground before them with a solid thud, cracking the scabrous asphalt. This one was tall, taller than Michelle and eye to eye with Terri. It put its hands on Terri's shoulders and pushed downward. Terri yelped in pain as it flipped and landed on her, wrapping its arms and legs around her body.

"It's breaking my shoulders," Terri screamed.

Michelle dived toward Terri and pushed her backward as hard as she could. They tumbled to the ground, the acrobat's head hitting the asphalt with a sick, cracking sound. Terri quickly scrabbled away from it, yelping in pain again as a knife sliced open her upper arm.

Monk turned in alarm in time to see a pair of knife throwing clowns capering toward them. They launched another pair of knives, one headed to Jackie, the other to Michelle. Suddenly she was on the ground, Michelle's body on hers. Jackie lay flat on her back beside them.

"Shit," Monk yelled, looking up in dismay.

Another acrobat was coming down before them, looming larger by the second. It landed directly in front of them and before Monk had a chance to react, sank a dagger deep into Michelle's chest.

Michelle silently stared down at it, blinking disbelievingly. She put her hand up to the handle and slowly pulled it out, hissing in pain. Blood dripped off the blade and out of the ragged hole over Michelle's heart. She slowly sank back and collapsed, the knife clattering onto the asphalt with an almost deafening clang.

"No, Michelle," Jackie shrieked, diving toward her at the same time Monk did.

Soon they were surrounded by acrobats and jugglers, all of them giving vent to soulless laughter that Monk almost ignored.

She rolled onto Michelle, listening for her heartbeat. It was faltering.

She looked at Jackie. "Jackie."

Jackie's face was contorted into a snarl of rage. She grabbed the closest one and it dissolved in her grip. The other clowns and acrobats stopped what they were doing and turned to her as one. They moved toward her but she made short work of them. As soon as they touched her she soaked them in and they dissolved into her.

Monk, her vision blurred by her tears, looked down at Michelle. Her clothes were soaked in blood but the skin of her chest had closed.

She looked as though she were sleeping. Monk leaned down and listened closely to Michelle's chest. She burst into tears at the sound of Michelle's heartbeat.

Her shoulders shook with the force of her sobs and she was only dimly aware of the warm body beside her, the strong arms that pulled her in close and soothed her. She felt Jackie's gentle kiss and looked up at her.

"We've got to get her out of here. *You* have to go as well. I can't stand this," Monk said. "I was selfish to call you here."

"I *wanted* to come, Monk," Jackie said with some asperity. "What makes you think *I* want you here? You think it felt good to watch you run around ahead of Michaels and Hellstrom, playing chicken with them? We love you every bit as much as you love us. We're in this *together*, Monk. You're going to have to get used to it."

"I know," Monk said. "I know." She felt completely unable to vocalize how much she felt for them. "Please," she said softly, tears starting afresh at Jackie's angry expression.

Jackie's anger faded and she put her arms around Monk, squeezing her hard. "Love you, Monk."

"Love you too, Jackie."

Jackie gently released her and knelt by Michelle. She picked Michelle up and they disappeared in a flash of light.

"C'mon, mate," Terri said. "Let's get this over with."

Monk allowed Terri to haul her to her feet and they walked on. Monk itched to look back but refrained. It hurt too much.

CHAPTER 18

MORIARTY SAT UP, Roth by her side, and watched the flash of light that signaled the dreamscape opening up.

"Huh?" Moriarty said, watching Jackie step through the breach, Michelle held in her arms. Michelle was covered in blood and unconscious.

"Oh, hell," Moriarty said, immediately getting to her feet, Roth beside her. "What happened?"

"We took a look at Autumn Park but it seemed to be empty. The only place that has the right kind of activity in it—the antibodies you were talking about—is that carnival world. We went there. We got attacked by clowns and jugglers."

Moriarty exchanged a glance with Roth, who still looked pale but her eyes burned with intensity.

"Michelle?" Roth said, gesturing toward Michelle.

"Got stabbed by a knife thrower." Jackie gently put Michelle on the sofa and kissed her forehead. "Monk and Terri are still in there."

"How's Monk doing?" Roth asked.

"She's alive but she's in bad shape," Jackie said. "She's tried absorbing a few constructs but that makes her sick. *Very* sick. She said she wasn't going to try it again until it was time to absorb a world."

"Can you cut another hole? Mack and I will go onto the dreamscape," Roth said.

"What about *you*, Roth?" Jackie asked. "You can't possibly have the energy to go in there and help."

"I have to," Roth said. "I have no choice."

Moriarty nodded. "Neither do I. Terri's afraid and worried."

"Worried about Monk?" Jackie asked. "What should we be worried about?"

"I don't know," Roth said. "What you've just told us doesn't sound good. We'll travel with them."

Jackie nodded, her eyes flaring yellow. She slashed a hole in the dreamscape. "They're headed to the center of the dome in the middle of the park."

Moriarty smiled. "Thanks. And don't worry. We'll take care of them."

"I know," Jackie said simply.

Roth and Moriarty stepped through the hole created by Jackie and turned to see it seal up behind them.

"Which way?" Roth asked.

Moriarty felt inside her bond for Terri. They were a short distance away from her.

"That way," she said, pointing down a dark, unlit path that led between endless rows of rotting rides and decrepit games booths.

"How are you *really* doing, Roth?" Moriarty asked.

Roth's cool façade slipped and Moriarty saw the pain in her eyes. "I miss Kilkenny. So does Rio. Physically, I'm just tired. The energy you've given to us has done us wonders. Rio will be waking up soon."

"And she's going to freak out when she realizes the bond to Kilkenny is gone."

"I know," Roth said.

"Do you know how to fix Kilkenny?" Moriarty asked.

Roth looked at her, fear in her green eyes. "No. I've never seen this. I've never really had anything to do with bond masters. We really *are* in uncharted territory."

Moriarty fought down her own uneasiness. *When push comes to shove all we can do is try. That's all that can be asked of us.*

They saw shapes in the distance and on both sides of them. Moriarty shifted her vision and looked at one of them. It was the fattest woman thing that Moriarty had ever seen, walking alongside a dwarf holding the leash of a thin poodle. There was something immeasurably crafty in the way the dwarf looked around at the rides. The poodle yawned. It had razors for teeth.

"You see that?" Roth asked softly. Moriarty glanced at her. Her eyes burned yellow.

"Yeah," Moriarty said. "All that does is tell me we have to get to Terri and Monk. Quickly. This way. They're just ahead of us."

Moriarty jogged, Roth beside her. Her body protested. She felt as though she'd overdone it and needed rest. She snuck a glance at Roth. She looked grimly determined.

In the distance, they heard Monk's voice. "Back to back, Terri."

Moriarty pushed herself and sprinted toward Monk. She heard a scuffle and felt Terri's grim determination and undertone of concern. Roth stayed by her side and Moriarty could hear her ragged breathing.

They rounded a final, rotting booth and Moriarty crashed into a spruiker. They both went down, Moriarty on top of him. Roth raced past her.

The man thing beneath Moriarty was still for a split second, and then tried to wrap his arms around her. She looked at him, saw his waxy skin, smelt an unpleasant undertone of rotting flesh. When she pushed against him she could feel muscle and flesh slide against each other and against bone. She almost recoiled with revulsion, but the desire to escape his foul presence took over. She lifted her arms, sliding beneath his grip and tearing at his arms. She tore the flesh off his biceps and then the arms from their sockets. He thrashed and his teeth snapped together with solid crunching sounds. She straightened and sat on him, tearing off his head with a brisk crunch. His thrashing became uncoordinated and slowed. She shot him a look of disgust.

She quickly looked up and scanned for Terri, Roth, and Monk.

They were in a grim triangle, fending off a swath of circus performers, carnival hands, and ride attendants. More were pouring in from all the alley ways. Terri and Roth had settled into an easy rhythm of tearing them to pieces, but Monk looked as though she was flagging. Moriarty's eyes shot skyward at the sight of the circus strongman, looking beefy, half rotten and blank faced, striding toward Monk with grim intent.

Monk saw him coming and tensed. He pushed aside the other half rotten freaks descending on her and pulled up a large hand to deliver a tremendous slap. Monk grabbed his arm halfway through his downward swing and twisted his forearm as hard as she could. It snapped with a grisly snapping sound and tore out of his elbow in a shower of fat, mucus, and blood. The bones peeked out of the stump. They looked as though they were crawling with maggots.

Monk, so pale she was almost translucent, braced herself against Roth's back and kicked at him. Roth easily bore her weight, calling back, "Are you all right there, Monk?"

"Fine and dandy," Monk called, sinking both feet into his stomach. He almost tore in two.

Moriarty's paralysis vanished. She flipped over the seething mass and landed in between Monk and Roth.

"What took you so long?" Roth asked.

"Spruiker," Moriarty said. "Wouldn't take no for an answer."

She tore at the blank-faced zombie things that came toward her in an almost unstoppable tide. She was soon dripping with sweat and breathing hard as she tore away at them.

"They keep coming," Terri said. She grunted and something near her tore and snapped with a sick crack.

Monk tore off the fat lady's head with a brisk snapping and tearing sound.

A body, sans head, sailed by, courtesy of Roth.

"Retreat," Moriarty said.

"Which way?" Terri asked.

"Toward the heaviest concentration of these things," Roth said. "This way."

Roth moved forward, Terri behind her. Monk followed Terri and Moriarty brought up the rear.

Hands grabbed at them, tore at their clothing. Moriarty lost count of the number of times she was yanked sideways. She kept moving backward, back to back with Monk. Suddenly they were free of the horde.

They stood on the steps of a ride, breathing heavily. The creatures stood in a semi-circle around the stairs, unmoving.

"What the fuck?" Monk asked, leaning forward with her hands on her knees. "Why aren't they coming after us?"

The crowd before them parted. The circus ring master made his way through the crowd toward them. He was close to seven feet tall and the most handsome man Moriarty had ever seen. He reached for Moriarty with blinding speed. His hands were on her arms and her feet were clear of the ground before she could react. He squeezed and she screamed as her bones creaked. His fingers dug into her shoulders.

She was dimly aware of shifting bodies behind her. She tried to move her arms, but it was too late. He pulled her arms out of her sockets. Suddenly a tall body slammed into both of them. The ring master did not move but his torso exploded in shower of blood and bone. Moriarty was quickly covered in his blood and she kicked at him.

His grip loosened and Moriarty found herself unceremoniously dumped on the rotting stairs. Roth and Monk bent over her. She looked up and saw Terri had a firm grip on him and he was dissolving into liquid and flowing into her. The terrible pain in her shoulders slowed down and stopped.

Terri immediately came over to her and knelt before her. "Mack?" she asked.

Moriarty was about to toss out a teasing comment but it died in the face of Terri's shaking and raw pain.

"I'm fine, lover. You did good." She held out her arms—mercifully healed and pain free—and Terri was in them, squeezing for all she was worth.

"I thought you were done for," Terri said. Every word sounded forced.

"I wouldn't let *anyone* touch her," Monk said softly. "I *know* what this feels like and I wouldn't stand by and let anyone else go through it."

"Over my dead body," Roth said. "Mack is my best friend. We've always stood together. That's just the way it is."

Terri looked around at them. "Thanks, guys."

Moriarty stood, bringing Terri with her. "We have to keep moving." She looked at Monk. Monk was pale and her skin had a grayish tinge. "You look horrible, Monk."

Monk blinked. "Thank you," she said after a moment.

"Can you feel Kilkenny?" Roth asked hesitantly.

"Yep," Monk said. "It's still the same sleepy, loving feeling as before. Her flame is staying steady. Not better, not worse."

"Flame?" Moriarty asked.

"Yeah," Monk said. "I have to funnel energy to her. I'm seeing her as a small flame in our bond. It started off as a spark but with the stuff I've absorbed I've now got a small flame. It's not getting better—or worse—so I'm going to throw a world at it and see if that makes a difference."

"Every time you absorb something you get sick. That's what Jackie told us," Moriarty said. "What's up with that?"

"I don't know, I'm hoping it's only backwash from silver poisoning," Monk said. "I have no idea what absorbing a world will do for us."

"If she goes you go, you know that, right?"

"I know. But it's not going to come to that."

"Good," Moriarty said. "I don't want to be breaking bad news to anyone's lovers."

"Time's getting short," Monk said. "We'd better get moving."

Roth held out a hand and pulled Monk to her feet. Monk swayed and Roth put a steadying hand on her.

"Where are we anyway?" Moriarty asked as they walked through the mouth of the ride.

"The ghost train," Roth said.

"Figures," Moriarty said, feeling Terri's hand slide into hers. She gave it a gentle squeeze and Terri pulled in close.

Monk's eyes flared yellow. "Follow me."

"You should let Roth go first," Moriarty said.

Monk shook her head. "You can't see constructs the way I can. Terri, shift."

Terri's eyes flared yellow.

"Look ahead of us. The ghost hanging from the ceiling that's supposed to drop on the train. It's got a blue sac around it. That's bad."

Terri nodded. "The walls in here are blue as well."

"Which means we stay on the tracks," Monk said.

They moved carefully forward in the darkness, taking the sudden curves slowly and avoiding the more obvious traps. They passed by an ancient, crumbling series of ghost train cars.

Moriarty stopped and eyed them. They looked like skulls that had been neatly cut in half. She bent forward and grimaced. They were made from bone, and were bleached white. She reached out and touched one. It felt almost warm. She pulled back her hand as though burned.

"Is that what I think it is?" Terri asked softly from beside her.

Moriarty nodded and Terri shuddered.

"Don't look," Roth said gently. "Or you'll begin asking questions."

"Like who did the cars come from?" Monk said.

Moriarty and Roth looked at her. Monk shrugged.

"I'm just glad that they're not alive," Terri said.

One of the cars squealed and jerked forward.

"Aw, shit," Moriarty said. *If I didn't know any better, I'd say those things just bit their way down the tracks. Fuck.*

"Couldn't have put it better myself," Roth said, eying the cars carefully as they jerked forward another couple of feet. She frowned.

"Can we just get the fuck out of here?" Monk said, backing away with the others as the cars jerked forward again. "I don't fancy being eaten by a skull."

"*Half* a skull," Moriarty said.

"Come again?"

"You said *skull*," Moriarty said, amazed at how even she sounded. "That's only *half* a skull. Not a whole one."

"Half, whole, who fucking cares?" Monk said. "Let's fucking get out of here."

The cars heaved forward and rolled down the tracks with a squealing, grinding sound that had all of them grimacing.

"Shit," Moriarty said. "*Run*."

They hared down the tracks ahead. Moriarty shifted her vision and carefully tucked Terri's hand under her arm. The grinding sounds from the cars became louder, undercut by a low moaning that set Moriarty's teeth on edge. *They* can't *moan. They don't have vocal cords.*

She stayed hot on Roth's heels, running as fast as she could, dreadfully aware of Monk's wheezing, strained breathing close by.

"Monk?" Moriarty panted.

Monk looked pale as death and stumbled along. Her yellow eyes shone with grim intensity and Moriarty knew she couldn't run much longer.

Up ahead of them a wall loomed. It was large and rust eaten but still solid. She glanced up and saw iron rings set into the ceiling.

"Grab on," Roth yelled, following the direction of Moriarty's gaze. "Mack. Jump."

Monk grunted as she flung her arms around Roth and hung on for dear life.

Moriarty felt Terri slide in close and grab onto her. She watched Roth carefully as she gracefully leapt into the air. Moriarty followed her. She held her hands up, feeling nothing but empty air. She suddenly felt cold metal under her fingertips and her hands closed around the rings. She levered her feet up, Terri clinging to her.

The train cars, snapping and snarling, roared down the tracks close behind them, and crashed into the doors.

The doors boomed and the cars shattered into a million pieces. Moriarty felt the rings in her hands give a little with a click she felt rather than heard.

She sighed with relief. "You down first, love," she said to Terri.

"No problem," Terri said.

Moriarty felt abruptly lighter as Terri let go and gracefully landed in the darkness below. Monk landed beside her with a grunt.

"You right down there?" Moriarty asked, letting go of the rings and landing lightly beside Monk.

Monk was on her knees, chest heaving with exertion. She nodded. Roth dropped neatly beside them. She silently held out her hand and levered Monk to her feet.

"We must have gone through another doorway," Roth said. "The ceiling is much higher than it should be if it was the real ride."

"Yeah, we did," Monk said, her yellow gaze travelling over the walls. "It almost looks like we're in a cave."

"No matter where we are we can't go any further here," Moriarty said, feeling Terri come up beside her and slip her hand into hers. She squeezed it gently.

"Yup." Monk nodded. "Backtrack and find another way?"

They all nodded and walked on. Moriarty studied the walls around them. They were rough and uneven rock, which meant they were in a cave. They went back the way they'd come and reached a fork in the tracks.

"Damn," Terri said softly as they started down the other fork. "I didn't even realize we'd turned."

"Neither did I," Moriarty said. "Forget the fork, I don't even know when we went through the doorway."

"I think the fork was the doorway," Terri said. "But now instead of going back through it, we seem to be stuck on *this* side of the doorway."

"Great," Moriarty said. "Why did it have to be a cave? It's so fucking *dark* down here."

The tracks curved gently downward and they stepped carefully.

"We've been walking for a long time," Moriarty said. "We should have come out the other side by now."

"I have no idea *where* we're going to come out," Monk said. "But you're right—wherever we come out is going to be close to where we need to be."

Moriarty shifted her vision. "What's up with the trap—*Monk*." She shifted her vision and looked at the place Monk had been and saw a hole in the floor. Roth had already stepped through it with grim intensity.

Moriarty shot forward and jumped down it, Terri close behind.

After a few stomach turning moments, she felt the ground under her feet and bent her knees to absorb the blow. Terri neatly and gracefully dropped down beside her.

"Don't move," Roth yelled.

Moriarty instantly stopped, bracing herself for the soft collision as Terri bumped into the back of her.

"What gives?" she called.

"Shift. You'll see," Roth said.

"Holy shit," Moriarty said softly. They were inside what looked like a gigantic grotto. Moriarty couldn't see the walls. Ahead of them were a series of small platforms, barely large enough for two people. They curved downward into the distance. There were gigantic spikes sticking up out of the ground far below them.

"We'd have been impaled if we'd taken a step forward, wouldn't we?" Terri said softly in her ear.

Moriarty nodded. "Roth. Are both of you all right?"

"We're both fine," Monk said, sounding a little winded. "There's a pinkish yellow haze down close to the bottom. I think we have to head through that. It's probably a doorway."

"Keep going, then," Moriarty said. "And watch for the bats." She pointed upward.

The air was swirling with movement and there was a glow of light far above them. She saw suggestions of wings silhouetted against it. *I hate to think what those wings are attached to*. She shuddered. Terri moved in close to her.

"I'm going to come down to a platform close to you," Moriarty said. She glanced at Terri. "Ready?" She pointed. "That one. I'll catch you."

Terri nodded. "Okay."

Moriarty studied the platform barely visible in the dim light below and in front of them. It was held up by giant, rusting chains that stretched up far above them into the eerie light. The bat things circled far above them.

She lightly pushed off the platform and headed for the other, further below than she'd have liked. She aimed for the chains. Suddenly it loomed up ahead of her and she grabbed the chains and dropped down lightly on the platform. It swayed a little.

"Now you," Moriarty said.

Terri instantly jumped off the platform and landed in Moriarty's arms. Moriarty grinned at her.

"Oh, shit," Monk yelled from the platform beside them. "Look up."

A bat thing broke off from the colony above them and spiraled down toward them.

"That's not real good, is it, Mack?" Terri said.

"Nope," Moriarty said. "Real bad, I think."

"Roth, get ready to grab on," Monk said.

"What? No. You've got to be kidding me," Roth said.

"Lighten up, mate. You only live once," Monk said and Moriarty could almost hear her grin.

The bat thing came down, and Moriarty almost sighed. It looked the way she'd expected it to look. It had gigantic leathery wings and a mouth that wouldn't close around razor sharp teeth. It had leathery skin. A pointed ear twitched. Dark eyes hunted for them. It squealed, and Moriarty clapped her hands over her ears.

"Follow us," Monk said softly. She leapt off the platform, Roth wrapped around her and grabbed onto the bat thing's legs. It flapped its wings hard for a moment, and then straightened them. It suddenly stilled and they slowly descended into the darkness, toward a source of light Moriarty could see below them.

"You've got to be fucking kidding me," Terri said.

"It kind of makes sense," Moriarty said. "I think Monk was right. We have to go down through the doorway below us. Anyone else going this route has to do the same thing. That includes Michaels and Hellstrom. You wouldn't want your creations killing you. Other people, yes, but not you. What's the best way to trap people on these platforms? Make it like the bats will kill you when they're really the way out."

"Psycho bitch," Terri muttered.

"I think we've more than established that," Moriarty said, grinning.

"Let's get our own flying lift," Moriarty said, jumping off their platform and heading toward the one recently vacated by Monk and Roth.

She landed, Terri a second or so behind her, and another bat from far above them broke away and headed downward. As soon as it got close to them, she felt Terri's arms slip around her. She jumped and grabbed the legs, laughing as she held on.

"What's so funny?" Terri asked.

"The legs feel like handles," Moriarty said.

"Figures," Terri said.

They swayed back and forth as they gently descended toward the cavern floor. Moriarty let go of the bat's legs when they were a couple of feet above the ground. The bat thing instantly ascended again.

Moriarty glanced at Terri. "That was interesting."

Terri nodded and rolled her eyes.

Roth and Monk rushed over to them.

"Crap," Monk said. "Are you guys all right?"

"Doing better than you, Monk," Terri said. "You look like shit."

Monk was so pale she was almost gray and her eyes were sunken in dark sockets.

She blinked at Terri.

Moriarty smiled. “How are you holding up, Monk?”

“Fine for the moment,” Monk said.

“You’re running on reserves,” Roth said shortly. She crossed her arms and eyed Monk mercilessly.

Monk shifted from foot to foot. “You know that.” She firmed her chin. She crossed her arms in an eerie imitation of Roth and looked her square in the eye. “Then how about we get this little show on the road?”

Roth nodded. “A fine idea.”

“How come I can see you?” Moriarty asked, peering at Roth’s deeply shadowed face.

“There’s light coming in from the doors over there,” Monk said, jerking her chin behind them and to the right. She held out her hand and a ball of light wavered into existence above it.

“Stop,” Terri said sharply. She held out her own hand and a ball of light appeared above it. Monk’s light guttered out. Terri’s light gained in brilliance until they could see ten feet a head of them.

“Look at those spikes,” Moriarty said softly. The light reflected dimly off them.

“Silver,” Roth said.

“Ouch.”

“Glad none of us fell, huh?” Monk said.

Moriarty nodded.

Terri moved ahead of them, and they went single file toward two doors about a hundred feet away from them. The doors loomed larger and Moriarty frowned.

“What the fuck?” she said.

“I don’t have an answer for this one,” Roth said. “Better let me go first.”

She approached the jarringly normal swing doors and cautiously pushed them. They swung soundlessly open and Roth stepped through them.

Moriarty tensed herself, holding Monk and Terri back. “In a minute,” she said softly to Terri’s questioning look.

After a moment the doors swung back open again. Roth appeared, holding them open, and light spilled into the cavern in a comforting square.

“Come on in,” she said. “Looks normal.”

Moriarty gestured for Monk and Terri to go ahead of her. They went and Moriarty took one long, last look around the cavern.

A series of platforms, suspended in the air by iron cables, hung all through the cavern, above an immense field of silver spikes. *Fuck. That could have been really bad. Not only could we have fallen, we could have gotten lost and stuck as well. Fuck.*

"You coming, Mack?" Terri asked from the door.

"Yeah," Moriarty said. She followed Terri into a corridor.

It was dimly it, and Moriarty blinked.

"This looks like an old hospital," Roth said, looking around.

Moriarty nodded. They were in an old corridor. A thick layer of dust lay on once white tile, disturbed only by their abrupt entrance into the world. Dim emergency lighting lit the corridor at irregular intervals. Close to them was a nurse's desk, bare of everything and covered in collapsed ceiling tiles.

"This looks like the plague world," Monk said, glancing at Terri.

"The what?" Moriarty asked.

"When I got drawn into the dreamscape with Wells, we ended up in a plague world. We outran a tidal wave and ended up in a hospital with a whole bunch of decaying, sick people." She looked around. "I think we're close." She pointed up the corridor. "This way."

"Where are we going?" Roth asked.

"There was a doorway between worlds in an operating theater. I can feel it. I can feel the doorway. I'm guessing that's where our dreamer is."

The light suddenly dimmed.

"There," Monk said, pointing behind them. A light went out in the distance and that section of the corridor was plunged into a terrible darkness.

Moriarty's senses went on high alert, and she shifted her vision. The world lightened for her again. The darkness faded a little and she was able to make out a shape. It was the shadow of a muscular man, standing immobile in the distance. He abruptly took a step forward, stopping beneath the next light. It winked out. More figures appeared behind him, seemingly bouncing off the walls. Their staccato movements made Moriarty queasy.

"How close are we?" Moriarty asked as Monk stopped without warning. Roth hit the back of her and she stumbled.

A light winked out a head of them.

"You see the figures in the darkness?" Roth asked.

"I see them," Moriarty said, tensing herself. *I have no idea how we're going to fight these fucking things.*

"There's a blue glow ahead of us and behind us," Terri said softly, looking both ways down the corridor.

"Look up," Monk said, keeping her eyes trained on the darkness.

Moriarty looked up. "Oh, dear."

There were skeletons above them, clinging to the ceiling tiles. Their eyes burned furnace red. One of them snapped its jaws together with a brisk, clicking sound.

"We can't go sideways," Monk said. "We can't stay. My gut tells me ahead." She turned to Roth, Moriarty, and Terri and grinned. "What's your pleasure?"

"How about *full speed ahead and damn the complainers,*" Moriarty said with a grin.

"Sounds like a plan to me," Monk said.

A skeleton dropped from the ceiling and landed on Roth, sinking its claws into her shoulders. "*Run*," she yelled, haring into motion.

She tore at the skeleton clawing at her and yelped in pain. Its ragged fingernails sank deep into her skin and its arms tore out of its sockets. Roth flung it at the wall close to them, and it exploded in a cloud of dust. She tore the remains of the arms off her, blood pattering on the ancient tiles beneath their feet.

They ran full tilt into the darkness and Terri immediately grabbed for Moriarty. "Help, Mack. I can't see a bloody thing."

"Grab onto my shirt and hang on," Moriarty said, lowering a shoulder and slamming into the man at the front of the cluster.

He grabbed at her with questing fingers and it burned where he touched.

Moriarty let out a war cry and kept plowing forward, Terri, Roth, and Monk behind her.

Hands came out of the walls, grabbing at them and tugging.

Terri hung onto her with grim intensity and she felt her tee shirt tearing.

Suddenly the terrible grasping stopped and Moriarty found herself in a stretch of dimly lit corridor again. Roth and Monk appeared by her side, breathing heavily. They were torn and bleeding from a dozen burnt scratches.

"That was fun, what'll we play next?" she asked with a grin.

"Are we still on the right path?" Roth asked, glancing at Monk.

Monk nodded. "Yeah," she said between gasps for air. "I reckon we're close now."

"Good," Terri said. "This is giving me the creeps."

"You just have to hang on a few more moments," Monk said. "And I suggest we move quickly again." She pointed upward.

There were shadows of hands on the walls and the ceiling tiles shivered. Skeletons appeared out of the darkness.

"We're out of here," Roth said shortly. "Go."

Monk jogged, the others close behind her. As they rounded a bend, a group of rotting doctors and nurses stood across the corridor, blocking the way.

Monk did not slow. She growled, dropped her shoulder, and bludgeoned her way through the crush. Doctors and nurses scattered like bowling pins. *That works and it's better than fighting.*

Roth glanced back at Moriarty. She shrugged.

The doctors and nurses slowly and painfully levered themselves to their feet and shuffled toward them, a slow moving tide of death.

"Fuck off," Monk said, exasperated, as a buxom zombie nurse grabbed for her. She tore its head off and flung it at a doctor. It left a smear of blackish blood as it bounced off him and hit the ground with a sick crack.

Roth and Moriarty exchanged a glance and shoved back the zombie things.

"We're on top of it now," Monk said. She stumbled to her knees at the door to what looked like an operating room. "I'm sorry. I'm so sorry. I can't anymore."

"We'll take care of these," Roth said. "Keep an eye out for us."

Monk nodded.

Roth, Moriarty, and Terri moved toward the zombies and began ripping and tearing. The corridor was soon awash in ancient blood and decaying body parts. Covered in blood and sweating freely, they went back to the door of the operating room.

Monk sat, chest heaving and swallowing convulsively. Her eyes fluttered open.

Roth bent over her. "Monk?"

"I'm fine," Monk said. "I'm just . . . tired, you know?"

Roth nodded. "We understand." She held out a hand and helped Monk to her feet. Monk sighed.

"We have to make a move," Moriarty said apologetically. She pointed up.

A pack of skeletons had formed and were crawling nimbly along the ceiling toward them.

"Let's just hope we get done before the antibodies try to kill us again," Monk said and the others nodded.

Monk pushed open the doors and led the way into the operating room. She suddenly stopped and Roth bumped into the back of her.

The inside of the room looked as sterile and clean as the outside was dirty and decrepit. There was a bed in the center of the room and three large lights shone down on it unmercifully, lighting up the figure. The figure had five intravenous lines going into its arms. It seemed so frail and pale.

"Oh, my god," Monk murmured. "This is bloody barbaric."

Moriarty nodded. "It is. That's why it's banned."

"Who's the governing body?" Monk asked.

"Never mind about that now," Roth said, approaching the bed. "We have to help this poor soul." She reached the side of the bed and hissed, grimacing.

"What?" Moriarty said, going to stand beside Roth, Terri close to her.

"Oh, no," Terri said softly. "It's an old woman."

"Oh, young one," Roth said softly. "That's not just *any* old woman."

Terri frowned.

"It's Sister Constance," Monk said. "Fuck."

"You mean *Saint Hatchet Face*?" Terri said, eyebrows raised in shock. She looked sick. Moriarty gently squeezed her hand.

"Yes," Roth said softly. "She looks so frail."

Moriarty studied her closely. She was no more than skin and bone, her skin so pale it was almost translucent. Her skin looked stretched across her skull and her eyes were sunken in dark sockets.

"Is she going to be all right?" Terri asked, smoothing her wispy hair away from her forehead.

"I don't know," Moriarty said. "She was old when she was turned. But since she *has* been turned, maybe she'll pull through."

"Let's get her disconnected from all this crap and get it into me," Monk said.

"No," Terri said, putting a restraining hand on Monk's arm. "You're not up to going first. You don't have the reserves to deal with anything if it goes wrong."

Moriarty nodded. "She's right, Monk."

"What about Kilkenny?" Monk demanded.

"You will get your worlds, young one," Moriarty said. "First try goes to Terri." She looked at Terri, studying her beautiful face. Terri's eyes were intense, almost wild. Moriarty leaned forward and kissed her, a hard kiss that was a promise of later passion. Terri moaned softly, returning it and pushing her body into Moriarty's. Terri nibbled her lips when they broke.

"For luck," Moriarty whispered. "Be careful."

Terri smiled at her. "I love you, Mack, and I'll be safe."

"How are we going to do this?" Moriarty asked.

"Take one of the needles out of her arm and put it into Terri's," Monk said.

Roth pulled over a visitor's chair and Terri sat down.

Moriarty looked at the IV bag. It looked as though it was full of light. A tube led up into the ceiling. She was amazed at how steady her hands were as she pulled the needle out of Sister Constance's limp arm and handed it to Terri. Terri's hand was as steady as a rock when she plunged the needle into her own arm.

The IV bag glowed brightly, and for the first moment or two Terri seemed fine. She suddenly went rigid and screamed. The bag shone as bright as the sun and Terri's chest heaved.

"Mack," she called, and Moriarty was instantly there, putting her arms around Terri and holding on hard. Her heart hammered in her chest in time with Terri's heart. She felt Terri's pain, felt herself become overwhelmed by energy. Moriarty grunted in pain as the energy shot into her like a flame from a flame thrower. It felt like it was burning her from the inside out, an unstoppable tide.

Roth's screams began a few seconds later as the energy from the world slammed into her, knocking her flat onto her back.

Terri sat slumped in the chair, out cold. Moriarty dropped to her knees beside Terri and the darkness claimed her.

MONK WATCHED AS Roth, Moriarty, and Terri all passed out. The bag connected to Terri's arm had gone dark.

Monk gently pulled the needle out of her arm and felt her forehead. She was cool. She gently scooped up Terri and slashed a hole in the dreamscape. She looked through the slit. The other side was her living room and it was empty. *Good.* She grabbed Moriarty by the collar and pulled her into the physical world. She gently laid the black haired woman out on the floor, then took Terri from the hospital room and laid her beside Moriarty. She put Roth on the couch.

"Jackie?" she called. "Jackie?"

A few seconds later she heard the sound of pounding footsteps as Jackie raced into the living room.

"Monk?" she said. She took in all the unconscious bodies in the living room and took a step closer to Monk. "Monk?"

"It's time to eat a world," Monk said. "Come with me."

Jackie nodded. She dived through into the dreamscape and Monk sealed up the hole behind her.

"Is that Sister Constance?" Jackie asked with a wince.

Monk nodded. "Yes. Terri took a world. Now it's your turn. I'll stay with you and I'll bring you back to Michelle. Okay?"

Jackie nodded. She looked uncertainly at Monk for a second, and then strode across the room to her. Monk suddenly found herself in Jackie's arms as Jackie kissed her. Jackie pushed herself into Monk's body and Monk found herself responding. When they broke, Monk held Jackie up and gently pushed her hair away from her forehead.

Jackie opened her mouth to speak and Monk put a gentle finger across her lips. "No, Jackie. No goodbyes. Whatever you have to say to me you can say it when we're together again."

Jackie nodded.

Monk gently pushed her down into the chair and went and read the labels on the bags. *Marsh world,* one said. Monk grinned.

"I have just the world for you." She gave Jackie the needle and Jackie put it into her arm. Jackie's back almost instantly arched and she sucked in a great, whooping lungful of air.

"Oh, my god," Jackie screamed as the bag glowed as bright as the sun and then winked out. She sat back in the chair, breathing hard.

"Hah," Monk said. "You're still conscious. How do you feel?"

"Like normal," Jackie said. "I feel like I've rested and slept a night."

A low moan from the bed drew their attention. Monk immediately crossed to Sister Constance, leaned down, and took her hand.

"Sister," Monk said softly as the old woman's eyes fluttered open.

"Miss Monkhouse," she said.

"You remember me," Monk said.

"Of course," Sister Constance said. Her eyes fluttered closed and she seemed to fade out for a second. Then she rallied and her eyes fluttered open again. "What happened to me?"

"Angela Michaels happened. She set a trap for us and used you to power it."

Sister Constance sighed. "She was always a horrible girl."

"Are you going to be all right?" Monk asked.

"I'll recover," Sister Constance said. "I just need some rest."

"I'm going to take over for you here and Jackie's going to take you home."

Sister Constance nodded and Jackie took a step forward.

"Miss Sharp," Sister Constance said.

"Hello, Sister," Jackie said with a smile. "Are you ready?"

"I'm ready," Sister Constance said. She looked at Monk. "Thank you, Monk."

Monk grinned. "You're welcome, Sister." She shifted her vision and looked at the flame deep inside her bond. It was still sleeping as she touched the needles in Sister Constance's arm. Sister Constance stiffened as Monk carefully pulled them out and put them into her own arm.

She was only dimly aware of Jackie pulling out of the operating room.

Monk fell to her knees, so tired she was ready to pass out. Footsteps pounded down the hallway toward the operating room as Monk felt for the flame. It wasn't a flame anymore, it was more like an ember. It saddened Monk and she felt the sting of tears. She remembered all of things she'd done with Kilkenny. They'd gone to the beach world where they'd first run into Jackie having a tea party. They'd waited for the wave to build and break and Monk had built them a bubble and they'd surfed on the biggest wave in all of human history. She'd sat with Kilkenny the first time she'd had her heart broken by an older girl at school, had listened to her as she talked hesitantly about Riordan Kendrick.

Don't go, Kilkenny, Monk thought as the doors to the operating room splintered under the force of the blows from the things trying to beak in. *I don't want you to go. I want you to stay with me.* She extended ghostly arms toward the embers.

The doors to the operating room shattered inwards, showering her with splinters and tearing at her skin. Ghouls slobbered and whined at the doors.

The embers flared again, and a ghostly pair of hands gently slipped into hers. Monk could feel every atom in every remaining world and pulled them toward her, pushing them into the flames.

The first ghoul crashed into her, clawing at her back and chest, ripping the skin to ribbons.

She felt a rushing sensation that swiftly overpowered her. She felt as though she was being burned from the inside out. Liquid fire ran through her veins and into the flame inside her, causing it to explode into fire. She burned, feeling her skin peeling away from her bones, as more fire flowed into her bond. The fire inside tore through her, a massive blaze.

Tremendous earthquakes rocked the operating room and the ceiling rained down in chunks of tile and concrete. Gravity slipped away from the world and she floated. The air became rarer and she had trouble breathing, but she still funneled energy into the fire inside.

It finally seemed to double up on itself and explode outward, singeing her very bones. The air disappeared and the ghostly arms from the fire pulled her in close, cradling her as she lost consciousness.

MICHELLE SAT ON the edge of the bed beside Kilkenny. She glanced at Riordan. Riordan's color had improved and her breathing deepened. She looked as though she were just sleeping.

She pulled the sheets back and looked at Kilkenny's wound. It was an ugly festering mass of slowly rotting flesh, and her torso had the same gray tinge it had before.

Suddenly Kilkenny's eyes shot open and her back arched off the bed. The wound tore open and black, blood laced with pus shot out of it and flowed down her body. The stench was terrific.

Michelle held her gorge leant over Kilkenny, and took her shoulders in a firm grip to still her trembling. Kilkenny suddenly stiffened and convulsed, then went limp.

Michelle carefully put her back on the bed, watching in amazement as the slow wash of blood stopped. Pink, healthy skin covered the terrible wound, slowly closing it over. The healthy color spread, washing away the terrible gray tendrils that were infusing Kilkenny's body.

She shifted her vision and studied Kilkenny's sparks. At first they were a dullish gold and finally they brightened and moved swiftly again. The dark grey streamer that came off the top of her head lightened to silver and spread off into the distance.

She did it. She actually did it. Michelle put a hand on Kilkenny's unblemished skin. It was cool to the touch. She'd healed herself.

Michelle sighed. *Thank god. Please be okay, Monk. Please be okay.* She settled herself down to wait.

KILKENNY SLOWLY OPENED her eyes for the first time in what felt like forever. She looked down at herself, at the arms that lay around her bare body. She felt full breasts against her back, as naked as she was. She felt a fire burning inside her, energy very different to either Roth or Riordan. This was pure passion and raw strength, and it felt *happy.*

She looked up to see Riordan's concerned gaze.

"Hi," Riordan said softly.

"Hi," Kilkenny said. "What happened?"

"Your silver cut flared up again."

"I can't feel you," Kilkenny said sadly. "Our bond is broken, isn't it?"

Riordan looked as sad as she felt. "It's broken."

"I feel like there's fire inside me. Who is it?"

"Monk."

"*What?*"

"Your silver cut nearly killed you and we weren't strong enough between the two of us to heal you. So Monk took your bond and went into the dreamscape to collapse it. She used the energy from all the worlds and gave it to you so you could heal."

Kilkenny looked down at where her cut had been and saw only smooth, unblemished skin. It felt strange not to hurt so much. She felt herself at loss for words. "Where is she?" she finally managed.

"I don't know," Riordan said. "She was still in the dreamscape in her physical body when it collapsed."

"Is she in Roth's drawing room?"

Riordan shook her head. "That was the first place we all looked."

Kilkenny nodded. "You, Riordan? How are you?"

"I feel fine," she said.

Kilkenny felt her insides unclench. "I'm glad." She shifted so she could see Riordan's face. "I made love to Roth in the dreamscape."

Riordan gently ran her fingertips down Kilkenny's face. She smiled. "I thought you might have. I'm okay with it. I love you. With all my heart."

"I love you, too." Kilkenny felt her paralysis disappear and she slid against Rio, claiming her lips in a deep and tender kiss, suddenly aware of how their bare bodies lay against each other. She felt Riordan's hands begin a gentle exploration of her body, and she did the same, marveling at Riordan's soft skin and lips, the warmth from her beautiful body.

Riordan broke their kiss, gently cupping Kilkenny's breasts and teasing her nipples. "I want you. But you're bonded to another. It's not right to make love now."

Kilkenny nodded. "I understand. It's like staring into someone's bedroom window."

Riordan smiled. "Yes, it is."

"I'm going to go and bring Monk back."

"You know where she is?"

"I think so. There are very few places that are really meaningful to Monk. I know where they are and I'm going there. I'll call Michelle and Jackie when I find her."

"All right," Riordan said.

"Will you go to sleep? And bring Roth and meet me in Roth's drawing room?"

Riordan nodded. "Yes. Will you bond with us again?"

"Yes," Kilkenny said, kissing her. "Yes. If you still want me."

"We do," Riordan said, her arms tightening around Kilkenny. Kilkenny shifted in Riordan's arms and snuggled into her. She lay with her head on Riordan's chest, listening to the comforting lull of her heartbeat. Riordan traced a pattern on Kilkenny's back and Kilkenny felt herself beginning to doze off.

"Feels good," she murmured, kissing the soft skin of Riordan's chest. Riordan's arms tightened around her and she drifted off.

Kilkenny soon found herself standing on a street that ran beside a flat, grey ocean. She could feel Monk's gentle tug in the distance. Gigantic, featureless sky scrapers lined the other side of the empty road. The sky was overcast and a steady wind rushed in from the sea, carrying the scent of brine. The warm ball of energy inside her felt her coming and the sense of happiness increased.

In the distance she saw a bus seat set in the middle of the road, and a figure sitting on it, looking out at the ocean.

She couldn't help herself. She ran toward the figure.

As she got closer, she could make out Monk, leaning back against the seat. She looked up when she heard Kilkenny. A broad grin creased her face, and she stood. She jogged toward Kilkenny. Kilkenny's heart beat faster and as soon as she was close enough, she launched herself at Monk.

Monk caught her easily and pulled her in close. She sat down on another bench nearby, Kilkenny in her arms.

She pulled back after a moment but when she took one look into Monk's bright, blue eyes, she burst into tears.

"I'm sorry, Monk, I'm so sorry," she said. "I didn't want to stab you with the silver knife. I didn't want to hurt you." She clutched at

Monk's shirt, burying her face into Monk's neck, taking in her musky scent and light sweat.

"It's at least half my fault," Monk said, gently soothing her. "I pissed her off and she pushed you forward. *I'm* sorry, Kilkenny, believe me."

"It's okay, Monk," Kilkenny said, wiping the tears from her eyes. "There was never anything to forgive."

Monk pulled her toward the bus seat and pushed her down. She sat sideways so she could see Kilkenny. "How are you doing, bud? In here." She tapped Kilkenny's chest.

"I'm okay on the inside. Can't you feel it?"

Monk grinned. "I can, actually. You're a very gentle person, Kilkenny, and that's why I worry about you."

Kilkenny felt her face heat. "I know what *else* you're asking. You're asking about Rio and Roth, aren't you? I know from being bonded to them that my heart is in good hands." She tilted her head and studied Monk. "I didn't know it was you holding me up, Monk. I thought it was Roth. I owe you more than I can ever repay for keeping me alive like that. I don't know anyone that would break their bond like that just to help a friend."

Monk was silent a long time. "It's simple for me," she finally said. "I don't have a family. I never really did. Then you, Jackie, Michelle, and Terri came along and not only did I find the best friends anyone could ever have, but I have two of the most beautiful women I've ever met in love with me. That means the world to me. The way you always just accepted me for who I was always blew me away. It is an honor and a privilege to help you, Kilkenny."

Kilkenny had no words to reply, so she settled for wrapping herself around Monk and squeezing hard. She called for Michelle and Jackie.

She soon heard the sounds of footsteps running down the road and looked up. Michelle was running toward her as fast as she could, Jackie by her side.

Kilkenny gave Monk a gentle kiss on the forehead and gently disentangled herself.

"Love you too, Monk," she whispered, gently squeezing Monk's hand, feeling Monk squeeze her back.

Monk stood and suddenly she was engulfed in Jackie and Michelle. Michelle almost immediately grabbed Monk and kissed her, long and hard and deep. Monk moaned softly. The steamy kiss continued and Michelle's hands wandered.

Kilkenny felt her face heat and suddenly remembered she had to be other places. Her eyes flared yellow, and she withdrew the silver sparks that formed their bond.

She thought of Roth and Riordan. She slowly disappeared from Monk's dream.

KILKENNY REAPPEARED IN the eternal late summer sunshine that shone down on Roth's mansion's rear lawn. She looked up at the house. She loved it. It was a mansion she and Monk had explored more than once on their trips to the dreamscape. Now she knew it was Roth's house and it added a new dimension to her feeling toward it. It had always felt like a haven, like their safe place. It still did—but now it also felt like Roth.

She jogged up the lawn to French doors. She looked down at her hands. They were trembling. She squared her shoulders and strode through the door, more anxious to see Roth and Riordan than she wanted to admit.

At first she thought the room was empty, but then she saw Roth standing by the empty fireplace, head resting on her hand, her elbow on the mantelpiece. She was smiling at Riordan, who was comfortably sprawled on the sofa. She straightened when she saw Kilkenny. Her eyes flared yellow.

"Rio. Roth," she breathed, as Roth strode toward her. Then Roth was on her, seemingly intent on kissing her off her feet. She shifted her vision, just as Roth took her bond and pulled it toward Riordan and her.

She moaned as she was suddenly swept away by the current between them. She was almost overwhelmed Roth's primal outpouring and Riordan's gentle love. She moaned into Roth's mouth as her knees gave way. They fell to the thick rug before the mantelpiece and Roth tore off her shirt and feasted on her breasts. She managed to tear off Roth's shirt and found herself being gently eased onto her back. She cupped Roth's bare breasts, squeezing them gently. Roth's hands parted Kilkenny's knees as Riordan descended on her. Kilkenny's mind dissolved at the soft touch of Roth's lips.

MORIARTY HIT THE button on her remote locking keychain and her Calais chattered briefly as the alarm disengaged. She slid in behind the driver's seat, Terri by her side in the passenger seat.

"Where to?" Moriarty said.

"Let's go back to my place," Terri said. She put her hand on Moriarty's thigh and squeezed gently.

Moriarty swallowed convulsively. "That feels good."

"It feels good to have you back again," Terri said.

Moriarty smiled. "I'm glad you accepted me so easily. I'd planned on a lot more groveling."

"No, I hadn't planned on making you suffer," Terri said. "Not when I want this as badly as you."

They quickly made it to Terri's house, guided by Terri's murmured directions. Moriarty drove up the driveway and stopped the car before the garage doors.

Terri got out, Moriarty following closely behind.

"Nice," Moriarty said, eying the two storey house nestled on an acre of land. The land looked perfectly groomed and manicured.

"Thanks," Terri said, unlocking the front door and standing aside for Moriarty to enter.

The inside of the house was like a gigantic loft. The floors were covered in thick, soft carpet and the walls were painted a light color. There were reproductions of old masters scattered over the walls. The furniture was light and airy. A huge skylight lay above the living room, making it bright and welcoming. A wide set of stairs, by the wall ahead of them, led to the upper floor. There didn't seem to be any ceilings in the house; just walls to divide the space into rooms. The overall feeling was open, spacious and comfortable.

"This is just beautiful," Moriarty said. "Wow."

"I like it," Terri said. She watched Moriarty carefully for a moment. "Are you going to kiss me and take me to bed? Because I'd really like that right now."

Moriarty's apparent paralysis broke. She kissed Terri, putting all her feeling into it. Terri's return kiss was as loving and raw as her own.

When they broke, Terri cupped her face in trembling hands and looked deep into her eyes.

"I feel like I want to crawl under your skin and stay there until it's time for us both to die," she said. "Not once has that ever changed for me."

Moriarty laughed softly. "Me neither." She plucked at Terri's shirt and Terri's breathing became ragged.

They did not last long enough to reach Terri's bedroom.

MONK LED THE way out of the dreamscape. Their exit led out of the office in Michelle's flat.

"Is it safe to wander around in here?" Monk asked.

"It's safe," Michelle said with a grin. "Terri and Mack were heading back to Terri's place. Roth, Rio, and Kilkenny are in our spare room. They're asleep."

Monk loved the way she could feel Michelle in their bond. "It's good to be back. Our bond," she added when Michelle gave her a quizzical look.

"I know," Michelle said. "I couldn't stand you not being there anymore."

Monk shifted her vision and watched Jackie collapse the doorway. She felt Michelle's arms slip around her waist. She shivered as Michelle nibbled her ear.

Jackie turned and looked at them uncertainly. Then her eyes took in Michelle's lean beauty and Monk herself. Monk felt her nipples harden under the weight of her gaze. She felt Michelle shift and hold out her hand. Jackie took it, and Monk led them into their bedroom.

She stared at Jackie, taking in her slim, elegant beauty.

Jackie bit her lip. "I don't know—"

Monk immediately put a finger against her lips. "There's no right or wrong. There's no scoreboard. Just us." She smiled. "Touch me."

She felt Michelle shift behind her, gently pulling her shirt off with shaking hands. Michelle took off her bra and caressed her breasts and nibbled her neck.

Jackie's seeming paralysis broke and she crossed slowly to them, unbuttoned Monk's jeans, and slipped them down her hips.

"I want," she whispered. She kissed the soft skin of Monk's belly, and Monk shivered as she continued lower.

Monk collapsed into Michelle's arms as Jackie knelt before her and gently took her.

CHAPTER 19

KILKENNY WOKE UP the next morning alone. Roth and Riordan had both headed out some time during the morning. She stretched luxuriously, marveling at the lack of pain in her side.

She got out of bed and went into the kitchen. Michelle leant against the counter, fully dressed, sipping on a cup of coffee.

"You want a cup?" she asked, lifting her mug.

Kilkenny nodded. "Yes, please."

Michelle got her a cup and eyed her expectantly. "How are you feeling this morning? Are you going to school?"

"I feel fantastic," Kilkenny said. "So yes, I guess I'm going to school."

"You need a lift?"

"No, no problem. Rio's going to stop by."

Michelle nodded.

There was comfortable silence for a moment.

"I wanted to apologize, Michelle," Kilkenny said.

Michelle stared at her. "For what?"

"I stabbed Monk with a silver knife. I nearly killed her." Kilkenny flinched as she said the words.

"It's all right, Kilkenny, I forgive you," Michelle said softly. "I understand that you didn't exactly have a choice about things." She smiled. "It's not me you have to apologize to anyway, it's Monk."

"I already did." Pause. "But it's just that I don't like hurting anyone. I hate it. And that would have . . . You and Jackie . . . Monk is my best friend."

Michelle looked at her for a moment, and then put down her coffee cup. She took Kilkenny's cup and carefully put it down next to hers. She pulled Kilkenny into her arms and held onto her. Kilkenny snuggled into her, scenting her perfume and Michelle herself.

"S'okay, Kilkenny," Michelle said. "It didn't happen. We all know you don't like hurting things. Our basic characters haven't really changed despite the change in species. Besides, think in the long run of all the good you can do for other shape shifters as well as for humans. Our lives are good. You also now have Roth and Rio looking out for you as well as us."

Kilkenny thought about it a moment. "Same with Terri and Mack, right? We're a pack now, aren't we?"

Michelle snorted a laugh. "I guess you could say that." She gently released Kilkenny. "I have to shove off and go to school."

Kilkenny nodded. "Have a good day."

"You too," Michelle said as she scooped up her mug and headed back up the hallway.

Kilkenny picked up her cup and headed off to shower. She was only a couple of minutes later than normal and half expected Riordan to be waiting for her when she was done.

As she showered, she thought of Roth and Riordan and the others, and realized she *wanted* them all to stay together. They really *did* feel like a pack. She'd been right when she'd said that to Michelle.

She pulled on her blazer and went back into the living room with her backpack slung over her shoulder. Riordan was comfortably sprawled on the sofa, waiting for her.

Kilkenny dropped her backpack by the counter and Riordan stood.

Suddenly they were both tangled together and Riordan was kissing her. Kilkenny's knees felt treacherously weak and Riordan's arms tightened, gently supporting her.

"Good morning," Riordan said when they broke.

"Hi," Kilkenny said. "It's good to see you."

"Even better to see *you*," Riordan said.

Kilkenny gently disentangled herself from Riordan.

"We'd better head to school or we're going to be late," Kilkenny said.

"Yeah," Riordan said. She gently pushed a strand of Kilkenny's unruly fringe out of her face. "You're so beautiful. I love you."

Kilkenny smiled. "I love you, too."

Riordan took her hand. "You want to climb down the outside?"

"I have my backpack," Kilkenny said with a grin.

"I'll go down first and keep an eye on you."

"I'm in a skirt."

"That's the idea," Riordan said. "Looking up works for me. That means I can see your—"

"Rio," Kilkenny cut in, snorting a laugh. "You're terrible."

"Yeah, but I'm good at it," Riordan said as Kilkenny grabbed her backpack.

"Yeah, you are."

Riordan took her hand and they left.

MONK STOOD AT the door to the convent and glanced back at Jackie. “You ready?”

Jackie nodded.

Monk felt her in their bond. She felt fragile and uncertain. She could feel Michelle, her gentle, loving strength cradling them.

“What’s the matter?” Monk asked. She took Jackie’s hands into hers.

“I feel different after last night. I love you,” Jackie said.

“I love you too,” Monk said. “Do you feel *good* different or *bad* different?”

“Good,” Jackie said. “Definitely good.”

“We can always talk later if you want.”

“Okay.” Jackie nodded. “I’m also not looking forward to,” she waved her hand at the door, “this.”

“I understand,” Monk said. “But I *have* to do this. I have to know she’s all right.”

Jackie nodded. “I also want to know how she managed to get taken.”

Monk nodded and squared her shoulders. “Here goes.” She pushed the doorbell beside the door and they heard it ring inside.

There was silence for a few moments and then the sound of footsteps coming up to the door. The door opened.

“Yes?” a young woman asked.

“My name is Therese Monkhouse and this is Jackie Sharp. We’d like to see Sister Constance.”

The young woman nodded. “She said you might stop by. She asked you be let in.”

“Thank you,” Monk said, moving past her into the shadowed hallway, Jackie close behind.

“This way,” the woman said, leading them up a set of stairs and along a long hallway to an end room. She paused for a moment, her hand poised to knock. She looked at them uncertainly. “Do you know what happened to her?”

Monk smiled. “I’m sorry, it’s not my story to tell.”

The young woman studied them for a few moments. “That’s no answer but it’s all you’ll give me, I see,” she finally said. “Will she be all right?”

Monk nodded. “I think so. I think she needs rest and good healthy food more than anything else.”

The woman nodded and knocked on the door. She paused a moment, opened it, and gestured for Monk and Jackie to go ahead.

They went into the room. It was bare, save for a picture of the Madonna and Child on one wall and a simple crucifix on the other. There was a single dresser, almost bare on top, save for a brush. The bed was equally simple, as was the single chair by its side.

Monk looked carefully at Sister Constance. She lay in the center of the bed, eyes closed, chest moving with deep, regular breaths. Her color was better than it'd been on the dreamscape, but there were still shadows around her eyes.

"She looks better than she did," Jackie said softly.

"I feel better, thank you," Sister Constance said dryly, opening her eyes. She glanced at the young woman. "Thank you, Grace."

"I'll be waiting close by if you need anything," Grace said, quickly glancing at them.

"Thank you," Sister Constance said as Grace backed out of the room.

The door closed behind her and there was silence for a moment.

"Come, sit down," Sister Constance said.

Monk gingerly sat on the edge of the bed and Jackie took the chair, looking uncomfortable.

"How are you feeling, Sister?" Monk asked.

Sister Constance gave her the ghost of a smile. "I've been better. This is nothing that won't pass." She looked at Monk, her eyes fading to yellow. Monk shifted her vision, as did Jackie.

"You're the same as me," Sister Constance said. "Are there more of us?"

Monk reacted before she could think. "Terri Warland. Michelle Coopersmith."

Sister Constance was silent for a long time. Monk could see by her distant expression that she was deep in thought. "Are we demons?"

Monk smiled. "It depends on your point of view. I'm not a demon, I didn't sell my soul to Satan and you can't drag me to a black mass any more than a Catholic one. But since I *am* a fucking faggot I guess I'm headed downstairs."

She could feel Jackie's eyes on her and when she looked, Jackie's mouth had dropped open slightly in shock.

"On the other hand," Monk continued. "That's me. What about *you*? You feel like an axe murderer or something? You feel unnatural?"

Sister Constance snorted a laugh. "You're terrible, Miss Monkhouse. You always were." She laughed. "No, I don't really feel any different to the way I was before . . . this . . . happened to me. If anything, I feel thirty years younger."

"God is the one who judges, not me," Monk said. "Live a good and virtuous life and you will be rewarded. Isn't that what all of you sisters used to tell us?"

Sister Constance nodded. "I suppose we did." She was silent for a moment. "What are we?"

"We're shape shifters," Jackie said quietly. "Werewolves. You're stronger and faster than you used to be and now you have complete control over your dreams. You can build them for yourself and for other people."

Sister Constance nodded. "Will you show me?"

Jackie was silent for a moment. "I will, if that's what you want."

"Thank you, Miss Sharp." She turned back to Monk. "What happened to me?"

"You got taken by Angela Michaels and another werewolf. They made you create worlds and keep them running."

Sister Constance flinched. "Did I hurt anyone? Did I hurt you?"

"No," Monk said. "*You* hurt nothing and no one. The people who used you weren't as nice, though. *They* hurt plenty of people."

"I'm now a lot more powerful than I was."

Monk and Jackie both nodded.

"You're not a maniac, Sister."

Sister Constance looked at them carefully. "Thank you, girls."

"I have a question for *you*, Sister," Monk said. "How did you end up in that dream?"

"I don't really know," Sister Constance said. "I was walking down to the school and when I got there it was deserted. I thought it strange, but then I heard people. It was Miss Michaels and a dark haired woman I've never seen before. I ended up in hospital with needles in my arm. I couldn't move. I was so weak . . . I think I might have fallen asleep . . ."

Monk and Jackie exchanged a glance. Jackie looked horrified.

"It's over, now, Sister," Monk said. "Those two won't be bothering you again."

"Thank you, Miss Monkhouse," Sister Constance said.

"We're going to go now," Monk said. She and Jackie stood. "We both hope you feel better soon."

"Thank you, girls," Sister Constance said, her eyes fluttering shut and her breathing evening out as she fell asleep.

Monk and Jackie backed out of the room. Grace was waiting for them.

"Did she tell you anything?" Grace asked.

Monk could feel Jackie's eyes on her. Monk shook her head. "No, but I think she's going to be fine. Really. All she needs is some rest."

Grace nodded and looked relieved. "Thank you. I'll show you out."

"Thank you," Jackie said.

A couple of minutes later they were standing outside the door.

Jackie heaved a deep sigh. "Thank God that's over and done with." She turned to Monk and grinned. "*I'm a fucking faggot and I'm headed downstairs*? Oh, geez, Monk. No wonder you ended up in trouble all the time when we were in school."

Monk grinned, her smile broadening when Jackie slipped her hand into her's and they walked back down the street toward Jackie's car.

"Can't help it, Jackie," Monk said. "I'm surprised. Looks like she doesn't hate me as much as I thought she did when we were in school. By the way, you're going to *train* her? Wow."

"I know," Jackie said. "But what would you rather have? A werewolf running around accidentally hurting people? Or a trained shape shifter who knew what they were doing?"

"I see your point," Monk said. "But I'm still not sure I could do it."

"You're going to have to work out how," Jackie said. "Because you're helping me."

"Uh," Monk said.

They reached Jackie's car and Monk paused as she climbed in. She stared at Jackie, feelings of unwillingness rising to the surface.

"Don't look at me like that, Monk," Jackie said gently. "You're good at that stuff. You helped me and Kilkenny, didn't you?"

"That's different. I *like* you both."

"I hope you do more than just *like* me now."

Monk got in the car and studied Jackie. "Is that really what you think? That I'd toss you over my shoulder like an empty beer can?"

Jackie shook her head. "I don't know what to think. All I know is that I can't think when I'm around you. All I can do is feel."

"Do you need some space?" Monk asked.

Jackie shook her head after a moment. "No. There's just a lot going through me right now. I crossed the line with you and Michelle last night. I lost my best friends and gained two lovers."

"Or you could say your two best friends are finally your lovers," Monk said. "I'm not sure what it's going to take to make this sink in, but we're together for keeps. We always have been."

"My mind understands that but my heart is a different story. I've had my share of crushes on people but this is the first time I've ever actually been in love. I'm crazy about you both but I feel really vulnerable."

It was a little awkward but Monk managed to pull Jackie in close. "I won't hurt you, Jackie. Neither will Michelle. I love you. I feel the same way about you as you do about me. You have to trust *me. Us*."

"I know," Jackie said. "This is just a first for me."

"I know what it feels like to have your world change," Monk said. "I had that the day after I first made it with Michelle. You just wonder when fate is going to rip it out from under you. Michelle and I are both adults. We're not kids. This isn't a game for us or for you. We're right here. We're all together now."

Jackie's arms tightened around Monk. "Thanks, Monk," she said after a while.

"No problem. You want to stuff around with me today?"

"I'd love to," Jackie said. "What do you want to do?"

"Let's go to the beach. Ice cream's on me."

Jackie smiled. "You're on."

KILKENNY SAT IN roll call and tried not to stare at Roth. She wanted to crawl inside Roth and not come out. It saddened her to see Roth's eyes so distant as they swept over the class and past her.

"Close your mouth, Kilkenny," Lauren Sonderby said, nudging her.

"I can't help it," Kilkenny muttered. "God, she's so *hot.*"

"I guess," Lauren said.

"What do you mean, you *guess*?"

"I'm straight, remember?"

"Oh. Yeah."

"Are the announcements boring you, girls?" Roth asked coolly.

"Yes," Kilkenny said.

"No, Miss Roth," Lauren said.

The bell rang, signaling the end of roll call. Kilkenny got up with a sigh. Lauren stared at her.

"Stay put, Miss Sharp," Roth said archly from the front of the room.

"What's up with you, Kilkenny?" Lauren whispered. "Shut *up* for God's sake."

"I know. I'm busted. I *should* have kept my mouth shut. I'm just tired. I'm going to apologize. I'll see you downstairs?"

"Good luck with that." Lauren nodded, scooping up her back pack and filing out behind the rest of the class.

Kilkenny leant against her desk and stared at Roth, who was leaning against her own desk.

"Come here, Miss Sharp," Roth said.

A couple of stragglers glanced back at Kilkenny, wincing.

Kilkenny approached Roth, backpack slung over her shoulder. Roth glanced at the door.

Kilkenny looked around. They were alone.

A picture of Roth's bare body rearing over her shot through her mind and she stared at Roth. The intensity in Roth's eyes was almost palatable.

"You don't know how badly I want to touch you right now," Kilkenny said.

"Yes, I do. I can see it in your eyes," Roth said.

"And I can see it in yours."

Roth sighed. "This is harder than I thought it would be. *Much* harder."

Kilkenny nodded. "It'd be best if we didn't do this while I was in school." She felt Roth's flinch. She gave Roth a sad smile. "But I could no sooner leave you alone than I could flap my arms and fly."

Roth grinned. "I understand." She ran a long finger down Kilkenny's face. "I love you."

Kilkenny smiled, gently trapping Roth's hand against her face. "I love you, too." She allowed her bond to soak into her.

She felt Riordan's gentle love and strength. Roth felt like an ocean of patience mixed with raw passion and love. The tide from her was almost overwhelming.

"I can hardly stand this close to you and not be able to touch you," Roth said. "I don't like us being strangers. I don't think I can do it. *Especially* when you look at me like you did in roll call today."

"I know," Kilkenny said. "What do you think we should do about it?"

"Take the job," a new voice said from the doorway.

They both looked over and saw Riordan standing there, smiling at them. She walked over and stood beside Kilkenny. "Take the job, love."

Roth smiled at her. "I already accepted."

"Excellent," Riordan said with a grin.

"What job?" Kilkenny asked, looking between the two of them.

"I saw Sister Constance before school this morning," Roth said. "I wanted to be sure she was all right. She told me that the principal's position at Corpus Christi was open. She asked me if I wanted it." She grinned at Riordan. "I told her I'd do it."

Kilkenny gaped at her. "You're a *principal*?" she finally managed.

"Normally, yes. I took a teaching position when I came here so I could meet you," Roth said. "I'm glad I don't have to keep teaching classes. I'd forgotten how horrible school children were. I like administration better."

"Wow," Kilkenny said. "What subjects do you teach?"

"Maths and science."

Kilkenny gaped. Roth and Riordan both laughed.

"Shut your mouth, Kilkenny," Riordan said. "You're catching flies."

"It means that by the end of the month I won't be teaching here anymore. Which is a good thing because I don't think us having sex in a classroom full of girls is such a good idea."

"What?" Kilkenny said.

"Keep looking at me like you did this morning and it's probably going to happen," Roth said. "The move will make things easier on us both."

"I'm going to miss you," Kilkenny said.

"You're going to see me all the time, young one, in the dreamscape."

Kilkenny gave her a smile. "Yeah." She felt her face heat. "I need to."

Roth and Riordan both nodded.

"We both do as well," Riordan said.

"Hey, so this is where you're all hiding out," Moriarty said, striding into the room. "I'm glad I caught you, guys." She dropped her books on the first row of desks. She looked at Kilkenny. "Don't I have a class with you now?"

"Klaatu barada nicto," Kilkenny said.

Moriarty laughed. "Good to see you, too." She glanced at all three of them. "You guys want to come to dinner tonight? Terri's place? Around six?"

"We'd love to," Roth said.

"So would I," Kilkenny said. "Can I bring Monk, Michelle, and Jackie?"

"I'll send you back to get them if you don't," Moriarty said.

"Cool," Kilkenny said, grinning back.

The bell rang, signaling the start of third period.

"That's our signal to move," Riordan said with a sigh.

Roth nodded and scooped up her attendance folder. Roth and Riordan both turned and looked at Kilkenny. The intensity in Roth's eyes ratcheted up a notch. Riordan simply looked as though she wanted to devour Kilkenny. Kilkenny gave them a brief smile, trying to force images of bare skin out of her mind. Roth smiled. Kilkenny felt herself color at her inability to control her hormones around either one of them.

Roth and Riordan began walking out of the room.

"Do you think the parents would mind if I gassed my seventh grade science class?" Roth asked.

"Yes, I think they would," Riordan said.

"Okay, just one, then. I could—"

"No, love."

"But—"

"*No.*"

Moriarty and Kilkenny exchanged a glance and laughed as Roth and Riordan finally went out of earshot.

"How are you feeling, Kilkenny? Better?" Moriarty asked.

"I'm feeling a lot better. Fully healed. I'm tired but that'll pass."

"Good," Moriarty said with a grin. "I was worried. I didn't want to lose you." Her black eyes were warm and kind.

"Thanks, Mack," Kilkenny said softly. "I don't want to lose you *or* Terri. I don't want you to go away." She put her arms around Moriarty and squeezed hard. Moriarty gently held her.

"Terri and I aren't going anywhere," Moriarty said. "And if we did I imagine we'd take the rest of our pack with us."

Kilkenny smiled. "Thanks, Mack."

She released Moriarty and drifted back to her seat and waited for her classmates to come in.

"HEY," TERRI SAID with a broad grin as she pulled open the front door. "Come on in." She stood aside and Michelle, Kilkenny, Jackie, and Monk filed in past her.

She led the way into the living room. Moriarty, Roth, and Riordan were comfortably sprawled on the sofas.

"Sorry, I just have to check on dinner," Terri said, heading toward the kitchen.

"Guys," Michelle said with a grin.

Roth and Riordan both gave them all hugs, leaving Kilkenny until last. Roth's gaze turned predatory as she approached Kilkenny. She kissed Kilkenny, leaving no doubt as to her intentions.

"God, knock it off," Jackie said with a wince as they broke. "Watching you is as psychologically damaging as watching Mum and Dad."

"Shut up," Kilkenny said, eyes glued on Roth. "I'll remember that next time you're staring at Monk's arse. Now *that's* psychologically damaging."

"Hey, leave me out of this," Monk said, backing into Michelle who was struggling not to laugh.

"Now, then, children," Moriarty said, scooping up Jackie and Monk and shepherding them into the kitchen. "Let's play nicely, shall we? How about we let Kilkenny stare at Roth's boobs in peace?"

Michelle and Riordan burst out laughing.

Michelle trailed behind the others into the kitchen and Riordan approached them, putting an arm around each one.

"She's right, you know," Riordan said.

"What?" Kilkenny asked, distracted by both of them.

"You *do* stare at Roth's boobs."

"What do you expect? I love them."

"Excellent," Roth said dryly, snorting a laugh. "You *only* staring at them is killing me."

"Tell me about it," Kilkenny said.

Roth and Riordan each kissed Kilkenny.

"Let's go and get some dinner," Kilkenny said softly. "Maybe we can do something after."

"You mean like chase cars or cats or something?" Riordan asked.

"Yeah, or bay at the moon. Take your pick," Kilkenny said.

Roth grinned and steered them both toward the laughter in the kitchen.

ABOUT THE AUTHOR

Jordan Falconer was born in Sydney, Australia, and from a very young age had an interest in ghoulies, ghosties and long legged beasties and all things that go bump in the night. After surviving Catholic school (twice!) she graduated from Sydney University with an honors degree in Psychology. She currently resides in California with her other half and three small, demanding dogs.

www.ingramcontent.com/pod-product-compliance
Lightning Source LLC
LaVergne TN
LVHW091036080826
845145LV00002B/522

* 9 7 8 1 9 4 9 2 9 0 5 5 4 *